Guilty Pleasure

Cherrell L. Bates

ISBN 10: 0692371451
ISBN-13: 978-0692371459

DEDICATION

Again, I simply dedicate this book to anyone who has ever had a dream. Let nothing stop you. If it's for you, it's for you. God will give you everything you need to make your dreams come true. Never ever give up.

ACKNOWLEDGMENTS

I want to thank anyone who has encouraged me in my journey. Whether you read "Yield Not To Temptation" or simply asked how the book was coming along, you motivated me. I will forever be grateful for your thoughtfulness and your support.

I must thank God. He's with me in all that I do. Without him, I would be nothing.

As always, I thank my parents, Gwen and John. Without them I would not exist.

I am thankful for all of my family and my friends.

Special thanks to Melissa and Stephanie for your advice

And finally, I thank my love, Quincy, for always pushing me along.

And to you, reading this book, thank you.

Love you all.

1

Quinton

"Do not speak evil against one another, brothers. The one who speaks against a brother or judges his brother, speaks evil against the law and judges the law. But if you judge the law, you are not a doer of the law, but a judge." James 4:11

Quinton

The room was full of smoke. The music was blaring. There were half-naked women everywhere. The ratio was definitely on my side. For every man, there were at least two women. I was not complaining about that.

I had taken down four shots of straight vodka. Now I was sipping on my third Rum and Coke. I didn't eat much today so this was definitely more than a buzz. I could feel myself slowly slipping out of control. Usually getting drunk wasn't my thing, but today had been a bad day.

I didn't want to come out tonight, but my boy, Tyler, insisted. I was a very social creature, but partying every night was his thing, not mine. Here I was, though, taking down drink after drink, trying to forget the pain that yet another woman had caused me. I was tired of the same old story. They said men were bad, but I had the track record to prove that women weren't too much better. Manipulative, gold-digging, dishonest women, who did nothing but used men for what they could get. If what you had wasn't enough, they proceeded to destroy you and not uplift you like a woman should.

I usually wasn't a bitter dude, but today, I was. I was frustrated. Enough was enough. Love was obviously not in my corner. I was giving up. It was pointless.

I sipped on my drink, trying to ignore the usual groupies. I wished for once I could just be incognito, but with my career, I was well-known across the city. They all knew who I was. They danced in front of me, flipping their bad weaves, twerking as if that was the only thing they could offer me. It was obnoxious and a turn off. Some women tried too hard.

I rolled my eyes when I realized that these two chicks were not going to disappear. I stood and headed across the room. I didn't want to be rude by saying something disrespectful. I did have a reputation to protect.

I headed back to VIP where Tyler and his boys were. Tyler had some chick in his lap. I stopped and stared at her because she reminded me of a girl from my past, but thankfully it wasn't her. This girl was cute, but she was not my type.

I sat down on the loveseat wishing I could get out of here, but I couldn't. I had too much going for myself to get a DUI, plus Tyler was driving tonight. I was tempted to order another drink, but I decided to stop. I wasn't trying to black out. I flagged down our waitress and ordered some wings. I needed some subsistence. It was time to sober up.

Thirty minutes later, I was in my own world, playing Texas Holdem on my phone when she walked in. Butterscotch complexion, curly hair, dark eyes, pouty lips and curves for days. She wore a fitted white dress. Oh my goodness, I thought. Why of all nights did she have to show up in this spot? I was not in a good state at the moment. She looked like trouble and I didn't need any of that.

She sat across from me. She smiled in my direction, pulled out her phone and proceeded to ignore me. I liked that. She wasn't a groupie. Now, I was even more intrigued.

I tried not to stare. I didn't want her to cuss me out. When you were that sexy, you had to be use to the attention, though. Men were like vultures and no matter how hard I tried, I wasn't any different.

My eyes kept falling on her lips. Naughty thoughts came into my mind. They were so pouty. They were made for kissing.

I tried to think of something to say, but in my condition, I couldn't formulate any words. At this point, I wasn't interested in holding a conversation with her. There were very explicit scenarios running through my mind. I wanted to do some things to her.

I was disappointed when she stood and walked away. I mumbled how stupid I was under my breath. I was not a shy person. I should have made something happen.

After a couple minutes, I found myself getting up and heading in the same direction. I found the mystery girl on the dance floor. I leaned against the wall. I was mesmerized at the way she moved those hips. I wanted to hold on to those hips. I wanted to do a lot of things with her that didn't involve dancing.

As badly as I wanted to leave earlier, I was disappointed when Tyler approached me. I shook my head and found myself following him. He was my only way out of here and I couldn't miss that boat. I turned to looked back at her once more and she was gone. Wow!

I was halfway across the parking lot when someone grabbed my arm. I turned around, ready to snap. I was not in the mood. I almost stumbled over my feet when I saw it was her.

"Well hello, Quinton. I take it that you don't remember me."

"Hi, I don't. I apologize." I couldn't forget someone like her.

"Christiana Michaels. From high school." My mind was blank. "We were lab partners. I drooled over you every day," she joked.

"Michelle!" We didn't call her Christiana in school, I thought.

"That was my middle name. I have embraced my first name these days. No more Michelle."

"Okay. You look incredible," I blurted. She had changed. She had gone from a plain-Jane to this. The girl looked like a model. It was amazing what time could do for a person.

"Thank you. I waited for you to say something all night."

"I am sorry."

"I saw you watching me."

"I apologize if I made you uncomfortable."

"You didn't. Look, I didn't flag you down to catch up."

"Then what's up?"

"I want you. You want me. Are we going to do this?"

"Excuse me?" Was this chick for real?

"We are grown. I am horny. And I can tell by the way you have been looking at me that you are to. Are you coming?" She walked away. What was I supposed to do? I said that I wasn't going to do this anymore, but she was offering. I couldn't turn it down.

I found myself telling Tyler that I would hit him up later. He gave me a head nod of approval and disappeared into the night. There was no turning back from my rash decision.

We rode in silence. I wasn't in the mood for small talk and

apparently she wasn't either. We both knew what this was all about.

We pulled up to a house in the suburbs. I followed her inside. She pointed to her guest bathroom and I was able to freshen up. When I opened the door, she stood before me in just her panties. She was incredibly sexy. She was thick in all the right places.

"Have mercy on me, girl."

"Let's go."

She led me to her bedroom and pushed me down on her bed. Tonight, I had no issue with giving up control. She did her thing and I held on to those hips like I had imagined earlier. She didn't disappoint. She gave me what I wanted and needed after my bad day.

Afterwards, she grabbed a shirt and disappeared into the bathroom. I took the opportunity and got dressed. I wasn't trying to hang around. I called Uber.

"Do you need a ride?"

"Nope. My ride is on its way."

"Cool." She started to brush her hair into a ponytail. I finally looked at the big ring on her finger. A sick feeling came over me.

"You are married?"

"I am."

"Wow." I frowned. She was obviously nonchalant about it. "Where's your husband?"

"Visiting his sick mother." I shook my head. I detected no guilt. She seemed cold.

"Wow, Christiana. Do you do this often?"

"Not that it's any of your business, but no."

I had looked at her with desire all night, but it took everything in me not to look at her with contempt. I didn't respect an adulterer. If I had known she was married then tonight would not have happened. How did I not see the ring? Obviously my vision and judgement had been affected by all that alcohol. I want sure if it was her confession, but now that I was sober, she wasn't as beautiful as I thought.

I was ready to go. I wanted to go to bed. I wanted this night to be over.

While this wasn't my first time hooking up with some random chick, doing this regularly wasn't my thing. I vowed to myself that this was my last time. While I protected myself, I was putting my health in jeopardy. One moment of pleasure wasn't worth an incurable disease.

I was relieved when I got home. I took a shower and went straight to bed. And as tired as I was, I was restless. I had too much on my mind.

I was lonely. I was on the brink of depression. I needed a change in my life.

Frustrated, I got up and took a sleeping pill. I had a busy day tomorrow. I was moving and I prayed that I didn't have to do it with a hangover. I am sure God wasn't too thrilled with my actions tonight. Being sick would serve me right.

I was moving in with Desiree. I am not sure how I was going to survive living with her. As much as I loved my girl, she was the main reason I couldn't sleep.

I was anxious. I was a little nauseated. Desiree was my weakness. She was like a drug to me. And unfortunately, she was the source of a lot of my pain.

Lord, please be with me.

Desiree

I climbed in the shower. It had been a long and stressful day, so I welcomed the water drops as they massaged my skin. I stood there with my eyes closed, willing my body to relax.

I should have been startled when I felt his arms slide around my waist. I had not heard him come into the house, much less enter the room. Instead of screaming, I leaned back and melted into his body. It brought me comfort and relief.

"You missed me?" he asked. I didn't say anything, I just nodded. "Good." As his hands moved agonizingly slow over my body, he whispered what he was going to do to me. I was glad that he could not see my face because his explicit words were making me blush.

Suddenly, he pushed me against the wall. He grabbed my arms and raised them above my head, ordering me not to move. As one of his hands grabbed my breast, the other lingered between my thighs. Before I knew it, my breath quickened and I moaned in pleasure.

It didn't take long before his world collided with mine. My hips begin to move to his rhythm. I closed my eyes and allowed myself to lose control. I surrendered to the passion.

When it was all over, I leaned against the wall and attempted to catch my breath. He whispered he would be back and I nodded.

After moments alone, I turned off the water and grabbed a towel. I walked into my bedroom and called for him. No answer. I panicked.

I ran through the house. There was no trace of him. I looked outside and the only car in my driveway was mine. He was gone. Again. This was getting old. Being left alone had unfortunately become the story of my life.

I collapsed on my couch and I cried. Why me? Did I deserve this? Did I deserve to be discarded over and over again?

I stood. In a rage, I begin throwing things across the room. The remote, a picture frame, an empty wine glass.

I was tired of being hurt.

Suddenly, my eyes opened. It was a dream. It was another erotic nightmare that took me through a rollercoaster of emotions. I sat up in my bed. I was frustrated because this was a reoccurring a dream. I usually had it every couple of weeks, but lately, I was having it more frequently.

Each time, a faceless man would sneak into my home. He would love me. He would bring me undeniable pleasure each time. He would then disappear, causing me heartbreak.

What did this all mean?

I stood and headed to my kitchen. I poured myself some wine to calm my nerves. I sat down in front of my TV and begin to mindlessly flip channels. There was no way I was going back to sleep. I would spend another long night on my couch, pretending as if another night alone didn't bother me.

"Desiree! Do you hear me!"

"Rayven, I hear you. Stop yelling."

"Well, will you answer me?"

"Give me a moment."

I got up from the table and headed to the bathroom before she could respond. I stood in front of the mirror and stared at my reflection. The color had drained from my face. Admittedly, I looked as if I had seen a ghost.

I had been through this before. I wasn't trying to deal with this again. I didn't need this at this point in my life.

I received a text from an unknown number every day this week. The text appeared harmless. It normally said something about missing me or about my appearance. I assumed that it was a wrong number and chose not to respond. Yesterday, I grew annoyed. I told the person that they had the wrong number; they replied back, "No, I don't."

I asked, "Who is this?" There was no response.

Today was different, though. I was surprised to look down at my phone and read, "You look so sexy in that jumpsuit. I love your hair like that."

I dropped my phone and started looking around.

"What is it, Desiree?" My best friend had asked. I was too panicked to respond. I suddenly felt as if I couldn't breathe. My chest began to tighten.

I ran to the bathroom because it felt as if I needed to escape. I ran as if I was being chased. I was running towards a temporary safe haven. I prayed that no one followed me.

Someone sending me a harmless text was one thing. They were a little annoying because I didn't know who the sender was, but I could deal with that. Someone obviously watching me was another thing. How dare someone take things this far? How dare someone invade my privacy?

I quickly became more pissed than scared. I didn't have time for this. I was stalked before and I was not about to go through this hell again. I was not going to give some idiot any power.

I texted back, "Look, don't start with me. Either tell me who you are or quit texting me." I than took a couple deep breaths and headed back towards my baffled friend. I think I had freaked her out.

"What the hell is going on, Desiree!"

"I'm sorry. I got a crazy text from Devin." I lied. I didn't even want to feed into my ordeal by telling Rayven. Talking about it would make me anxious.

"Devin? What does his trifling ass want?" Devin was the last guy I had dated. He had did me pretty dirty after I had put my all into the relationship. He slept with a couple of my so called girlfriends and tried to steal from me. He hid behind the façade of being a good God-fearing man, but like many Christians, he was the biggest hypocrite I had ever met.

"He asked to see me. I had to set him straight." I hated lying, but I didn't know what else to say.

"I can't imagine what you said to him with that temper."

'Right!" I laughed it off.

We were at our favorite pizzeria in the mall. I watched in disgust as my best friend took down her sixth slice of meat lover's pizza and her eighth chicken wing. I was savoring my second slice because I did not want all the extra calories going to my booty. I had plenty of curves already. Admittedly, I was a hater.

This chick ate like this every day. I had no idea where the food went because she still remained a size four. I had to struggle to maintain my size eight. It was hard because I was not naturally slim. I was in the gym four days a week. I had every right to be in my feelings right now. Who wouldn't?

"Are you ordering dessert?" She asked, finally looking up.

"Nope, I am straight. My metabolism is nothing like yours. I can't get down like that," I laughed.

"Whatever, Des, you are not fat. You are a sexy curvy goddess."

"I know I am not fat, but if I eat like you do, I will be."

"Whatever." Rayven rolled her eyes and switched away from the table and to the front of the restaurant. I watched a group of high school boys break their necks to stare at her. Sometimes I was so envious of her. She was a gorgeous woman.

Wow. Why was I so insecure lately? I felt stupid.

"You are actually letting this man come live with you?" Rayven asked, rejoining me at the table. I rolled my eyes. She had been on my case about this for the last two weeks.

"Yes, Rayven. Quinton will be staying with me. What is it that you have against Q anyway?" This was getting exhausting. She was holding a grudge, but wouldn't tell me why.

"I hardly know the man. I just don't like him. Why is he staying with you again?"

"Do you have a thing for him?" I asked, trying to make sense of her disdain.

"How insulting! He's not exactly what I am looking for." She wouldn't look at me. She was blushing. I knew she was lying.

"Okay." I laughed. "Calm down. He's actually getting a house built. It won't be ready until next year. Staying with me will save him money. That's all."

"Good for him." She didn't sound sincere.

"Can we just be real for a moment, though? Did you guys have a fight that I don't know about? Did Q ever disrespect you in some way? What went down between you two, Rayven?"

"I am not going to sit here and give you the reason that you are looking for." She shrugged. "I am just not feeling him like that. He's a womanizer."

"And?"

"And? You would cry more than that if you were one of the poor women that he played."

"You're right, but I am not one of those women, Ray. Plus, if a man tries to play me, then something of his will be catching flames. I was about to let Devin have it a couple months ago."

"Oh, that's right. You are on that Waiting to Exhale level." She found that hilarious. "You loved Angela Bassett in that movie."

"You know my temper."

"I do and I am scared of it."

"Quinton's a bit of a player. I am not condoning it, but there's nothing I can do about it. I will always be his friend, regardless." She shrugged. "He's a good person, Rayven." Why was I defending him to her? It was pointless.

I understood that Quinton was a player. He was a gorgeous man. He was very successful and very popular in the city. Sadly, women threw themselves at him on a regular basis. Like any other man, he rarely turned an attractive woman down.

Admittedly, he didn't appear interested in settling down. He was focused on enjoying life. And while as his friend, I felt it was time for him to calm down and find a good woman, he was grown. He could do what he wanted to and I wasn't going to judge him for it. His decisions didn't affect me. Plus, we were all sinners, I thought.

"You can preach to me now, Desiree Harris, but what are you going to be saying six months down the line when you get played?"

"We're just friends!" I rolled my eyes. This chick was ridiculous. "Nothing could ever come between me and Quinton."

"He's definitely not good enough for you."

"I wouldn't say that. He's just not my type."

"He shouldn't be!" I just stared at her and shook my head. We were all friends once. In college, the three of us would hang out. I am not sure how things changed so unfavorably.

"That man is delicious, though!" She did smile on that.

"Yeah, I can admit that. He's freaking sexy. He looks as if he knows how to please a woman. There has got to be a reason these women trip so hard over him."

"Yeah. I am sure he can please a woman." My mind started to drift into unchartered territory. If I knew that I would not ruin my friendship with him, I would be willing to find out. I knew myself, though. I became emotionally attached to men.

"When you find out, Des, please don't spare me any details."

"I am not giving Quinton the cookie."

"Yes, you are." I frowned at her. What was my best friend implying? She was making me sound easy.

"Why do you think I would jeopardize my friendship with Q just to get some good loving? There are plenty of men out there that are willing to please a woman."

"True, but you won't be in the same house with those other men. You will be with Quinton. You both are young, hot and sexy. And I am sure you are both horny." True. I was very horny and was going through a drought.

"Quinton would not be into a woman like…."

"Shut up, Desiree. I have not seen such a beautiful woman with such low self-esteem. Females who don't look half as good as you, are conceited as I don't know what. Will you quit with these insecurities."

"Whatever, Ray."

"Excuse me!" Rayven called out to two attractive men who were passing by. Of course they stopped. My best friend was breathtaking.

"Well, hello," the sexier one spoke up and approached the table.

"This is my best friend, Desiree. Will you please tell her how beautiful she is?" I was going to kill her.

He looked over at me and smiled.

"Baby, you are beyond beautiful. Look at that smile. What's your name?" Five minutes later, Justin Johnson was walking out with my number in his phone, promising to call.

"Thanks a lot, Rayven. Sometimes I want to slap you."

"What? You should be hugging me with gratitude. Justin was gorgeous. You could stand to go on a few more dates."

"I am thankful, but that was a little humiliating."

"I couldn't resist."

We sat in silence for a few moments. I reflected a little. I thought about my relationship with Quinton. We had been through a lot together and while I was definitely secretly hot for him, I was not willing to go there.

"Rayven, you are quick to judge Q, but you are always breaking some poor man's heart. Why are you being a hypocrite? You think it's wrong for Quinton to play women, but you are essentially doing the same thing to men."

"Well, I am doing women a favor. Some of these men deserve to be played."

"No one deserves it."

"Look, I am upfront with mine. Can Quinton say the same?"

"I really don't know. I honestly don't pay as much attention to his love life as you seem to do."

"Then you are choosing to turn a blind eye."

"Whatever, Rayven. Are you ready?"

"Sure," she said, standing. I followed her lead. "Just be careful, Des. You are an emotional person with a big heart. Please don't let Q pull you into one of his games. Don't get your heart broken."

"You have a great imagination. Stop worrying."

"Okay, if you say so. Now let's go shop until we drop."

"I am right behind you."

As we headed out the door, those same high school boys that were looking at Rayven earlier were breaking their necks as we walked by. One of them called out to Rayven. She turned around and said, "I am not going to jail over you!"

"I was talking to your girl," he said, smiling at me.

"You are talking to me?" I laughed. I was surprised.

"Yeah, I am talking to you, baby."

"Sweetheart, how old are you?" When he didn't answer, his boys fell out their chairs laughing at him. I grabbed Rayven's arm and pulled her out the door. She started laughing uncontrollably.

"Why are you laughing so hard? They were staring at your booty when you walked by."

"Yeah, but they didn't try to get at me, baby."

"Just shut up. You get on my nerves!"

A sick feeling came over me as I read the letter in my hand. First, the text messages, now this. There was no return address. It was just an envelope with my name on it.

Desiree,

I can't stop thinking about you, sweetheart. I wish we could be together. You looked beautiful today. I didn't mean to frighten you.

Missing You,
The one

My hands trembled as I held the letter. I read the letter over and over again. What was going on? Now this person knew where I lived. Did I truly have a stalker or was someone playing a cruel joke on me?

I was not dating anyone. This didn't seem like a letter from an admirer. This felt very wrong. This was not sweet or romantic. This was creepy. I felt relieved that Quinton was moving in

"Desiree!" Rayven screaming my name caused me to jump. I quickly threw the letter in my nightstand. If this continued to be a problem, I would contact the police.

Rayven and I were cooking dinner. Baked chicken, mashed potatoes, broccoli and made from scratch biscuits. My mouth was watering before we could finish. Rayven, who had just devoured a bowl of my left over spaghetti, started complaining again.

"When is he supposed to get here?" she asked, leaning against the counter. "It's getting late."

"Sunray," I said, calling her by her nickname, "please stop."

"Look, I would be very content if the man decided not to show up. It's bad enough you made me cook dinner for him."

"Why? He is not staying with you." She just gave me a blank stare. "Well, sweetheart, I do not think you have to worry about that." I looked up at the sound of a car pulling into my driveway. Sure enough, an Infiniti pulled up beside my house. A van pulled up behind it. "Here they are now."

"They?"

"Quinton and his boy, Tyler." Rayven rolled her eyes.

"Oh so now I have to deal with two of them?"

I ignored her and headed to my front door. I reached it just as Q started to bang on it.

"Quinton, stop trying to break my door down."

"Forgive me. I thought maybe you didn't hear me."

"If you break it, you are fixing it." He pulled me into a bear hug and kissed me on the forehead.

"What's up, baby. I am sorry that we are late. Tyler held us up."

"Des, it really wasn't my fault entirely. Blame Q too."

"What does it matter?" I asked. "You both are cool, Tyler."

"What's up, beautiful? Come on over here and give a brother a hug. I threw my arms around him. "How are you doing?"

"I am alright. How about yourself?" He smells good, I thought.

"Oh, I am good. I am just a little tired, thanks to Quinton."

Quinton spoke up. "Stop lying, man. It's your own fault."

"Yeah, uh huh. I plead the fifth."

All three of us turned as Rayven entered the room. She had her pocketbook with her. Okay, now she was taking things a little too far. Was she really about to leave? I was ready to go off.

"Where are you going?" I asked. "Are you leaving?"

"I want wine and you don't have any. Would you like anything?"

"I am cool, as long as you share that wine with me."

"Cool." She then proceeded to walk past us all.

"Hello, Rayven." Quinton spoke to her with a smirk on his face.

"Quinton." She didn't glance his way. I almost laughed when Tyler grabbed her hand.

"Sweetheart, what's the matter?"

"Nothing." She was forced to stop and look at him.

"Something's wrong. Did you have a bad day? Your man tripping or what?"

"Could be any of those." Her eyes had brightened.

"It has to be. So, how are you doing, Rayven?"

"I am okay. How are you?"

"I am wonderful. I am Tyler by the way." He offered his hand and she actually shook it.

"Rayven. Nice to meet you." She managed to smile. "Des, I will be back shortly." She looked back at me.

"Okay. Don't take all day. I know you are hungry." A huge grin suddenly appeared across her face.

"You already know." With that, she was gone.

"Wow." Tyler turned to me. "What's with your girl?"

"Who knows," I said, shrugging. "Don't pay her any attention."

"That chick just doesn't like me." Quinton spoke up.

"Quinton, don't you go worrying about Rayven."

"Oh, I am not. I could really care less whether she likes me or not. I haven't done anything to her." There was a strangeness in his eyes but I didn't call him out on it.

"I know." I just shrugged. "She can be hard to deal with."

"Yep, so what smells so good?"

"Dinner." I laughed as Q and Ty peered into the kitchen.

"What's for dinner?"

"Baked chicken, mashed potatoes, broccoli and biscuits. Don't y'all have something to do?"

"Can't you bless us with some of that good cooking?"

"You both know you are welcome to have some."

"Thanks!"

"Sure. Why don't y'all start bringing Quinton's stuff in? I have to finish up some things and we do have to wait on Rayven."

Quinton frowned, but didn't say anything. Instead, he and Tyler disappeared outside. It was time to move in.

As I stared after them, an uneasy feeling washed over me. Was having Quinton in the house going to be a good thing? With my bad dreams and crazy stalker, I was relieved to have him around. However, I was extremely attracted to him. Would I be able to keep my desires at bay?

I quickly shook my head as I headed to the kitchen. I could do this. Nothing was going to happen. I was not going to ruin my friendship with Quinton over some hormones.

"You got this."

2

Secrets

"Nothing is covered up that will not be revealed, or hidden that will not be known." *Luke 12:2*

Desiree

Thirty minutes later, we all sat down and had a civilized dinner. Ray was decent towards Q. I could tell that it was not quite sincere, but I could deal with that. He said he didn't care, but I think he appreciated it. He was smiling. I was convinced at that moment that the two of them had a thing for one another.

After dinner, while we were cleaning up in the kitchen, I caught Quinton and Tyler checking my best friend out from the living room. Jealousy washed over me. I had been feeling it a lot lately.

Men loved her. Why would these two be any different? Just because Rayven wasn't Q's favorite person, didn't mean he couldn't recognize the beauty in her. She was 5'10" with curves for days. She had cocoa brown skin, long reddish brown hair and hazel eyes.

"A lot of sexy in this room," I mumbled under my breath.

Quinton and Tyler were both gorgeous. I had watched countless women literally fight for their attention since high school. Desperate, immature, thirsty women. It was insane.

Even I had flipped over Tyler's chocolate complexion and devastating smile when we first met. Those dimples drove all the girls wild back in the day. Plus, he was tall at 6'1" with an athletic build. Grey eyes, wavy hair, and a goatee. All of it was sexy to me.

I may have found it all too sexy once. I laid eyes on Tyler as a teenager and lost my mind. I stared at him in awe. I was tongue-tied. I was crushing hard. It was puppy love.

In the beginning, he didn't notice me. All that changed the night of the prom. I was standing outside alone. Because of my date, I was having a horrific night. I was practically in tears, wanting to go home.

I jumped when Tyler approached me. My heart started beating faster than it should have. Why was he here?

"What are you doing?" he asked.

"Nothing."

"Why are you out here alone?"

"Getting fresh air."

"Are you crying?"

"No," I lied.

"Yes, you are." He reached out and touched my cheek. "Why are you crying?"

"My date is being a jackass."

"He is known for that. You want me to go in and rough him up? I will do that for you."

"No, I will be fine."

"You look beautiful."

"Thank you." My cheeks were burning. I was glad that it was dark outside. "So do you," I blurted.

"Thanks for noticing, Desiree."

I was not prepared when he kissed me. It was sweet and gentle.

"I'm sorry. I always wanted to do that."

"It's okay."

"It was nice."

"I agree." I smiled and looked away.

"I would love to hang out with you, but I don't want to be rude to my date."

"I understand."

He disappeared for the night. I was left in shock. I was left wondering what just happened.

I walked back into my prom and proceeded to ignore my date. I sat in the corner, wishing Rayven was here. We didn't attend the same school. If she was here, then she would have deserted her date just to make sure I was okay. That was the type of friend she was.

I watched Quinton and Tyler dancing in the middle of the room. Girls were all around them. They were the two hottest dudes in school. Everyone wanted a piece of them. I was no different.

After the last dance, I quickly headed towards the door. I didn't want anyone to see me. I was about to call my sister to come get me and I would crash at her apartment, but someone grabbed my arm.

"Tyler, what is it?" I frowned.

"Where are you going?"

"Home."

"I will take you."

"You don't have to. Where's your date?"

"She got a little tipsy. She left with friends."

"Oh."

"Come on." Before I could respond, he grabbed my hand. He opened the door to his BMW.

"Whose ride is this?"

"My dad's."

He didn't take me home. He took me to a private spot by a lake. He turned on some Usher and pulled me out of the car.

"May I have this dance?"

"What are you doing?"

"I know you didn't have a good time tonight. Let me make it up to you." Wow, I thought.

We danced together under the stars. Every few moments, Tyler would kiss me. I melted with each kiss.

I am not sure how it happened. I don't think Tyler had planned on anything more than kissing happening between us, but teenage hormones got in the way. Before I could think clearly, my dress was around my waist and my underwear was coming off. Against his dad's BMW, Tyler took my virginity.

Neither of us talked about that night. Sometimes, we would share a look, but nothing more. I never told anyone. I didn't tell Rayven and I didn't tell Quinton. To be honest, I am not sure how Quinton would like knowing that Tyler and I had been intimate.

I looked over at Quinton and shook my head. What T and I shared was over ten years ago. Shamefully, these days, Quinton was the one to get me hot and bothered. Sometimes, I would stare at him and would have to leave the room to get myself together. Why did God have to make one man so attractive?

He was tall just like his best friend. He was 6'3" with an incredible body. Mocha-Brown complexion, hazel eyes, a bald head. Everything on that man was perfect.

I turned slightly to see him biting his lips. Goodness, I loved those lips. I turned away quickly. Whenever he did that, I would get turned on. This time was no different.

I didn't realize that my mind had drifted until I almost dropped a glass. My cheeks got hot. Thankfully, no one noticed.

An hour later, Rayven and I were sitting on my couch, sipping on Moscato, watching the Real Housewives of Atlanta when Quinton approached us with a proposition.

"Ladies, we are heading out tonight, would you like to join us?"

"Hmm, I don't know." I didn't know if I felt like going out. I was content with getting tipsy on my couch tonight. Did I feel like getting dressed up and coming home with throbbing feet?

"What else are you doing tonight?"

"This!" I laughed.

"Oh come on, you can do that any other night."

"I thought you both were tired?"

"Been a little stressed lately. I just want to have some fun."

"You don't need us to have fun."

"Come on, come out with us. We haven't hung out in a while."

"Okay, fine. Stop begging."

"Cool. See you ladies later then. Come on Tyler; let's get this bookcase built in the next two hours."

"Coming." I blushed when Tyler leaned over to kiss me. "See you later, beautiful."

"Stop flirting."

"Can't do that."

"Do you actually like the attention, Desiree?" Rayven asked as soon as they left the room again.

"Why do you ask?"

"Your face is red. This happens every time a man flirts with you. I don't get why you are blushing over him of all people." The bitch had returned.

"You don't know Tyler. How are you going to judge him?"

"He hangs with Q doesn't he? I can guess his character."

"I am going to ignore that. Are you going out with us tonight?"

"Maybe." Don't do us any favors, I thought. At this point, I could care less.

"You should come."

"I said maybe."

I was relieved when Rayven went home. She was giving me a headache. I wasn't in the mood for her foolishness. I had too much to worry about. Like my stalker. That was stressing me out.

I jumped when my phone rang. I had been deep in thought, so it frightened me. I frowned at the unrecognizable number. First the text, then the letter, now this. I prayed this was someone I knew.

"This is Desiree."

"Hey, beautiful. I was starting to think that you weren't going to answer the phone." As soon as I heard his voice, I smiled. This was the fine dude that Rayven had embarrassed me in front of today. Justin. I was surprised when he asked for my number. Now I was floored that he actually called me.

"Hey, Justin, how are you?"

"I am good, sweetheart. I am glad to hear your voice.

"Really," I giggled. "I can't believe that you actually called me."

"Baby, I am definitely a man of my word. If I tell you that I am going to do something then I am going to do it."

"That's good to know."

"So, what's up? Do you have a man or what? You are probably worth it, but I am not trying to have some dude get at me over you."

"I am single, don't you worry."

"Good. I am so glad to hear that. So we are hooking up, right?"

"Isn't that the reason that you are calling me? Don't you want to hook up with me?" I was surprised at my own boldness.

"I wanted to know what you were up to tonight. Are you busy?"

"Well…."

"Sounds like you are." He sounded disappointed.

"I am sorry."

"Yeah, me too."

"If you had called two hours ago, I would have been all yours."

"Sadly, I had intended too, but I got caught up with the family."

"I understand."

"Look, I still want to do this."

"Me too."

"Good. I am not from around here. I am actually visiting family, so I am only here for another two weeks. I do promise that I am going to take you out. Can I call you tomorrow?"

"You may."

"Okay, cool. I will be thinking of that pretty smile all night."

"You are too sweet."

"There is more where that comes from. You have fun tonight."

"I will. You too."

"I will try my best. Goodnight."

"Goodnight."

"Who's Justin?" I jumped. I didn't know Quinton was in the room. He sat down on the couch beside me. I was surprised when my entire body tensed up. That was not a good sign.

"Wow, Q! You scared me."

"Don't avoid the question. Who is Justin?"

"Justin is a guy I met today."

"Look at you smile when I say his name."

"He's really cute. I haven't been on a date in a while."

"Whose fault is that?"

"I haven't really had the opportunity."

"Yeah, right. I don't believe that for one second."

"It's the truth."

"No, you play hard to get, but I am happy for you. You deserve to meet someone. You seem to be genuinely interested."

"Thank you."

He stared at me as if he wanted to say more, but didn't. I frowned. Quinton was never someone to bite his tongue. Not around me anyway.

'What is it, Q?"

"Nothing. I have lost my train of thought. "I really came to say that we are leaving in an hour. Can you handle that?"

"I can." He reached over and squeezed my hand. A strange feeling washed over me. I felt butterflies. That was a sign of trouble to come.

"Good. See you in a few." I was glad that he didn't noticed. I walked to the kitchen to grab another glass of wine before heading to my bedroom.

I showered and then slid on my new turquoise dress from today's shopping excursion. I usually didn't feel overly confident, but tonight felt differently. Today, I could appreciate the reflection staring back at me

Suddenly my phone rang. It was my best friend.

"Hey, Sunray."

"What's up, Des?"

"I am just getting ready. Are you on the way?"

"No, I am not. I won't be able to make it."

"You have got to be kidding me, Rayven. I gave up a chance to go out with Justin because I thought that you were going tonight."

"Are you serious? He called already?"

"Yeah, he did."

"Oh, I am so sorry, Des. Is he going to call you back? Will there be another chance."

"Yeah, tomorrow."

"Whew!" I heard her breathe a sigh of relief. 'I am glad that I didn't completely blow it for you."

"Rayven, why aren't you going?"

"My period came on and I am just not feeling it. My stomach is killing me so the only place I am getting dressed up for is my bed."

"Okay, I can understand that."

"Good, so do you still love me?"

"I still love you."

"I love you, too. What are you wearing?"

"That turquoise dress I brought."

"Yes, girl! You better work that! You are going to be killing them in that dress."

"I don't know about all that."

"Will you shut up for once? Don't start that BS tonight."

"You know how I am. I am sorry."

"Take a selfie and send it to me for approval."

"Okay!" This best friend of mine was a mess.

"Alright, sweetie, I am going to lie down. You go have fun. Shake what mommy gave you and get a number or two."

"I will try."

"You deserve it."

"You are right. I do."

"Wow!" That was Quinton's reaction when I entered the room.

"What? Do I not meet your approval?"

"Yeah, you do," he said, staring. I was not use to such a reaction from him. My face started to get hot.

"Stop staring. You have seen a woman in a dress before."

"This is you, though."

"What's that supposed to mean?"

"Desiree, you look beautiful, chill out." Quinton staring at me like that made me feel uneasy. I couldn't handle how intense his eyes were at the moment. I detected something unrecognizable.

"Thanks. So are we ready?"

"We have been ready. Where's Rayven?"

"Not coming." His smile disappeared. I knew his assumption.

"Oh, is that so?" His eyes had darkened a little. "Why is that?"

"It's not because of you, Quinton."

"Are you sure?" He didn't believe me.

"I am positive."

"Alright." I was relieved to drop it. "Let's roll."

Quinton

I walked behind Desiree as we headed to my car. I was glad that she couldn't see the way that I was looking at her. I couldn't stop staring at how that blue dress clung to every curve on her body. When did she get so thick?

Full breast. Coke bottle curves. A round booty. Thick thighs.

Her walk was mesmerizing. She moved as if she was moving to the rhythm in a song. A slow seductive song.

I took a deep breath and then looked up to the heavens. I didn't want to go through this with her again. I didn't want to experience those feeling of hurt and despair again.

I needed to find another woman to focus on tonight. I was going to grab the first beautiful scantily clad woman I saw. I was not planning on looking Desiree's way.

As I drove us towards downtown, I tried not to let this situation with Rayven bother me. I didn't appreciate the blatant disrespect. Some things had gone down between us in the past, but that was years ago. It was definitely time for her to stop holding a grudge. We were adults and I wasn't into playing these high school games.

Eventually, I was going to have to approach her. Now that I was going to be staying with her best friend, I suspected that she would be around a lot. We couldn't go on like this anymore.

What was my next move? I wasn't sure, but a change was going to come. Either she was going to chill with that attitude or I was going to cuss her high maintenance ass out. I really didn't want to do that because I didn't want to cause any more drama. Des would be pissed with me.

Next to my mother and sister, Desiree was the most important woman in my life.

Desiree

We headed to downtown Charlotte to a hot new club named Belvie's. Apparently, it was the place to be on a Friday night. The line was long and the place was packed.

As soon as I set foot through the door, I was ready to move to the music. Dancing was always my thing. I never left anything on the dance floor. By the end of the night, I would be drenched in sweat and my heels would be in my hand.

A sexy Dominican with big arms pulled me to him as I walked by. I danced with him and then two of his buddies. After taking a break by the bar, I was pulled to the dance floor by Tyler. I went from dancing with Tyler to Quinton to Tyler and back to Quinton.

"Slow it down, girl," he whispered in my ear.

"Keep up!"

We had a blast. I was disappointed when he walked away. I could not wallow too long. I turned around and slammed into Justin.

"Hey, beautiful. Look at you, girl. That was one lucky man."

"Who, Quinton?"

"Quinton," he repeated, as if he knew who that was. "I take it you know him?"

"Oh yeah, we have been friends since we were kids."

"You sure that's not your man."

"Oh, gosh no!" I frowned at him, but he laughed.

"I was just checking. Sweetheart, you look amazing tonight."

"Thank you, Justin."

"You are welcome. I was wondering if I could try keeping up with you on the dance floor. I don't do much more than a two-step, but I can try."

"Let's see what you can do."

I danced with Justin the rest of the night. It was fun. I needed this after some recent stress. I was looking forward to his phone call. He had whetted my curiosity. I was interested.

I was little bummed when he had to leave with his boys. I smiled as he kissed me on the cheek and promised that he would text me later. I didn't have time to feel lonely, though. Quinton's arm slid around my waist. It startled me.

"Q, you can't come up behind me like that."

"I thought my man was never going to leave."

"Why did you want him to leave?"

"You owe me a dance. Come here." As he pulled me closer, a slow song came on.

"Too bad for you."

"No, we are still going to dance."

"Fine. Watch where you put your hands." I was a little nervous. I didn't know if I liked being this close to my friend. He was devastatingly attractive. While Q and I were friends, I was no different than any other female. I wanted him.

"It's part of the dance, Des." I took a huge breath and tried not to melt in his arms, but in the end, I surrendered to him. I was tired. I leaned into him, actually laying my head on his shoulder.

"Are you tired?" he finally whispered.

"Yeah and my feet hurt."

"I guess so. You danced with every man in the room. Are you ready to go?"

"Yes," I said, actually yawning.

"Let's go. Stay close." He grabbed my hand and I leaned against him as we pushed through the crowd.

"What about Tyler?"

"He's not coming home with us."

"He's getting lucky?"

"Something like that." I rolled my eyes. That didn't surprise me. "Do you want to stand here while I get the car?"

"Please," I nodded. My feet were killing me. I was not trying to make that long walk across the parking lot.

"Alright. Hold tight." Quinton had made two steps when some drunk dude approached me.

"You got a man?" he slurred, almost stumbling into me.

"Yeah," I said, staring at him, horrified.

"I see no man," he said, grabbing my hand. Before I could handle the situation, Quinton was back by my side.

"I don't think so, partner. Keep your hands to yourself." He gave the dude a slight shove so that he would back off.

"Hey!" The dude lunged for Quinton.

"Back up, little man." The dude stopped, scratched his head and walked away.

"Come on," Quinton said, pulling me. "Of course I can't leave you for two seconds."

"It's not my fault."

"No, it's that freaking dress's fault!"

"This dress is not that bad!"

"I didn't say it was bad at all. But that dress and those curves are a lethal combination and some men can't handle it." I didn't respond.

"Wait! Let me take these shoes off."

"Do your feet hurt that bad?"

"Yes sir!" He shook his head and then lifted me in his arms. He scooped my 5'8", one hundred-fifty pound frame up with no issues.

"Really! I didn't ask you to carry me."

"Shut up and be grateful."

"You have been working out? Still living in the gym I see."

"You know how I do."

"You smell so good."

"Stop flirting with me, Desiree."

"Get over yourself! It's just a compliment." He smiled

"You mean you don't secretly want me?" I kissed his cheek. I did, but I wasn't about to admit it to him. How would he have reacted if I had actually told him yes?

"No sir! I love you, but I am not in your fan club. I am not one of your groupies."

3

Resistance

"Flee from sexual immorality. Every other sin a person commits is outside the body, but the sexually immoral person sins against his own body. Or do you not know that your body is a temple of the Holy Spirit within you, whom you have from God? You are not your own, for you were bought with a price. So glorify God in your body."
1 Timothy 1:10

Desiree

When we arrived back at the house, I was so tired that I handed the keys to Quinton. Once inside, I stumbled to my bedroom and collapsed on my bed. I was annoyed when Quinton decided to not only follow me, but take a seat beside me.

"You do have your own bedroom." I turned away from him.

"Your bed is comfortable." He ignored me and lay beside me.

"Yes, it is, but so is yours."

"Don't you want to share? We could cuddle tonight."

"I don't think so."

"We used to sleep in the same bed."

"Yeah, when we were kids. Now, I sleep alone."

"By choice?" Quinton was worse than Rayven at prying in my business. I turned over and stared at him. He stared at me with his eyes darker than normal. I didn't respond. "You aren't going to answer that, huh?"

"Do I need to?"

"Every woman wants some company." I hope that he was not offering anything. I didn't want Rayven to be right about him.

"Yeah, but..."

"Not from me, huh?" he finished for me. "I am just messing with you. You're like a little sister to me."

"Quinton, we have the same birthday."

"I am two hours older, though."

"Wow." Quinton leaned in closer to me. Was he trying to smell me? "What are you doing? Stop that! I know that I need a shower."

"What are you wearing? That smell has been driving me crazy all night. What do you have on?"

"I don't know if I should tell you."

"Why not?"

"Then every woman in Charlotte will smell like me."

"Whatever. A woman has to be pretty special to get perfume from me, Desiree."

"It's called Bella."

"Bella! I like that. You have the scent all over my shirt."

"Oh, I am sorry. Would you like me to wash your shirt?"

"Come on, Des. Who do you look like? My Mother?"

"I was just trying to be polite."

"Uh huh. I enjoyed our dance earlier," he said, reaching out to rub my cheek. I could feel myself blushing.

"Did you?"

"Yeah, why are you blushing?" Did he have to call me out?

"I didn't realize I was."

"You are." We just stared at each other. I was so attracted to him right now. Was I tired and tripping, or was I tipsy from all the rum and cokes. My body felt so hot right now. Was this desire?

"I didn't know you danced so hard."

I am glad he finally said something. Things were getting awkward between us.

"There is so much that you don't know about me, Quinton."

"I am going to make sure I learn those things." I didn't respond. I just stared back at him. What was that supposed to mean? I had to be tripping. Other than an occasional compliment, I was not used to him flirting with me in anyway. I think it was my imagination. Or maybe I was craving his attention.

"What are you thinking?" I asked after a moment of silence.

"I think maybe I should keep my thoughts to myself. I don't want to offend you in anyway."

"I will take your word for it."

"Good." He stood up. I was relieved because I didn't like the way my body was reacting to him. I was not used to this. Quinton was like my brother. I closed my eyes and turned over again.

"Hit the lights will you?" I was so tired that I was tempted to fall asleep in my clothes. I did not want to get up.

"Wait a minute, sleeping beauty." What now?

"Yes, Q."

"Are you hungry?" I was.

"I am alright, sweetheart." Why did I lie to him?

"I know you are hungry." I almost jumped off the bed when he reached over and rubbed my stomach.

"I suppose something to eat sounds like a good idea right now."

"I know. Go put your pajamas on and meet me in the kitchen."

"Sure, let me take a quick shower."

"Cool, I'll be doing the same."

My mind drifted to us together in a shower. How enjoyable that would be right about now.

Oh goodness, Desiree. Maybe, I needed a cold shower. What was going on with me?

As the warm water hit my bare skin, I started to feel slight sexual tension. I was aching for the caress of a man's hands. It had been a while for me. I felt neglected. Maybe Justin could help me out.

I slid my hand across my own body thinking about the possibilities. The compromising positions. The new highs.

Where had this come from? Why was I feeling this way? I was usually able to control my desires.

"Quinton." That sexy man. He had the ability to get me all worked up. Was this how it was going to be with him living here? I hoped that I could snap out of it soon because I wouldn't be able to deal with any tension between us.

Frustrated, I shut off the water and I climbed out of the shower. The water had turned cold and it was no longer enjoyable. I toweled myself dry and walked back into my bedroom. I stood in the middle of the room naked, staring at my door. It was unlocked.

I headed to it so that I could lock it. Knowing Quinton, he would come in without knocking. That would have been humiliating. I would have sent him packing once again.

I walked over to my dresser and opened my bottom drawer. I pulled out the vibrator that Rayven had given me for my last birthday. I hadn't opened it or used it. I held it in my hand for a moment. As I stared down at it, my mind began to drift. Should I? For some reason, I could not do it.

I quickly threw it back in my drawer and slammed it shut. I touched my face and it was hot. I felt guilty thinking about it. I couldn't convince myself to ever use it. I wanted the real thing.

I rubbed myself down in baby oil. In just my panties, I stared at my reflection in the mirror. Maybe I had lost some weight. I was never happy with my body. I was curvy and I had to accept that. I didn't mind the boobs. I didn't mind the booty. I just wished my thighs didn't rub together so much. I wished my stomach was flatter.

I sighed and grabbed my tank and boxer shorts. I usually slept nude. I loved how my silk sheets felt against my skin. I had a house guest tonight, though. I would be covering up.

I went to grab my bra but decided against it. It was just Quinton. He had seen me look much worse. I didn't really care how I looked right now to him, especially since it was 3:00 in the morning. I gathered my hair in a bun, slid my feet into my favorite pink slippers and headed down the hall.

Quinton was lying in the middle of the living room floor in just boxers. Cute little M&M boxers. I giggled to myself. How adorable. I shook my head and rolled my eyes when he looked at me. He just gave me a smile. He knew what he was doing.

He was on the phone. I knew he was on the phone with Tyler when I heard the topic of conversation turn to this female with the banging body. I wondered what she looked like. What kind of woman would turn Tyler's head? Rayven?

I shrugged to myself and walked to the kitchen. I poured myself a glass of wine. I then made myself comfortable on my couch, while eavesdropping on their conversation. I took the opportunity to allow my eyes to run freely across Q's body.

Wow! When did his body get like that? From where I sat, it was nothing short of perfection. That body was a piece of art. A tempting piece of chocolate. A woman's fantasy. At least mine.

I imagined rubbing my hands across his pecs. His stomach. His arms. I stared at where his boxers hung low and my mind went there. I began to think about what he had to offer down below. My eyes finally drifted to the bulge. Oh my goodness.

I had to take a big gulp of wine. What in the world! I didn't like acting like this. This was not me at all.

I was thinking about going there with Q and that would not happen. Never. Not that he was offering. Something told me I was quite out of his league.

I almost dropped my drink when his head turned suddenly. He stared at me with narrowed eyes. My hand trembled slightly. My face felt hot again. I turned away and took another sip. I prayed that he could not tell what I was thinking.

"I will talk to you later," he said, finally ending his conversation. "What are you looking at, Desiree?" Did he really ask me that?

"I was looking at you," I admitted. "Can I not look at you?" I stood quickly and headed to the kitchen. He followed.

"Why are you running from me?"

"I am not running. I need more wine."

"Is that it?" I didn't realize how close he was until he grabbed my hand. He forced me to look up at him. I just stared back into those eyes of his. He knew how beautiful of a man he was. Why did he feel the need to tease me?

"Why are you holding my hand?"

He didn't say anything. He reached out and touched my face. I felt like every inch of my body responded to that innocent touch.

"You...." He started to say something and then stopped.

"What?"

"Never mind." He kissed my forehead and walked away. Wow.

"What are you doing?"

"Fixing us something to eat, remember."

"Oh."

"You want pancakes?"

"How did you know?"

"We know each other, don't we?" he said, looking over his shoulder. "Don't you think that I remember that you love pancakes?

"You're right. Nothing can hit the spot like some pancakes."

He stopped to look at me. "You haven't met the right man."

"Quinton." I was so hot. I wanted to come out of these clothes. "Two very different spots, my friend. Dirty mind."

"That wasn't too dirty." He turned back around.

"Uh huh. When's the last time that you had some?" When did I get so bold? Sex was not a topic that came up too often between us.

"Too long!"

"Really? What's that?"

"Last month." I didn't believe him. He turned away.

"Oh my goodness, really?" I would play along.

"To me that's a while. Don't judge me. How about yourself?"

"About four months." He literally dropped a fork. I shook my head. "You said no judgment."

"It's been that long? Why?"

"I don't know! Leave me alone!"

He stared at me. Oh gosh! If he wanted it, I would have thrown myself at him. I am not quite sure why.

"Was it good for you? Your last time?"

"It was... I can't remember." Why was he being this nosy?

"Wow," he laughed. "What kind of men are you being intimate with?" There he was staring at me. I felt as if he was undressing me with his eyes. I knew it was my imagination, though. Why would he do that to me?

"Shut up, Quinton."

"That must have been a selfish man, Desiree. If it was special, you would have remembered."

My mouth was so dry. We had to get off this topic.

"So did Tyler get lucky?" Well it wasn't a 360, but more like a 180. I was hoping we could stop focusing on me.

"Were you eavesdropping, sweetheart?"

"It was hard not to, sweetheart," I sad, mocking him.

"Now look who is nosy."

"You really can't say anything."

"Whatever. Yeah, he got what he wanted."

"Didn't sound like the goods were worth talking about."

"You really were hanging on to my every word."

"Come on, tell me."

"You want all the glorious details."

"Yeah go ahead and run it past me."

"Wow, you keep surprising me tonight," he laughed.

"I am full of surprises."

"Are you?"

"Quinton, enough about me please." I was getting desperate. I felt as if I needed another shower at this point.

"You sure you won't get offended or become judgmental."

"No, talk to me like I am one of your boys."

"I can't do that. You aren't one of my boys. You….."

"I'm what? No, no, never mind. Talk."

He told me how Tyler met this beautiful Puerto Rican girl visiting some friends from Miami.. She had the long hair, the chest, the tiny waist and the booty. This was Tyler's type of woman. Her name was Sophia.

Sophia and Tyler were making out at the club earlier, so they knew they were going to leave together. They went back to her girl's spot. The party continued there. The chemistry was explosive, so Ty knew he was going to be a very happy man by the end of the night.

They made out on the couch before Sophia led him to the bedroom. They stripped down, she pushed him on the bed and then did a sexy dance for him. He was practically whispering, "I love you" before the main show begun.

That's when she made the ultimate mistake. She tried to jump on the pony without a saddle. Tyler demanded that she grab a condom, but she put up a fight.

"I am on the pill."

"No condom, no loving, baby."

Tyler loved when his women could put the condom on for him. She fumbled. Already, frustrated, Tyler had to take matters into his own hand. He was on the verge of leaving at that point.

Sophia climbs onto the saddle and attempts to show how she could salsa in the bedroom, but she quickly lost control. He told her to slow down, but she screamed, "Keep up". He took the steering wheel and decided to drive a while but she was still trying to drive from the passenger seat.

"She had rhythm on the dance floor, but her moves in the bedroom were a fail."

"So what did he do?" I found the story hilarious.

"He rolled off of her and told her that he was out. He told her that his wife was expecting him."

"Really, Tyler? Not cool."

"No, it wasn't. I agree."

"So what did she do?"

"She was pissed. She cussed him out in Spanish. She threw a couple things at him. Tyler remained calm, got dressed and told her to work on some things and walked out.

"He got out alive?"

"Yeah, he called me before he pulled out of her driveway."

I dropped my head into my hands. I started laughing so hard that tears were falling down my cheeks.

"This is not funny. I should not be laughing at my boy," Quinton said, shaking his head. He had been laughing with me.

"It's hilarious and you know it, Quinton."

"You better not tell him that I told you. He would kill me."

"You know that I couldn't do that. How would I bring that up?"

"I trust you. Poor, Tyler."

I didn't feel sorry for him. That's what he got for trying to hook up with some girl who he knew nothing about. I didn't quite understand how people could do one night stands. You could catch diseases too easily these days. It was not worth it. One night of pleasure in exchange of something incurable did not sound like a good deal.

I sat at my kitchen table consumed with my own thoughts for a while. I looked at an old copy of Cosmopolitan while Quinton played chef. I tried desperately not to look at him in order to remain clam.

"Come here, Desiree."

"What is it?"

"Come taste this." I stood and walked over to him. "Open your mouth." I did, so he could feed me.

"Oh!" I rubbed my stomach because his pancakes were delicious. "Give me more, please." My eyes were closed, so I was surprised to open them to find that he looked amused.

"What!"

"Don't do that in front of me."

"Do what?"

"Make love to your food."

"Does that turn you on?" When I blurted those words, I instantly regretted it. I wanted to take it back.

"Very much so," he whispered. He was kidding me.

"Whatever. I want pancakes."

"Here." I took the plate, took my seat, thanked the Lord above and went to work. We both ate in silence. As Quinton put it, I made love to my food. Afterwards, he looked at me and smile. "You have a little syrup on the corner of your mouth."

"Do I?" I went to lick it.

"You don't quite have it. Would you like my help?"

"Yeah, why don't you come help me?" I was surprised enough when he grabbed my face, so when he leaned in to me, I almost fell out my chair. I closed my eyes as he kissed the corner of my lips.

"Did you get it?" I whispered.

"I think so." He didn't move his face back. Our lips kind of just hovered near one another as if we were both daring the other to go for it. I was tipsy and horny. What was his problem?

"What have you been drinking?"

"Nothing," he said, pulling back finally. "Why do you ask?"

"Because you have apparently lost your mind."

"Nah." He laughed, pulling completely away. I was relieved, but a little disappointed at the same time. "We haven't done anything wrong," he said, grabbing our plates and heading to the sink.

"Leave the dishes until tomorrow, I will get them." I stood and headed to the living room. I grabbed the remote, fell back on the couch and started flipping channels. Moments later, Quinton joined me. I was glad he didn't sit too close to me.

"Thanks for cooking."

"You are welcome." Neither of us said anything for a while. Something strange flowed between us. I wasn't sure if it was tension, guilt or disbelief at the fact that we almost kissed.

"What's wrong?" I asked, sensing something was on his mind.

"Nothing is wrong?"

"Just tell me. You look sad." I reached over and touched his cheek. He grabbed my hand and kissed my palm.

"I am tired of being alone."

"What! Are you being for real?"

"I am always honest, Desiree." He gave me this look.

"What are you looking for? A girlfriend? A commitment?"

"Can't I want that?"

"You can, I am just finding all that hard to believe."

"What makes you say that?" He didn't look too pleased with me.

"Settling down with one woman has never been your thing."

"Can't a man grow up and change up his style?"

"I suppose."

"I was not ready for a commitment at first. Now I am."

"I am still not quite sure that you are ready."

"Wow, thank you, Des."

"It's surprising. You date a lot of women."

"I have been in a serious relationship."

"Did I know you?" I knew that I was making him angry, but I had to be sure. I had seen Quinton break many hearts.

"Yes, you did," he actually snapped. "Why is it hard for you to believe that I want the same things out of love that you do?"

"I am sorry, Q."

"Are you?" He didn't look at me; he just kind of stared off into space. I moved closer to him and rubbed his shoulder.

"I am. I was not trying to hurt your feelings."

"Are you sure about that?"

"Yes. Have you been in love before?"

"I have been in love before. I have never felt loved in return." That was a horrific feeling. I knew that from firsthand experience. Not being loved in return could drain you. It made you feel hopeless to the point where you avoided looking for it anymore.

"You are still young."

"I am almost twenty-seven."

"That's still young."

"Don't try to sugarcoat things. I am twenty-seven and I have never experienced love."

"That doesn't mean anything. You still have a lot of life ahead of you. There's plenty of time, Q."

"No, time is running out. I feel like a life without love is a life passing me by."

"Please don't feel that way."

"Look, I know what I have done in the past. I have been reckless. I have made many mistakes, but I am ready to move past all that. I have had a change of heart."

I looked at him and finally the disbelief was drifting away. He was being sincere. He had to be.

"I need one woman, Des. I need a woman who wants to be my queen. Someone who will love me through my flaws."

"You will find her."

"I have been telling myself that for the last year now."

"Well if you have to keep telling yourself that for another year, you need to do it."

"Don't say that. That's a long time."

"I am sorry, but it's true."

"I want to experience the unconditional love of a woman right now, not years from now."

"I know."

"I want someone to hold at night. Someone to wake up to. "

"You can have any woman that you want." Did he understand how devastatingly attractive he was. Despite his womanizing ways, I thought he was a good person. Everyone deserved to feel loved.

"Thanks, but not any woman," he said, rubbing my thigh. I grabbed his hand because even that was turning me on. "Many women seem to just want to hook up. I know that's on me too. These aren't the women that I want to settle down with."

"You keep going after the wrong women. Where do you usually pick up your women?

"Anywhere. Clubs, restaurants, the mall."

"Nothing good comes out of club. Look at T tonight."

"You are right," he laughed. "What else am I supposed to do? Going to the club is part of my career."

"Get hooked up."

"None of my boys are trying to help."

"How do you know?"

"I know them."

"Oh. Well, maybe I can help you out."

"How?"

"I can hook you up."

"You have someone in mind."

"Sure. I know plenty of good single women."

"Send them my way, sweetheart."

"So, you would like that?"

"Yeah, baby."

"Okay. I will see what I can do for you."

"Thank you." He pulled me into a hug and I swear I melted. I just inhaled his scent and willed my body not to react.

"Do you have a type?" I asked, pulling away.

"Someone who looks just like you."

"Like me?"

"Yes, Desiree, you are incredibly beautiful." My face turned hot again. I couldn't help it. I reached up and touched my cheeks.

"Am I?" This was news to me.

"Yes. Stop blushing. Start believing that."

"Thank you, Q."

"Can she have your lips? Can she be thick like you? Can she…"

"Stop, Q." I stood. I had to get away from him for the night. I had started imagining what it would feel like to cuddle up to him.

"Where are you going?"

"I am going to bed. I am really tired. It's like 4:30."

"Okay. That does sound like a good idea, but I am not quite sleepy. Why don't you stay with me a while? We can cuddle." Before I could respond, he was pulling me down beside him. "Come here." I took a deep breath and laid my head against his shoulder. Why was he torturing me?

"Just for a little while."

"Let's see if we can find a movie."

"Cool." I remembered him turning on the TV and flipping channels. A picture of a young Michael Jackson flashed across the screen. Little MJ singing "I want you back" was the last thing that I remembered.

4

Tempted

"Watch and pray that you may not enter into temptation. The spirit
indeed is willing, but the flesh is weak."
Matthew 26:41

Quinton

I woke up with the TV glaring in my face. I was so out
of it that I didn't know where I was at. For a moment, I thought I
that I was at some chick's house and we were cuddled up on the
couch after some fun. I looked over and I realized that I was
snuggled up with Desiree.

This was not bad at all. I was holding a beautiful woman in my
arms. A woman that meant something to me. I should have been
feeling pretty lucky. I wasn't because I had come to the realization a
long time ago, that this was the closest I would ever get to her

"You are so beautiful," I whispered aloud, staring at her sleeping
face. She had been driving me crazy all night. When I saw her in that
blue dress earlier, it did something to me. When we slow danced
earlier, I didn't know what to think. When we almost kissed in the
middle of her kitchen, she almost sent me over the edge.

I was trying hard to play it cool around her. I was trying to keep
my desire at bay. If she knew how much I just wanted to feel those
lips of hers on mine, she would flip. She would have cussed me out
and sent me packing if I followed through with kissing her.

Des and I had been friends since we were kids. I would often tell
her that she was like a sister to me, but it was the farthest thing from
the truth. Often, I found myself staring at her, yearning for
something I couldn't have. I wanted affection from someone who
wasn't willing to give it. The story of my life.

"I am not good enough for you."

"Hmmm?" Did she hear me? I was relieved when her breathing told me she was really asleep.

She didn't respect me. It was obvious. She hated how I dealt with women. I could not really blame her. I knew what I did was wrong. I wasn't sure why I hadn't been able to get my act together. My mother had taught me so much better. If she knew what I had done over the years, it would break her heart.

"Time for a change," I whispered.

Desiree shifted again against me. I thought about pulling her completely in my arms and keeping her there but I knew she would resist. I sighed, almost feeling defeated. I decided that I need to just get her to bed and maybe go take another shower myself.

I stood and scooped her up in my arms. She wrapped her arms around my neck and whispered, "I know how to walk."

"I know that."

I took her to her bedroom and laid her on the bed. I was not thinking straightly, when I leaned down and kissed her on her lips. It was a peck, but nonetheless, I had kissed her. Her eyes flew open.

What did I do that for! I stared at her as she stared up at me. I prayed that she was not going to slap me or throw me out. Where would I go?

She sat up.

"Quinton? Why did you kiss me?"

"I don't know why, Des. I am sorry." My heart was beating fast.

"Are you?" No

"Yes."

"Okay." She just continued to stare at me. I needed to get out, but my feet weren't moving. "That's not how you kiss a girl." Before I could respond, she grabbed my hand and pulled down beside her. She grabbed my face and pushed her lips against mine.

It didn't last long, but long enough. And it was better than I had imagined. The type of kiss that left you speechless. The type of kiss that could lead to so much more.

"I don't know why I did that?" She said afterwards, moving away. I wasn't sure why she did it either, but I sure did appreciate it. "Quinton, why did you let me do that?"

"I don't know why. I wanted you too."

"You shouldn't want to kiss me. I am your little sister, remember."

"Not anymore. Not after tonight. I can't look at you like my little sister. You're too beautiful. Too sexy. I notice too much." Her face started growing red.

"Don't tell me that."

"Stop being shy, you just kissed me."

"You kissed me first."

"I did. I don't regret it."

"I….we should go to bed."

"You're right. Goodnight, Desiree."

"Goodnight, Q." I leaned over, kissed her forehead and got out of her room as quickly as I could. I headed to the kitchen because I needed water. I took down two glasses before heading to my bedroom. I climbed into my bed immediately and tried to go to sleep.

I couldn't. I was restless. I couldn't fight it. I turned on the TV and tried to focus on anything besides Desiree. That didn't work.

Why? Why did I just kiss that woman when I knew that it was going to leave me wanting more? More was not something that I was willing to pursue. Not with this woman. Our friendship meant too much to ruin over some chemistry that we obviously had.

It couldn't have just been on my behalf. I know I kissed her first, but she kissed me back. She took things to a level that I would have never imagined. She threw herself in my arms. Both felt good.

"Why did I kiss her?"

Because of that blue dress. Because she felt good in my arms when we danced. Because she smelled so good. Because I wanted to.

I was staying here for almost a year. If I didn't find some other chick to focus on, this was going to be one long year. I was going to have to do better than I did tonight at controlling my temptations. I couldn't go there with her, no matter how much I wanted to. I had to let this go.

I had been pushing aside all these cravings I had for Des over the years, but now we were under the same roof. I am not sure if I should've been praying to God, but I needed strength. I was not sure how I was going to be able to do this. Stay away? I didn't want to.

"She's beautiful."

She was my kind of woman. Curvy and thick in the right places. She had it all, the boobs, the booty, the thighs and that itty bitty waist. She was 5"8' with a cocoa brown complexion and sexy long jet black hair. She had beautiful light brown eyes and a pouty smile.

The craziest thing about it was that she didn't realize how beautiful she was. I couldn't begin to understand that. She was the kind of woman that took your breath away. I had watched men openly stare at her. Maybe she was just being humble.

When was the last time I had been intimate with a woman that meant something to me? A woman that could make me smile even when she was not around. A woman that made you erase all the other numbers out of your phone. A woman you would do anything to make happy.

The last couple of women I had been with had been big disappointments. In every way possible. Some were jealous and possessive, others were in it for the perks, and some were just dull and stupid. They didn't satisfy all of my senses.

I had been really into a girl I met two months ago. Kaylen. We went out every other night for two months. I really liked her and was for once looking towards the future. Yesterday, she told me she was going back to her ex. We were done just like that.

And then there was Christina. An adulterer. She was nothing, but a waste. I wished last night would have never happened.

Frustrated, I realized that I was still thirsty. I headed back to the kitchen. Once there, I took down two glasses of water. What was going on? Why couldn't I get enough? I almost felt feverish.

"I need to go to bed."

On the way back to my room, I walked right into her. She stood in the middle of the hall in just a tank top and some boy shorts. Oh my goodness. She had to know I was up. Did she not care?

"What are you doing up?" I asked.

"I can't sleep." I can't either. On the account of you. "What are you doing up?"

"I was thirsty. Were you headed to the kitchen?"

"No, I wasn't headed to the kitchen."

"Where are you going?" She had a bathroom in the room.

"I heard you were up."

"Yeah."

"I am going to regret this."

"Regret what?"

"This," She said, backing me up into the wall. For the second time tonight, she kissed me. What was she doing to me? Why?

I wrapped her completely in my arms. I kissed her back as if she was all mine. It lasted forever. I didn't want her to stop.

"Those lips of yours," she said, finally pulling away.

"My lips? What about yours? You can't keep doing this to us."

"What am I doing?" she said, backing up to her bedroom. I don't know why but I reached out and grabbed her waist.

"Starting this fire between us."

"I don't mean to," she said, looking down.

"Sure," I said lifting her chin. I leaned over and kissed her again. "I like the way kissing makes me feel."

"But you shouldn't."

"What can I say?" I shrugged.

"We can't cross this line again. Tonight is it!"

"I agree." Did I?

"Okay, good. Well, goodnight." She threw her arms around me. I clung to her for as long as she let me. How could something feel so good make you feel this bad afterwards?

"Night, Des." She smiled at me and disappeared in the room.

I turned and headed back to the kitchen. I needed more water.

I woke up later on that day around 2:00. It took me forever to fall asleep, but I finally did. I got up and immediately headed to the bathroom. I drank a gallon of water the night before.

I found a shirt and headed to the front of the house. I figured that I should show my face. Hopefully things weren't going to be too awkward between me and Desiree.

She was in the middle of the kitchen in a short yellow dress. Mercy! Not first thing in the morning. I never noticed her in all these dresses before.

"Well hello, sunshine." She was cheerful as she greeted me.

"Hello, beautiful. What are you doing?"

"Making a sandwich. Do you want half?" Before I could respond, she was handing me the other half.

"Thank you. So are you headed out?"

"Yes, I am."

"Where you headed?"

"I have a date. With Justin."

"Who's that?"

"He's the guy that I met yesterday. I was dancing with him."

"How can I forget him? He was in your face the entire night."

"You and I spent plenty time together on the dance floor."

"He took time away from me."

"You were okay."

"So you are spending the rest of the day with him."

"We are just hanging out for a couple of hours. He has things to do. He's not from around here."

"Oh okay. I am sad that we aren't spending the day together."

"Well I will be home early if you want to hang."

"Cool.

"You are going to get tired of me. We live together now."

"I doubt that."

She looked incredible in that dress. I was feeling some type of way. Jealousy? That couldn't be it. Envy? Maybe.

"You look beautiful, Desiree," I finally blurted

"Thank you." She blushed, looking away quickly. I shook my head. She couldn't have possibly been that humble.

"So where is this Justin guy taking you."

"I don't know. I don't mind surprises."

"Good to know." She just smiled at me.

"About last night." Here we go.

"What about it?"

"We should forget it ever happen, I suppose."

"That's going to be hard."

"You think so?"

"Yes."

"Well maybe push it to the back of your mind."

"That's going to be hard too."

"Oh." She looked defeated. "What are we going to do about it then? I am sorry I kissed you, Quinton."

"I'm not."

"You aren't?"

"No, I am not."

"What are we going to do?"

"I am going to think about last night and smile."

"Really?"

"Yes, I am. It's okay if you smile too." She smiled shyly.

"It was nice. I have no problem admitting that."

"Yeah. We will hold on to the memory and move on. Deal?"

"Deal. You aren't going to tell, Tyler are you?"

"Our secret, Desiree. I wouldn't do that to you."

I was a little bummed out that she was leaving. I didn't have any plans. It would have been cool if we could have hung out. Then again, maybe it was good that she was leaving. A little distance was needed after last night. We both had fires burning within us.

I couldn't let her get involved with me. Things would get so sticky. Neither of us needed that. We needed to keep our friendship drama free. When I move out a year from now, I intend for us to still be friends. I wouldn't forgive myself if I messed that up.

I watched Desiree walk out holding hands with the dude from yesterday. I really did feel jealous. Well, maybe it was more envy than anything. I would give anything to be out with a woman right now. Instead, I was home alone on a Saturday with no plans. Tyler was busy. I could go see my family, but I wasn't in the mood.

I just gave in to my thoughts of my inadequacies. At how because of my background, I would probably never be with a good woman The good ones didn't respect me.

I suppose I couldn't blame them. I had dug my own hole. The way I had treated women over the years, even I had to admit was quite ridiculous. I was praying that the good Lord above would grant me with another chance at finding love. I was finally ready to stop running. I was ready to claim my Queen.

It was time to put down these chicks I had been dealing with. They didn't care about a man. They said that I had broken hearts, but my heart had gotten broken as well. Some chicks just wanted me to break them off some. Some just wanted to be taken care of. They didn't want to be loved by me.

I started to get mad. Was my past always going to hold me back? I deserved the chance to redeem myself. I shouldn't always have to suffer the consequences.

I had a lot going for me. I was pretty decent looking. I had a fun personality. I had a good job. I was building my own house. I was educated.

I would cook for my woman. I would nurse her back to health if she was sick. I would massage her tired feet after a long day. I would take the clothes off my back if she needed it.

I would wash her car. I would clean her house. I would take care of her financially. I would keep her satisfied in the bedroom.

I volunteered. I had ambition. I went to church and praised the good Lord above. I had what it took.

I got in the shower and stood there for the longest. The water felt good. It washed away some of my anger.

Somehow my mind drifted to Desiree and last night. Those kisses. Her sweet, soft, pouty lips.

I would never be able to look at her the same. All of that had been shattered last night. She would consume my mind for a long time. It would take another woman for me to stop yearning for her.

"I wonder if Justin will get a kiss." I hated that. I didn't want anyone to feel the way I felt last night when she kissed me.

I turned off the water, hopped out and dressed in a hurry. I had to get out of here. I felt suffocated. I needed to focus on something else. I didn't want to spend the rest of my day thinking about Des.

I got in my ride and just drove. Minutes later, I was pulling into the driveway of my baby mother's house. Almost four years ago, I made the mistake of get ridiculously drunk and hooking up with a woman who I detested. Three months later, she was telling me that she was having my baby. Seven months after that, she was delivering that baby and I was demanding a paternity test. I was the father.

I was not ready to be anybody's father. At 23, I still felt like a little boy. My son was a blessing. He changed my life and my outlook on it. I had no choice but to grow up and become a man. I went out and got myself together to support him. I was doing pretty well and as far as I was concerned there was nowhere to go but up.

Before I could get out of my car, my baby boy was running of the house.

"Daddy," he screamed.

"What's up, little man." I got out and lifted my pride in joy in my arms. I kissed his forehead as he threw his arm around my neck.

Quinton Jr was the splitting image of me. His complexion was like mine. He had my gray eyes and my smile. No one could ever tell me that this little boy was not mine. This was my heart.

Before I could even reach the sidewalk, my son's ghetto mother came to the door. She wore some ludicrously short booty shorts, a sports bra, and fuzzy slippers. She had extremely long weave and long lime green nails. Why was this chick so flashy?

She glared down at me before speaking. She sucked her teeth and said, "Quinton."

"India." I stopped on the step below her.

"And what do I owe this surprise to?"

"My son of course."

"Oh okay." She gave me this crazy look. She had it in her head that I wanted her. I was not going say anything today, though. I wanted to be civil. We didn't have the best relationship.

She turned and headed into the house. I followed.

"He has been asking about you all week."

"Has he?"

"Yes he has."

"Well, do you mind if I take him for a few hours?"

"That's cool. As long as you have him back by 9:00 tonight."

"I will."

"Alright. Come on, Quinton, let me get you ready."

"Nooo," he yelled when I went to sit him down on the floor.

"Go little man and get ready. You can hang out with me today."

"Okay, yeah!" He jumped down and went running behind his mother. Ten minutes later, I had my son in his car seat and was heading to my parent's house.

"Daddy, where are we going?"

"To see Grandma and Papa."

"Yeah!" He clapped his hands in excitement. What kid didn't love their grandparent's house when they were little? Grandparents always spoiled you rotten.

All my family seemed to be visiting at the same time. My nineteen-year-old little sister, Peyton, was in town for the weekend from UVA. My thirty-year-old big brother, Mike, was over with his wife, Tonya and their kids, Jaden and Joelle. It was like our Sunday get together, but on Saturday.

I decided that Lil Quinton and I would just chill at the folk's house for the rest of the day. I thought that it would be good for my son to play with his cousins who adored him. His hateful mother didn't take him out much. She was always worried about herself and burdening some babysitter.

While he played, I pulled my brother Mike to the side. This thing with Desiree was really bothering me and I couldn't get it off my mind. I wanted to get his opinion. He told me what I needed to hear.

"You need to stay away from that girl."

"You think so?"

"Yeah, if you need to get some, go get it from someone else. Don't jeopardize anything by hooking up with her. That's sloppy."

"I know. That woman is beautiful, though."

"Yeah, I know. I know how you love beautiful women, but you can't afford to hurt this one."

"You are right."

After playing all day and eating all the sugar his grandma had forced down his throat, I took my exhausted son back to his mother's. I tucked him in and got into it with his mother. She reeked of weed and alcohol. She needed to be sober around my son.

"Go ahead with that mess, Quinton."

"You are high and tipsy. You knew I was bringing him home."

"You have no right to come in here and tell me what it is that I can and cannot do in my own house."

"I have a right to speak up when it pertains to my son."

"I wouldn't care if I had five of your kids, you still do not need to concern yourself with what I do."

"Keep your voice down."

"For what!"

"Daddy!"

"See, you woke him up," I said, heading to my son's room.

"You should have dropped him off and left. You wanted to come in here and start an argument over something stupid."

"The way you raise my son is not something stupid."

"Whatever!" She walked into her bedroom and slammed the door. I was sure she had a dude in there.

I walked into my son's room, picked him up and rocked him back asleep. I tucked him back in and walked straight into India's room. I didn't care what dude she had up in there.

"Oh, you are just making yourself too comfortable in my house. Now what!" There was a naked dude stretched out on her bed. I paid no attention to him and he paid none to me. My issue was with my son's mother, who now stood naked in the middle of the floor.

She switched over to me and tried to push up on me. I wanted none of that. Nothing about her turned me on.

"From now on, I ask that you be sober around my son. You owe it to him to be aware of your surroundings."

"I am aware, Quinton."

"Not aware enough."

"Whatever. Why don't you stay awhile?" she asked, trying to push up on me again.

"No."

"You can be here when Quinton wakes up. He would love that." She was not looking out for our son. She was looking out for herself.

"I don't think so, India."

"What? You're too good for me now? You use to hit this."

"All of that is part of the past. I have moved on to better things.'

"What? You have a woman now?"

"Yep." I lied to her so that she would get out of my face.

"Who are you fooling?" She laughed. "I seriously doubt that you have settled down." Wow. Even my baby mother was clowning me.

"And I seriously doubt that you know anything about me."

"You better not have some whore raising my child." A whore probably could do a better job than you, I thought.

"Don't worry about who I date."

"I want to meet her!"

"Bye, India!" I turned and she was on my heels.

"I mean it!"

It was time to go. I tried being civil with her, but that was almost near impossible. I didn't want things to get out of hand. India would call the boys in blue in a minute. God knows I didn't need that. India wasn't worth me getting locked up.

I went and kissed my son and headed for the door. India was still following me, naked. She practically came outside.

"I need money."

"And..."

"Can, I get some?" I had given her my child support for the month and then some. She was tripping

"Nope. You better go in there and ask that dude you just gave your cookies to."

"I just sucked...."

"Bye." I got in my car and shut the door. She flipped me off and slammed her door.

What a horrible environment my son had to grow up in. If I could take my son from her, I would, but I couldn't exactly prove that she was an unfit mother. I did believe that my son needed his mother, despite my strong dislike for her. The courts would agree.

When I pulled back into Desiree's driveway later on that evening, Justin was coming out of the house. I didn't like seeing that. I wanted to be the only man to come out of Desiree house. I pulled myself together quickly.

"What's up, man?" I didn't want to be rude.

"Hey man. Justin Jones," he said, offering his hand. I took it.

"Quinton Alexander."

"Quinton Alexander?" He frowned at me.

"Yep." I knew where this conversation was heading.

"Are you the Quinton Alexander from off of Hot 107?"

"The one and only."

"Oh I didn't realize that Desiree was talking about you." Why would Desiree bring that up? He didn't need to know anything about me. All he needed to know was that if ever decided to disrespect my girl, it was going to be me and him.

"You aren't from around here, right?"

"Right, but I am always up here. I am from Atlanta." I didn't really care. "I hear that you are pretty popular."

"I am known. It comes with the job," I shrugged.

"I would love that job."

"It's cool." I loved my job. It helped blessed me in many ways, but I was going to be humble about it. I wasn't in the mood for a whole lot of questions.

There was something about him that I didn't particularly care for. Or maybe it was because I was jealous. Jealous that he got to spend the day with her and I didn't. It didn't matter why I didn't like him, I just didn't.

"So you and Desiree are good friends?" Obviously.

"Yeah, I have known Des most of my life."

"She seems wonderful."

"She is."

"Yeah, I am sure you know that." I wanted to tell him that you had to be a heck of man to land her. I also wanted to let him know that I didn't think he was man enough. I just kept my mouth shut.

"Yeah. Well nice meeting you, my man. Take care."

"Same to you."

Desiree was on the couch when I walked back inside. When I saw her, all the tension from tonight disappeared. Seeing her face just made me smile.

"What's up, beautiful?"

"Hey, Quinton."

"I see my man just left. How was your date?"

"It was nice." Her face lit up. She must like him, I thought. "I really like him. He was such a gentleman."

"I am happy to hear that. I would be angry if he disrespected you." Did you kiss him? I was scared to ask. I was pretty sure I knew the answer. "So, are you going out with him again?"

"Yeah, I am. Speaking of dates. I have a girl for you."

"Do you?" I wasn't as excited as I should have been. Sadly, I didn't have much hope. "Who is she?"

"Laiyah. I saw her today, she asked were you single."

"Oh okay."

"Don't worry. She's cute."

"Does she look like you?"

"Nooo. Put this number in your phone." She recited the number to me and I saved it. "Call her soon so you two can hook up."

"Alright, I will." She stood up. "Where are you going?" I grabbed her hand.

"I...." She just stared down at me. I don't really know how it happened. I don't know if I pulled her in my lap or she climbed into it, but the next thing I knew, she was straddling me. We were kissing again. Her hand was under my shirt and I was rubbing any bare skin I could find.

This was definitely not taking my brother's advice. This was not good. This was not good at all.

5

Laiyah

"Wrath is cruel, anger is overwhelming, but who can stand before jealousy?" *Proverbs twenty-seven:4*

Quinton

I made sure I called Desiree's friend, Laiyah, the next day. The way I had been feeling about Desiree these last couple of days, had me feeling desperate to find another woman to focus on. I was only twenty-seven, but I felt like I needed to settle down as soon as possible. I wanted to have a stable life for my son.

I was ready to experience love. I wanted it now. My patience was running thin. It was my time.

I dialed Laiyah's number and fell back on my bed. By the second ring, my throat was feeling dry. Why was I nervous? I was not someone who got nervous. Since I turned sixteen, I never had a problem with asking out a female. Maybe because this was important to me. I was in search of a commitment.

By the time the sixth ring rolled around, I was about to hang up. I was not into leaving messages. Just before I could press end and the disappointment could settle in, she picked up on the seventh ring.

"Hello." She answered the phone winded. What was she doing?

"Hello. May I speak to Laiyah?"

"This is her." I had that feeling.

"How are you doing, Laiyah. This is Quinton."

"Quinton!" Her voice definitely changed when she said my name. It got sexier.

"I am Desiree's friend."

"Oh, I know who you are."

"Really?"

"I have had my eye on you for a while. You are a sexy man."

"Thank you. So what's up with you, Laiyah?"

"I was just here waiting on you to call." I teased.

"So you knew I was going to call?"

"I had a feeling that you would."

"A confident woman. I like that."

"Well, you look like a man that likes having fun, so I figured you would be down for a good time."

"A good time?" I needed clarification.

"Not like that," she laughed. "Not on the first date."

"How did you know that I was going to ask you out on a date?"

"Why else would you call me?"

"I don't know. Just to see what you are about."

"True, but I know you are curious. You want to know what I look like. And I am not going to send you a picture. I want this to be a true blind date."

"Not fair. You know what I look like."

"That's because you are the Quinton Alexander."

"Don't say it like that."

"How else do I say it?"

"So do you want to get together soon?"

"Of course I do. You won't regret asking me out."

"Wow, you are sure of yourself."

"I thought that was a good thing."

"Oh, it is. It's surprising."

"I have a lot to be confident over. I am a beautiful woman."

"I bet." We shall see. "So, what were you up to before I called?" I was curious. I wanted to know why it took her so long to answer her phone. Why was she out of breath?

"I was running on the treadmill."

"Oh okay. When can I see you, Laiyah?"

"When do you want to see me?"

"As soon as I can." She was right, I was curious.

"Excitement. I like that. When are you free?"

"Whenever you are?"

"Well, I am pretty busy this week." Please don't tell me that I was being set up for more disappointment. Rejection. Nah. I could tell that she was into me. She wanted to see me. "I am still going to make time for you."

"Glad to hear that."

"How about we do lunch tomorrow?"

"What's for lunch?"

"I like you, Quinton," she laughed.

"Lunch is good."

"I thought it would be. You don't go on air until night, correct?"

"6:00 to 10:00."

"Okay. So how about we meet at Reese's? 1:00?"

"That works."

"Good. Well, I better get back to my workout."

"Okay, I won't hold you any longer."

"See you tomorrow, Quinton."

"Alright then, Laiyah."

I needed this date, especially after the heart break from the last girl I was into. I intended to bounce back quickly.

"I called Laiyah," I said, walking outside where Desiree was.

"Did you? Are you two hooking up or what?"

"Yeah, we are."

I was mesmerized because Des was washing her car. I am not sure what turned me on the most. Was it the fact that she was woman enough to wash her own car? Or was it because she was wearing tiny UNC Chapel Hill shorts and a white tank?

"That's what I want to hear. Does it seem like the two of you may have something in common?"

"I think so. That outfit is killing me." I blurted. I didn't mean to. She turned to me and blushed.

"What do you mean?"

"Sexy as hell. Why do you blush when I compliment you?"

"I am not use to attention from anyone."

"Are you kidding me? You could have any man that you want."

"You must have me confused with someone else." I frowned

"I am talking about you, Desiree. You are so beautiful and it's a shame that you don't even realize it."

"I don't think I am ugly by any means. I am nothing special. I am not one of those girls. Men don't notice me." Oh my goodness, I wanted to shake her. She couldn't be serious right now.

"You are the same woman that I had to fight at least five dudes to get a dance with the other night."

"That's because I have the right moves on the dance floor."

"No, it's because you are so sexy that it doesn't make sense. I can't keep my eyes off of you."

"Don't say that to me, Quinton." She turned her back to me. I walked over to her, grabbed her waist and turned her around.

"Why not?"

"I don't know." Her face was red. She wouldn't look at me. She started biting her lip.

"Look at me."

"Don't make me." I lifted her chin. "You shouldn't notice anything about me."

"Just because we are friends doesn't mean I can't notice your beauty. How you affect me." I shouldn't have said that.

"Affect you? What does that mean?" It means that my entire body reacts every time you walk into the same room.

"You have the sweetest lips." She bit them.

"You shouldn't know that."

"I shouldn't, but I do."

"Are you going to kiss me?"

"Should I?"

"You shouldn't." I dropped back from her. "But I want you to." I kind of smiled and pulled her into me. We kissed right there in the middle of the driveway. She pulled away first. We stared at each for a couple of moments and she gave me a small smile.

"For someone so shy, you sure are aggressive." She giggled and then turned back to her car. "Why do you keep kissing me, Desiree?"

"I kiss you because I want to."

"Why?"

"Q, you know you are gorgeous right. I am attracted to you just like every other female out there."

"Really?" She looked at me and laughed.

"You are a confident man. I am sure that didn't surprise you."

"I am confident, but not every woman is attracted to me and that's okay."

"Everyone loves Quinton Alexander."

"I don't want every chick to want me." I hated groupies. "I just never imagined that you would be attracted to me." I guess even I had insecurities. Especially when it came to this woman.

"I'm just going to be honest. I am horny and I would love to go there with you. You just do something to me." I stared at her without any words. Why did she just tell me that?

"I…"

"Please don't respond to that, Quinton. Let's not make things too awkward between us."

"But…"

"When are you and Laiyah going out?"

"We are going to lunch tomorrow." There was so much I wanted to tell her, but I couldn't. Maybe I would have offered her too much temptation. A kiss was one thing, but going further than that was a line she wasn't willing to cross

"Cool. Where are you guys going?"

"Reese's."

"I love that place." We should go sometimes, I wanted to say.

"You want some help?" I was being rude.

"I can handle it."

"Are you sure?"

"Yes."

"Okay."

I sat down and tried not to think about kissing her. I tried not to think about what she just told me. I thought about Laiyah and falling in love. I thought about Quinton Jr and his crazy mother. What could I do about that situation? Things with India were getting out of hand.

I thought about telling Desiree about my son, but something stopped me. I was going to keep my mouth shut like I had been doing for the last three years of my son's life. I never told her because I felt as if she looked down on me enough as it was. I didn't want her to see me as the typical baby daddy. I loved my son, supported him and would give him the world if I could.

If I told Desiree, she would have been pissed. I knew I was going to have to tell her eventually, especially since my son was almost three. I wasn't quite sure when the right time would be, but I would wait until it presented itself.

"Why did you think that I would be into Laiyah?" In a daze, I listen to her tell me how Laiyah was beautiful, funny, intelligent and someone who had it together. As she put it, this woman was someone that I needed in my life.

"Okay, I trust you. Who taught you to get your ride that clean?

"My ex." When I thought of her ex, I thought of Anthony. He was the one who had crushed Desiree's heart. If I saw him in the streets today, I would knock him out. I never liked him. He was definitely not good enough for her.

The look on her face told me she was thinking about him. I didn't want her to focus on him, so I stood.

"Are you finished?"

"Why do you ask?"

"Come on, I will take you to Sweet Frogs." Her eyes lit up.

"I am ready."

I went to bed early that night. One reason was so I wouldn't be tempted to make a move on Desiree. The other reason was because I had a busy day. I had to run errands the next morning. My date was 1:00 that afternoon. Then I had to pick up little Quinton from the daycare. After all of that, I had to work tomorrow night from 6 to 12. I had to do my show plus two hours of the Slow Jams.

Wow. I was in an unfamiliar situation. I had not gone on a date where I was not looking to gain something in the end in a while.

I really wanted to impress this girl, Laiyah. I took a little extra time to get dress. I settled on dark jeans and a nice button down with some Wallabees. I put on some Curve because I always had good experiences with the ladies when I wore it.

I was at Reese's at 12:50. I was rarely late. Plus, I wanted to make a good first impression. If I liked her, then I was definitely going to ask her out on a second date. I didn't have time for games.

It would have been nice to know what she looked like, but unfortunately, I didn't have much to go on. She texted me to tell me she would be wearing a black skirt and red blouse. That's all I had to go on. I didn't like that fact that she had the upper hand over me.

I was paranoid, thinking she was going to sneak up on me in any minute. I was not going to be able to get a good look at her before she approached me. If she wasn't my type, I couldn't exactly make a run for it. I would have to endure the whole date.

Laiyah was early too. Her eyes lit up as soon as she walked through the door. I knew it was her. She had this huge grin on her face as she quickly approached me.

Immediately I thought that she wasn't my type, however; she was a lovely woman. She had a caramel complexion with curly black hair. Fake hair and fake nails. She had green eyes which were obviously contacts. She had a large chest. That didn't look real. What was authentic about this woman?

She was on the slender side. She didn't have much of booty. I didn't like that at all.

She was wearing the hell out of her tight skirt and fitted blouse. She was very pulled together. I did like that. She had a sexy walk. She had a great smile and nice pouty lips.

"Hey, Quinton." Her voice sounded higher in person.

"What's up, Laiyah?" I said, leaning over to kiss her cheek

"And how did you know I was Laiyah?"

"You knew my name."

"True, but I could have been one of your groupies. You are the Quinton Alexander."

"Stop that."

"I will try. Shall we find a table?"

"Let's do that."

"You were early," she said once we were seated.

"Yeah, I hate being late."

"Me too."

Halfway through the meal, I was not too sure about this girl. She didn't impress me. I couldn't pinpoint the exact issue, but something didn't feel right. I was not sure if I wanted to see her again.

She giggled a lot. At any and everything. She was laughing at things that weren't even funny. That annoyed me. It was a turn off.

I was also irritated at her picking over her salad.

"Just a salad?" I asked when she ordered.

"I'm not that hungry." I left it alone. Admittedly, some salads these days were very satisfying, but everyone knew that you didn't come to Reese's for a salad. She was picking over a few pieces of lettuce and some cucumbers. I had issues with that.

My mother was an award winning Chef, so I grew up eating very well. I loved food and had a large appetite. Going to new restaurants and trying new foods was my thing. I needed a woman who could get down with that.

I spent $12.00 of my hard earned money on her salad and her ice tea for her not to appreciate it. She barely drank the tea. Reese's had some of the best tea in the city. What was wrong with this chick? I was ready to force half of my sandwich down her throat. I almost said something but I didn't want to be rude to Desiree's girl.

The conversation was lacking. I am not sure what happened to the flirty and witty girl on the phone yesterday. Today, she failed to bring anything to the table. I was doing all of the talking.

"Something is missing from this chick," I said to myself when she went to the bathroom. A personality.

I knew by the time she walked back to table, that I would not be asking Laiyah out again. This was a sorry excuse for a date. She was not my type. Miss Fake didn't do anything for me.

I was not going to let on that I was not feeling her. Usually, I would, but I was attempting to be civil. There was no reason to be rude. She was still a nice person. I was just not into her.

Well," she said turning to me after I walked her to her car.

"Yeah." What was I supposed to say?

"Thank you, Quinton." She leaned over and kissed me on my lips. Dag! I should not have let her do that. Now, she was going to think something was possible between us. I didn't care how nice her lips were, this date was not good enough to seal with a kiss.

"No problem."

"We need to go out a night next time." Why did she think that I was going to ask her out again? "Maybe our next date will end with something more than a kiss."

Wow! Was she offering sex? This time I was not willing to bite the bait. I don't think that I could be intimate with her. I was not overly attracted to her. She was no Desiree Harris.

"Okay." That was all I said. I would not be calling her again.

We said our goodbyes and I was on my way. Man, I was so disappointed. That date was a big fail. I was agitated because I was becoming more and more impatient with this love thing.

I was going to talk with Des about why she thought it would be in my best interest to hook up with Miss Giggles. I needed to educate her on what kind of women I liked. I still had faith in her, though.

I stopped by the music store to kill time. I had another hour before it was time to pick up little Quinton. There were some new artists out that I wanted to check out.

"How are you doing?" A cute chick walked past me in the store.

"Fine." She smiled at me. What's good with you?"

"Not much. In here trying to see who is out these days."

"Me too." Her name was Fallon. She was pretty sexy. She had a quick sense of humor. She appeared to have it all together. I didn't hesitate asking for her number.

After buying a couple CDS, I went and picked up my son. I took him to Mickey D's, brought him a Chicken Nugget Happy Meal and let him play a while. We hung out, talked and laugh. I spoiled him by buying him a few treats before taking him home to his mother.

After dropping him off, I headed to the station. I did my thing across the airwaves for the next six hours. By the end of night, I was exhausted from answering phones, asking trivia questions and tripping with some local celebrities. I loved my job, though.

I got home around 1:00 in the morning. I intended to head straight for bed, but was surprised to find Des still up. She was lying half-awake on the couch in front of the TV.

"What's up, girl?"

"Hey," she said, smiling up at me.

"Why are you still up?"

"I was waiting on you."

"Why?" I asked, taking a seat beside her. "Do I have a curfew?"

"I want to hear about your date," she said, shoving me.

"Desiree, why did you set me up with that girl?"

"What! You didn't like her?"

"Not at all."

"What was wrong with her?" she asked, laughing.

"Why are you laughing? Why did you do that to me?"

"No, it's not like that, Quinton."

"Are you sure?"

"I am not that mean."

"What's wrong with her?"

"You don't like fake?" She was still laughing.

"No. I don't want to insult your girl too much, so I won't tell you what else I thought about her.

"Truth be told, she is not really my girl."

"Huh? What do you mean? You hooked me up with some chick that you didn't even know?"

"No, it's not like that either."

"What? Wait. I am confused."

"When I go out with the girls from work, she tags along. She's not exactly part of the clique, but we aren't rude enough to leave her out. We figure the more the merrier."

"That doesn't explain why you hooked us up."

"Well, I didn't really choose her for you. She knows you off the radio. Everyone at work knows that we are close. When she found out, she freaked out. She basically begged me to give you her number, so I gave in. I thought she was pretty enough and she is a nice girl, so I was like why not? I knew you were on the lookout."

"Oh okay. I guess I understand."

"I don't know her well enough to know whether or not you would be into her."

"It's okay."

"I am sorry." She leaned over to kiss my cheek.

"Don't worry, we're still friends."

"Thank goodness!" She smiled.

"She was so fake, Desiree," I blurted once again.

"I know. Not much is real about her. Let's move on from Laiyah. I have two more ladies for you."

"Cool. Do you know them?"

"Yes, these are my girls."

"Good. Now, we are talking." I quickly saved both numbers.

We sat there a moment, staring at the TV screen.

"Thank you for allowing me to stay with you. It means a lot."

"I like having someone around. I like that we get to hang out."

"Me too."

She rubbed my head, kissed my cheek and stood.

"Bedtime."

"You are right. I am tired." She grabbed my hand after turning off the TV and lights. We walked down the hall together.

When we got to her bedroom door, she just stared at me.

"Goodnight, Quinton." I saw the longing in her eyes.

"Goodnight, Desiree." I wanted to kiss her, but just kissed her forehead. I didn't have the nerve. She just smiled and disappeared into her bedroom. I stood there and just stared at her door.

"Lord, please help me."

Des and I were at the gym the next evening, goofing off when Laiyah walked in. I had my arm around Des because we were sharing a good laugh. Ms. Fake decided to jump to conclusions.

"Hello." She looked angry. Her face was red, her eyes were dark, and she had her hands on her hips.

"Laiyah." I didn't feel like talking to her, but here she was.

"Hey, girlie!" Desiree appeared more cheerful.

"I thought you told me that you two were just friends, Desiree?"

"Yes, I did say that."

"So, you lied!"

"No, I didn't lie to you, honey, it's the truth. What's this about? Why are you tripping all of a sudden?"

"What is going on here?"

"Wait a minute, Laiyah." It was time for me to get her straight. "What's with this confrontation? Why are you all up in Desiree face getting hostile? Like she said, there is nothing going on here."

"It sure didn't looked that way."

"I don't really care what it looks like." I was about to go off.

"You seem to be all up on her."

"So?"

"Laiyah, really you can't be serious. We were just laughing…" I am not sure why Desiree was trying to explain, but Laiyah cut her off.

"Do I look like a fool?"

"Yeah," I mumbled. Desiree elbowed me in my side.

"You are really over-reacting."

"If there's something going on, why are you wasting my time?"

"No one is wasting your time," I said, speaking up. You are wasting mine, I thought. This whole conversation was ridiculous.

"I feel as if you two are playing me."

"Sorry that you feel that way." Desiree was getting annoyed.

"Right."

"Laiyah, you are not making sense. If something was going on between Quinton and I, why would I give him your number?"

"I don't know. Do you two have an open relationship? Or maybe you are just stupid like that."

"Excuse me!" I grabbed her hand. If Laiyah said one more thing, Des would be liable to smack her.

"Maybe you didn't realize how much you wanted Quinton until you realize that I was likely to take him."

"Laiyah, let's get one thing straight. If Quinton was my man, you wouldn't have the chance to take him. Secondly, you don't really have a chance in…."

"Okay." I pushed Des behind me. I didn't want things to get out of hand because any drama could get us kicked out. This was my gym

"I am not trying to be rude, Laiyah, but you are out of line."

"Excuse me!" She looked offended. I laughed in her face.

"You really don't know either of us like that."

"I…"

"You are not my woman. You have no potential of being my woman. You don't even have the potential of being a hook up. I am not interested in pursuing anything with you, so you really have no basis to come in here with that bullshit."

"I…"

"Nah, there's really nothing else you need to say. We went on one date. It lasted an hour. What are you thinking? I don't like you. I find you fake. I don't plan on calling you. There's no second date. So, it looks like you are the one wasting time with your nonsense today."

"Go to…"

"Nice seeing you too, Laiyah. Let's go, Desiree, I said, grabbing her hand and pulling her to the door. "Desiree, why did you hook me up with that woman?"

"I am sorry! I had no way of knowing that she was psycho!"

"Yeah, she was insane."

"Luckily you didn't like her and asked her out again. If she was this jealous after a lunch date, imagine if you two started dating! That relationship would have gone nowhere!"

We looked at one another and just starting laughing. I was laughing so hard that my side started hurting. Nothing was all that funny, but the situation was just that crazy.

"Let's go to Cold Stone's," she finally blurted.

"Cold Stone's? We are just coming from the gym. How healthy is that?"

"Look, I can drop you off at the house, but I am going to Cold Stone's to get me a Brownie Obsession."

"I can't let you go alone."

"If it makes you feel better, we will split one."

"Deal!

6

Revelations

"For nothing is hidden that will not be made manifest, nor is anything secret that will not be known and come to light." Luke 8:17

Quinton

When I called Desiree's friend, Lark, she didn't appear to be very outgoing. She was a quiet girl. I really wasn't into quiet chicks, but since I was not trying to be too picky, I decided to go with it. I asked her out anyway.

I am not too sure if she was all that interested in me. It almost felt as if she was accepting the date just to be nice. For some reason, that made me want to see her even more. I guess it was true what they said about men loving a good challenge.

"So what did she say?" Des asked when I hung up the phone.

"She said yes, but are you sure that she is interested in me?"

"Why do you ask? Are you complaining about Lark before you have had the chance to meet her?

"No, I am not. She seems nice."

"She is. She's a sweetheart."

"It just seem like she really didn't want to go out with me."

"That's not it."

"Then what is it?"

"She's probably more reserved than you are used to. She can be on the quiet side."

"How quiet?"

"She's not a mute! She just a little shy."

"Oh goodness."

"Please don't cancel. You need to try different types of women."

"I agree. I wouldn't do that to you or her."

"Thank you."

"I am willing to see what will transpire between us."

"You never know. Plus this will be good for her."

"What do you mean?"

"She hasn't been out with a man in a while. She really deserves it. She is such a wonderful person. She has had her heart broken."

"How recent?"

"Six months."

"What happened?"

"This jerk, Kevin. He and Lark were supposed to get married this summer. She found him getting it on with his best friend in their apartment. In their bed."

"Wow. Typical."

"His best friend was a dude, Quinton." I just stared at her on that one. I didn't know how to respond.

"Did she get tested?" I finally asked.

"She did. Negative, thank the Lord."

Wow. It's damaging enough to a woman's confidence when she finds her man cheating on her with another woman. To find him cheating with another man could possibly destroy a woman.

"So, you are hoping that I can help mend her broken heart."

"Make her feel good again. Treat her like she should be treated. She's going to flip when a sexy man walks through the door." She stared at me with that look as she bit into a nacho.

"I want to make you feel good," I blurted. She dropped that nacho. She didn't respond. She just continued to stare at me. "No worries. I will make sure your girl has a good time."

"Thank you, Quinton. This means a lot to me."

"You never know, Lark may be the girl for me."

"She might. These nachos are on point. Come sit down and eat some with me. I don't need all of these going to my booty."

"Men like that," I said, pulling up a chair.

"I know," she said, winking at me," but I have plenty."

"I have been meaning to ask you something?"

"What's that?"

"Why doesn't your girl, Rayven like me? What's up with that?" Deep down, I knew why. Something had gone down between the two of us in the past. I am not sure that Desiree knew about that.

"I don't know. Rayven doesn't have good sense sometimes."

"So, you are admitting to me that she doesn't like me?"

"Yeah, I am," she said, not able to look me in the eye. "Q, you may not believe me, but I don't know why."

"Wow."

"The excuse she always gives me is that she doesn't like the way you treat females."

"I get that, but she doesn't have much room to talk. Every man she dates, she ends up playing him. She has dealt with several dudes that I am cool with. They all say the same thing about her."

"Do dish. I am curious. What's being said about Rayven?"

"Are you sure you want to know?"

"Yeah. Is Rayven a whore?"

"Nah." I laughed at the expression on her face. "They say that she's uses them for everything that got, yet she doesn't care about them. She dumps them like trash on a Monday morning. I am sorry, but your girl is a gold-digger."

"Are you for real? That's what they are saying?"

"I have heard that coming from several dudes."

"Wow. I kind of suspected that. I didn't realize she was getting a reputation, though. I don't know how I feel about that." She stared into space for a moment. "Quinton, honestly, I think the whole you being a player thing is just an excuse. I think Rayven likes you. She wants to be with you."

"I think you are wrong." I prayed that wasn't true.

"Every time I tell her that, she blushes."

"She doesn't like me, Desiree."

"I think you like her too." I just stared at her. She couldn't be serious. Where did she get that absurd idea from?

"I am praying you aren't serious."

"I am. Q, you two could be missing out on something special."

"Desiree, there is no way. I am not into your girl. I don't particularly care for her these days."

"Why don't you like Rayven?"

"She's very rude and she is disrespectful."

"So you don't like her because she doesn't like you?"

"And she has a bad attitude."

"She does, but she is good person." I begged to differ. I believed actions spoke louder than words.

"Okay." I wasn't going to respond. I wanted her, not Rayven.

We kind of stared at one another. That tension had returned. Was I going to have to deal with this every night? Every single night, there came a point where we both wanted to go there, but weren't willing to make that move.

"We can't," she said, speaking up. "We're friends. We have been for way too long. We can't destroy that. You mean too much to me."

"I agree. It's hard though, Desiree."

"You think I don't know that. I'm struggling, Quinton."

"Me too."

"You can have any woman that you want. You…"

"Don't start with that. That's not true."

"You are the Quinton Alexander. You can roll your eyes at me all you want, but the truth is that you have groupies."

"I do value my health." Is this how she thought of me? She thought I was willing to get it from anywhere?

"Well, that's good."

I lay in bed that night wishing Desiree was next to me.

"This is crazy."

She wasn't just another beautiful woman to me. The sound of her voice excited me. Her laughter brought me joy. It was the simple things. It was scaring me

I was finally able to start thinking about my son. Sometimes I felt as if he was the only thing in my life that I had did right. He was my future. He deserved to have a drama free life and I am sure that was not going to happen while he was under his mother's roof.

Sometimes I believed that India didn't even deserved to be called a mother or a woman for all that matter. As harsh as it sounded, she was nothing but a partying whore. She was addicted to drugs, alcohol and sex. She would admit that to you in a minute. I didn't want to think that way about any woman, especially the woman who had given birth to my child.

She asked for it, though. She brought strange men around my son. She was drunk around my son. She was high around my son. I was scared for Quinton Jr. Eventually something was going to go wrong. I felt it in my heart.

No child deserved to be raised up in that kind of environment. He deserved a home where his mother spent time with him, baking cookies and watching Sponge Bob. He should have been the little man of the house, not locked up in his room because his mother had someone over. He deserved to be with me, his father. I appreciated every moment that I spent with him.

Sometimes, I wanted to take him away from India. Other days, I just didn't feel like going through the court system. I wasn't sure how easy it was going to be to prove her as an unfit mother. I didn't want to resort to hidden cameras or private detectives. Plus, I was a young black man. The courts didn't exactly like my kind.

Quinton needed his mother. He deserved to have his mother get it together so that she could raise him right. She didn't want to listen, though. I tried to tell her these things for our son's benefit, but she wasn't trying to hear me.

Sometimes I got angry with myself for not doing it right. It would have been nice to raise him the way I was raised. I was raised in house with my mother and father in the same household. It was a household full of God and love.

I didn't dwell too much on how my son was born. His mother and I weren't together, but he was still a blessing. I had a son. I didn't know if I was going to have any more children.

I still hadn't told a whole lot of people about Quinton. The only people who knew were my family and Tyler. I tried on many occasions, but I couldn't tell Desiree or most of the women I dated. I told a few women that I had a son and they walked out of my life quickly. I learned to keep my mouth shut.

It was easy lying to women that I didn't know. It made me sick to my stomach thinking about lying to Desiree. It made me sick to my stomach thinking about telling her. I knew I had to.

I got up because I could not sleep. I needed a snack, so without turning on any lights, I walked to the kitchen. Once in there, I turned on the light and I see her. She was sitting on the counter in just a tank top, eating ice cream. My body reacted to that sight.

She stared at me while licking that spoon.

"Well, don't just stare. Would you like some?" Yes I would, I thought. She was talking about the ice cream. I was talking about her.

"What kind do you have?"

"Butter Pecan." Our favorite. She dipped the spoon in the container and pointed it in my direction. Delicious

"Thank you."

"You are welcome." I just leaned against the counter and stared at her. "You smell so good, Quinton."

"So do you." I pushed hair out her face and restrained from kissing her. "What are you doing up?"

"I couldn't sleep. What about you."

"I am hungry. I came to fix something."

"What are you fixing us?" I smiled.

"My version of a Philly Steak and Cheese. Does that sound good?" She gave me a huge smile.

"It does. And some fries."

"Wow, girl, are you pregnant?"

"Yep, with your baby."

"Oh okay. When's our little girl due?"

"How do you know it's a little girl? Don't you want a little man? Every man wants a son." Now was a good time as any.

"I have a son." I confessed before backing out. I couldn't keep it a secret any longer, especially since I was living under her roof.

"Right." She didn't look close to believing me.

"I am not lying to you, Desiree. I have a little boy."

"What! No, you don't. You wouldn't keep that from me!"

"Hold on." I jogged to my bedroom and grabbed Quinton Jr.'s picture off of my nightstand. When I got back into the kitchen, I pushed it into her hands.

"He looks just you," she finally whispered.

"He does."

She frowned at me for a moment. I could tell that her mind was blown and she was letting it sink in. She didn't seem to know what to say. She finally jumped down and shoved me.

"Quinton!"

"I know and I'm sorry."

"Are you! How could you? I can't believe you kept this from me. What's up with this!" She looked as if she was going to cry.

"It's inexcusable, Desiree. I should have told you."

"We're friends, Quinton!"

"And you mean the world to me." I tried to grab her hand, but she pulled away. She went to push past me, but I grabbed her waist.

"Quinton, please let go of me."

"I don't want to." I pulled her to me. She fought me, but eventually settled in my arms. The chemistry between us had won. She stared up at me. She looked as if she wanted to slap me, but that familiar desire had returned to her eyes.

"Desiree, listen to me. Please, I am asking you to." She stared at me and didn't respond. I pushed her against the counter. "Desiree." I kissed her forehead, tempted to just lift her in my arms and take her to my bedroom. I could feel her relax

"Explain what?" she whispered. I moved away because I could hear the hurt in her voice. I felt like less of a man. "How are you going to explain the fact that you have been deceiving me?"

"Let me try." I thought she was going to leave, but she didn't.

"I am not sure I want to hear your reason."

"Yes, you do."

"I just don't see how you are going to explain to me how you kept the fact that you were some child's father away from me." I suddenly felt like she had lost all respect for me. This was killing me.

"I know and I feel stupid about all this."

"How old is he. Two? Three?"

"Quinton Jr is almost three."

"For three years, I didn't even know that there was a Quinton Jr in the world." This time her lips were trembling. Was she about to cry? She was breaking my heart.

"Please don't cry," I said, closing my eyes. I couldn't stand this.

"Don't tell me not to cry."

"I hate this. You are one of the most important women in my life and I don't like hurting you."

"How often do you lie to me? If I was so important, then how could you keep this from me?"

"It's because you are so special to me that I didn't tell you."

"That doesn't make sense."

"You probably shouldn't listen to what I have to say. I don't deserve it, but I hope you give me a chance."

I was surprised when she threw her arms around my neck and kissed me. I pulled her in my arms and kissed her back for a long time. I was disappointed when she pulled away. She grabbed my hand and led me to the table.

"Let's sit down. Tell me about Quinton Jr. Tell me why you kept me in the dark."

"I figured that if you knew that I had a kid, you would be disappointed in me. I was humiliated."

"Are you for real?" She looked at me as if I was crazy. "I can't believe that's what you think."

"I'm a fool."

"Yes, you are. I've never looked down on you in any way. I am not quite sure where you got that from. I think you are a wonderful man and I love you dearly."

"I love you too."

"I have never been disappointed in you."

"I don't know. I care so much about how you think of me."

"I understand. I feel the same way."

"We've always talked about me being a player. Maybe it was a guilty conscience. Rayven hates me because of it, so I figured…"

"I am not Rayven, Q. You and I have known each other since we were ten, not you and Rayven. Come on! We are like family."

"Then we need to stop kissing." She gave me this guilty look.

"I know. We need to work harder, Quinton. We can't have sex. You want it. I want it. It can't happen."

"I am trying my hardest."

"What you do with women has nothing to do with me. If I thought that you were a bad person, I wouldn't set you up with my girls. These are my friends."

"True."

"Tell me about your son. Who is his mother?"

"India Smith."

"India Smith!." A look of disgust came over her face and then she covered her mouth. "I am sorry, Quinton."

"No offense taken. I can't stand the woman."

"Why were you messing with her?"

"I am ashamed to say alcohol was the reason. I was pissy drunk and she looked pretty good at the moment." She laughed.

"I have seen her little boy. Well, your little boy. He's precious."

"Looks just like his old man," I joked.

I sat there and told her the whole story. How I got drunk and had a night of passion with India. Ten months and a paternity test later, I had a son. I was a little embarrassed revealing the details, but I felt relieved. It felt good to get all of this off my chest. I was appreciating her understanding.

"I want to see him," she said when I finished.

"You can see him any time you like."

7

Boundaries

"For this is the will of God, your sanctification: that you abstain from sexual immorality; that each one of you know how to control his own body in holiness and honor, not in the passion of lust like the Gentiles who do not know God" *1 Thessalonians 4:3-5*

Desiree

When I left my job as a receptionist at Johnson, Jones and Smith, a highly respected law firm in the area, early on a Thursday morning, I was leaving for good. It had been a wonderful two years at the small close knit firm, but it was truly time to go. Monday, I was starting my new job as part of the marketing team at Pink Legacy Records. It was a new up and coming female owned record company in our city. It had only been in existence for a year, but was backed by some of the hottest artist in the industry. It may have been a risk, but I was in search of something new and fun.

It was only 10:00 in the morning when I walked out the law firm, so I headed home. I wanted to relax a while before I ran errands. I had a nail appointment, a hair appointment and then I was heading to the mall to find something sexy to wear. Justin was taking me out tonight and I wanted to make a good impression on him.

The mailman came early today. I opened the mailbox to find another envelope. It had been a couple weeks, so my heart sank when I saw that my creepy admirer had not disappeared.

"Why me?"

I walked inside to my bedroom. I threw my stuff on the bed and I slowly ripped opened the envelope.

Desiree,

Congratulations on your new job, baby. I am so proud of you. I have been thinking about you lately. I would love to feel you in my arms. I would love to kiss you. I want to make love you to you. Beware of Quinton.

Missing You,
The One

"Sick bastard!" I didn't have time for this. I threw the letter in the nightstand with the other one. I turned and left the room. I was going to try my best and ignore it.

I thought Quinton would be home, but the house was empty. I started unbuttoning my blouse as I turned on the TV in the living room. One of my favorite TV shows caught my attention, so I ended up flopping on the couch in just my bra. I wasn't thinking that Quinton would return.

He did. When he walked in the house, I was in my red lacy bra and my black pencil skirt. I didn't have time to cover up.

"Hey, um…" He just stared at me.

"Sorry." My face turned red. "I got distracted." I grabbed my blouse and attempted to cover up.

"It's your house."

"True, but I don't live alone anymore."

"Desiree, I don't mind."

"Yeah, but you should." I smiled sheepishly and stood. "I should go change."

"What are you doing home so early?"

"Last day, remember?"

"That's right." I finally took in his shorts and sleeveless shirt. He had been running. I am not sure why that turned me on.

"I am getting out these clothes." I needed to get away from him.

"Okay. I am going to shower." Can I join you?

I needed to stop focusing on Quinton these days. For the last two weeks, I had been staring at him like a sixteen-year-old girl with a crush. I made out of character comments. I told him that I wanted him. What was wrong with me?

I couldn't throw myself at him. Of course he was going to take it. What man wouldn't? I wasn't that type of girl, though. I wasn't that confident. I am not sure where all of this was coming from, but I didn't like any of it.

I was standing in the middle of my room, staring at myself in the mirror. I looked deranged.. I didn't recognize myself.

"I need to get dress and get out of here." I took off my skirt and started looking for one of my favorite sundresses. I was set on wearing it, so I become extremely frustrated that I couldn't find it.

"Oh my goodness!" I realized my dress was in the dryer. Thinking Quinton was still in the shower; I opened the door and ran to my laundry room. When I found it, I attempted to make it back to my room, but he came out in the hallway in just a towel.

"Quinton!" Why! I was in just my underwear. He was naked under that towel! This was not helping with my resistance.

"Desiree." He moved towards me. I held up my hand.

"It's not a good idea," I whispered.

"You are standing here, in your underwear, looking…."

"Looking like what?"

"Like the woman I want to be with right now."

Against all judgment, I dropped my dress and moved towards him. I practically jumped into his arms. He kissed me with so much passion that I didn't know what to think. His hands moved freely over my body. I let him. I wanted it. I couldn't fight it anymore. I didn't care about any consequences.

He lifted me up and we moved towards the living room. His lips didn't leave mine as he laid me on my back. He fell on top of me. An intense yearning continued to move over me, causing me to lose all sense of judgment. All I could focus on was how every part of my body had awakened to his touch. How with just his kiss and his caresses, my body was floating.

"Des," he whispered. His lips moved from my lips to my neck.

"Yes, Quinton. You want to…."

"No, please don't stop this. Don't fight this."

"Okay."

"I shouldn't enjoy kissing you this much."

"Why do you?"

"I…" I stopped him. I wanted to feel his lips on mine. My hand lingered on his towel. I wanted to pull it off, but was scared to.

His hand started to caress my leg wrapped around him. It burned against my thigh as is slowly inched upward. I stopped breathing in anticipation. I closed my eyes because his hands lingered between my thighs.

"If you let me touch you there, there's no turning back, sweetheart." I opened my eyes. He was staring down at me with so much desire in his eyes.

"Do you want to, Quinton? Do you want us to turn back? Tell me," I said, sliding my hand across his cheek.

"No, I want to make you moan. Let me do that for you." I was a little startled. All the women in the world and he wanted to be with me. Despite me being surprised, I was even more turned on. I didn't say anything. I just grabbed his hand and started to lead him to where I wanted to be touched.

"I don't think that I ever wanted someone so badly."

Right as we were about to surrender and allow the passion between us to explode, there was a loud bang at my door. We both jumped. We were tangled so we rolled off the couch onto the floor.

"You have to be kidding me," I whispered.

"This is crazy. Are you expecting someone?"

"No." We stared at each other. I didn't really care who was on the other side of the door. I wanted to be with Quinton right now. I needed this. I moved towards him. "I don't hear anything."

He pushed his hand through my hair and pulled my head towards his. "I want you, Desiree Harris. I shouldn't, but I really do."

"I don't know why you do."

"You are the most beautiful woman. I care about you, I…."

"Shush." I cut him off because I didn't want him to say anything he regretted. Moments of passion could make you say crazy things.

Quinton sucked on my bottom lip as he unhooked my bra. As I sat there, with my breast exposed to this gorgeous man, in just my panties, I felt unusually confident. I knew he wanted me. He was attracted to me. He wanted to please me.

"I love these," he said, kissing and caressing my breast.

"Do you?" I asked, rubbing his chest."

"Yes!"

"Your lips are amazing," I whispered as he begins to kiss me again. He kissed me softly, gently, and passionately. I could sit here in his arms and let him kiss me all day. That was scary. I couldn't wrap my brain around it.

"My lips? Your lips are amazing, Des. So soft, so pouty."

"This is crazy." I closed my eyes and relished in the pleasure for a moment. That was interrupted by another loud bang at the door. "No, please go away." I mumbled

"I am not going to stop." He pushed me on my back and with his teeth, he begin to slide my panties down my leg. My breath quickened. This was about to happen. I was now naked.

I yanked on his towel and just like that he was naked too. I had known this man for seventeen years and would have never imagined that we would share this intimate moment together. We were about to cross that line.

I pulled him to me. He stared into my eyes. He rubbed my face.

"Why are you looking at me like that?"

"I don't want to forget this moment."

As he was about to enter my world, there was another bang on the door. Some chick started screaming Quinton's name.

I sighed in defeat. This was not going to happen. I was being deprived of something that I wanted so badly.

"It's for you."

He buried his face in my chest before whispering, "I know."

He pulled away in frustration. I feel you, baby, I thought. I sat up too. Realizing I was naked, I became embarrassed and attempted to cover up the best I could with my arms.

"I am so sorry," he said, taking notice.

"It's okay." It wasn't. "Who is it?"

"India." Wow.

"I guess you better get that."

"I guess so. I am so sorry."

"Stop apologizing." I stood all of sudden and he handed me his towel. I wrapped it around myself in a hurry. I was annoyed because this chick kept banging on my door. "Please, Quinton, answer her!"

"Okay." He ran down the hall to get clothes. I gathered my clothes and headed to my bedroom. He was fully dressed before I could reach my door. He grabbed my hand. "I will make it up to you."

"We will see," I said. I tried not to show him my frustration. The distraction was probably a blessing in disguise.

"Do you have plans tonight? We could…."

"I will be with Justin." I was surprised to see the disappointment on his face. He dropped my hand. He couldn't honestly be jealous.

"I guess we missed the opportunity."

"Why do you say that?"

"I have this feeling." He threw me a look and headed towards the door as India continued to bang. He looked as irritated as I felt.

I walked into the bedroom and shut the door. I reopened it slightly when I heard India's voice. I was being nosy.

"What's up, India? How did you find me?"

"It's a small world, Quinton. I asked around."

"Why?"

"I think that I have the right to know."

"What concern is it of yours?"

"For your son's sake, Quinton. Please, don't act stupid."

"What are you doing here? Come here, little man." Wow. Quinton Jr was in the house. The fact that Quinton had a son was still hard for me to wrap my mind around. I wanted to see the little boy so badly, but at the moment, I didn't have clothes on.

"I need you to keep, Quinton."

"Why? I do have to work tonight, India. I am not going to keep him so that you can go messing around with some random dude."

"Kiss my ass, Quinton. I do not have time for this shit!" Whoa, I thought. Why was this chick cussing around her kid?

"Watch your mouth around my son."

"Whatever, Quinton. Don't even start this shit tonight. I don't understand where you get off telling me what I can and can't do."

"I just ask that you have some respect."

"Whatever!"

"India, why can't you keep Quinton tonight?"

"My mother is in the hospital, okay," she said, sounding worried. "I don't really know any details yet. I thought it would be best if Quinton not tag along. He doesn't feel that good as it is."

"I am sorry to hear that, India."

"I know. So will you keep him or not?"

"Yeah, no problem. My mother can watch him tonight."

"That's cool, Quinton. Thank you."

"You are welcome."

"So you are staying with some whore." Whore? I wasn't anybody's whore. She obviously knew nothing about me.

"She is a woman. She is not a whore," he said, quickly defending me. "Don't put her in the same category with yourself." Oh wow. Did he really go there?

"Once again, kiss my ass."

"I said chill with the language."

"Why do you always have to insult me, Quinton, like you are so much better than me?"

"I am just speaking the truth. I personally think that you can do so much better for yourself."

"Why are you taking up for this chick?"

"She's my girl. I would do anything for her." That was good to know. Not that I would ever try to take advantage of Q.

"I use to be your girl."

"Yeah, use to be. That's all part of the past."

"Forget you. What's this chick's name? Desiree Harris. I remember her uppity ass." Uppity? Why was she tripping about me? This chick had better be glad that I was not decent or I would have joined Quinton and gave her a piece of my mind.

"Des is not uppity. She is just on a higher level than you. She has her life together." Wow, I didn't know that Quinton was so blunt. There was obvious disdain towards his son's mother.

"I am not arguing with you. How long are you staying here?"

"I don't know, India. A while. That's all you need to know."

"Just tell me, Quinton."

"I will let you know!"

"Quinton!"

"Desiree!" Oh crap. Why was he calling my name?"

"Yes, Quinton." I said, opening my door wider.

"Can you come here for a minute please?"

"I will be there in a minute." I grabbed shorts and a jersey off the floor. I headed down the hall.

I looked right at India when I entered the room. Girlfriend was a hot mess. Her purple weave, matching finger nails, and her booty shorts were all a joke. What a shame.

"I am not uppity," I blurted. "Just a little high maintenance."

"What's the difference?"

"There is a difference. Look it up! That's what Google is for." Why was I letting this chick get to me? I just couldn't understand why women couldn't get along. I admitted there were times I could get a little hateful. Sometimes my confidence was low and I got a little envious, but not in the case. I just could not stand India.

"Desiree," Quinton spoke up, "You don't have to explain yourself to this girl. She doesn't know anything about you."

"Whatever, Quinton!" she snapped.

Quinton pushed his son into my arms. "Des, take my son, will you? Come here, India." Quinton grabbed her and started pushing her towards the driveway

"Don't touch me!"

"Just walk," he said, shoving her a little. "I will be back, Des. Daddy will be back, little man." Before either of us could respond, they were both out of the door. Wow. What was I supposed to do?

Little Quinton took one look at me and his adorable face started to scrunch up. His little arms reached towards the door.

"Daddy!"

"Oh, sweetheart, daddy will be right back, okay? I promise. Don't cry." He stopped, looked at me and pointed to the door. "Yeah, your daddy's coming. What's your name?"

"Quinton," he responded softly. He was precious..

"And how old are you?"

"I'm three," he said, holding up three fingers. Wow, he was smart. I remember Quinton saying that his birthday was soon and he was almost three.

"Are you hungry?" I asked, trying to distract him from the fact that his father was missing.

"Yes. I am very hungry."

"What do you want, sweetie?" I headed towards the kitchen.

"Crackers." Thank goodness I had those. I reached in the cabinet and handed the little boy crackers. He eagerly took them. I wasn't sure if he was going to eat them, but he did.

Wow. I could not believe this moment. This was Quinton Jr. My Quinton had a son and I was just learning about it. As far as I was concerned, he had deprived me three years of getting to know this little boy. I would have loved him. I would have loved to spoil him.

"You really do look just like your father?" He smiled at me shyly and laid his head against my shoulder. He had his father's eyes and his smile. He was definitely going to grow into a heartbreaker.

Quinton Sr. finally walked back in the room.

"Thankfully, she is on her way."

"Good. He wanted crackers. Was that okay?"

"Yeah, he's fine." Q took his son who was reaching out to him.

"He said he was hungry."

"I bet. He eats like me. All the time."

"He is growing." I started to back away. Why was I feeling nervous? This was just a kid. He wasn't judging me.

Quinton actually grabbed my hand. "Where are you going?"

"Nowhere."

"Little man, guess who this is?"

"Who?" The little boy started to eye my suspiciously

"This is Des."

"Des?"

"This is daddy's friend."

"Hi," he said, waving at me

"Hi, sweetie!" My heart started to melt. I was in love already. "Quinton, he looks just like you."

"Yeah, I know."

"I can't believe you didn't tell me. How could you keep him from me?" I was starting to get upset.

"I am sorry," he said, reaching out to touch my cheek. "I know I messed up, Desiree. I didn't mean to hurt you."

"I know."

"Quinton, tell Des that daddy is so sorry."

"My daddy's sorry."

"I know."

I watched Quinton affectionately talked to his son for a while. I saw him in a way that I had never seen him. As a father. I loved it

When Quinton Jr started to get sleepy, his father laid him down for a nap. I followed him to his bedroom in a daze. I leaned against the door and watched Quinton tuck his son in. As I watched, something pulled on my heart strings. I wanted my own child.

I was childless and Quinton was a father. The self-proclaimed player. I couldn't believe it, but Quinton appeared a natural.

He looked up at me and smiled.

"I think that I am going to take a nap too. You want to join us?"

"Tempting, but I have some things to tend to."

"Really?" Did he actually look upset?

"Yeah." I blew him a kiss and headed down the hall. He grabbed me before I could reach my bedroom.

"Wait a minute, Desiree."

"Yes." We stared at each other. I saw the desire in his eyes. I looked away. "No, Quinton."

"I'm not going to make a move on you with my son here."

"Glad to hear that."

"I just wanted to apologize this one last time. I am sorry about everything. About India showing up. At how you met my son."

"I know, Quinton. It's fine. I must admit that I have to get use to things. And I didn't appreciate your baby mother banging on my door! Still, I am good. I am not going to be angry about it."

"Thank you. That's a relief." We continued to stare at one another with all the sexual tension between us. He stared at my lips.

"Just kiss me, Q."

"I didn't know if you wanted me too. I..." I grabbed him and kissed him first. He pulled me completely in his arms. When I felt things heating up, I pulled away.

"Let's not start anything that we can't finish."

"Yeah, two times in one day would be too much to handle."

"You are right." I turned towards my bedroom and he followed. "Maybe it's a good thing we didn't go there, Quinton."

"Why do you say that?"

"We said we weren't going to cross that line."

"I keep trying, Desiree, but every time you come in to the same room, I just want to do the unimaginable with you." I was baffled.

"Why, Quinton? You can have any woman you want."

"I want you and you are just going to have to try and understand that. This is not about any other woman. This is about you."

"I..."

"You are so incredibly beautiful, when will you get that?" My face got hot. I grabbed it.

"Stop, Quinton. I can't...."

"I will tell you that you are beautiful every single day until you get tired of me telling you. I will not stop." I just stared at him.

"I think you are beautiful," I finally blurted.

'Thanks," he said, giving me this sexy grin.

"You are welcome." I turned quickly so he couldn't see my face. I headed towards my closet. "I need to find something to wear."

"So you are going out with Justin?"

"I am."

"I take it that you like him."

"I do."

"Will this be something serious?"

"We only went on one date, Q. I don't know about all that. I do know that I enjoyed being with him."

"Please don't sleep with him." I turned, startled by his request. "Are you serious?"

"Yes, very."

"Why not?" I challenged.

"I don't want you to."

"Quinton!"

"I am just being honest."

"Wow." I couldn't sleep with Justin, I barely knew him. As much as I was craving intimacy with a man, I wasn't about to turn into a whore. I wasn't going to tell Quinton, though. "Don't you worry about it," I joked.

"I am not. You won't. That's not your style."

"You don't know everything about me."

"I plan on finding out."

"Do you? Are you pursuing me, Quinton?"

"Yes."

"Stop it!"

"No. I wish I was Justin tonight. I would love to take you out."

"Quinton!" My face was so hot. What was going on? Why was Quinton saying this stuff to me? "You are going out with my girls and they are like me."

"Okay. True. I need that."

I stood in the mirror, playing with my hair. I had an appointment a little later and was wondering what I could do with it.

"What do you think? Should I wear my hair up or down?"

"Up. Do you like when a man kisses your neck?"

"Of course." I watched him cross the room. I closed my eyes as he wrapped his arms around me. He kissed me softly on my neck. I tried desperately not to melt "I could really use a back massage." I was trying to get his lips off me.

"I can take care of that. Are you tense?" Because of you.

"Yes." I lifted my arms so he could pull my jersey off.

"Go lay down."

I reluctantly did so. I closed my eyes as his hands momentarily took me to heaven. He was seducing me. Once again, every part of my body was at his full attention. I was so sexually charged that his touch began to turn torturous.

"Enough," I said, rolling over and grabbing his hand. I had to get away from him.

"Okay." He stared down at me and then leaned down to kiss my bare breast. I arched my back a little to allow his tongue to sweep across my nipple.

He was going to make me lose control.

"Please, stop torturing me," I whispered to him.

"My precious, Desiree," he said, rubbing my cheek. "There is so many things that I want to do to you. You have to let me do want I want to do to you."

I was so turned on.

"Quinton."

He leaned down to kiss me and it was on. For the second time today, he was on top of me, touching me. We made out for a while.

Finally, he pulled away.

"We should stop this now before we can't."

"You are right. Get off me."

"Okay." He kissed me quickly and then jumped up. I jumped up quickly too before he could do anything else. 'Sorry about that."

"You are not."

"You're right. Feels too good."

"Yes it does." That was an understatement. I smiled shyly and then turned my back again. I walked over to my dresser and pulled out the first pair of underwear I could find. I needed to get dress.

"You are wearing those." I looked down at one of my favorite black lacey boy shorts.

"Yes, I guess so. Why?"

"Please, don't let him see you in those."

"Why?"

"I don't want him too," he answered honestly. "I will be thinking about you all night in those."

"Time to go, Q." I laughed. I need to get dress. It was already 1:00 and my appointment was at 4:00. I had to run some errands.

"Fine, if you insist on leaving."

"Shush, you will be okay without me."

"Whatever. Have fun with my man. Not too much, though."

"Thank you, father."

"I am not your father, sweetheart. I want to love your body, so please don't call me your father."

"Goodbye, Quinton."

"Bye Desiree."

I stared at the shut door. I was in shock. This couldn't be real.

Why was he flirting with me? Why was he kissing and touching me? Making out with me? And why was I letting him? This was crazy. We had agreed not to go there, but yet we almost did. Twice!

I knew I had gotten involved in something I should not have, but could I stop now? I wasn't sure I could. We had reached the point of no return. We wanted it too badly.

We were going to go there. It was inevitable. My celibacy would be ending soon at the hands of my devastatingly handsome friend. I just hoped that once we started, that we would find a way to stop. That we could give into our desires just once. After that, it would be out of our system. And then we could both move on.

"God, I hope so."

What would Rayven say if she knew what was going on under this roof? She had warned me. Wow. I hated when she was right.

8

Propositions

"My son, keep my words and treasure up my commandments with you; keep my commandments and live; keep my teaching as the apple of your eye; bind them on your fingers; write them on the tablet of your heart. Say to wisdom, "You are my sister," and call insight your intimate friend, to keep you from the forbidden woman, from the adulteress with her smooth words." *Proverbs 7:1-5*

Desiree

What went on under my roof was going to stay between Quinton and I. I was not trying to tell Rayven anything about what had developed over the last couple of days. I knew how she would react. Negatively.

I knew that it was messy to get involved with Q, but I was grown. Ray would not respect that. I loved her dearly, but sometimes I didn't want to deal with the chick. We often didn't see eye to eye.

This situation with her and Quinton was baffling. She offered no valid reason for disliking him, blaming her dislike on his womanizing ways, but she essentially did the same thing. Every time I called out her audacity to judge, she would shrug and tell me, "Men deserve it, Desiree." Well, thanks to women like her, so did women.

"Does Rayven really want Quinton?" I thought so. It would explain everything.

"Does Quinton like Rayven?" I had a feeling he did, but then again, why was he trying to get me in his bed.

Who was I kidding? He was a man. Despite the feelings that I suspected that he had for Rayven, I was a woman that was offering him something that he wanted. He wasn't going to refuse that.

As inexplicable as it was, there was undeniable chemistry between us. I am not sure where it came from, but I desperately wanted to explore it. It was unchartered territory. I had sexual tension for a man that I had never felt before.

"Why did it have to be Quinton Alexander?"

I couldn't tell Rayven any of this. I didn't want to hurt her. I knew she was going to be jealous. I didn't have any time for drama, especially with my best friend. It was not worth it.

I trusted Quinton. I knew he wasn't going to kiss and tell when it came to me. He cared about me too much.

"Desiree Harris, you have got to get out of here."

I started to gather my things in a hurry. Why was I sitting here focusing on Quinton when there was another man I should have been focusing on? I rushed out the house and to my car. I turned up the radio and backed out of my driveway. As I sang along to an old Luther song, my mind finally drifted to this sexy man who I was going out with tonight.

Yes, I had gone out once with Justin, but I was excited for this date. I hadn't dated anyone since Devin. As Rayven would say, I deserved this. I worked so hard, but played so little. I wasn't quite sure what Justin had planned, but tonight I was ready for anything.

"Where has the time gone?" Time was getting away from me. Why was I rushing, when I got off at 10:00? Quinton. I grew annoyed because I didn't want to focus on him anymore. I turned up my radio and proceeded to block him out.

After some quick errands, I stopped quickly in my favorite store on the way to the nail salon. I had twenty minutes to find a cute little dress. I walked out empty handed and frustrated, deciding that I had plenty of dresses at home with the price tags on them.

I headed to Divine Nails. I had an appointment with Jennie, my regular manicurist. I was always a firm believer in taking pride in my appearance. Sometimes, I wasn't quite sure how beautiful I was, but my mother had always taught me to use this world as my runway.

"Sweetie, you walk around as if you are the most beautiful person in this world and other people will believe it."

It didn't matter what I really thought. It didn't matter that I was really insecure. It didn't matter that I was unhappy with my nose or with my body. I took care of myself because I had to.

Despite the pride I took in my appearance, I still felt as if I couldn't measure up sometimes. I blushed when a man smiled at me. I become tongue-tied when I was complimented in anyway. I couldn't shake the bad habit.

"When will you realize how gorgeous you are?" I could hear Rayven words in my head. My best friend would tell me how beautiful I was, but I always discarded her compliments.

And when did Quinton start to notice me? He had been full of compliments these last few days. I wasn't sure how to handle them.

I just knew that I loved the way he kissed me. I loved how he touched me. I loved seeing the desire in his eyes. I loved the way he could make me feel. I loved that he wanted me.

Oh mercy me. I kept replaying today's events in my head. It was so hot. It was so sexy. I desperately wanted more.

I started to shift uncomfortably in my seat. My face was burning. I needed water. I prayed that no one could tell what I was thinking about. I was turned on.

I pulled out my phone and found myself texting him. "I can't stop thinking about earlier. Can you?" Why I asked him that, I didn't know. I just wanted to see if he was struggling like I was.

Two minutes later, he responded. "Des, I can't think of anything else. I am not sure why, but I need you. So badly. Just know if I didn't have my son tonight, I would be trying desperately to get you to stay home. I want to please every inch of you."

I threw my phone in my purse as if it had burned me. Why did he text that to me. He had put images of what could be in my head. I closed my eyes and could feel his lips on me.

"Desiree, it's good to see you." Jennie! My eyes opened and I jumped up. What a welcomed distraction.

"Hey, Jennie. I am glad to see you, girl." I truly meant that.

I followed Jennie to one of those comfortable chairs and told her to hook me up with my regular. I loved a French manicure. It went with everything. I lay back in that chair and enjoyed my massage. I forced myself to concentrate on the items in my closet and not Quinton Alexander. What was a girl to wear?

I left the nail shop and drove directly to my hair appointment.

"Hey Des," my beautician, Corrine said, hugging me. "It's been a minute, girl."

"I know!"

Corrine kept me distracted by entertaining me with stories of her crazy neighbor. I didn't have time to think because I was laughing the entire time. I definitely appreciated the distraction along with the sexy curls that she had hooked me up with.

On the way to my car, an older gentleman, who had to be at least thirty years older than me, attempted to get at me. I had to admit that he was a nice looking man in his obviously expensive suit. He appeared to have it together and was standing by a pretty nice Mercedes Benz. If sugar daddies were my thing, I would have been excited. I would have hit the jackpot. Dating senior citizens was not my thing, so I was going to have to let him down gently.

"Hey, baby girl. Where are you headed?"

"Home."

"Why don't you come here for a minute?"

"I am sorry, but I am in rush," I said, amused.

"Well, you are beautiful woman and I was wondering if you needed someone like me to take care of you?" Wow.

"No," I said, trying not to laugh. "I have someone to do that." I was talking about myself of course.

"Maybe I can help him out. Why don't you give me a shot? I think you could handle it." How would he know?

"He doesn't like to share," I said, actually stopping to look at him. This could not be happening. I took in his appearance and noticed the obvious bugle in his pants. Down boy!

"Are you sure about that?"

"Yeah, I am sure." My eyes landed on his wedding band. "I don't think that your wife would appreciate your offer either."

"Oh," he said, obviously embarrassed. "How would she know?"

"Because you don't appear to be too quick on your game or you would have taken that ring off."

"Nothing to hide, baby girl."

"Maybe you have nothing to hide from me, but what about your wife? Would you go home to her and tell her about me?" The look on his face said it all. "Look, we are all sinners, but I draw the line at adultery. Have a good day."

With that, I turned towards my car. I put a little extra movement in my hips. Why not give him a little show? I looked over my shoulder as I climbed into the driver's seat. He was still staring. I blew a kiss at him and he smiled.

Give it up, old man. Stay true to your wife and respect your grown kids. I laughed as I sped past him.

"What a fool!"

I walked through my door at 6:30. The house was empty of course. I am sure by now that little Quinton was with his grandmother. His father was probably at work. As soon as I turned on my radio, Quinton's deep voice flowed through my home.

I walked to my bathroom and turned on the water. I wanted nothing more than a bubble bath, except for Mr. Alexander himself. I walked out my bathroom to hear him talking about a female.

"This goes out to a special woman." Who was he talking about now? "I hope you know who you are?" Did she? He had so many fans. "You're the only thing that's been my mind lately. I keep telling you how beautiful you are and I am going to make you believe it."

"No, Q." He couldn't be talking about me.

"I know you love this song. So here it is, baby." When "Beauty" by Dru Hill came across the sound waves, my face turned red. He knew I loved this song.

I shook my head and went to enjoy my bath. I let out a sigh of relief when I sank down into my tub. Warm, lavender scented bubbles surrounded me. I needed this. I needed to relax.

I laid there singing along to the songs Quinton played, imagining him beside me. I laughed at his jokes like I always did. Quinton, I thought, you are too much, in more ways than one.

I didn't know what I was doing when I reached over and grabbed my phone. I wanted to mess with Quinton a little as he stated to take calls. I wanted to have a little fun. I got through.

"You are on the air with Hot 107. What can I do for you tonight? What's been on your mind lately?"

"Well, a whole lot actually."

"Is that so?" he chuckled. "Who is this on my line?"

"Who do you think it is?"

"Is this my beauty?"

"It may just be."

"Hey, baby. Why are you playing with me in front of all my listeners tonight?"

"Those weren't my intentions. I just wanted to thank you for my song. Only you would know how much I would love it. I have to show you how much I appreciate it a little later." I was shocked by my own behavior. I didn't even try disguising my voice.

"You don't owe me anything, but I am appreciative." I could tell he was smiling.

"Good to know."

"I'm glad you were listening, beauty. I meant what I said earlier."

"I know you do. Can you do something else for me?"

"And what's that?"

"Play me another song."

"My baby is greedy."

"I want to dedicate a song to you. Another oldie, but goodie."

"And what's that?"

"Will you play "Ask of You" by Raphael Saadiq?"

"I can do that."

"Thank you."

"In case you don't realize what's going on, people, my beauty has made my night. Apparently, this goes out to me. I just need one last thing from you, sweetheart. Tell me the only station to bring you the hottest Hip Hop and R&B songs all day long."

"The sizzling Hot 107."

"Are we your favorite?"

"My only."

"And who's your favorite man of the hour?"

"You, Q Alexander, you."

"Please believe it."

I smiled as I hung up the phone. Q called me immediately.

"Hey there."

"Why did you hang up?"

"I thought we were finished."

"No, we are never finished." Wasn't that the truth? "You realize what you just did in front of the whole city?"

"You started it."

"I did. I wasn't sure if you were listening." There was a pause. "Are you sure that you have to go out with Justin tonight?"

"Yes, Q, I am sure."

"I wish it could be me and you." I almost said, "Me too"

"And little Quinton?"

"He would be fine at my mother's house."

"Plenty time for me and you, Quinton."

"I know. I am just craving."

"Me too," I answered, honestly.

"What are you doing?"

"I am taking a bath."

"A bubble bath?" He knew me so well.

"Yes, actually."

"Do you know what I could do to that body of yours while you are in that bath tub?" I closed my eyes and put my head back.

"Don't make me think about that. You aren't here to fulfill any of that, Quinton."

"I would say have fun tonight, but I don't know if I mean it."

"I wouldn't do that to you," I laughed.

"Have fun, Des. He better treat you good."

"He will. Justin is a gentleman."

"If you say so. I love you, Desiree Harris."

"I love you too, Quinton Alexander."

"Okay people. That was "Ask of You" by Raphael Saadiq. I think my beauty for her dedication. Please know how much I will miss you tonight. Here's the newest one from John Legend."

After my bath, I rubbed myself down in my favorite vanilla scented lotion. I sprayed my favorite perfume. I put on my sexiest underwear. I had to do it right tonight.

I looked over at my clock and realized that I had over an hour before Justin would be knocking at my door. Not knowing what to do with myself, I set my alarm and then decided to take a quick nap. I didn't get much rest today.

Forty-five minutes later, after realizing I couldn't sleep, I was fully dressed. I kept pacing my bedroom, constantly rechecking my appearance in the mirror. As always, I was feeling insecure. I threw up my hands in frustration, grabbed my clutch and walked out of my bedroom. I was not about to change, so this was going to have to do.

I had chosen a hot pink mini with a lacey white tank. My favorite part of my outfit was my gold Jimmy Choo sandals and matching clutch. I knew the outfit was hot, so I was going to feel hot in it. Rayven always told me that I had an incredible sense of style, so I was going to have to trust that I made the right decision.

I was anxious. I didn't know why. This was not my first date. All of the nerves should have been out of the way. I just wanted to make sure that Justin stayed interested. I wanted him to like me.

I am not sure what we were going to do tonight. Justin just promised that he was going to make it special. I was not sure how he was going to top our first date. When we met over the last weekend, it was carefree and laid back. I laughed and smiled the entire date. And it ended like a first date should; with a great first kiss.

I was really digging him. He seemed like a good guy, who had it together. He was a thirty-year-old club owner from the ATL. He was educated. He had graduated near the top of his class form UNC Chapel Hill. He was smart, intriguing and hilarious. He was easy on the eyes with pretty brown eyes and a sexy grin.

I waited fifteen minutes on my couch because I was ready. Justin showed up right on time. I jumped up immediately when he rang my doorbell. I stopped at my mirror in my foyer to check my appearance once more. Here goes nothing.

"Hey, you!" I was smiling before I had the door opened.

"Gorgeous." He leaned over and boldly kissed me. It took me by surprise, but I loved it. It was quite pleasant.

"Thank you."

"You are welcome. This is for you," He handed me a pink rose.

"Thank you kindly. My favorite color." I leaned over and kissed his check. "Be right back." I went to stick the rose in a vase of flowers I already had and then quickly rejoined him. "I am ready."

Justin took me this upscale soul food restaurant downtown. Over candles and a live jazz band, we had a romantic meal. I loved it. We held hands and enjoyed getting to know each other.

Afterwards we went to dancing.

"You say you love dancing."

"I do!"

"Well how about you show me some moves."

"My pleasure!" I had a blast. I had an even better time at the end of the night when we slow danced under the stars besides his car in an empty parking lot. We danced to the sounds of R. Kelly coming from his car stereo. When we stopped dancing, he held me closer and kissed me for a long time.

"Wonderful," I whispered to him.

"I agree. Look, I am enjoying being with you. I am not ready for this night to end. I don't know how you would feel about this, but would you like to come back to my cousin's spot? I home alone all weekend. We can watch a movie."

"A movie?" Netflix and chill, I thought.

"Yes, that's all, I promise. I will be on my best behavior. I just think it would be nice to cuddle up with you." That did sound good.

"Okay, Justin, I am going to trust you. Let's do this."

His cousin lived in a nice townhouse not too far from me. We turned on his cousin's big screen. Justin popped some popcorn. We cuddled up and watched an old Denzel Washington movie.

When it was over, we made out a little. After that, I remembered laying my head on his shoulder and closing my eyes. That was the last thing I remembered. We fell asleep holding each other.

9

Infatuation

"I adjure you, O daughters of Jerusalem, that you not stir up or awaken love until it pleases." *Song of Solomon 8:4*

Quinton

I don't think Desiree realized how much she had made my night. She had been the only thing on mind the entire day. I wasn't sure if she knew how much today affected me. I was pretty messed up over what had gone down between us earlier.

I took a risk that morning when I told her how much I wanted to kiss her. I never imagined that she would jump in my arms. I never imagined that she would allow me to kiss her the way I kissed her. I never imagined that she would allow things to proceed so far. I never imagined her wanting me as much as I wanted her.

Twice today, we almost had sex. And twice we stopped. Brutal.

My brother had warned me. "Stay away from Desiree, little brother. Don't cross that line." I tried to take heed, but I couldn't. How could I? She wasn't making it easy for me.

It was hard to resist a woman who lived under the same roof. It was hard to resist a woman when every time she walked in the same room, your whole body reacted. It was hard to resist a woman who made you want her with just the sound of her voice. A woman who had everything that you desired and more.

I dedicated that song because that's how I felt about her. The song represented exactly what was in my heart. Desiree was unaware of how beautiful she was. She was unaware of how much I wanted to make her mine.

"I can't believe she called the radio station." That blew my mind. She didn't even try to hide who she was. Anyone who knew her should have recognized her voice. If she was that nonchalant, what did that mean? Could she have possibly felt the same way that I did?

I doubted it. She was attracted to me, which was obvious. I could turn her on. I could make her moan in appreciation. I could ignite that same fire in her that was in me. Despite all that, I doubted she felt the same way about me.

I sighed in frustration. Was she really out with another man? Justin. I hated it. It literally made me sick to my stomach. Why? I didn't want to go home knowing that she wasn't there. She should have been with me.

If I didn't have Quinton Jr tonight, I don't think that I would have bothered going back. What would have been the point? It would have been torture. I would have crashed at Tyler's place.

I needed to focus on my son, I thought, pulling into my parent's driveway. Despite his mother acting like a fool earlier, I was grateful that he was with me. While I expected him to be sleeping, I needed to cherish every moment that I had with him.

"Daddy!" Quinton Jr came running full speed towards me as soon as I set foot through the front door. Wow, he was wide awake. I was in for a treat after all.

"Hey, buddy."

"Hi, daddy."

"What were you doing?"

"We made cookies!" That explained everything.

"Thanks a lot, mother." She approached us in the foyer.

"I am sorry. This is my grandson and I will spoil him as I see fit. I don't get to see him often."

"Still, ma. You have set me up big time."

"You will be okay."

"Yeah, but your grandson will keep his father up all night."

"No, I won't, daddy. I promise."

"We will see, little buddy," I said, kissing his cheek. "Did you behave for grandma and papa today?"

"I did. I was a good boy."

"He was an angel as always," my mother quickly cosigned.

"Just like his father."

"Okay, son." She gave me a smirk.

"Don't try to play me, mother."

"I am not, I just beg the difference, sweetheart." She shrugged. "I love you both. Time to go now. Mommy is tired."

"Thank you for everything. I appreciate you as always."

"Good! Give grandma a kiss. I will see you next time, sweetie."

"Bye, Grandma."

"Bye! Be safe Quinton. No speeding!"

"I will mother. Love you."

Quinton wasn't too bad. I took him home. I gave him his bath. I read him a book and he was out. All by midnight.

After he fell asleep, I walked around the house in circles, trying desperately to find something to do. I was trying not to focus on what happened earlier in the living room, on the couch and on the floor. I tried not to think about what happened in her bedroom. I tried not to think about Desiree at all.

I sat down on the couch and closed my eyes. Desiree had been consuming too much of my mind for years now. I had to find a way to shake this crush. I had to fight this infatuation. I had to stop lusting for her.

I was like all of her other admires. I observed her from afar, never thinking I would get a chance. From the sidelines, I watched many men approach her, but never get the time or day. I had always wanted to make a move, but never had the courage until she kissed me that night. That just made me bold.

It was freaking me out, though. I had been through this once in my past. There came a time in college when I wanted to approach her. I wanted to cross that line. I didn't have the chance to. Before I could reveal what was in my heart, she had shut me down. She would never know my full intentions of that fateful night.

After that night, I pushed aside any emotions I had towards her. I had been winning the infatuation fight, but then I moved in. I knew these feelings I had tried to lock away, were going to resurface.

I wasn't prepared for that nervous feeling in my stomach when I saw her in that little blue dress. I wasn't prepared for the funny feeling in my heart when we slow danced together. And then she kissed me and she had messed me up completely.

"This can't be happening."

I would do anything for Desiree. I always made sure she was happy. I always made sure that she was by my side. Besides my mother and my sister, she was the one constant female in my life. She had been there for seventeen years. I could not lose her.

If I just wanted sex, I could easily get some of that from plenty of women. Who was I fooling, though? This was not just about the sex. This was about so much more.

My phone ringing was a welcomed distraction.

"What's up, man. Why are you calling me so late?"

"Whatever, Q, I know you aren't in the bed."

"That's not the point. At this time of night, I could have been. Where's the respect. You would cuss me out if I did it to you."

"Chill, Q. Stop tripping."

"What's up, T? What do you want?"

"I am sorry, but I had to call you and tell you about Desiree."

My heartbeat quickened.

"What about her? Is she alright?" If Justin had harmed her in anyway, he was about to get a beat down. I would kill him.

"She's fine. Don't get worked up."

"What then? Is she with you?" I got really paranoid.

"Heck no. I wish, though."

"Huh?" I would beat Tyler ass too. I wasn't going for that.

"Look, Q, I saw her tonight and I have decided that there's only one word that can be used to describe a woman that beautiful."

"What's that, my man?"

"Sinful, Q."

"That nice, huh?" I asked, slowly. I didn't like knowing that she had gone all out for Justin.

"It has to be a sin for a woman to be that beautiful." And she was naturally that beautiful. I had seen this woman with her hair up and without an ounce of make-up on. Even then, she could take your breath away.

"What did she have on?" I was sweating.

"Okay, I was with this chick, Camille, tonight. Man, I will tell you about her in a minute."

"Good sex?"

"Yes indeed."

"Oh okay," I laughed. "Back to Desiree." She was the only chick I was worried about. I wasn't concerned about Camille.

"I was all over Camille in the corner when Desiree walks in with this little dude. Who is that, Q?"

"Justin," I mumbled. "Scrawny, isn't he?" I was acting like a chick. I was straight up hating.

"I am not sure what he could do for her, but moving on. Desiree looked so incredible that it didn't make any sense. You missed it tonight, Q. You thought that little blue dress was nice!"

Oh gosh. I was practically salivating at the lips.

"Short skirt, sexy lace top, sexy heels. She did something to me."

"Man." I laughed, nervously. I didn't respond to his comment. I didn't even want to think about Tyler coming on to Desiree. I also didn't want him to know how much agony I was in right now. I needed her here. I just wanted to see her face. Hear her voice.

"Has she always been this beautiful?"

"Yes." My throat was dry.

"And she had some moves. She was working little dude on the dance floor." I didn't even want to think about it. "I would have loved to show her some of my moves."

"You can't handle, Des." My jealousy was getting the best of me.

"Maybe not, but I would have loved to try."

"Don't talk like that about my girl." She was mine.

"Whatever, I am going to get me some of that." No he wasn't. I would end our friendship if he so much as touched her.

"Stay away from Desiree. She doesn't need any of your mess." Desiree Harris was way too good for Tyler.

"Man, why are you tripping? Why are you so uptight tonight?" Because Des needed to be with me and she was with someone else.

"No one is tripping."

"Yeah you are. Stop fronting like you don't want some of that too." I wanted to tell him not to label her as a piece of ass, but my scolding would have given myself away.

"Nah, T." I wasn't going to tell him how much I wanted to. What went on between me and Desiree was going to stay between us.

"I can tell that you are lying."

"No you can't."

"Go somewhere with that noise. You are telling me that you don't want Desiree?" I did, and in a matter of time, we were going to be together. I was determined.

"Nope."

"You sure looked as if you did the other week."

"Look, I didn't say that I wasn't attracted to her. I am not blind. The girl is gorgeous and her body is banging, but that's my homie."

"So if she came home and offered you some, would you turn it down?" Heck no. She had already offered and if it wasn't for my crazy baby mama, I would have already explored my lust for this woman by now.

"I…"

"You stumbled. I know you are lying."

"Okay, I would take it, so what. Neither you or I will get that close to her."

"Speak for yourself."

"Come off your high, T. She is not giving you the time or day."

I couldn't even stomach what he was saying.

"Okay, man. Is Justin getting some?" I hoped not.

"How would I know?" I could have done without this entire conversation. I should not have picked up the phone. "Tell me about Camille." I wanted Tyler to stop talking about Desiree.

He obliged. He gave me all the details.

"Wow man. I need to get some myself. It's been a minute." It hadn't been that long. I went home with Christiana the other week.

"Yeah, you need to get off this celibate crap."

"For what? I am trying to find me a girl."

"One chick?"

"You need to settle down, T."

"I am not ready. Too many beautiful women out there."

"Alright fine, suit yourself. Keep on playing."

"I will. I am sure you will fall back on your ways."

"I am not trying to."

After hanging up with Tyler, the loneliness really settled in. I hadn't been intimate with a good woman in a while. I was not use to this, so I was a little bothered. I had to solve this. Soon.

"Daddy!" That brought me out of my thoughts.

"Coming, little man." Quinton Jr was standing on my bed in tears. "Dry it up! What's wrong?"

"I am sleepy!" I walked around with him for about twenty minutes until he fell back asleep. I slipped him back in bed and then settled back on the couch. My mind drifted back to college when I started to see Desiree in a whole new light.

Desiree knew some of my deepest secrets, but I never told her how I felt. Without me saying a word about my feelings for her, she destroyed me. She made me lose all hope in love. She was the real reason why I had been running from commitment. She did it all without realizing.

I remembered the day that I started seeing Desiree differently. It was the beginning of spring semester, senior year. I was chilling in my apartment, taking a break from a paper I was writing. I was in the kitchen, trying to find something to eat when there was a knock at the door.

"Go away," I mumbled. I was thinking it was my annoying neighbor from downstairs. She had been trying to hook up with me. I wasn't interested in her, but she didn't seem to get the point.

The knock grew louder. Ready to cuss the chick out, I headed to the door. I jerked it opened.

"Not right now, Simone."

"Do I look like her?" Desiree turned her nose up.

"Des! I thought you were going to be Simone. She has been bothering me all day."

"I told you that I could handle that," she laughed, pushing past me. "That's what you get for flirting with her at that party. I warned you that she was crazy."

"Yeah, yeah, I should have listened. What's up, girl?" I asked, shutting the door behind her.

"Nothing much. I thought I would come see you. I am bored," she said falling on my couch.

"Is that so?" My eyes lingered on her legs. She was wearing extremely short shorts and a very tight tank top. Mercy. Was Desiree always this thick?

"It's good to see you." I sat across from her. Her eyes had an extra sparkle to them. I stared at her for moment and started to get lost in them.

"What are you staring at?" I didn't know what to say at the moment. I was surprised at my own self.

"Are you wearing make-up?"

"No, Q. Why are you all of sudden in my face?"

"You are beautiful."

"Okay, Q." She rolled her eyes. I was confused at her insecurity.

"You don't have to believe me, but you should," I shrugged. I stood and headed back to the kitchen.

"Where are you going?"

"To fix something to eat. You want some."

"Yes," she mumbled. I fixed a foot long steak-um and cut it in half. When I rejoined her in my living room with plates in my hand, she was crying.

"What's wrong?" I hated when Desiree cried. It did something to me. I sat the plates down on my coffee table and pulled her to me. "Why are you crying, Desiree?" I turned her face to mines.

"Nothing is wrong, so don't worry about it."

"Don't come in here and bullshit me. Your face is red, your eyes are puffy and you have snot hanging out your nose"

"Shut up, Quinton." She pulled away, but laughed a little.

"What's wrong, baby girl."

"That bitch is going out with my man." I didn't realize Desiree had a man. I never met the clown.

"Huh? Wait, back up. Who?"

"Brianna."

"Oh." Brianna was Desiree's high maintenance roommate. I disliked her strongly. Many did.

"Chick doesn't know who she is messing with!"

"Chill, Des." Her eyes were dark with anger. I knew she had a crazy temper, but she didn't lose it often. It was not a look I saw much and I was not trying to see what could go down. "When did you get a man?" Considering we were close, I would have like to think that I would know when she was dating someone.

"Well, he is not exactly my man," she admitted, sheepishly.

"Huh? Now I am confused."

"I am talking about Anthony, Q."

"Oh." Desiree, for some reason unclear to most, had this big thing for this loser, Anthony Thompson. He played on the basketball team with me. While I got along with everyone on the team, he was the one dude I could not stand. He was too arrogant for his own good. He thought he was a star, but wasn't.

"Yeah," she sighed. "Drama."

"What happened, Desiree?"

"Brianna is going out with him. That's what happened."

"Wow." Everyone knew Desiree had a crush on Anthony, including her roommate Brianna. They were supposed to be girls.

"How could she?" I thought it was a good thing. I figured that they both deserved each other. Anthony was not good enough for Desiree. I didn't vocalize that because she was already upset. It was not something that she wanted to hear.

"I agree, that's really messed up."

"Who are you telling? I can't be mad at Anthony because he can date whoever he wants, but Brianna knew how I felt. She was supposed to be my girl."

"Yeah, but you are the only person who likes her. That girl has a reputation and you know it."

"Yeah, but what happened to being loyal to the one person who had your back."

"If it's not in her, it's not in her," I said, shrugging.

"I just can't believe that she did this to me. She went behind my back and she already gave him the cookie. I am so pissed right now."

"Yeah, I can tell. So what exactly did you say to her?"

"I called her a whore. I denounced our friendship and told her I did not want to associate with someone that I couldn't trust."

"That's all. You weren't hard enough." Brianna deserved more than that. Desiree was just too good of a person.

"Be honest with me, Quinton. Is Brianna cuter than me?"

"There is nothing cute about that girl."

"I thought she was the cutest thing to walk the campus of NC State." Who was she kidding?

"Desiree, that's you." I was serious. My girl was one of the most breathtaking girls on campus. She held that tittle deservingly.

"That's not funny." She didn't smile at me.

"I am not joking around in anyway. You need to learn how to take a compliment, Desiree, seriously." Her face turned bright red. She touched her cheeks.

"I am sorry. Thank you, Quinton."

"You are welcome. As far as Brianna goes, I don't really find her attractive. That's just me."

"Obviously, Anthony does."

"Well, he obviously doesn't have good taste in women." I shrugged. And you obviously don't have good taste in men, I thought. "Anthony is a fool not to notice how wonderful you are."

"Aww thank you," she said, throwing her arm around me. "You always know what to say to make me feel better."

"Uh huh." This feels nice, I thought. I was enjoying this simple hug a little too much. Just as I was tempted to bury my face in her neck, she pulled away.

"And do you know after I said what needed to be said, she actually slapped me."

"She did what!" Brianna had lost her mind. If she was a dude, I would have been ready to go duel it out. "Are you okay?"

"I think she scratched me." She turned her face and there was a little tiny scratch near her eye.

"She took things too far," I said, kissing her cheek.

"Don't worry. I jumped on top of her after that. I didn't hurt her, but I pinned her down for a while. I warned her that she better not put her hands on me again. I left her crying in her room. I had to cool off. I actually sat out on the steps by your door before knocking."

"It's a wonder that you didn't knock her out."

"Q, you know I am not a fighter. Only when I have to."

"Right." We sat there, eating our sandwiches for a few moments without speaking. I tried to think of something that would make her feel better, but drew a blank. "Where are you going?" I asked when she stood up.

"I guess I should head back. Thanks for lunch."

"I don't think so. Not right now."

"But…"

"You are going to chill with me right now." I grabbed her arm.

"Look, Quinton, I am a little tired, very angry and I am still hungry. Let me go."

"You're still hungry? Me too. Come on, let's go to IHOP." Her eyes brightened. "Don't front like you don't want some pancakes, Des." I rubbed her stomach. I knew she had a special place in her heart for them.

"Sounds good," she said, actually biting on her lip. I looked away because that turned me on for some reason.

"We will get you pancakes and then a sundae afterwards."

"Now you are talking. Thank you, Q. I love you."

"I love you too."

I spent the rest of the day trying to make her laugh. I hated seeing her cry. I always did what it took to make her happy. It had always been that way.

I also spent the day noticing things about her that I had never noticed before. I noticed that when she smiled, I smiled. I noticed how infectious her laugh was. How when she talked, you hung on to her every word.

Our waiter was obviously an admirer. He was practically drooling, his eyes never leaving her face. How did he know she was not my girl? I wanted to grab him by his shirt, but I didn't. He looked as if he was still in high school. I could not afford hurting a minor.

I should not have been turned on when she touched me. I should not have stared every time she licked syrup off her lips. I should not have moved my chair closer to hers when she wasn't looking. I should not have taken every opportunity to reach over and caress her hair or leaned in to inhale how good she smelled.

Hanging out with Desiree was a stress reliever for me. I needed this time with her. I was not looking forward to our night ending together. I wanted her to stay with me.

I thought Des had a good time and that she had calmed down about the today's incident. When she stopped in front of her apartment door, she looked as if she was going to beat it down.

'Well, I am not about to let you back in there. You and Brianna are going to get into it again and I don't trust that chick. She may call the police and I will have to come bail you out. Save us the trouble."

"I have no choice. What do you suggest I do?"

"Just stay with me tonight. Just one night."

"Okay, but I need some stuff."

"I will go with you. Give me your key."

Brianna and Anthony were cuddled up on the couch. I knew Des was hurt by what she saw, so I wished I had of just dragged her to my place from the beginning. I was glad that I was with her. I was sure that Brianna was doing this to be spiteful.

She looked over at Desiree who just pushed past me and into her bedroom, ignoring both Brianna and Anthony. I glared down at her and she quickly looked away. She knew I didn't respect her.

"What's up, Alexander," Anthony said, acknowledging me.

"Thompson." I detested the dude. This is who Desiree had a thing for? I couldn't begin to understand why.

"She tried to bring an ally," Brianna mumbled.

"Consider yourself lucky I am here, Brianna and shut up." She did. She crossed her arms and stared at the screen.

"What's this about?" Anthony asked, curiously.

"Keep your girl in check and don't worry about it." He looked over at Brianna and shook her head.

"I don't do drama, Brianna."

"Anthony, don't worry about Quinton."

Before I could say anything else, Des breezed back in the room.

"Coming, Q. Give me a minute." She walked over and stood in front of her TV. She started rummaging through her DVD's.

"Really, Desiree!" Brianna screamed. Des ignored her. I shook my head as Anthony obviously checked out Desiree's behind.

"Here it is," she said, finally holding up the DVD in her hand. "We can go now. Bye Anthony." Desiree smiled at him.

"Bye, Desiree," he said, watching her every move. I was starting to get highly agitated.

"Wow, Desiree," I said to her as we walked outside. "No words for you sometimes."

"You adore me!"

"I do."

Des changed into more short shorts, and we snuggled up on the couch to watch her DVD. It was a Kevin Hart stand-up special.

She fell asleep in my arms. I stared down at her and frowned. I was not use to how she was making me feel today. I wasn't use to these reactions. To these emotions. I had to do something about it.

I knew I was in trouble the next night. Desiree and I were at a house party. Everyone was in the basement. Desiree was playing pool against this chick name Rita. When she won the game, she practically jumped in my arms. I held on and didn't want to let go

"I deserve a prize," she said, leaning back to look at me. "What are you going to give me?"

A kiss. Some loving. Anything you want. The world.

Where did that come from?

"Let's start with a drink and then we will talk about it."

10

Wounded

"There is no fear in love, but perfect love casts out fear. For fear has to do with punishment, and whoever fears has not been perfected in love." 1 John 4:18

Quinton

After the night of the house party, I didn't see Desiree for a few days. I was used to seeing her every day. I was worried and I didn't understand why. After debating with myself, I picked up the phone and called her.

"Hey, Quinton," she said, picking up immediately.

"Hey, Des." I was nervous and I didn't know why I would be.

"What are you doing?"

"Missing you," I blurted. Why did I say that?

"Really?" I was relieved to hear a smile in her voice.

"Yeah, I am starting to think that you have been avoiding me."

"No. I have been studying. I have to keep these grades up."

"You deserve a break. Come see me."

"Anything for you, Quinton."

I don't know why I had to see her, but I did. I wanted a glimpse of that smile. I wanted to hear the sound of her voice. I wanted to touch her. I was feeling desperate.

She banged on my door moments later.

"It's open." She walked in with her yoga pants and fitted tank. She was very low key, hair in a pony-tail, no make-up on her face, and she still made my heart beat a little faster than normal.

"Hey, you." She floated directly in my arms without me asking for a hug. I was surprised when she didn't pull away immediately. She laid her head against my chest. "I forgot to say, I miss you too."

"Don't say it, unless you mean it."

"Shut up, Q. You sure know how to ruin the moment," she joked. I sure did because she pulled away.

"I am sorry."

"Uh huh." She leaned over and kissed my cheek and then took a seat on my couch. "Come sit with me." She grabbed my hand and pulled me down beside her.

"So what's up with you and Brianna?"

"I don't talk to the girl. She does her thing and I do mine. She goes into her room and stays in there if she knows I am home. She is scared to even look at me."

"Desiree, you got that girl all messed up," I laughed.

"Oh well. She got herself messed up."

"So I take it that there is no rekindling the friendship."

"No, I am done with Brianna. Some of the girls won't even talk to her. Especially Rayven. She better not say two words to Rayven."

"No one likes Brianna. You were the only one cool with her. Everyone else tolerated her."

"Wow, really?"

"How did you put up with her for so long?"

"Until now, she was cool with me, so I was cool with her."

"That's because everyone loves you."

"Obviously not everyone."

"She just doesn't value friendship, Desiree."

Things blew up with Brianna that next week. A teammate of mine was having a get together. We were all watching a big game between Charlotte and Brooklyn. Unfortunately someone invited Anthony. He unwisely brought Brianna.

Anthony and Brianna were caught having sex in the bathroom. Idiotically, they didn't lock the door. Desiree's girl, Logan, didn't bother to knock. I think she knew what was going on and intentionally opened the door to initiate drama..

Brianna ended up screaming and running out the apartment, humiliated. Anthony comes out the bathroom, yelling with his pants around his ankles.

"Dude, we don't want to see that," my boy, Trey, yelled out.

"Anthony, we didn't know you were so well endowed," Logan said, laughing.

"You better believe it," he said, pulling up his pants. I couldn't stand him. He was conceited as I don't know what. "Why did you do that to, Brianna?"

"No one is worried about her," Logan said, crossing her arms. "She disrespected Des and no one is going to stand for that."

"What did she do?" he said, looking over at Des. Her face had turned red and she turned away.

He obviously didn't realize that Desiree had this thing for him. I didn't get it. He didn't deserve a woman like her. The more I thought about it, the more jealous I got.

When no one said anything, he shook his head.

"I don't have time for the drama that you ladies involve yourself in. Let me go find this chick and take her home. Goodnight."

Later on, Desiree and I were alone outside on the balcony.

"That was funny. I never seen Brianna run so fast," I said.

"I know right. Was that a little too mean? I didn't know Logan was going to do it, but should I feel bad, Q? Tell me the truth."

"No. She betrayed your trust. She physically attacked you."

"You are right. I am not going to feel bad," she said, sliding her arms around my neck. I pulled her closer by grabbing her waist. "Thank you, Quinton."

"You are welcome, baby."

I'm not sure who kissed who, but the next thing I knew, we were kissing. I had never enjoyed kissing another woman so much. I wanted her. I wanted to be with her in every way possible.

Suddenly, she pulled away. We were both breathless. She looked at me, terrified.

"Why are you kissing me, Quinton?"

"The same reason you are kissing me."

"I don't know why."

"Me neither."

I didn't expect her to kiss me again, but she did. She kissed me with aggression and passion. Her hand slid up my shirt and I grabbed her butt. I was fired up. With a condom in my pocket, I was ready for anything. We could take this as far as she wanted to take it.

I wasn't ready for her to pull away, but she did.

"Stop that, Q."

"You kissed me. What's up, Des?"

"Well, we shouldn't be kissing."

"Why not?" I knew that was a stupid question.

"Why do you think?"

I couldn't stop thinking about that kiss the rest of the night. I thought about it while trying to finish up some homework. I thought about how her lips felt while I was in the shower. I was still thinking about how good it made me feel when I went to bed.

I laid there. Awake. I couldn't fall asleep. She had my mind messed up and I was not sure why.

There was a bang at my door around 2:00 in the morning. What was this! Who could possibly want to bother me at this time of night? I angrily jumped out of the bed and to my door.

"Who is it?" I asked. It better not be Simone.

"Me, Quinton!" I opened up the door, quickly.

"Desiree!" I grabbed her by the arm and pulled her in. "Is everything okay." She nodded. "You sure nothing is wrong?"

"Yes, I am sure. Q, I...."

"Then, what in the world! Why...."

"Shut up, Quinton. I needed to see you."

"Why?"

"I want you to kiss me." I went to do so, but she stopped me. "No, listen. I want you to kiss me. Kiss me for all it's worth because you can't do it again."

"Wow, okay." I had mixed feelings. I desperately wanted to kiss her, but I knew as soon as she left, I was going to be left thinking about her. I was afraid that I was not going to get any sleep.

Could I really kiss her only once?

"Why are we in this moment, Des? Why are you here for this?" I needed to know.

"Because I am so attracted to you, Q. I need this. It feels good when you do it." I was glad to know that I could make her feel good. "Q, please." I pulled her to me and I kissed her like she was my woman. I kissed her with urgency. I was hungry for her.

When I pulled away, she looked up at me. She was trying to catch her breath as she reached up to touch her lips. I realized how roughly I kissed her.

I was not satisfied and I am not sure she was. I pulled her back in my arms. I kissed her just as passionately, but slowly. I wanted the both of us to savor this moment. I would never forget this and I wanted to make sure she didn't either.

"Quinton," she whispered against my lips.

"Yes," I answered. I couldn't stop. The more I kissed her, the harder I fell for her. She completely embraced me and I shivered. Why did that feel so right to me? I pulled her closer, not ever wanting to let go of her.

Why couldn't I take her to bed with me? Not for sex. I would have loved to hold her all night long and then wake up next to her.

I whispered her name. I almost protested when she pulled away

"We better stop now."

"Thank you." I touched her cheek and placed a peck on her lips. "Have a goodnight, Desiree." She reached up and touched my lips and then kissed my cheek.

"Goodnight Q. Let's try not to make this weird in the morning." With that, she walked out of my apartment. I walked outside and watched her run down the steps to her second floor apartment. When I heard her shut her door, I shut mine.

The damage had been done.

The sweetness of her lips lingered on mine the rest of the night, the next day and two weeks later. I couldn't forget how her lips felt if I tried. I couldn't stop thinking about how good it felt to have her arms around me.

No woman had kissed me like that. I wanted that type of kiss every time I saw her, but I had a feeling that I was not going to get that chance again. When I saw her, she acted as if it never happened. I was pretty sure that's how she wanted it to be.

Despite that, I was left thinking maybe she didn't enjoy the kiss as much as I did. Maybe I didn't affect her the same way she affected me. Maybe I hadn't kissed her as well as I thought.

As quickly as I thought that, I erased it from my mind. I refused to believe that. The way she moaned her appreciation, the way she dug her fingers into my back and the way she looked at me afterwards, were all indications of how much she enjoyed it.

Maybe I was tripping because I wasn't just attracted to my friend, but I was really digging her. I wasn't satisfied with being her boy anymore. I wanted to date her. I wanted to be with her. I wanted to call her my woman.

What was this? A crush? More than that? It had to be because usually I wasn't afraid to pursue a woman. Desiree was an entirely differently story. She scared me to death.

She made me feel insecure. I couldn't seem to impress her. She consumed me and I didn't like it.

It bothered me so much that I called Tyler to help me figure out my next move. T had been my best friend since the eighth grade. He went to school in VA.

"You are tripping over some chick, Q! Say it isn't so."

"I would be lying."

"Q, we are one of a kind."

"What does that mean?"

"We are players." I wasn't really a player. "We don't settle."

"I know."

"And we sure don't trip over chicks."

'True, but I think I love this one." There was silence on the other end. Even I was taken aback by what I had just said. I hadn't quite admitted that to myself. Still, I knew that as soon as I admitted it, it was true. My feelings for Desiree were very real.

"T, this is the first time I admitted that. I know this is crazy."

"I don't even know what to say. Quinton, we don't fall in love."

"Yeah, well I wasn't planning on it. It just happened."

"How does it just happen?"

"I don't know, man."

"Maybe you are mistaken."

"There is no mistake here." I explained to him how I been feeling lately. How no matter how hard I tried, I couldn't seem to get her out of my mind. I couldn't stop thinking about that kiss. I had stopped talking to all other girls. I didn't want anybody else.

"Was the kiss that good?"

"The best, hands down."

"Wow, it sounds like you have it bad."

"Now you hear me, T?"

"What's this chick's name? Who is this chick that is trying to make you settle down?"

"Desiree." There was silence on the other end. "Tyler did you hear me? I am in love with Desiree."

"Yeah, I hear you. I don't know what to say. We have been around Des since middle school. I thought we were all just friends Then again they say friends make the best lovers. At least you picked a chick worth falling in love with."

"Yeah, so what should I do?" I usually didn't ask Tyler for any female advice because I figured that I knew everything there was when it came to dating women. This was new territory. This was love. Tyler probably was not an expert on love. I usually turned to Des when it was something serious, but in this case, that was out of the question.

I wanted Tyler to suggest a way I could get over Desiree. That was all I wanted to hear. He baffled me when he didn't give me that.

"Tell her, Q. Tell Desiree how you feel."

"What!"

"Hey, why not?"

"Because you are always talking about how you are against love. Why are you trying to encourage it? You need to be my boy and help me figure out a way to get over this chick."

"I am not going to do that. Don't get over it. Don't run."

"Tyler, you are sounding like a hypocrite."

"Look, I never said that I was against love. Love is a wonderful thing and one day I will want it, but right now, I am not ready. I have to grow up."

"Who says that I am ready?"

"You are not me, Q."

"Whatever, T, I taught you everything that you know."

"Why do we have to go there?"

"I just wanted to remind you."

"Whatever. Stop trying to fight love. Tell her."

"I can't tell Desiree how I feel about her."

"Why not?"

"Tyler, you wouldn't understand."

"I might understand more than you think."

"If I decide to settle down, it has to be with a woman who has some sort of feelings for me."

"I hear that, but…"

"And I know that she doesn't feel the same way about me."

"How do you know that? She let you kiss her."

"We were hot for each other that night. That's it."

"I don't care what you say, Quinton. Be a man and tell this woman how you feel about her. I don't know much about love, but I do know that you can't just get over someone. Explore it."

I thought about what Tyler said all night. I just couldn't see any point in telling Des how I felt. I didn't have the courage. No one wanted to be rejected.

Plus, I wasn't ready. I couldn't settle down with anyone. Not right now. I wanted to graduate and get established before I thought about settling down with any woman.

By the time I went to bed that night, I decided not to tell her. I didn't see any point in it. It would be in both of our best interest for me to keep my mouth shut.

She was starting to bother me, though. The thoughts of her were taking up too much of my day. I was starting to lose my sanity.

Every day was the same. She was on my mind when I opened my eyes each morning. She was on my mind while I should have been paying attention in class. She was a distraction at basketball practice. She kept me from doing my homework. She was the last thing on my mind when my head hit the pillow at night.

This was getting ridiculous. Something had to be done about this. This was a serious problem that needed resolving.

No other female existed to me when she came around. My heart felt funny. My stomach was in knots. I didn't like the feeling. I didn't like how she was changing me.

I had lost control. I had lost my mind. Desiree possessed that along with my heart.

After another week of this, I couldn't take it anymore. I was starting to think that maybe Tyler was right and that maybe you couldn't fight love. So after a night where I sat on the couch and stared at a blank TV screen for thirty minutes, I decided to tell her. I was about to be a man about it.

I took a shot of Hennessey, grabbed my key, opened the door and headed for her place. I stood in front of her door for a few minutes before knocking. Internally, I was having a conflict. One part of me told me to knock and the other part told me to walk away.

Usually women didn't make me nervous. I was never shy. I was not easily intimidated.

This was Desiree, though. This was love. I was scared of loving Desiree. I had never felt this way about anyone. No one had warned me that it was going to feel like this.

I had to tell her, though. She would want to know about my struggle. I didn't want to fight anymore.

I knocked.

"Who is it?" She yelled after a moment.

"Quinton."

"Come in, Q."

Her apartment was practically empty.

"What happened? Did you get robbed and forget to tell me."

"She paid her half of the lease for the remainder of the semester and left." She started laughing. "She said that she couldn't stand being around me."

"Whatever to that. I know that you are happy."

"I am beyond happy."

"Okay. I have something to tell you," I blurted as I followed her into her bedroom.

"What's that? Come zip me up while you are talking."

I took in her strapless black dress. It hugged every curve in her body. Her appearance made my heart beat ten times faster. My entire body reacted.

She was so beautiful.

"Okay."

She walked over to me, giving me that smile that I adored and turned her back to me. My hand shook as I zipped her dress. I had to control myself. I would have loved to slide that dress down her body until it hit the floor. Then I wanted to kiss every inch of her.

"Where are you going?" There was sinking feeling in my gut.

"Just heading out for a while. Thank you, Quinton." She gave me a hug that didn't last long enough. She smelled nice and sweet. I would remember that smell the rest of the night.

"No problem. With who?"

"You are nosy."

"I am. Who are you going out with?"

"A friend." I was panicking inside and hoped that it didn't show on my face.

"Male or female?"

"Male. Who are you trying to be, my father." This could not be happening. Not right now.

"No." I could tell my face was red. I needed to calm down. "You are going out on a date?" It was obvious, but at this point, I didn't know what else to say.

"What do you think?"

"I was just asking." My chest was tightening. I felt hope slipping away. She didn't belong to me, but I felt like she was being snatched right out of my grasp.

"Anything else?"

"With who?"

"Anthony," she blurted.

"What the hell!"

"Don't yell and don't you start!"

"What's wrong with you?" I was so angry.

"Just drop it! This is none of your business!"

"What! I can't care about you. I can't be concerned!"

"Stop yelling!"

I felt so sick. I was pissed. I had no right, though.

"Why would you go out with him after what he…?"

"Quinton, you wouldn't understand."

"Obviously not." Why did I choose this woman to fall in love with? I love you, Desiree. Why couldn't she understand that? How could she not tell? I was never good at hiding my feelings.

"Look, it's not like Anthony knew how I felt."

"That's not the point. You tell me that you want a good man. You say you are sick of these trifling dudes. Why would you choose this one?"

"I know you are not talking." Ouch. I see how she felt about me.

"Don't put me in the same category as Anthony."

"Then where do I put you?"

"If you think so poorly of me, and Anthony and I are the same category, why go out with him? You wouldn't go out with me."

"Quinton, I wouldn't go out with you because you are Q." I felt like she had just punched me in my gut.

"So what are you saying? I don't deserve a woman of my own?"

"I didn't say all of that."

"What are you saying?"

"You don't know anything about love?"

"What does that have to do with anything?"

"The ultimate goal of a relationship is love, Q. It's not always sex." I just stared at her. She thought so lowly of me. She didn't realize how much she was hurting me.

"I think love sucks," I mumbled.

"How would you know?" Because I love you and you are saying this to me. "Don't stand up here and talk about love to me, Q."

"It's not for me, I guess. What does love have to do with Anthony? You love him?" If she said yes, I doubted that I would be able to control my reaction.

"No." Her face turned red. I closed my eyes in horror. This had become the worst night.

"Are you sure?"

"Quinton! Drop it!"

"Fine. Do whatever you want."

"I will. It is what I want. Now let it go."

"It's forgotten," I said, heading towards the door.

"Where are you going?"

"To let you get ready for your date," I mumbled.

"Quinton!"

"Yes." I stopped at her door with my hand on her doorknob. I was slowly suffocating. I was struggling to breathe properly.

"Are you mad at me?" I could hear that she was scared. She came up behind me and wrapped her arms around my waist.

"Why would I be?"

"Quinton!"

"Desiree, please let me go." I turned slightly and she was giving me a panicked look. She was pleading with me. There was nothing I could do any differently. She had ripped my heart out.

"Please don't act like this." She looked as if she was about to cry.

"Like what?"

"Like you are mad at me. What did I do?" Destroyed me. I reached over and pulled her to me. I pressed my lips against her forehead for a moment.

"I am not mad." I turned for the door once more, but she grabbed my hand.

"You said that there was something that you wanted to tell me."

"Maybe later."

"Please…"

"Desiree!!!" She gave me a wounded looked. "Have a good time. Don't worry about me."

"I…"

"You wouldn't understand!" I opened her door and left without looking back. I ran up the stairs and back to my apartment.

I fell on my bed and stared at the ceiling. Of all the women in the world, I had to fall for this woman. Why did I allow her to rip me to shreds like that? It was nothing like hearing that the woman you loved would never date you, but she would date someone you detested.

Anthony! She wanted Anthony. She put me on a lower level than him. If she knew about some of the things that he had did to women, would she go out with him then? I had some stories.

"Why are you doing this me?"

The night I wanted her the most, she belonged to someone else. The night I was ready to unleash my heart to her, she unknowingly rejected me. She had destroyed my faith in love. I would never get to be with her.

No woman had ever made me feel this way. No woman had ever made me fall in love with her and then made me feel like shit for doing so. I was experiencing heartbreak like never before. The pain was unbearable.

"Don't fight love," Tyler said. Obviously, I had no choice because love didn't want me. It rejected me. Love was fighting back and it had already knocked me out. There was no getting up from this battle.

I had to fight it. There was no reason for me to hold on to it. I obviously couldn't have it. Forget it.

I lay on my bed for three hours. I had no desire to do anything. I was trapped in this room with my feelings and my emotions. Deciding I needed air, I finally got up. I was going to go for a ride

I grabbed my car keys and without another thought, I headed out the door. I ran down the steps and my nightmare continued. I wished at that moment that I had not left my apartment.

There was Anthony with his arms around my love. He had my love pushed against his car. He had his hands and lips all over my love. The woman that I loved.

It was so painful to watch, but I couldn't look away. Every kiss they shared destroyed me. I had never experienced this amount of sadness. I could feel my world crumbling around me.

"Quinton." I hadn't even notice Rayven when she walked up. She was standing there with keys in her hands as if she was about to head up the steps.

I didn't say anything. I just stared at her. She looked at me confused and then at the kissing couple. It took her a couple moments, but she eventually figured things out. Her eyes grew big.

"Oh, Quinton." I could tell she knew how I felt. She shook her head and then reached for my hand. I don't know why, but I took her hand and followed her upstairs. She led me inside her apartment.

"You love her?" She asked, shutting the door behind me. When I didn't answer her, she said, "You do. I am sorry. I know that must have been hard to watch. I am sorry you had to see that. She's really stupid for going out with him"

She pushed me down on her couch and stood over me. I just stared at her. She had this look in her eyes. I knew what that look meant. She was horny.

"Would you like me to help you forget her?" I should not have nodded, but I did.

She climbed into my lap and kissed me. I kissed her back. The next thing I knew, we were pulling each other's clothes off. I was sliding my hands over her naked body. I was kissing her bare skin.

Despite it all, I was still thinking about Desiree's lips. I kissed her best friend, desperately wanting Desiree in my arms. I wanted to make love to her. Not Rayven.

I held on to her hips. It all felt good, but every time I closed my eyes, I could only think of Desiree. This wasn't working.

Rayven got on her knees afterwards and looked up at me. So I didn't have to look in her face, I closed my eyes. For a moment, she made forget Des. She took away my troubles. I was focused on Rayven and Rayven only.

When it was all over, reality settled in again. I sat up straight and realized that the loving Rayven offered me, hadn't comforted me. I accepted her gift because she was the closet I would ever get to Desiree. I had used her best friend.

Rayven sat beside me and placed her head on my shoulder.

"Are you still thinking about her?"

"Yes," I admitted. It was the first word I had spoken to her.

"I take it that I didn't help you forget."

"No, you didn't." I looked away when I saw the hurt in her eyes. She was wrong to think that she was going to help me forget this woman who I loved. Sex could make your forget someone in the moment, but once it was all over, the pain would still exist.

"I am sorry, Rayven," I whispered. I stood and pulled on my clothes. She didn't respond. She turned away. I sighed and headed straight for the door. I didn't look back.

I didn't know the chick wanted me for herself. If I had known that I was going to hurt her, I would have never gone into her apartment. I would have never unwrapped the gift she offered me. Now, I felt even worse, if that was possible.

I walked back into my apartment. I sat on my couch and dropped my face into my hands. I did something that no woman had made me do since my mama did when I was a little boy. I cried. I cried for myself. I cried for Desiree. I cried for Rayven.

Now, here I was, almost five years later. I was getting pulled into dangerous territory again. I was starting to think about my good friend a little too often. I did not like where I was headed.

I was not about to do this to myself again. I was going to find me a woman soon before Desiree made me lose my mind again. She had hurt me once and I was not going to let her do it again.

I wanted her desperately, though. This time around, I knew she wanted me. Could I resist her? I doubted it.

11

Nonchalance

"Let no one say when he is tempted, "I am being tempted by God,"
for God cannot be tempted with evil, and he himself tempts no one.
But each person is tempted when he is lured and enticed by his own
desire." James 1:13-14

Quinton

Before I went to sleep that night, I promised myself that I would chill. There was no way that I could afford to start tripping over Des again. It was not good for my sanity.

As much as I wanted to explore the chemistry between us, I was going to stop pushing for it to happen. I was going to lay back and allow things to progress naturally. I just hoped that we were coming from the same place.

When I woke up the next morning, I didn't see Quinton Jr. How did he sneak out of here?

"Quinton!" No answer. Maybe he had gotten up and fell asleep somewhere. "Little man." I was worried.

"Quinton!" Desiree. "Come here. To the living room."

I walked to the living room and there was my son cuddled up in Desiree's lap. They were sitting on the floor watching the Disney Jr channel. Little man was enjoying a Pop-Tart. He was so absorbed that he didn't even realize that I had entered the room. I laughed.

"Hey, Quinton."

"What's up, Des?" I took in her shorts and her tank. As I had been days these last few days, I was instantly turned on.

"When I got home, he was standing in the hall. He said that he was hungry and that he wanted to watch Mickey Mouse Clubhouse. I couldn't resist. I took him and here we are. Was that okay?"

"That's perfect. That's what he loves to do. Thanks for doing that. He usually wakes me up."

"It's okay. Hey, little man. It's daddy." I laughed when he waved at me. He wasn't trying to leave Desiree's lap. I couldn't blame him.

"Hey, buddy."

"Hi, daddy."

"What are you laughing at?" Desiree asked.

"He likes you."

"Really?" Her eyes grew big.

"Yeah." I sat down beside them on the floor. "Quinton." This time my son moved away from Desiree to settle in my lap.

"Hey, daddy," he said, throwing his arms around my neck.

"What are you eating?"

"A Pop-Tart."

"What kind?"

"Blueberry."

"My favorite. Can I have a bite?"

"No, daddy. Get your own."

"Okay, fine," I chuckled.

I looked over at Des. She gave me one of those sexy smiles that drove me crazy. The mischievous one. I wonder what that meant.

"How was your night?" I really only wanted to know one detail.

"It was cool."

"What did you guys do?"

"Dinner. Dancing." She offered no details.

"What else?" I was going to make her tell me.

"What do you mean what else?"

"Did you sleep with him?"

"Are you really that nosy, Q?"

"Yes, I am. I have to know."

"I don't kiss and tell, remember?"

"Did you or not?"

"No, Quinton. No cookies for Justin." She didn't understand how relieved I felt. "Does that make you happy?"

"Yes."

"Why would it?" She gave me a look of shock.

"You know why. Don't play like you didn't know how I felt. I didn't want you to go out with him period."

"Yeah, you were being jealous."

"I was very jealous. I thought about you all night. I missed you."
This was not playing it cool. What happened to that plan?

"I missed you too." She leaned over and kissed me. It didn't last
long. We wanted to respect the fact that I was holding my son.

"You should have been here with us."

"I couldn't, Q."

"Yes, you could have."

"No." She moved closer to me and kissed me again. Did Justin
get to kiss these lips too? I hoped not.

"Did you kiss him like that?"

"What Justin and I share does not compare to what me and you
share, Quinton. Don't worry about another man when I am with
you." I couldn't help it. I didn't want her to be with another man.

"Okay, beauty."

"I can't believe that you put me out there like that on the radio."

"You are the one who called in."

My son looked at me and then at Des. He climbed out of my lap
and moved closer to the TV. I guess our conversation annoyed him.

"Little man, don't get too close."

"I won't."

"Come here," I said to her. I practically pulled her into my lap.

"You are so greedy," she whispered against my lips.

"You have to show me some appreciation, remember?"

"You are right. I do."

Desiree slid her hand under my shirt while we kissed. I reached
my hand up and unhooked her bra. I took her breast in my hand and
caressed them.

"I love these." We kissed for a while. I was disappointed when
she pulled away, but I understood. Things were starting to get hot
and heavy. "Why did you stop?" I teased.

"Because of that precious little boy," she smiled.

"Good reason. You wait until he is back with his mother."

"I am looking forward to it." She smiled as she stood up.

"Where are you going?"

"I am hungry. Would you like something?"

"What are you fixing?"

"Some eggs and bacon. Who knows what else?"

"Yeah, I would love some of that. Desiree?"

"Yes, Quinton," she said, stopping at the door.

"Would you like to go to the zoo with me and Quinton?" I couldn't help it. I just wanted the woman with me. I was still trying to figure out what playing it cool meant. I wasn't sure if I could.

"Sure. I will hang out with you boys." She smiled and disappeared into the kitchen. I leaned against the couch and shook my head. What was I going to do?

"Daddy." Quinton walked over to me and sat beside me.

"Yes, son."

"I love you."

"I love you too." He was the best thing that had ever happened to me. "Little man, do you like Desiree?"

"I like Desiree, daddy. She is pretty."

"Yes she is."

"Do you really like her, daddy?"

"I like her a lot." More than anyone would ever realize.

"Me too. I really like her. I want to play with her, daddy." I found that hilarious. So did I!

"Not at much as I, kid. Guess what we are going to do today."

"What!" He was so excited that it did something to me. I loved seeing the joy on his face. His mother didn't do anything with him.

"We are going to the zoo!"

"To see the tigers!"

"Yes, and the lions, elephants and giraffes."

"Yeah, daddy! You are the best."

"Thanks, kid!"

Des brought breakfast to us. We ate it as we watched cartoons with my son. We didn't say much. She just kept looking at me with desire in her eyes. It was driving me crazy, but I didn't say anything.

After breakfast, I took a shower while Desiree played with Quinton outside. I watched them from the window. He adored her, I could tell. His eyes grew big whenever she talked to him. I knew today that I was going to get overlooked.

I put on my white tee, some khaki shorts, and my favorite Jordans. I sprayed on some Versace, Des's favorite cologne. I knew she was crazy about it because every time she smelled it, she would hug me and whisper how good it smelled. I wanted desperately to get one of those hugs today.

When I walked outside, Desiree was chasing Quinton Jr around the front yard. She looked over at me, smiled and waved.

'Run to daddy." He came running towards me full speed with his arms outstretched. I lifted him in the air.

"Little man, it's time to take a bath."

"I want Desiree to do it," he said, whining.

"Des has to go and get dress so that she can come to the zoo."

I was finishing putting on Quinton Jr's clothes when Desiree walked in. He ran from me with his arms opened towards her.

"What do you have, kid, that I don't?" I joked.

"Don't even start. You get plenty attention from me," she said, giving me a knowing look.

"Not enough. I want more," I said, giving her a knowing look of my own.

I looked her up and down. She was as sexy as ever in her fitted lilac sundress.

"You are so beautiful," I blurted. I couldn't help it.

"Thank you," she said, blushing as always. "Do you want me to drive?" she offered once outside.

"No, I don't."

I took Quinton from her and got him settled in. She was still standing by the car when I shut the door. She was eying me.

"What?" I asked. She didn't say anything. She just wrapped her arms around my neck and sort of buried her face in my neck. "What's this for, Des?"

"You smell so good. That smell drives me crazy." I smiled. I had achieved what I wanted. "Did you wear that for me?"

"Of course," I said, opening her door.

"Thank you. Such a gentleman."

"I try."

After getting behind the wheel and starting the car, I looked over at Des before backing out. As she smiled back at me innocently, I could feel that familiar feeling tugging at my heart.

"What, Q?"

I didn't realize that I was looking at her strangely.

"Nothing." I took a deep breath. I was in trouble.

I was right; my son didn't pay me any attention. He adored Des. He didn't want her to let him go.

I adored Des for being so patient. She didn't complain about holding him when I knew she had to be tired. I got tired after holding my son for long periods of time. When she started shifting him in her arms a little too often, I started thinking I was not being fair to her.

"Desiree, let me take him for a while."

She handed Quinton Jr to me and gave me a grateful smile. Before he could start crying, I walked him over to the tiger display and started pointing. I had to get his attention away from Desiree.

She stood back. When I turned, she was smiling at me. I stared back, thinking how she was incredible. As I walked over to her, I urged myself to calm down. I needed to take a step back from things.

She grabbed my hand and once again, I was putty.

Eventually Quinton started getting tired, so we headed home. I dropped Des off before taking my son home to his mother. I wasn't sure what kind of battle I was going to have to deal with today. I wasn't too keen on seeing her again.

Surprisingly, India was cool. I got the feeling that she was worried about her mother. She took our sleeping son out of my arms, smiled and said thank you. She walked away, told me goodnight and I saw myself out.

With the way I was feeling, I didn't want to head straight home. I stopped at Frieda's, a nice little bar uptown. I sat down alone and enjoyed a beer while trying to focus on something else. I managed to talk to this cute little chick named Brittany. She wasn't my type, but she was nice to look at and she proved to be a great distraction. I appreciated her.

She gave me her number. I knew I wasn't going to call, but I didn't want to hurt her feelings. I only pretended to save her info.

I drove around an hour before heading home. I convinced myself that it was time to stop avoiding the situation. I was hoping that she was in bed, so I could get my mind right. If she wasn't, I was going to have to learn how to be a man about our situation.

She wasn't in bed. She was on the couch asleep in front of a very loud TV. I picked up the remote as I stared at her. She was in just a tank and some panties. Was she doing this to me on purpose?

I stood over her, imagining every curve on her body, willing myself not to touch what my eyes were enjoying. Instead, I reached down to rub her cheek. I touched her lips, wishing she was awake so I could feel them on mine

I jumped back when she moved. Slowly, she opened her eyes. She smiled up at me.

"Hi, Quinton. Where have you been?"

"Hey, girl." Breathe, Q. "Why aren't you in bed?" I avoided her question. I didn't want to lie to her, but I didn't want to explain to her that I was driving around because she was making nervous.

"I didn't think that I was tired. I was trying to watch TV, but obviously I passed out. I was a little lonely." She sat up.

"I am sorry. I had stops to make and I didn't anticipate them taking so long." I hated lying to her

"I thought you were coming back." There was disappointment written all over her face.

"They were unexpected."

"You don't have to lie to me, Quinton," she said, calling my bluff. "If you had to stop by some chick's house, just say it." Is that what she thought? She was the only chick I wanted to be with tonight. I was scared to, though.

"Desiree, I didn't go to some chick's house."

"You don't have to defend yourself to me." I didn't know what to say, so I didn't say anything. After a couple of moments, she finally stood. "Well, I suppose, I should go to bed."

"Yeah, you seem tired."

"Okay." She gave me this crazy look. "Goodnight, then."

"Goodnight." My heart dropped as she walked past me and down the hall. I longed to follow her, but I didn't.

"Desiree." I panicked all of a sudden.

"Yes," she said, giving me a hopeful look.

"Never mind. I will ask you later." I chickened out.

"Are you sure?" Her face fell.

"Yeah, I am sure."

"Fine. Bye." Just like that she was gone and I was left there, feeling stupid.

I headed down the hall. I stopped in front of her door. I was tempted to knock and make the move we both wanted me to make, but I opted out. I hung my head and headed to my room.

I stood in my shower ten minutes. I tried to calm my nerves. I tried desperately to get some clarity. Frustrated that I couldn't find any, I climbed out, toweled off and wrapped my towel around my waist. I headed to the kitchen.

Whenever I felt anxious, I wanted food. I needed something comforting right now. I started making myself a peanut butter and jelly sandwich. I had sat down to enjoy it when she walked in. She walked in wearing a robe, but it was wide open. She was topless.

She was intentionally torturing me.

"What are you doing up, Des?"

"I heard a noise," she shrugged. "I came to see what it was."

"And you weren't scared?"

"Nope."

"Desiree. You knew it was me."

"I didn't," she said, giving me that mischievous look of hers. I held my breath as she started moving in my direction. If she touched me, I was going to lose it. She stopped directly in front of me.

"Are we playing it cool now?" She was calling me out.

"What are you talking about?"

"Quinton, please don't act like that. You said you wanted me, now you are acting as if you don't. All of sudden, you are scared to touch me, to kiss me."

"That's because…"

"You are trying to be laid back about this whole thing. You are trying to play it cool, right? I am going to play your little game."

"Huh?" I didn't intend for this to be a game. I was just trying to regain some sanity. Right now, she was making it worst.

"Shush." She grabbed my face and gave me a quick kiss. Before I could kiss her again, she moved out of reach. She grabbed my hand, and while holding my gaze, she slid it down her body, stopping on her thigh. "Just know I was so ready for you."

"Desiree!"

She started shaking her head and backing up.

"No, Quinton, we are going to do things your way."

"Des, I don't want to play any games with you."

"We are going to see how long we can hold out. Maybe in the end we won't have to go there."

"No." I stared at her. "Is this your way of trying to tell me that you just don't want to go there anymore?"

"Don't you get mad with me, Quinton! You wanted to play games all of sudden. I am just following your cue." I didn't like seeing the hurt on her face. I tried to think of something to give her insight to how I was feeling, but I couldn't. She walked out of the room.

She couldn't possibly think that I didn't want her. All had she to do was give me that look and I was at her mercy. How could she not realize that I would do anything for her? That included pleasing her.

I finished my sandwich, grabbed a beer and headed down the hall. I felt defeated. I drank my beer and stared at the ceiling. I tried to think of something else besides seeing her in that robe. When I realized that wasn't going to happen, I desperately tried to figure out my next move in dealing with this situation.

Thirty minutes later, I had not come up with a solution. Once again, Desiree had complete control over me. Right now, all I could do was surrender.

I lay there completely still, in my feelings, until I fell asleep.

I was relieved not to be around her the next few days. She went out with Rayven the following night. The night after that, I was going out with Des's girl, Lark. We had postponed the date twice, but we were finally going to make things happen. I wasn't too sure about our chemistry, but I was curious. I was ready.

I thought about Lark all day. She proved to be a great distraction from Desiree and my frustration. I wondered how she looked. Would we hit it off? Could I finally have some luck with a woman?

Around 7:30, I was climbing into my ride to pick her up. My car was in date mode. I had cleaned it from top to bottom. I had put in a new air freshener. The air conditioner was on full blast and I was playing sexy slow jams. I was ready for her.

She lived across town in the suburbs. As soon as I pulled in her driveway, she was walking out of the door. I got out as soon I as put the car in park. I figured the least I could do was open the car door.

"Hey, Lark, how are you?"

"I'm great." She gave me a quick hug. "How are you, Quinton?"

"I'm good."

She was actually very attractive. She was tall with a short curly fro. She showed off her curves in a tight fuchsia dress. I took notice of her sexy legs. I appreciated her pedicured toes in her heels.

"Wow." Desiree had done well

We went to dinner. Unlike, the first time we talked, she was talkative, funny and witty. I was into the conversation. I was laughing the entire time. I was digging her. Not as a woman that I wanted to date, but as a friend.

When we got back to her place, I found myself going in for the drink she was offering. I was enjoying myself, but I knew there was no chemistry between us. She had to feel that. I didn't want to give her the wrong idea. At the end of the night, if she wanted a kiss or she wanted to see me again, I was going to have to be honest.

She startled me when she said, "Look, Quinton, you are a gorgeous man and like Des said, you are wonderful. I just don't think we are for each other." Wow. I was not sure if I was more surprised or just relived.

"I was thinking the same thing," I blurted.

"Whew! Good. I am glad we are on the same page. I think you are really cool," she said, flopping down on the couch. "We should definitely hang. I am single now, so I have a lot of time on my hands. I need to get out more regardless."

"I'm down with that. So what happened with dude?" I asked, boldly. Des had filled me in, but I wanted to hear it from her.

The next thing I knew she was giving me all the details of her messy break-up. She told me how she was engaged to her high-school sweetheart. She came home one day to find him in bed with his best friend. A man. Brutal.

"This was the day before our wedding. They ran off together to our honeymoon destination. Aruba. What a bitch!"

"You will find someone better."

"Thank you!"

Eventually we hugged and I was on my way. When I got home, the house was dark. Initially I thought Des was asleep, but I saw light coming from under her door. When I walked past her room, I could hear music and her talking on the telephone. I assumed with Rayven.

I headed straight to my shower. I really needed one to help me relax. Hopefully it would help me get some sleep tonight.

After getting out of the shower, I realized I was thirsty. I wrapped a towel around my waist to head to the kitchen. On the other of the side of my door was the object of my desire.

'Hey, Quinton," she said, giving me that smile of hers.

"Hey, Desiree." I tried to stop the big grin, but I could not. I was happy to see her. "What's up with you?"

"Chilling. What are you up to?" she asked, pushing past me.

"I just took a shower."

"I see that," she said, giving me this look. "Are you tired?"

"I am not tired. Are you?" I asked, shutting my door.

"I feel good," she said, falling onto my bed. I took in her itty bit shorts and see through tank top. She had her hair down. There was gloss on her lips. She was breathtaking as always. I wanted her so badly, that my throat felt even drier. "How was your date?"

"It was good actually, but…"

"But what?" she said, rolling her eyes.

"She was beautiful, funny, and smart."

"What? That's not your thing?" she asked, sarcastically.

"We mutually agreed that we didn't have chemistry, Desiree."

"Really?" she asked, surprised.

"Really. We didn't have the chemistry that you and I have."

"You and I." She just stared at me. I knew what she was thinking. She wanted me as badly as I wanted her. If she made the move, it was on tonight. I wasn't worried about playing it cool.

"So what was Rayven up to?" She gave me this look.

"Rayven? I haven't talk to her. Why do you ask?"

"I heard you on the phone. I assumed you were talking to her."

"Oh, that was Tyler."

"Tyler?" I didn't like that one bit "Why would you talk to him?"

"He called me because he said you didn't pick up. I told him you were on a date, but he held me hostage on the phone."

"What did yall talk about?" I asked, trying not to sound annoyed.

"Sex. His girlfriends."

We sat there in silence with all the sexual tension in the world between us. I wanted to make that move, but I couldn't. She had rejected me and in the back of my mind, I could never forget that. She would have to make the move. I had yearned for this woman five years now.

Finally realizing that I was torturing myself, I stood.

"Where are you going?"

"My throat is dry. I am going to get something to drink. You want something?"

"Sure, I want something." I headed for the door. "No, Quinton. I am not thirsty." I turned to look at her. She gave me that look, standing up on my bed. My mouth fell open as pulled her shirt off. She stood before me topless, with her hands on the drawstring of her shorts. "Are you taking this tonight or not? Or are we still playing it cool?"

I moved for her, quickly.

"At least pretend you want me," she giggled as I knocked her down on my bed.

"Let's get this straight," I said, pulling on her shorts. "I could never pretend to want you. I always want you."

"Do you?" she asked, kissing me.

"In the morning. In the afternoon. In the evening. Every night."

"Show me then."

"Yeah, I can show you," I said, sliding her panties off. Once again, she was naked under me. Nothing in this world was going to stop me tonight.

I proceeded to kiss every inch of her body. She moaned and kept whispering, "Don't tease me."

"Shh," I said, pinning her hands to my mattress. I looked up at her and saw her eyes dark with desire. I stared in them for a moment. She wanted me right now and I didn't want to forget this moment.

I had wanted to be with this woman for so long now and this was my chance. I fell in love years ago and tonight I was finally able to show her a form of love. She was going to love me in return.

"Come here," she whispered. Wrapping my arms around her, I went to kiss her. And with all the pent up emotions, I kissed her with everything I had. "I like that, Quinton." She reached down and pulled my towel off. "Now love me."

And I did, for hours. Over and over again. When it was all over, it was almost 3:00 in the morning. We lay beside each other, gasping for air, dripping in one another's sweat. I looked over at her, hoping that I didn't disappoint her. I smiled because she was smiling up at the ceiling. I reached for her hand and she squeezed it.

"Come here." She moved closer, laying her head on my chest.

"Was it everything you dreamed of," she joked.

"That and more," I said, seriously.

" You know, you drive me crazy, Quinton Alexander."

The feeling was mutual.

She fell asleep in my arms. I laid there wide awake, listening to her breathe. I couldn't sleep. Too much on my mind.

"Now what am I going to do?"

12

Aftermath

"Do not be conformed to this world, but be transformed by the renewal of your mind, that by testing you may discern what is the will of God, what is good and acceptable and perfect." *Romans 12:2*

Quinton

I was on cloud nine in the days that followed. I finally had my chance with Desiree. She lived up to every fantasy I had of her.

I couldn't stop thinking about how it felt to kiss her. How her body felt. How she tasted. How she smelled.

I couldn't stop smiling.

Tyler asked me why I was so happy, but I couldn't tell him. This was not some random chick, this was Desiree. She was too important to disrespect. I would not kiss and tell when it came to her.

It wasn't just about the sex, though. When I looked at her, I longed for so much more. She would never know that. I would never find the courage to confront her again. This intimacy between us was going to have to do.

I wanted to make another move on her, but I didn't. I was scared too. Maybe one time was good enough for her. Maybe that was all she needed. So I would sit back and play it cool yet again.

A week went by and she had made no move. She would kiss me, though. It was addictive. One night, snuggled up on the couch, we kissed for twenty minutes straight.

I came home one morning after running errands. Desiree was in her kitchen. She was pacing the floor, on the phone with Rayven. She looked over at me and smiled when I entered the room. I headed to the fridge because every time I laid eyes on her, my mouth got dry.

"Rayven, hold on for minute. Someone is knocking at my door." I didn't hear any knocking. I didn't realize she was behind me, so I jumped a little when I realized that she was standing there. Wow.

"What's up, Des?" Without a word, she grabbed the back of my head and pulled me to her for a kiss.

"I just wanted to say hello to you, Quinton."

"Well, hello."

"Rayven, I am back. What were you saying to me, now?" I don't know what made me do it, but I walked over to Desiree and grabbed her by the waist. "Quinton!" She laughed. "I already said hi."

"I didn't quite hear you." I grabbed the phone. "Give me a minute, Rayven."

"What! Desiree, stop playing with that boy and talk to me." I placed the phone down on the counter. She was annoying.

"What are you doing?" she whispered, at the same time, sliding her arms around my neck.

"Like I said, I didn't hear you," I kissed her again, passionately. "Next time you kiss a man hello, you do it right, woman."

"I won't make that mistake next time."

"Good girl." She just smiled and pick up the phone.

"Rayven, I am back. Oh calm down!"

I rolled my eyes. It was time for Rayven to let things go. She offered and I accepted. She knew I didn't intentionally set out to hurt her in anyway. She sure knew how to hold a grudge.

'Rayven, would you like to talk to Quinton because I am not about to tell him that." She looked over at me and rolled her eyes.

'Tell the chick to get over it," I said, loudly. I didn't want to be rude, but enough was enough.

"Do you hear that? Get over it. Rayven, I will hang up on you. Move on with the conversation already. Q is not worried about you."

I laughed and headed to my bedroom. I tried to take a nap, secretly hoping that she would join me, but she never did. After realizing I could not fall asleep, I found a good movie. Afterwards, I hoped in the shower and then headed out to pick up some dinner. After dinner, I headed to work.

I went to work and enjoyed myself. I tripped with Deejay Fresh, my partner and crime during my show. Up and coming local artist, Calila, who was drop dead gorgeous, surprised us with a visit. She chilled with us for half of the show.

A lot of women called in to flirt with us like they did every night. They were just mere groupies that I wasn't interested in. I did manage to get a phone number from one of the interns. She had been eyeing me all night, so I decided to give her a chance. I was still looking for the right woman to distract me from Desiree Harris.

The rest of the week went by smoothly. I went out with two more of Desiree's friends. I enjoyed both of their company, but sadly, I didn't hit it off with either of them. I was starting to think that maybe I was the problem. I couldn't understand why I couldn't get past the first date.

Initially, I went out with Marissa. She was a cute girl with a nice booty, but she was a little too ratchet for me. She was wide open, so she had me laughing all night. I could hang with her, but I didn't want to date her.

At the end of the night, she tried to thank me by offering me a sexual favor. I turned it down. The only woman that I was seeking intimacy from was Des.

I went out with Michelle two nights later. She was Des's cousin. Des gave me her number while rolling her eyes.

"Look, you can go out with Michelle if you want to, but when things don't work out, don't come complaining to me about it."

"Huh?"

"Please don't blame me for anything."

"It doesn't sound like you care for your own cousin." I laughed at that. "Why would you try to set me up with her?"

"I am not really trying to set you up, Quinton. I am just delivering the number to you."

"I take it she knows who I am."

"Quinton, please, the whole city knows who you are. You met Michelle. You obviously don't remember her."

"Is she as beautiful as you?"

"She resembles me. Our styles are definitely different."

"Do you two get along?"

"We do. She gets on my nerves, but she is clueless to the fact."

"Wow. Why are you bothering to give me her number?"

"I owe her a favor. The girl would do anything for me. Every time I see her, she asks about you. She always asking what type of woman you are into. She wants to know who you are seeing."

"Did you tell her that I am into you," I said, grabbing her hand.

"No," she said, blushing. "Look, maybe I am wrong about you liking her, but you have been forewarned."

By the end of my date with Michelle, I could see where Des was coming from. The girl was nuts and I didn't have time for that. I was entertained, but for all the wrong reasons. I was laughing, but it was at her expense.

She was lovely to look at. Desiree was right to say that they resembled. They were around the same height, had the same complexion and a similar smile. Their styles were different. Desiree was edgy, sexy, and contemporary; this chick was a walking gap ad. Nothing was wrong with that, but I was not into the girl next door. I wanted the bombshell.

She threw her arms around me like she knew me. I did remember meeting her once like Desiree mentioned, but we weren't cool enough for her to be throwing herself at me. She started rubbing on my head and I was immediately uncomfortable.

I laughed at her throughout dinner because I didn't know what else to say. Something was very off about her, but I tried not to show it on my face. I didn't want to disrespect her in anyway. She was a part of Desiree's family who I had grown up around.

She tried to kiss me when I dropped her off, but I wouldn't let her. "No, Michelle, that's not cool."

"Why not?"

"I don't feel as if this is the right moment."

"Well, when is that?" she asked, placing her hand on my leg.

"I don't know," I said, pushing her hand away.

"Okay." She looked hurt. "Can you walk me to the door?"

"Sure." I didn't want to, but I didn't want to be rude. I could not do that to any woman despite how much I disliked her.

"Are you going to call me?" she asked, once we got to the door.

I sighed. I didn't know what to say at that moment. I didn't want to hurt her feeling, but I had a feeling that I had already done so.

"Sorry, Michelle, but I don't think I will be calling you." I had to be honest. I wasn't prepared to see tears forming in her eyes. I felt terrible. "Look, you are beautiful and you are nice, but I don't think that we are right for each other."

"Fine." She was pissed. She stood there with her arms crossed and stared at me. How awkward was this?

"Please don't be angry with me. I am just trying to be honest with you." I was trying to smooth things over but she didn't seem very receptive. She continued to stare at me.

Oh my goodness. This chick needed to take her ass inside. I didn't have time for this. I wanted to go home and see what Des was up to. I took a deep breath because I was starting to get angry.

"Maybe it's best if you head inside," I said, trying to coax her. She didn't move. "Suit yourself, sweetheart. You are being immature. I don't have time for this." I rolled my eyes and headed to my car.

I backed out of her driveway and blew my horn at her. I couldn't care. I didn't lead her on in anyway. I was looking for love and I learned early in the date that she couldn't provide it.

"Man, I should have listened to Desiree."

When I got home, I walked straight into my bedroom, kicked off my shoes, pulled off my shirt and headed straight for Des's bedroom. The door was open slightly, but I still knocked. I wasn't that bold.

"Come in, Quinton."

"What's up, girl. I should have..." She was in a towel. I swallowed hard. "Wow. Is this a good time?"

She stood in front of her mirror, brushing her hair, but she stopped to look at me. She frowned.

"Why do you ask? You should have what? Wow what?"

"I should've listened to you. That date was a total waste of my time." She giggled and then returned to brushing her hair.

"Didn't I tell you? I warned you."

"I know. She was quite annoying, but oddly enough, I found myself laughing at her the entire night." She laughed.

I sat on the edge of her bed and just watched her. I was mesmerized. I was imagining what was under the towel. I thought about everything that I was longing to do to her at this moment.

I wanted to go there again with her. That night we shared had definitely whetted my appetite. I was hungry for much more.

"Why are you staring at me?" She put her brush down.

"I don't know why." She walked over to me and climbed into my lap. "Because you are beautiful," I said, wrapping my arms around her. I kissed her shoulder. She lifted my face so that I would kiss her.

"Have I told you that you have the softest lips?" When I kissed this woman, my mind could not focus on anything else.

"No you haven't. Tell me," she teased.

"Well, you do." Not knowing if she was going to resist, I pulled her towel off, letting it fall to the floor. She smiled down at me.

"You had me worried," she whispered. I went to respond, but she stopped me. 'Shush, Quinton." She pushed me down on the bed.

"Okay, then."

It was another unforgettable night.

When Desiree left my side the next morning, I knew it. I desperately wanted to pull her back beside me, but instead I found myself watching her disappear into her bathroom. When her door shut, I rolled over and fell back asleep.

When I awaken hours later, it took me a couple moments to focus. I was still in Desiree's bed. I sat up and called her name. No answer. I looked at the clock and realized that she had gone to work. It was late morning.

"Dag. What did she do to me?" I smiled and climbed out of bed.

I was starving, so I headed straight for the kitchen. I grabbed a bowl of cereal and settled in front of the TV. I wasn't there long before I heard my phone ringing. I ran down the hall to my bedroom to get it. I was pleasantly surprised when I answered it. It was the cute little intern, Farrah, who I had been flirting with at the station.

She informed that she was tired of waiting on my call and had decided to make the first move. I had been focusing on Desiree and hadn't allowed myself to focus on her, so I was glad that she stepped up. I needed this. We made plans for the night since I was off.

Farrah seemed looked a good girl. She reminded me of Desiree. And while my beautiful friend may not allow me get any closer to her than in the bedroom, I would always want more from her. The least I could do was find someone like her.

Maybe she could be the chick to succeed in actually getting my mind off of Des. Not today, though. After last night, she was all that I was going to think about.

Desiree

I hadn't been quite right since I slept with Quinton. My mind admittedly felt as if it was gone. I just found it impossible to think straight whenever the man was around. He had this effect over me that he should not have. I didn't like it. It kept me frustrated.

I couldn't believe that I allowed myself to go there with him. I had crossed that line that should not have been crossed. I was treading in very dangerous waters and if I wasn't careful, I was going to find myself drowning. Who was going to save me?

I was almost ashamed at how attracted I was to him. I was embarrassed at how badly I wanted to be intimate with him. I was embarrassed that he knew how much I wanted him. I was humiliated by this whole ordeal.

I had always had a crush on Q, but had managed to keep that information to myself. I was never one to put my business out there like that. There were some things that I didn't even want Rayven to know. She would lecture me if she knew how I felt about him.

Every woman had a thing for Quinton Alexander. He was a beautiful man, but I didn't intend on being one of his groupies. I was his home girl and I cherished our friendship dearly. I wasn't trying to jeopardize any of that because of some raging hormones.

I had always wanted to go there. Even as a sixteen-year-old girl, I would sit there and stare at him just as much as I had stared at Tyler. He was always gorgeous. By the time I was twenty-one-years-old, I knew how badly I wanted him. No other man in my life could even compare to his sexiness.

Was it that beautiful body? That sexy mocha-brown skin? That bald head or gorgeous hazel eyes? Could it be that devastating smile?

It was all of that and then some. I sighed. I was in my office, feeling hot and bothered. I had been distracted since I had arrived.

"Why couldn't you leave me alone, Q?" I asked, standing as I stared out of my office window. "Wow, I am hot."

I walked over and locked my door. I unbuttoned my shirt, tempted to take my blouse off, but decided not to. I opened my bottled water and drank it all.

It wasn't the temperature in the room that had me feeling like this. I was on fire. I sat down in my chair once again. Quinton was invading my thoughts. Sex with Quinton. Already, he had my body yearning for him when he wasn't around.

I had managed to keep myself and my hormones under control until we reached college. Yes, there had been many times that I wanted to just throw myself at him, but I didn't. I never knew whether or not he wanted to go there. I didn't want to run the risk of being rejected. I wasn't the most confident woman in the world.

Quinton would flirt with me, sometimes shamelessly. He had even been known to get a little fresh with me, but I had considered all that harmless. What wasn't harmless was the night we kissed in college years ago. All rational thinking flew out the window.

I remembered we were at one of our basketball player's apartment, watching a big game. My backstabbing roommate came in with my crush and I was furious. My girl, Logan, always looking for trouble, followed the couple to the bathroom. She opened the door and exposed the couple having sex. To my satisfaction my roommate, Brianna, left out humiliated and crying. I didn't feel bad humiliating her and I didn't feel bad when she moved out a week later.

Later on that evening, Quinton and I stood outside on the balcony. We were tripping over what had happened one minute and in each other arms the next. He pinned me against the balcony as he kissed me. I kissed him back eagerly, not knowing who had really started the kiss. It didn't matter. I just knew how good it felt.

Despite how good it felt in the moment, it had scared me. I pushed him away. We both laughed it off. I attempted to ask what the deal was, but neither of us had any answers.

I tried to forget that kiss, but I couldn't. I was hoping that Quinton's mind was focused on it too. I found myself running to his apartment at 2:00 in the morning. I wasn't thinking straightly.

I told him to kiss me, kiss me good and not to do it again. And he did. It was incredible. I let him do it once more before pulling away. While I was tempted to go to his bedroom, I put a stop to it all. I couldn't allow us to go there. I was not willing to take that risk.

That was five years ago. And I had done well in keeping my desires at bay. I never gave Quinton any indication to how much I wanted him. He hadn't given me any indications either until he moved in. He had only been in the house a little over two months and we had already crossed so many lines. That scared me.

"God help me!"

I stood and started pacing.

The sex was amazing our first night together. I couldn't stop thinking about it. Despite how it made me feel, I assumed it would be a one-time deal, but he came to my room last night and shamefully, I made a move on him. I allowed him to pull that towel off of me and then I took control. I wanted him to crave me as much as I did him.

This morning, I hesitantly pulled away from Quinton and dragged my behind to work. From the moment I got here, all I could think about was him. Why? Why was I allowing him to distract me like this? I wasn't getting any work done. This was not fair! I was sure that he was not thinking about me right now.

Frustrated, I started buttoning my shirt. I had to get out of here. I needed a temporary change of scenery to get my mind right. I fixed my clothes, my hair, grabbed my purse and was out of the door.

I had barely put one foot in front of the other when I bumped into this fine brother, Malik. He was new here at Pink Legacy. We had both started around the same time. He was always flirting with me and I was always blushing. I was flattered that this sexy man was digging me. He had made that evident.

"Hey there, beautiful. What's up with you?"

"Hey, Malik. I am just heading out to lunch."

"We really need to plan to have lunch together one day."

"You should come with me. Lunch for two is much nicer."

"I would love to, but I got to deal with this meeting."

"Oh." I tried not to show my disappointment. I was so embarrassed. I couldn't believe that I had asked him out. "Maybe another time." I turn to walk away because my face was hot.

"Wait," he said, grabbing my hand. "Are you free tonight?"

"Tonight?"

"Yeah, don't look so surprised. You know how much I want to take you out. I have been in your face since the day I met you."

"Well…"

"Don't think about it. Let me take you out tonight. I will plan something nice, I promise."

"Okay. I will allow you to do that."

"Whew." He sounded relived. "You had me sweating, Desiree. I will drop by your office later and we can sort out the details."

"Sounds good, Malik."

"Yeah it does. I will get at you when you get back."

Malik had barely moved when Quinton came out of nowhere.

"Quinton Alexander, is that you."

"Malik Williams, what's up, man?"

"I am here making this money."

"I see that."

I could not move. The fact that Quinton and Malik knew each other shocked me. They appeared to have been friends. I looked back and forth between them.

Quinton looked nice today. He wasn't flashy, just clean in his jeans, a t-shirt and a UNC fitted. It didn't take much for him.

I wanted him. Right now. He hadn't even spoken to me yet.

Wow. This was ridiculous. Why was he here?"

"What are you doing here, Q?" Malik vocalized my thoughts.

"To see this lovely woman," he said, finally turning to me. When they both looked at me, my eyes grew big and my face burned. My knees felt as if they were going to give out. I grabbed the wall.

"Desiree?"

"Oh, yeah," Quinton said, stepping towards me.

Oh my goodness, my mind was screaming. Was I really standing here between these two fine men? One who I had just been intimate with. The other who I hoped to get close to.

"You two aren't together are you?" Malik asked.

"Desiree is my girl." Quinton didn't offer any more explanation.

"Oh good. I am taking this one out tonight."

"Oh are you?" Quinton gave me this look. He didn't like that.

"Look, I have to go. I am late. Talk to you both later."

"Okay then, Malik." They hugged quickly.

"Quinton, what are you doing here?" I asked him.

"Too see you. You left me this morning." He stepped closer.

"I had to," I whispered, stepping back. Why was he doing this to me? I didn't need this right now.

"Because," he smiled, taking my hand and pulling me down the hall. "I haven't been able to stop thinking about you."

"Seriously, Quinton?"

"I just wanted to see you." He looked so serious. It scared me. I shook my head in disbelief.

"Was it that good?"

"Yes," he said, sliding an arm around me. I wanted to melt. "I wanted to take you to lunch. We should spend time together out of the bedroom."

"Now, we are talking. I am so hungry."

"I bet. What would you like? Pancakes?"

"No. You pick."

"Okay. So you are going out with, Malik?" He asked as we rode down the elevator.

"Yes." He just looked at me. "You don't like that?"

"Not really." I didn't push it any further

140

Quinton and I just picked up sandwiches and chips from a deli spot in our building. We ate outside on the patio. It was a nice day out and I adored the sunshine.

I definitely enjoyed my food and my time away from the office, but this whole little lunch date was defeating the entire purpose. I was leaving the office so I could get my mind off of Quinton, but here he was sitting across from me.

He kept undressing me with his eyes. He would touch me innocently on my face, squeeze my hand or grab my thigh. It was all driving me crazy. I wanted to tell him to stop, but I didn't. I didn't want him to stop. When I couldn't take it anymore, I stood.

We got ice cream cones and walked back to my office. I enjoyed it. It was the only time that I stopped focusing on Quinton. I was a messy eater and I had to make sure it didn't drip on my silk blouse.

"You don't have to walk me all the way, Quinton." I didn't want him to leave, but I needed to get away from him.

"Are you really trying to get rid of me?"

"No, I was being nice."

"Well, so am I."

"Fine. I have no problem with that." I was lying. I sighed in defeat and linked my arm through his.

Quinton followed me all the way into my office like I knew he would. Here we go! Please don't do this to me. Not now.

I knew his intentions when he shut and locked the door.

"What's up, Quinton?"

"You know what's up."

"Don't start this, right now," I pleaded.

"Desire, I just want a goodbye kiss. I have to have it."

"I think that you are full of it," I laughed.

"Just a kiss," he said moving me towards me."

My mind was screaming no. My body was telling him to bring it on. I wanted his kiss.

"Kiss me then." Here I go again. I was giving into him so easily. I wasn't sure if I knew how to say no to him.

"Come here." He yanked me towards him. He wrapped both arms around me. In his arms is where I wanted to be.

Of course the kiss turned into so much more. Quinton pinned me against my desk. He practically had my skirt around my waist and shirt off. His lips had moved from my mouth to my body.

"You said just a kiss," I whispered, feeling like I couldn't catch my breath. I had my hands planted firmly against his chest.

"I can't help myself. You make me lose all self-control."

"You can't do me on my desk, Quinton."

"Are you telling me no?"

"I...."

He whispered what he wanted to do to me on my desk. His words were explicit. I wasn't use to that. I was so hot that I felt faint.

"Quinton," I whined.

"I love the way you say my name."

"No, Q, baby, please stop." I pushed him away.

"I am sorry." He looked embarrassed.

"You know I want you. I always do. I can't have you right now. We can arrange something later." My hand lingered on his cheek.

"You and I have plans tonight." He looked frantic.

"Stop!" I pulled him around my desk and pushed him in my chair. I tried to ignore how knowing he had plans tonight made me feel. I shook my head. I was not about to get jealous.

I stood in front of him, readjusting my clothes. He just stared at me. I stared back at him. Unspoken words lingered between us

I finally leaned down and kissed him. I kissed him long and hard. I then whispered in his ear. "If you want me as bad as you say you do, you will find a way to have me."

"Trust me, I will."

"We will be making arrangements then?"

"Yes."

"Good." I stood up straight and he stood. He pulled me to him and hugged me. I tried not to melt

"I have never met a woman like you."

"I am sure you haven't." I smiled to myself.

I straightened his clothes, sliding his hat back on his head. I wrapped my arms around his neck and laid a quick soft one on him.

'Now go, Q, please. I have work to do. I will see you later."

"Okay." He rubbed my back as he stared at me. He kissed my forehead. "See you later, baby."

When the door shut behind him, I fell into my chair. I grabbed my head. I wanted to scream.

"No, no, no!" Quinton had just ruined my day in a big way.

13

Unstable

"My inward parts are in turmoil and never still; days of affliction come to meet me." Job 30:27

Quinton

When I left Desiree's office, my mind was racing. I didn't know what to do so I just drove around the city. I needed to get my mind off of her and what I had just done. If I went back to her house, I was not going to be able to focus on anything else.

"Wow, Des." I turned up an old Maxwell song on the radio. Why did I go to her office?

I woke up. I had my cereal. The next thing I knew, I was heading to her job. I did it without thinking. To see her in that fitted white blouse and red skirt was worth it.

I spent that entire meal thinking about making love to her on her desk. I kissed her not knowing if she would be receptive. She allowed things to get pretty far, but in the end she pushed me away. As much as I wanted it, I appreciated that. If we had of went there, it would have ruined my day. I would not have gotten anything done.

I didn't want to go down this road again. I didn't want to endure the emotional turmoil. I wasn't sure if I could survive it this time.

"I don't know how I did it the first time," I said aloud.

I never intended on falling in love so early in my twenties. Ty and I were always on the same page, so I felt crazy calling him to tell him that I was in love with Des. He made me feel crazy, but still he encouraged me to tell her how I felt. I was scared out of my mind, but I worked up the courage to tell her. She rejected me like no other woman did in my past without me uttering a word about my feelings.

She destroyed any hope I had in being with her. She didn't say it, but I felt as if she told me that I didn't deserve love.

I felt stupid telling Ty that I was joking. I told him that I really wasn't in love. I told him I was bored and wanted to see his reaction. It took a while to convince him, but in the end, he laughed it off.

I struggled to get over her. It was hard being around her each day as if I didn't feel anything. It was hell watching her falling in love with Anthony. She had insulted my character, yet loved someone like him. I was forced to be a spectator when I didn't want to be.

For the rest of senior year, I continued to love her. I didn't bother with any females. I stopped dating around. I concentrated on school, graduating and finding a job. My grades soared.

After graduating, I returned to the scene. I dated as many women as possible. I returned to my old ways. I had no choice.

Here we were five years later and nothing had changed. I was still not over this woman. I was setting myself up by getting involved in this sexual affair between us. I didn't know how to not want her.

This woman had hurt more than she would ever know. Yet, I still ached for her. I still longed for her. I wanted her like no other woman I had ever wanted before.

Now she was going out with Malik. He was much more of a ladies' man than Tyler and I would ever be. Although, we went to two different schools, we befriended him in high school. We were freshmen and he was a senior. He taught us everything that we knew about women. He knew how to get what he wanted.

The thought of Malik with Des made me sick to my stomach. I didn't like her going out with any man, but this was killing me. I was trying desperately to push it to the back of my mind. I had a date with Farrah tonight and she didn't deserve having me distracted.

I turned up the radio and attempted to enjoy an old Jay-Z song. I turned up the air conditioner and continued to ride around on this blistering hot day in Charlotte. I wasn't ready to allow Desiree to ruin my day and I wasn't ready to go home.

I called India and asked if she mind if I picked up my son from daycare. She didn't. She seemed too relieved about not having to deal with him. Knowing India, she was probably somewhere hooking up with some dude who she barely knew.

I didn't like disrespecting her. After all, she was a woman and she was responsible for bringing my greatest gift into this world. I just had so much pent up frustration over India. Messing around with her was still one of my biggest regrets in life. I loved my son and would never call him a mistake, but I wished another woman had given birth to him. There were times that I wanted to take Quinton Jr away from her and raise him myself.

Quinton Jr made my day when I stepped onto the playground. He came running at me at full speed, screaming, "Daddy." His unconditional love was a blessing to me. I had my son, now all I needed was the good woman.

We went to the mall. I brought him some clothes, some Jordans and a new toy. I treated myself to a nice button down to wear on my date that night. I found myself walking into hallmark. I picked up a card for Des just to let her know that I was thinking about her. I also picked up her favorite chocolate from the Godiva store.

I was headed out the mall when something in the Victoria Secret window caught my attention. A little see through pink number. Pink was Desiree's favorite color and I loved seeing her in it.

What was I trying to do? Seduce her? Maybe.

I didn't want to push her away. You didn't just buy any woman a card, expressing how you feel. And you definitely didn't just go out and buy lingerie and expensive chocolate for just a friend. I just wanted her to know that I was not trying to play her. I was coming from a sincere place and she meant to world to me.

I took Quinton Jr to McDonald's and brought him a chicken nugget happy meal. I let him play around in the play area for a while. I sat there and thought about Farrah. I really liked her.

Of course I yelled at India. The house was a mess and smelled like weed and vodka. There was a naked dude lying on her couch. She yelled back and told me to mind my own business. I refused to leave until the dude left. India then attempted to swing on me.

The only thing that stopped her was Quinton Jr crying. I gave her this look and headed to him. It took me a while to comfort him, but when I did, I headed straight out of her front door. She cried as I walked past but I ignored her. I was furious.

I would've done anything to take him with me. I wanted him out of this unstable environment. I didn't know what I was going to do, but I was going to figure it out. I knew my son deserved better.

I got home and went for a run. I had to get rid of this aggression. I needed to have a good time tonight with Farrah.

I got back to the house and jumped in the shower. I was momentarily washing my worries away. It was time to start focusing on Quinton.

I shaved. I put on my best cologne. I slipped into my button up and dress slacks. I was ready.

I sat down for a minute and closed my eyes. I actually prayed for a goodnight. I had been having bad luck with the ladies and I needed just one to change all that around.

I laid Desiree's gifts on her bed. I stared down at the treat from Victoria Secret. I wanted her to wear it for me and no one else. I would lose my mind if she wore it for Malik or any other dude.

Realizing that my time was slipping away, I grabbed my wallet, my keys, and I headed to the door. One thing my father had taught me was to never be late, especially when picking up a female.

Before I reached the door, Desiree walked in. I grew excited. All of sudden, I wanted to stay with her. I knew she had plans, though.

"Look at you," she smiled. She was checking me out. "You look too good to be true."

"Thank you."

"Come here." She touched my cheek and leaned over and gave me one of those sweet kisses that only she could give. "Just a little something to keep you thinking about me." I was serious.

"That's really not fair."

"Maybe not." She leaned over and did it again. "Go have fun, darling. I will see you later I hope." She turned and walked away from me before I could pull her back in my arms. Frustrated, I left.

Why me! I took a couple of deep breaths to get my mind right.

"Farah, not Desiree. Desiree, get out of my head!" I repeated these words over and over again.

When I pulled up outside Farrah's townhouse, I sat in the car and said another quick prayer. After a couple deep breaths, I headed to her door. To my pleasant surprise, she was ready.

She looked lovely in a short white sundress. It accentuated her coke-bottle shape perfectly. She wore her jet black hair down and her make-up was thankfully minimal. It all complimented her smooth butterscotch skin. I felt lucky.

"You look beautiful tonight, Farrah." I led her to my car.

"Thank you, Quinton," she said, leaning over to kiss me as I opened my car door for her. Wow. She smelled good. I wouldn't forget that smell the rest of the night.

We went to this new exclusive restaurant uptown called Urban Spice. I had heard that the food was pretty good and that the atmosphere was nice for a date. I wanted to impress Farrah.

She appeared impressed. She definitely ate well and I appreciated that. She was charming and I found myself hanging on to her every word. She made me laugh.

After dinner, we headed to a comedy show. I couldn't concentrate on the comedian because she was snuggled up close to me. Her hand rested firmly against my thigh. It felt nice.

She invited me in for a drink. She disappeared after pouring me a rum and coke. She said she wanted to be comfortable. I didn't expect her to return in lingerie. She wasn't Desiree, but she displayed something quite pleasant.

She obviously wanted to take it there, but I wouldn't let her. The old me would have taken what she was offering, but I was looking for something real, not just some good booty.

I told her that she looked incredible and pulled her in my arms. We made out for a long time. It was great. It was just what I needed.

"I can't believe that you didn't try to sleep with me."

"I want to get to know you, Farrah."

"I like that. Are you staying tonight?"

"Not tonight, sweetheart. I don't think that would be a good idea. I do have to get up early."

I wanted to see Desiree.

"Well, turn the lights off and lock the door when you leave, sweetheart. I am going to bed. Bye, Quinton" She kissed me and headed towards her bedroom.

I was disappointed when I got home and Desiree wasn't there. The house was dark. I walked past her bedroom and called out her name to make sure she wasn't in bed. Nothing. I was annoyed.

I walked to my bedroom and stretched out on my bed. I stared up at the ceiling and tried not to think about Desiree being out with Malik. I knew they would kiss and that made me nauseated. If he tried anything else, I was going to lose my mind. Malik was not good enough for her. Plus, I didn't like sharing.

Why couldn't she be with me and no one else?

I got up to take a shower. I made myself go to bed afterwards. I still couldn't sleep. I sat up in my bed and turned on the TV. I stared at the screen without seeing what was on it, feeling all the tension in the world. I was getting a headache.

I was relieved when she got home. I heard the front door open. I turned off the TV to attempt to get to sleep. I had just closed my eyes when there was a knock at my bedroom door.

"Quinton, are you asleep?" Desiree opened the door slightly.

"What's up, Des?" I asked, sitting up and turning on the lamp.

I sighed when I took in her short yellow dress. Her hair was curly. She was breathtaking. I was sick thinking about how she wore that for my boy.

She didn't say anything. She just crawled onto my bed and kissed me hard. As much as I liked Farrah, nothing could compare to this.

"Thank you for my gift." She whispered against my lips.

"You are welcome, baby." I almost pulled her back into my arms when she pulled away, but I didn't. "You are going to kiss me like that and leave?" She smiled at me and walked towards the door.

"Goodnight, Q." She was gone before I could protest any more.

"God, please help me."

Desiree

I wanted to stay with Q tonight, but I was too tired. We both deserved better than that. If I couldn't put forth good effort, I wasn't going to try, especially when all I could think about was sleep.

I pulled off my clothes as soon I stepped back into my bedroom. I put on a tank top, used the restroom and then washed my face. I pulled my hair up into a ponytail and then I climbed into bed.

I was exhausted, but I lay there restless. I hated this. My body wouldn't allow me to go to sleep.

Frustrated, I got up and headed to the kitchen. When I couldn't sleep, I ate. I poured myself a big bowl of Apple Jacks and headed to the living room. Let's see what TV could do for me. Usually, I would fall asleep watching it.

Give Quinton a few more minutes and he would be in here, checking on me. I wanted that. I wanted his company. Moments passed and he didn't come. That annoyed me.

I sat there and focused on my date with Malik. I had a great time. I was digging him and was excited to see him again.

After work, I came home to find a gift on the bed. I didn't know what was more shocking; the fact that Quinton gave me such an expressive card or the skimpy lingerie. I thought it was sweet how he remembered that I was crazy for Godiva.

I took it that he wanted to see me in that lingerie. I could arrange that for him. I could put on a show that he would enjoy.

Pushing Q out of my mind, I got myself psyched for my date. Things hadn't worked out with Justin, so I was hoping things would work out. I deserved to go out with someone and have a good time.

So I found a cute little yellow summer dress that I had never worn. I curled my hair. I put on my favorite lip gloss. I grabbed my purse and waited for him in the living room.

As I sat down in front of the TV, there was a knock at the door. Wow. Was he really ten minutes early? He was fine, intelligent, and prompt. He had it going on, I had to admit. I was into him.

"Malik," I said, opening the door.

"Desiree, you look too good to be true."

"Thank you. You are early."

"Yeah, being late is not my thing."

"Okay. Would you like to come in, Malik?"

"I am okay, sweetheart, let's ride."

"Cool." I locked the door and took the arm he offered. "How was the rest of your day?"

"I spent the rest of it thinking about you," he said, opening the door to his truck.

"Honestly?" I asked, skeptically.

"Yes, honestly," he said, shutting the door behind me. When he got into the driver seat and turned on the ignition, he turned and gave me a huge smile. "I have wanted to ask you out for a while."

"Why didn't you?"

"I didn't think that you would say yes."

"Scared of rejection?" I joked.

"Yeah because I liked you. I don't want to mess this up either. Now that I finally get the chance to take you out, I am going to make it worth your while."

"Worth my while, huh? Where are you taking me, Malik?"

"Do you trust me?"

"Should I?"

"Yeah, you really should."

"Well, okay, I am going to trust you."

"Well just trust that I am going to show you a good time."

"You better."

He took me to an upscale restaurant downtown called Century. I wasn't use to such high class dining. The waiters and waitresses wore suits and dresses. They catered to your every need.

A live jazz band played soft romantic ballads. We held hands over candlelight. We laughed while sipping wine. The only time we didn't talk was when we enjoyed our filet mignon. I smiled shyly at him while he stared at me seductively over chocolate cheesecake.

The place had a long waiting list, but somehow Malik managed to get us a table in the corner. I was impressed. I was also impressed by his ambition, his ability to hold a conversation and his ability to make me laugh. I loved his sarcastic humor and witty comebacks.

By the time we left the restaurant, he had won me over. He wanted to know more about me. I wanted to know more about him.

He took me to a cozy little lounge. We ordered drinks and snuggled up on a loveseat in the corner. He whispered sweet things in my ear. I giggled like a school girl. He sung to me. I was mesmerized. I was glad he couldn't see my face because it was hot.

We went back to his place. I made it clear to him that we weren't going there tonight. He respected that. I sat on his couch and stayed far away from his bedroom. Things did heat up on the couch when he kissed me. I didn't mind because his lips were everything I imagined them to be. His kisses were addictive.

After realizing it was 1:00, I informed him that I needed to get home. We did have work in the morning. He kissed me on my cheek and asked me, "Do you have to go?" I knew he was teasing because he was standing with his car keys before I could answer him.

Malik took me home. He walked me to my front door. He kissed me goodnight and whispered, "See you in the morning," and was on his way. I walked inside and headed straight to Quinton's bedroom. I wanted to thank him properly for his thoughtful gift.

Now it was 2:00 in the morning and I was pigging out on a bowl of cereal. My body was exhausted, but sleep had evaded me. I knew I was going to be tired tomorrow. I was going to looked like crap. That was no good considering Malik was going to be in my face.

I smiled when Quinton entered the room.

"Hi, Quinton." He frowned as he took a seat beside me.

"Why are you up?"

"I can't sleep."

"What did you get into tonight?" he asked, with accusing eyes.

"That has nothing to do with it."

"Was your date that good?"

"Quinton," I whined. I sat down my empty bowl and climbed into his lap. "Help me. I want to go to sleep, but I can't."

"Wow." He kissed my forehead. "Come to bed with me."

"How's that going to help?"

"None of that. I want to hold you until you go to sleep." I stared at him. Was he serious? Could I be next to him and not take it there.

"Again, how's that going to help?"

"It will," he said, stroking my hair. "Are you coming?"

"Okay." He stood with me in his arms, managing to turn off the TV and the lights. He took me to his bedroom. "I trust you."

"Good." He laid me in bed and climbed in behind me. He kissed me quickly and then reached for the light. He pulled me to him. "Close your eyes, Des."

I did. I laid my head on his chest. He rubbed my back. I fell asleep listening to his heartbeat.

I woke up the next morning alone. I lay in Quinton's bed and thought about him before getting up. If he didn't have plans tonight, I was going to wear that pink little see through number for him. If he had plans then I was going to be highly disappointed.

I spent a little more time in front of my closet that morning. I decided on a cream pencil skirt and a red blouse. I took longer than usual on my hair and my make-up. I was dressed to impress today.

Malik followed me in my office when he saw me. He kissed me. It was a pleasant way to start off the day.

"You look beautiful."

"Thank you."

"Can I take you to lunch?'

"Of course."

"Great." He kissed me again and was on his way.

The morning flew by. The next thing I knew, Malik was knocking on my door. We went to a nice Italian spot downtown.

My good day ended there. I thought I was going to spend the night with Quinton, but he had plans with Farrah. I didn't have plans so I spent the night alone in my own bed. My pink lingerie stayed in the bag. There would be no show tonight.

The rest of the week flew by. By 4:00 Friday, I was in my car headed home. I wanted to get out of my work clothes and just chill. I was in need of a long bath. After my bath, I was going to order Chinese. After that, who knew what I was going to get into. I was praying that Quinton would stay at home for once.

I pulled another letter out of the mailbox when I got home.

Desiree,

I am angry with you. Who is Malik? Still, I adore you.

Missing You,
The One

I stood there for a second. This was beyond unsettling. How was this person finding out every detail of my life? This had to be someone who was close with me. If this was a joke, someone was in for it. I was going to find a way to take them down.

I was surprised to find Quinton home on the couch. After finding the letter, I was relieved to see him. I didn't want to be alone.

"What are you doing here?"

"I was off today."

"What are you up to?"

"Just relaxing, Des."

"I see. Are you going out tonight?"

"I am. I don't really have anything else to get into. T and I are going to hit up Belvie's."

"Oh okay." I became preoccupied with another piece of mail. I didn't want him to see my disappointment. What a letdown.

"You should come."

"Nah,' I said, quickly. I don't know why I said no because I had nothing else to do. I just wasn't sure if I was in the clubbing mood. "I am going to chill tonight."

"Oh," he said, staring at me as if he didn't believe me. "Well I guess there's nothing wrong with that."

"Nope." I headed to my room and fell on my bed. I was glad it was the weekend, but things weren't going the way I wanted.

I jumped up. As much as I wanted him, I wasn't going to sulk over Quinton. I needed to relax. I stripped and jumped into my tub for a nice long bath. I almost fell asleep. I decided to get out so I could take a nap.

I was standing in front of the mirror in just my panties when he walked in. He stared at me and I stared at him. I made no attempt to cover up. What was the point?

"Are you sure that you don't want to go." His face looked red.

"No sir. I am not in the mood."

I tried not to notice how good he looked in his button up, jeans and Wallabees It didn't matter what he wore. He was just too sexy for his own good

"You look good," I blurted turning back towards the mirror.

"You look better."

I found the nerve to look up at him through the mirror. His eyes met mine and then they started focusing on my backside. His head actually tipped to the side. "What are you staring at?"

"This tattoo." He reached out and touched the tattoo on my back. My skin tingled. I jumped slightly as he began to repeatedly trace it with his fingers. He was exciting me.

He finally stopped and leaned against the wall beside me.

"Are you really just going to stay home?"

"Yes. You don't believe me?"

"I thought maybe Malik was coming over." So he was jealous. I tried not to smile. I was amused.

"Not tonight. He is out of town."

"Did he treat you good? He didn't try to pull something did he?" I wouldn't tell him if he did.

"Yes, he did and no, Q."

"I have to make sure. I really wish that you were coming."

"Why?"

"I want to be around you. I will be thinking of you all night."

I was all too aware of his finger rubbing my thigh; however, I jumped when his finger slid inside the edge of my panties. I tried to stand it, but I couldn't. He was torturing me.

"Stop that!"

"No," he said, grabbing by my waist and pulling me to him. He kissed me long and hard. He knew I liked it that way. It left me breathless. "Are you going to be home when I get back?"

"Yes."

"Don't go to sleep."

"Why?"

"It's been too long, Desiree. I need you." I needed him.

He kissed my forehead and was gone. I stared after him and smiled. That's what I wanted to hear.

I jumped when my phone rung.

"Hello."

"Hey, girl."

"Rayven, where have you been?"

"Busy!"

"That's no excuse."

"I know! Let's go to Belvie's"

"I don't know, Sunray. I am not exactly in the mood to go out."

"Come on, it's the weekend, doll. It's been a hard week for me and I need to wild out a little. I deserve this and so do you."

"If I don't go, that doesn't mean that you can't go."

"Des," she whined. "Who else am I supposed to go with? Please, I haven't seen you in forever. Don't you miss me?" She was throwing a guilt trip on me. It worked.

"Fine."

I chilled for another hour and then found myself getting ready to do something that I told Q that I didn't want to do. I hadn't seen my girl in a minute, though. I didn't want her to go by herself either.

I dressed in a short pink dress. It was strapless. I let my hair down. I applied eye liner and my favorite lipstick. I was doing it up. I always ran into someone in Belvie's. I had to look my best.

At 11:15, I left to pick up Rayven. She ran to the car in her itty bitty green dress. She was as gorgeous as always. She threw her arms around me once inside.

"I missed you!"

"Good!" I said kissing her cheek.

When we walked past the bouncer, Rayven blew him a kiss, so we got in free. As soon as I set foot in the door, a tall ball headed brother pulled me to him. My night had begun. I had forgotten that I didn't want to be here.

An hour later, I was heading to the bathroom when I heard my name. I turned and Quinton stood before me, shaking his head.

"Hi, Quinton," I said, sheepishly.

'What are you doing here? You made it clear to me that you didn't want to be here."

"I didn't. Rayven wanted to come," I shrugged.

"So you decided to come for her, but not for me."

"I am sorry. Don't be mad."

"My feelings are a little hurt." He tried to shrug it off.

"Are you having fun?" I said, grabbing his hand

"I am. Come dance with me."

"I have to pee."

"Okay, but I will find you later."

I was dancing with my eyes closed, when he wrapped his arms around me. I knew it was him without looking. I could tell by his touch, his cologne. His lips grazed my ear and I smiled.

"I found you."

"You did." I turned and threw my arm around his neck. He danced with me for the rest of the night.

I dropped Rayven off and headed straight home that night. I headed straight for the shower. I slid into that pink number and climbed under my sheets. I waited.

When it was 4:00 in the morning, disappointment started to settle in. I was starting to think that he wasn't coming. The club had closed at 3:00 and it only took twenty minutes to get home. Jealousy hit me as I thought of the possibility of Q hooking with some chick.

As soon as I closed my eyes, I hear the door. It was 4:15. He was at my door within a minute. I closed my eyes when he peeked in and pretended to be asleep. I wasn't going to make it easy for him. I smiled when I heard him sigh in frustration.

I stayed in bed until I heard his shower running. I headed to his room. I sat on the edge of his bed and waited. I sat up straight when he turned the water off. Moments later, he emerged in his towel.

"Desiree!" He was surprised, but desire was in his eyes.

"So you made me a promise."

"I did."

"Come undress me and do what you said you were going to do."

The next day I hung out with Quinton and Quinton Jr. He asked and I accepted his invitation. I didn't have anything else to do. Plus, I appreciated the time I got to spend with his precious little boy. I was falling in love with him.

After going to the pool and having a picnic in the park, we were in the grocery store, picking up something to cook when Quinton said, "There's Farrah."

"Oh." I didn't like how that made me feel. "Well, are you going to say hi?"

"I…" He looked at his son who was asleep on his shoulder.

"Give him to me." I took the little boy and shoved him slightly. "Just go." Q deserved to be happy despite how jealous I felt.

"Thank you, Des."

I eyed her. She was a lovely girl. He knew how to pick them.

"Farrah, what's up, girl?"

"Quinton! Um, hi!" She looked nervous.

"How are you?" He went to hug her, but she backed up. What was that about? "What? I can't get a hug."

"I don't think that's a good idea."

"Why are you acting funny? Don't act like we haven't being seeing each other all week. What kind of games are you playing?"

"Farrah, baby, I found what we need." A rather large man emerged out of nowhere. He wrapped his arm around her waist.

"Okay, honey." Her face turned red. Wow. Drama.

"Who are you?" The man asked Quinton.

'I am Quinton. Who are you?"

"David. Who are you to my wife?"

"Wife? Farrah, you didn't tell me that you were married."

What did we have here? Not just a cheater, but an adulterer.

"Answer my question, Quinton." He stepped in my friend's face.

"No need for confrontations. I am just a friend."

"Why don't I believe you?"

"I am not sure why, but that's really not my problem."

"It will be if I find out that you are messing with my wife."

"David, there's no need for you to be in my face, man."

"What is going on, Farah?" he asked, turning to his wife.

"Nothing, David! I promise."

"Did you or did you not sleep with this punk?"

Okay. It was time for me to intervene. I switched a ring from my right hand to my left. I headed straight for the threesome.

"Quinton, honey." All attention turned to me. "Can you take little Quinton. He is getting heavy. I was thinking we should pick up something instead of cooking. I am hungry. Are you ready?"

"Who are you?" David asked.

"Desiree, and what's it to you. You don't know me."

"Sorry," he said, throwing his arms up defensively. "Are you Farrah's friend too?" Farah's eyes pleaded with me. What a pathetic excuse for a woman.

"I know nothing about your wife and don't care to."

"Are you my man's woman?"

"I am!" I moved towards David. He backed up. "Will there be any more questions?"

"Nope."

"Good, Quinton, are we ready?"

"Yep." He grabbed my hand and we headed for the door

'I'm sorry, Q," I said to him when we reached the parking lot.

"For what?"

"You liked her."

"I will bounce back." I stood outside the car as he placed his son in his car seat.

"You will and you find someone more deserving." I said once he was finished. He just stared at me. He had a strange look on his face. "What? Why are you looking at me like that?"

"You are right?" He traced my lips with his finger.

"Why tease me?"

"I don't mean to."

"Yes, you do, Quinton. You…" He cut me off with a kiss.

14

Relinquish

"Let all bitterness and wrath and anger and clamor and slander be put away from you, along with all malice. Be kind to one another, tenderhearted, forgiving one another, as God in Christ forgave you."
Ephesians 4:31-32

Quinton

Messing around with Des was going to ruin me. I don't think I realized what I was getting myself involved in that first night we kissed many weeks ago. It wasn't just about the intimacy or the chemistry. I had feelings for this woman. Every day in the back of my mind, I knew that I was going to end up hurt. Even if we put a halt to all the kissing, the making out, or the sex, I would still end up hurt. I couldn't avoid it.

I thought about her entirely too much. I could barely get things done. I knew it was bad when one day I spent ten minutes in her driveway, daydreaming about her, before going inside.

She was home when I walked in. She was in her kitchen, fixing a sandwich. I took one look at her and knew something was wrong. She had a frustrated look on her face.

"Hey, Desiree. What's up with you?"

"Nothing much," she shrugged. She didn't bother to look at me.

"What's going on with you, Quinton?"

"Right now, I am just trying to figure out what's wrong."

"Nothing."

"Desiree," I said, sliding an arm around her waist. "Why are you lying to me? I can see it in your eyes."

"It's your boy, Malik."

"Oh." She had gone out with him every day for the last couple of weeks. I didn't say anything to her about it, but it was burning me up inside. I couldn't sleep at night because she wasn't home. I didn't want to imagine her in his bed, but I did. I didn't want to share her with any man, much less someone I called my friend.

Malik did not deserve this woman.

"Did he hurt you?" I would rough him up nicely.

"I am not heartbroken. I am just pissed and very frustrated."

"What did my man do?"

"He comes into my office today, looking as if someone died. He shut my door, kisses me, sits in my chair and then pulled me into his lap." I wished she would have spared me the details. "Then he tells me that we are over."

"Huh?" I didn't know what else to say. Did she expect me to be sad about this? I wasn't.

"Apparently, his ex is pregnant. They are getting back together. They want to be a family."

"Are you serious?" I could not believe what I was hearing, but it didn't surprise me. Knowing Malik, it all made sense. He never stayed with one woman long.

"Very much so."

"Wow." I couldn't talk against Malik. The same thing had happened to me. I just didn't want to be with my son's mother. I was surprised that Malik was so careless, though. He didn't want kids.

"Was it Meelah?"

"The name does sound familiar." She rolled her eyes.

"Malik and Meelah do have history." She was the one chick that he couldn't stay away from. To Malik, Meelah was his Desiree.

"Why did he have to pull me in the middle of what they had? I mean if this woman is pregnant with his child, then I applaud him for stepping up. He should. I am just angry that he even asked me out when he was still messing with his ex the entire time. I am not about all that, Quinton."

"I agree that the two of you shouldn't have gotten involved." I hated every minute of it. "Don't worry about it, girl. You don't need a man like Malik in your life anyway."

"You are right."

"You really liked him a lot, huh?" I was worried. I was scared that she had fallen for my boy in a short amount of time."

"No, that's not it," she said, staring off into space. "Please, we only went out for like three weeks. I am just tired of being alone, Quinton. I am getting lonely."

"Say what?" I found what she was saying hard to believe.

"Don't make me say it again."

"I don't believe you."

"Why not? You say that you get lonely."

"I do. Very much so."

"I am like you, Quinton. I want to be with that right person at this point in my life. The lonely nights are getting old."

"We have spent many nights together?" I teased.

"Yes, I have spent many nights with you." Not enough. "I need love, though." I stared at her and shook my head. If only she knew.

"So do I." Give me yours, please.

"I think that's sweet." She squeezed my arm.

"I think you are sweet."

"Q, why do you insist on flirting with me?" She was blushing.

"I can't help myself around you." That was the truth.

"I love your eyes," she said, finally looking up at me.

"I love more than your eyes." I wasn't thinking when I blurted that to her, but I meant it. She smiled. "I love that smile of yours."

"Do you?" she asked.

"Any man would love you. You could have any man that you want. You just don't realize that."

"I don't know where you are getting you information from."

"I have been around you for years. You have broken a lot of hearts." I spoke form experience.

"Quinton Alexander, I have never broken anyone's heart."

"You don't know that."

"Whatever!" She reached for her sandwich and took a bite. "This is wonderful. Taste," she said, holding it out towards me. I took a bite. It was delicious.

"This does hit the spot."

"Keep that half. I am not going to eat all of this."

"Thank you. What are you up to? Are you busy?"

"Not really. Why?"

"Do you want to ride with me really quick? I have to check on the house."

"I would love to see that."

"Let's go."

"I love this," she said as soon as she sat foot through my door.

I watched her as she ran through the six bedrooms, the three and half bathrooms, the dining room, the kitchen, the living room, the playroom for my son, and a den. I was amazed. Her eyes were wide with excitement. I was surprised by her reaction, but her approval did mean a lot to me.

"This is going to be so lovely when it's all done, Quinton."

"I sure hope so.

"I am so proud of you. You are doing so well for yourself. You are going to be a homeowner. What an achievement."

"I am just doing all of this for my son."

"And that's wonderful." She kissed my cheek and then wrapped her arms around my neck.

"I am his provider. I am still missing something."

"What's that?" You, I thought.

"A good woman."

"Quinton, you will find a good woman to settle with."

"I know. I am just anxious. When I want something, I want it. I am ready to have a family."

"Seriously," she said, actually stepping back to look at me.

"Yeah, is that hard to believe?"

"No, that's just very grown up of you. I…" Her phone rang. "Sorry, I need to take this," she said, rolling her eyes at her phone

I stared at her as she walked out on the deck. And I couldn't stop myself from imagining how my life would be with just her, Quinton Jr. and I. With a loving son, a beautiful woman, a great home and a job that I loved, I would not want for anything else. I would be incredibly blessed.

I was thankful that she couldn't see me because I was staring her down. She was still in her dress from work. Wow. She could never look bad.

"Oh, Desiree," I sighed.

I wanted her in this house. I wanted her to be waiting for me when I walked through the front door. I wanted her in my bed at night and waking up with me in the morning. I wanted her around, so Quinton could have someone positive to look up to. I wanted her to have my kids.

"Where is this coming from?" I mumbled.

"My Quinton is growing up," Desiree said, rejoining me. She stared back at me. She stood there with her hands on her hips, biting down on her bottom lip. She was taking it all in.

"What?" I finally asked. "What's on your mind?"

"I think that I am ready for that."

"For a family?"

"Yeah. I want to be someone's wife. I want to be the mother of his kids. I want to move into a house like this." I stared at her as I swallowed hard. "We want the same things, Quinton."

I want you. Do you want me?

I leaned against the counter, staring at her.

"Come here." I was surprised when she did. She floated into my arms. The way she kissed me was addictive. I didn't want her to stop. I held her as tightly as I could.

Goodness, she smelled good. What was the name of that perfume? Bella. I could never forget that smell. It haunted me.

We ended up on the floor. She was on top of me. I was desperately trying to get her naked. She was unbuckling my belt. All the while, her lips never left mine.

"We are getting too use to this, Quinton," she whispered. "Me to you. You to me."

"What's wrong with that?" I asked, rubbing her hair.

"Eventually, we have to stop this."

'What's the rush, beauty? Who are you with?" She stared down at me for a moment, her eyes searching mine.

"I guess you right now." That's what I wanted to hear.

We both lay there afterwards, breathless. I heard her whisper, "Amazing." I couldn't have agreed more. After a couple of moments, I thought she was still basking in the pleasure, but I turned to look at her and she had a panicked looked on her face.

"What's wrong?" She stood in a hurry. She started fumbling for her clothes and pulling them on. What just happened? "Desiree?"

"Nothing, Quinton." I stood and started to do the same. I watched her, feeling confused.

"Desiree." I grabbed her hand before she could move away. "What's wrong? Did I hurt you?"

"Quinton, I never have sex with anyone without a condom. It's messing with my mind a little."

I didn't respond for a moment. We had been careless. I usually never made that mistake. I was just so caught up in the moment with this woman. Still, despite how I felt, I wanted to comfort her.

"Look, Desiree, it's going to be okay. Believe me when I say that you can trust me."

"I do," she said, nodding.

"And I trust you."

"Great. You should. I am clean, but, Q, I am not on the pill right now." She started breathing hard. She was becoming hysterical.

"I hear you. Calm down. You aren't going to get pregnant." Of course I couldn't guarantee that, but I had to say it.

"We better not."

"Give me a hug." She did, laying her head on my chest.

"I am the first woman you were intimate with in this house, she whispered moments later. I wanted her to be the first and only.

"Thank you for being that woman," I said, kissing her forehead.

"Uh huh. Let's go home."

She may have felt better, I thought as we headed to the car, but I didn't. I was terrified. I couldn't afford to get another woman pregnant. Not even if it was Desiree Harris.

After talking to Tyler, we decided to drive down south to Myrtle Beach for the Fourth of July weekend. Some of his people had a beach house, so we were gamed. Of course we invited Desiree. Desiree invited Rayven. They both happily accepted.

We hopped into Tyler's Tahoe on that Thursday night and we were on our way. I had been stressed lately, so I was looking forward to the get-a-way. I needed this.

I was worried about Rayven ruining my trip. Could I really spend four days with a woman who insisted on being outright rude to me? Could I handle her attitude without snapping? Was Rayven going to be able to get over herself and have a good time?

I was pleasantly surprised. Rayven jumped in the truck with a huge smile. She was cordial, even speaking to me first. She told jokes all the way down the road and had us all laughing. It was the first glimpse of her personality that I had seen in years.

Still, I thought that her good mood was temporary. I figured she would be back to her old ways within the next twenty-four hours. I had no reason to think that she would all of a sudden get along with me. I had given up on that happening a long time ago.

She proved me wrong. The next day brought positive confrontations. It brought changes.

We were all chilling, watching TV in the living room when Rayven touched my arm.

"Quinton, do you think we can talk privately."

"Yeah, that's cool." What was this about, I thought. "Let's step outside." We headed outside to the deck. "What's up?"

"I think that it's about time that we reconcile, don't you?"

"Excuse me?" Did I hear her correctly?

"I am tired of this battle. I don't want to fight anymore."

"Yeah, I would love for all of that to end," I admitted.

"Admittedly, all of this had been on me. I think that it's time that I be an adult and apologize to you for my behavior."

"I accept your apology. I apologize for ever disrespecting you."

"I accept."

"Tell me this, though, Rayven. Why did you dislike me so much?" I knew why, but I needed for her to vocalize it.

"Well," she sighed. "That night you saw Anthony kissing on Des in the parking lot." I hated talking about that moment. I couldn't forget that image if I tried. "The night me and you...."

"What about it? How did I upset you?"

"I wanted you, Quinton, if you didn't realize that." I did after the fact. "I had feelings for you."

"Rayven, you had to know that I didn't realize that."

"I know you didn't. I spent all of junior year trying to make you pay attention to me, but no matter what I did, you didn't seem to recognize my existence. I saw you that night and I saw how vulnerable you were. I wanted to take advantage of you."

"What?" I laughed, nervously.

"Look, I saw that look on your face. I saw the hurt in your eyes. I wanted to be the one to make you feel better. You are a man, and I knew you would take it. Sex always makes you feel better."

"And it did."

"I foolishly thought I could make you forget about Desiree."

"I appreciated that, Rayven. That was a bad night for me and for a while, I didn't think about how I felt. What happened between us was nice, but my feelings, and my emotions..."

"Ran deep," she finished. "Look, deep down, I knew there was no way I could really make you forget about her. I was just being naïve. Because of that, I was embarrassed."

"Why?"

"I don't know," she shrugged. "I was worried about how you thought of me. Did you think I was easy? Did you think that I was a whore? I just threw myself at you. I offered you my body as if it was a stick of gum."

"Don't put it that way. I didn't think of you as easy at all. After seeing the hurt on your face, I thought maybe you liked me. I walked away because I was incapable of dealing with my emotions. I thought because I did so, you despised me."

"You are right in a sense. Honestly, I felt like I had made a fool of myself. I couldn't look at you the same way again. It was just easier for me to give you the cold shoulder. It was easier for me to be a bitch. I am intimidated when I am around you."

"Rayven, I promise you that there is no need for that."

"I can barely look at you sometimes. It's like when you walk in the same room, I lose all self-confidence."

"I don't understand that. Why let me make you feel that way?"

"I really can't explain to you why."

"You shouldn't. You are an incredibly beautiful woman."

"Thank you." She actually blushed.

I took her hands in mine. "Rayven, I didn't think any lesser of you. In fact, I thought that I had hurt you, so I wanted to apologize to you. When you didn't want to talk to me, I was confused. I thought maybe I had taken advantage of you."

"No," she said, shaking her head vigorously. "I am sorry, Q."

"It's okay. I understand now. You haven't called me Q in five years. I miss that. I miss you. Before that night, we were friends. I want that back."

"Me too. That's why I thought it was important to talk to you."

"I want you to know that I appreciated what you did for me. Your intentions were to help that night and you did. I needed that. You allowed me to escape my feelings for a while. If you had not of come when you did, I would have kicked Anthony's ass that night."

"You looked like you were extremely capable of doing that. Honestly, I knew I couldn't make you forget Desiree. I made a move on you when I knew nothing was going to come out of it. I may have been hurt by my failure to do so, but I definitely was not surprised."

"Why may I ask?"

"I had been watching you for weeks before that night. I saw the way you looked at her. I saw how you went out of your way for her. Your eyes would light up. You loved her, didn't you?"

"No." I don't know why I lied.

"Why are lying to me?"

"I'm not lying?" I laughed nervously.

"I saw tears in your eyes. I thought you were going to cry." I did. "That was more than a crush. You don't have to admit that to me, though. Love is special and I understand if you want to keep that to yourself." I sighed.

"Okay. I did love Desiree. I loved her very much. She almost destroyed me. Will my secret be safe with you?"

"I am not going to say anything. I haven't all these years."

"Thank you." I leaned over and kissed her forehead.

"So why didn't you tell her."

"There was no point. Nothing would have come out of it."

"You don't know that. Maybe you could have saved her from making that mistake with Anthony."

"Very true," I laughed. I didn't reveal that I had attempted to. I didn't reveal how much Desiree's words had hurt me.

"Maybe we should go back in. They may suspect something. They probably think that we are going at it."

When we walked in, Desiree and Tyler were sitting close on the couch. Her head was on his shoulder and his hand on her leg. I had to take a deep breath. Seeing that made me sick to my stomach.

"What's up?" Desiree said, throwing a concerned look our way. "Is everything okay?"

"Everything is good," Rayven said, speaking up.

I was eying Tyler's hand. If he so much as moved that hand an inch, I didn't know how I was going to react. I made sure to sit on the other side of Desiree.

She quickly relieved me of my jealousy. She moved close to me. She wrapped her arm around me and laid her head against my shoulder.

"You smell good,' she whispered.

"Not as good as you."

Rayven forced her way between Desiree and Tyler. I watched Tyler rest his hand comfortably on her leg. I realized that Tyler was being Tyler. I was sure that I had nothing to worry about.

Later that night, we decided to hit up a nice restaurant

and then Senor Frogs. I danced with many women, but my eyes were continuously roaming the room until I found Desiree. Naturally, she was surrounded by a group of dudes. As far as I was concerned, she was the most beautiful woman in the room.

I stopped dancing with one chick and headed straight to the bar. I wanted to have a good time. I didn't want to spend my entire night sulking over my friend.

She was killing me with that outfit. She had on ridiculously short shorts, a sheer blouse and extremely sexy stilettoes. There wasn't an eye in the room that hadn't checked her out.

After getting my drink, I lost sight of Desiree and I panicked a little. I took my drink down, slammed the glass on the bar and started moving through the crowd. I was worried. If anything happened to her, someone was going to pay the price. I was slowly losing control of my emotions. I had started shoving people out of my way

I had to chill because I didn't want to start anything.

"What's the deal, man." I had almost knocked one dude over.

"I am sorry, my man, I tripped."

"Whatever. Just watch your step." I walked away from that quickly. I didn't have Tyler near me to back me up. That would have been an unfair battle considering he was surrounded by his boys. I wasn't for leaving South Carolina with an ass-whooping.

Just as I was about to give up on finding her, I felt a familiar hand grab mine

"Quinton, I have been looking for you."

"Here I am."

"Good. I want you to dance with me." To my luck, a slow song came over the speakers. It was almost closing time.

"Why?" I teased as she pulled me to the dance floor.

"Because we haven't been alone all day."

"I know, baby." I pulled her into my arms and held her close. We moved to an old Backstreet song. She sang in my ear.

In the backseat of the car, she fell asleep in my arms. I could hear that familiar voice in the back of my mind. It was cautioning me to be careful. Or was that my heart? Either way, it was inevitable that I was going to get hurt.

Later on that night, after the girls had gone to sleep. Tyler and I sat outside, throwing back some drinks.

"So what have you been up to, Q?" Tyler asked.

"You know, working hard, trying to provide for little Quinton, fighting with India. It's all the same old drama."

"That chick hasn't chilled yet?"

"Not at all. I still have to fight her every time I see my boy. Sleeping with her was without a doubt my biggest mistake."

"Well, you got a blessing from it. You have your son."

"You are right. Sometimes I wish I could just take him and run. I could do better on my own."

"Maybe one day she will mess up."

"Maybe. What's been up with you?"

"Working, trying to save for a house like you."

"That's what's up, T. Are you seeing anyone?"

"Nah. I haven't been able to date much. Been working. You?"

"No one. I really like this one chick, but it's not like that. Just a little crush." That's all he was getting.

"Nope, Q, you have a crazy look on your face. How much do you like this chick?"

"I like her a lot." She was everything.

'Do you love her?" Where was this coming from?

"I might," I admitted.

"Are you for real?" he asked, throwing me a baffled looked. I didn't say anything. "Tell her," he said after a moment of silence.

"I can't do that."

"Don't be a punk. A little rejection is not going to hurt you."

'I am not her type, man."

"Oh." He looked as if he was thinking. "So it sounds as if you are ready to settle down."

"I am."

"You should go for this woman, Q. I have to meet her."

"One day." I wasn't ready to tell T anything about Desiree.

"Believe it or not, Q, I think I am ready to settle too. I have been doing a lot of thinking."

"You should? We are getting too old for this." We were both going on twenty-eight.

"We are not that old, Q," he laughed. "I am getting tired of this game, though. I want to settle down with some woman and I want her to love me unconditionally."

"I agree. I want that too."

We both sat in silence. I looked up at the starless sky, thinking about the same ole. Quinton, India, and Desiree. I was falling fast in some dark hole. This time, there was not going to be a way to climb out of it. Still, knowing this, I couldn't stop myself from jumping in.

"Desiree is so beautiful," Tyler blurted.

"Yeah, she is," I said, shifting uncomfortably in my seat. Why was he bringing her up?

"I mean wow, Q."

"So is Rayven," I said, quickly.

"She is. I have been watching Desiree, though."

"Really?" It was all I could say. I didn't like where this conversation was going.

"Yeah, Q."

This could not be happening. He was going to make me lose my mind. I didn't want him anywhere near her.

"I have never told you this, but I had a crush on Des when we were in high school."

"Seriously, dude. I would have never guessed that."

"Why not?"

"You didn't pay her attention. She was our little sister."

"I never thought of Des as my sister. I really liked her."

I didn't respond. I didn't like where this conversation was going. I know we graduated over ten years ago, but if I found out something happened between him and Desiree, I was going to go ballistic.

"What are you saying, T." He didn't respond for a moment. I started to panic. I looked over at him to see if I could read the expression on his face. I couldn't.

"Nothing, Q. I was just reminiscing."

Something didn't feel right.

15

Confessions

"Therefore do not pronounce judgment before the time, before the
Lord comes, who will bring to light the things now hidden in
darkness and will disclose the purposes of the heart. Then each one
will receive his commendation from God." *1 Corinthians 4:5*

Desiree

I didn't know about anybody else, but I was having
myself a good time. I needed this. I needed this time away. I was
grateful that Quinton had extended the invitation.

The night before had been a good one, so we all slept in late the
next morning. I had been awake for over twenty minutes, but I didn't
roll out of bed until noon. Realizing that I had to pee, I finally forced
myself to get up. I stumbled to the bathroom.

I was standing in front of the mirror, brushing my teeth when
there was a knock on the door.

"Desiree." Thankfully, it was just Quinton. I was standing there
in my underwear.

Q walks in, fully dressed in his t-shirt and khaki shorts. He was
laid back, but still so devastatingly sexy. I was instantly turned on. By
the look in his eyes when he took in my lack of clothes, so was he.

"Good afternoon, Quinton."

"You are just getting up?"

"Well, I didn't get to sleep until late."

"Right," he smiled. He gave me a knowing look and bit his lips a
little. Don't do that to me. That turned me on too.

We both blushed, knowingly looking at the bed. Quinton had
snuck into my room in the early morning. One thing led to another.

"T and I going to go get something to eat. We are starving. We are downstairs waiting on you two."

"You should have let me get to sleep last night."

"I couldn't help it."

I stepped back into the bathroom and finished brushing my teeth. I had barely sat my toothbrush down when he jumped for me.

I wrapped my arms around him, closed my eyes and gave into the pleasure he was offering.

"Why did you let me do that?" he asked, scrambling to fix his clothes afterwards.

"For the same reason you did it." I grabbed a t-shirt.

"What would you like to eat?" he asked, smiling.

"You know what I like. Rayven eats anything."

"Alright then, let me go before T comes up here."

"Good idea."

He laughed and disappeared out of the room. As soon as he left out, there was another knock at the door.

"Dessie."

"Come in, Rayven."

"Hey." She frowned at my appearance. "Q saw you in that?"

"What? I have on a t-shirt."

"A t-shirt that is barely covering your lady parts. A t-shirt that I can see through."

"Quinton wasn't looking at anything," I said, turning away. I didn't want her to detect that I was lying.

"Sure. He is a man. You are a woman. He noticed."

"The boys are going to get us something to eat."

"Praise God for that. I am starving."

"Me too. You look like crap," I blurted.

"Des, you don't look too hot yourself right now." That's because Quinton had messed my hair all up.

"You still love me."

"I don't know why. What's the deal today?"

"I don't know, but I am trying to put on my cutest bikini and stare out at the ocean."

"Sounds like a plan," she said, leaving out.

I chose a hot little pink number. Nothing too scandalous, but it fit perfectly. Over it, I wore tiny white shorts

"Sunray?" I knocked, but walked into her room. I became instantaneously envious. She looked gorgeous in a barely there red number "Wow, Rayven?"

'Don't say anything. You know that I am cute today. This suit is hot. I had to have it."

"It is, my friend, but can you really call that a swimsuit?"

"Victoria Secret call's it one."

We were sitting downstairs, watching TV when the boys returned with bags of Wendy's. I rubbed my stomach. I was starving.

"Thank goodness," Rayven said, jumping up. I laughed as I followed behind her.

'Wow.' Tyler eyes grew wide as he took in her appearance. "Rayven, we like this."

I tried not to roll my eyes. Of course my best friend was going to get their attention. She was the type of woman that could make any male drool. Even females turned their heads when she walked by.

I was taking my seat when Quinton grabbed my hand.

"There aren't many words to describe what you have on?" Only I heard it. I laughed. I turned my face because it was burning again.

After lunch, the four of us headed down to the beach. We fooled around in the ocean a little bit before Rayven and I took a seat on some lounge chairs. The boys joined in a game of football. I figured that my best friend and I could catch up while enjoying the view. Men with no shirts, tackling each other to the ground.

"Look at this, Desiree," Rayven blurted.

"I wouldn't mind tackling a few of them myself." There was one in particular. I couldn't take my eyes of Q in his black trunks.

"Forget that! I want to get tackled."

"I know that's right," I laughed loudly.

"Yeah, so what have you been up to, girl?"

"Not much." The only situation I had was with Quinton, and we were keeping that a secret. "I want to know what's up with you. You've been avoiding me. I call you and I get nothing."

"Girl, it's not even like that."

"What is it like then?"

"It's just that I have had so much going on in my life lately."

"And since when did you stop sharing all of that with me?"

"I had to deal with the emotions before I could reach out."

"What kind of emotions?" I was feeling concerned.

"So many," she said, shaking her head. "These last two and half weeks have been trying. I have cried more than I would like to admit. It has been a rollercoaster ride for me."

"Ray, why didn't you come to me?" I grabbed her hand. "I am your best friend." She squeezed my hand and gave me a small smile.

"I know, but I had to deal with it myself."

"I understand. So what's the deal?"

"Well," she said taking a deep breath. "Mike called me."

"Wow."

Mike was Rayven's ex. Like Anthony had done to me, he had broken her heart. She foolishly thought that he would be the one. Everyone did because he was the first man to get her to commit.

He appeared to be good for her. He appeared to have it all together. He was gorgeous, intelligent, and quickly moving up the corporate ladder. He appeared to love Rayven to death

Rayven trusted him with all her heart and she should not have. With some detective work, we found out that Mike was being unfaithful. He was cheating with Selena. We considered her a friend.

Of course Rayven wasn't going to take things lying down. She could have run home and cried, but she didn't. She walks into Selena home with me on her heels. We caught them red handed. She almost knocked Selena out cold. She slapped Mike around a couple times.

Once outside, she headed over to Mike's truck and slashed all four tires. She did the same to the chick's car. I had to grab her when she was proceeded to bust some windows. I didn't want any neighbors to call the police. I dragged her ass home.

Mike didn't come outside to face the woman that he supposedly loved. That really hurt Rayven. That's what sent her over the edge.

Mike did show up at Rayven's apartment hours later with a friend. They screamed at one another. There were tears. And then they were over.

I was there to pick up the pieces. I provided the shoulder for her to cry on. I was the only one to see how much Mike had hurt her. It took her many months to get back in the game.

"And what did he say?' I finally asked once I got over the initial shock of hearing his name again. I prayed that Mike was not trying to get Rayven back. There was no way that she could possibly trust this man again. She could not allow this man to destroy her once more.

"He wanted to see me. He asked me out to dinner."

"I take it that you went."

"Yeah," she said, quickly wiping away a tear. "I know what you are thinking. I should not have gone."

"Why would you give him the privilege of seeing you?"

"I don't know." She shrugged. "I wanted to see him." She paused for a moment to gather her thoughts. "I needed to see him. I wanted closure. I regretted that things didn't end more amicably."

"Okay, so what happened?"

"I don't know what I was thinking. I actually wanted to believe that he wanted to get back with me. And it's not like I wanted to get back with him. I just wanted to be able to tell him hell no and to get out of my face. Cussing him out would have been amicable enough for me."

"Wow, Rayven. What happened next?"

"Des." The tears really started falling. "I don't even know why he felt the need to tell me that his first child was born last month."

"Oh, wow." I was speechless."

"Not only that, but he is marrying the baby's mother. Selena."

"Oh, no." I covered my mouth quickly. It was probably not the best reaction, but it was authentic. She had blown my mind.

"I know. Crazy, isn't it?"

"I am so sorry," I said, quickly composing myself.

"For what?" she said, still wiping away tears. "I cannot believe that I am acting this way."

"You are hurting, babe. I think that it's perfectly fine that you are acting this way."

"I am supposed to be over him, though. This was over two years ago. If he doesn't mean anything to me, then there is no reason for me to be this emotional. I mean why should I care if his marrying that whore or that she just had his kid?"

"You loved him and it wasn't five years ago, it was two. And just because you feel that you are over this man, it does not mean that when he comes around again that you can't feel something for him. You have so many memories with him."

"I know, but I don't want to," she whined.

"Sunray, it's okay. You can cry," I said, wrapping my arm around her shoulder.

"I have already cried it out. I cried last week. I cried this week. I am all cried out, Desiree. I don't need to cry anymore."

"I agree then. If you have already mourned, then don't even think about him, her, or their kid. Just know that you can do better. So what did you say?"

"I gave him a hug, told him congratulations and I excused myself. I left."

"I am proud of you," I said, squeezing her hand.

"Thank you. There was nothing else he needed to say to me."

"You are right."

"And then on top of it all, I had a STD and a pregnancy scare."

"Rayven, what's going on with you!"

"Let me explain. Well, I have been seeing this dude, Cameron. He is so sexy and I have been breaking him off the cookie. Girl, he was everything!."

"Ray! What happened?"

"Well, the chicks started calling my phone. They are all telling me the same thing. This dude is a whore. When I confront him, he doesn't have anything to say at first. He stands there, looking all stupid in the face. Then he tells me that he may have gonorrhea from some other chick that he had been messing with."

"You didn't wrap it up?" I was about to lecture.

"I did, but apparently they hadn't. Still, condoms can fail, so can you imagine how mad I was. I chased him around my house with a knife. I was crying and screaming at him. I had never been so scared in all of my life. If I had of caught him, I was going to cut him."

"Wow, Rayven, that's dramatic."

"Drama seems to follow me. Thank goodness, the doctor called me earlier this week. I am all clear. No STD for me. I am clean."

"Hallelujah, Rayven. What's the deal with you being pregnant?"

"Well the doctor pulled me off the pill a month ago because they were making me sick. Basically, my period is late. I am scared to death, but I keep taking test and they all say negative. Still, no period, though. I don't know what's going on?"

"Stress. It happens."

"True."

"You should have allowed me to be there for you. You didn't have to go through all of that by yourself."

"Des, I am a whore."

"Shut up, Rayven. I don't associate with whores."

"Des, I have been whoring around for years. I am definitely not proud of that. I didn't want you to look down on me."

"Rayven, I said, taking her hand. "I am not in the judging business. I am your girl. I am your big sister. You know I love you."

"I know, but still I don't want you to think any less of me for making such stupid decisions."

"I don't give a crap what you do, Rayven, I am not going to think any less of you. You are still my BFF. It's time to change your mentality. From now on, you come to me when you need me. Do you hear me?"

"I do now." She hugged me. So," she said, after a moment of silence. "You sure nothing has been going on with you?"

"Nothing,' I said, pretty quickly.

"I don't believe that. Who have you been messing with?

"No one really," I said, throwing a look in Q's direction.

"What does that mean? You are lying. What are you hiding?"

"Nothing, Rayven. I am serious.

"Desiree, I know you better than that. I don't believe you. You mean to tell me that there has been no one since, Devin?"

"Well, there is this one guy."

"Let the truth be told."

"His name was Malik."

"And how did you meet this dude. At Belvie's?"

"Nope. I worked with him. Malik and I started at Pink Legacy around the same time. And since we were both the new kids on the block, we talked a lot. We looked out for each other."

"Get to the juicy."

"He flirted with me because he had a thing for me. So one day, I got confident and I asked him out for lunch. He said no, but he invited me out to dinner."

"How did that go?"

"Well, he took me to Century's." I nodded because Rayven gave me an impressed looked. "After that we went to a cozy lounge. I went back to his place, but we just made out. We didn't go there."

"I had a great time. He was a gentleman. We went out a couple times after that. Each time was better than before."

"You are talking in past tense. Why aren't you still seeing him?"

"So apparently he had just gotten out of a serious relationship. Suddenly his ex walks back into his life, pregnant. They got back together. He says they are going to get married and be a family."

"That sucks for you, but not a bad deal for him and her."

"Yeah, I just felt like he wasted my time."

"I hear you, but move on. You will be fine."

I didn't tell her about Quinton knowing Malik. I figured that she would have something to say about that. I didn't want any lectures.

"So have you stayed out of Quinton's bedroom?"

"Yes!" I said, quickly. I prayed to God that it didn't looked as if I was lying. "Why would I go near his bedroom, Ray!"

"No need to get defensive. I was messing with you."

"Speaking of Quinton, what's going on with you two?" I wanted us to move from the topic of Q and I being intimate.

"What do you mean, my friend?"

"Why are you being so nice? Something is going on and I want to know what it is."

"I know you do," she said, laughing. "Do you promise that you will keep that pretty little mouth of yours shut?"

"Huh?"

"Look, please don't say anything to Quinton about this. I trust you, Desiree. Don't do me dirty on this one."

"Okay, fine." I didn't understand the urgency in her voice. What was the big deal about the two of them making up?

"Back in senior year, I caught Q in a vulnerable moment."

"Huh?"

"Look, it's really not my place to tell you about that. I wouldn't know if I hadn't walked in on it. I don't think Tyler knows."

"Okay," I said, slowly. I felt a little uneasy. I didn't like not knowing what that moment was about considering Quinton and I was supposedly so tight.

"Well, I can tell you that it was over a female."

"Quinton?" I frowned. "Vulnerable over some chick?"

"Yeah. I walked up to him when he was hurting. Because I liked him. I took advantage of him."

"What! You liked Quinton! And you didn't tell me?" I was feeling hurt. Q and Rayven were my two dearest friends and they both had kept me in the dark. "You have kept something like that from me? How could you?"

'I am sorry, Desiree."

"Are you?" I didn't believe her.

"Des, don't be mad. The only reason I didn't let you know how I felt about Quinton was because of his reputation. You know how he was. I thought that I was a fool for liking him, but I did."

'And what do you mean by you took advantage of Quinton? You gave him the cookie, Rayven?"

"I did!"

"What! You slept with Quinton!" She quickly covered my mouth. I was a little loud.

"Shut up! Don't let him know that we are talking about him?"

"Sorry." We both looked in his direction. He was being chased with a football in his hand. Good. "So what happened? Did Quinton blow you off afterwards? Is that why have been at odds?"

"Actually, the other way around."

"Huh? I am so confused."

"Des, he cared about this chick so much. He wasn't focused on me. I tried my hardest to make him forget her, but I couldn't. And when he left that night, I was so humiliated."

"Why?"

"I just felt small. I could not bring myself to look at him. Being hateful to him has protected me. It's been my shield."

"Dag and he never knew why?"

"He kind of knew why, but he didn't fully understand. He didn't realize that I had a thing for him."

"And I take it that he does now."

"Yeah, I pulled him aside yesterday and told him how I felt. I figured it was time to move on."

"So now you two are cool?"

"We are."

"That's a blessing. I am still a little blown by all this."

"I can tell. You should see your face."

"I can't believe you slept with Quinton." I repeated. I prayed that she couldn't tell how uneasy that made me feel. "And you have some nerve. You were making all of those jokes about me giving him my cookie and you had beaten me to it."

"I know. I said it because I always believed that Q had a little thing for his Desiree." Well, he did. I wasn't going to tell her, though.

'Whatever to that."

"I see the way he looks at you." So she had noticed? "And I see the way that you look at him. You want some of that." I did. I had already gotten some of that. I had just gotten some hours ago.

"Sunray, please." I had to change the subject before I gave myself away. "So how was it?" I asked.

"He's packing if that's what you are asking." I knew that.

"Was it good?"

"For what it was worth. He wasn't into me."

"So you mean to tell me that I am supposed to look into this man's face and not say anything?"

"That's right, Desiree Harris, you promised me."

"Yes, I know. I just hate you for telling me this."

"I love you too."

After that conversation with Rayven, I was in my feelings for the rest of the day. Even though I wasn't really surprised that she had a thing for Quinton, I was hurt that she never admitted it to me. And to make matters worse, she had slept with him.

And then I was hurt by Quinton's secret. Who was this chick? Why did she have him vulnerable? Thinking back, I couldn't recall him being serious about anyone.

Obviously he wanted to keep his love life personal. T didn't even know about this mystery girl. Still, I was bothered that I was not in on something and Rayven was. That didn't make any sense to me.

Was I jealous? I wasn't going to lie, I was. I loved my closeness with Quinton. And thinking that Rayven could get as close to this man as I was, didn't settle too well with me. I always wanted to be his number one female friend. I didn't care how selfish that was.

What really made my stomach hurt, was the fact that we had both slept with him. I don't know how most women would feel, but I wasn't too keen on sharing my men with my best friend.

I was tempted to put a stop to all the intimacy between us. I wasn't sure if I could handle it. When I laid eyes on him, I wanted to blurt out that I knew about him and Rayven, but I didn't dare.

As soon as he brushed his hand across my thigh, I was putty in his hands. I quickly pushed aside the worrying. I pushed aside the past. I was not concerned enough to stop what was going on.

After a night where every time Tyler and Rayven turned their back, Q was kissing on me, we ended up in his Jacuzzi style bathtub.

"Are you having a good time?" he whispered in my ear as he massaged my bare skin.

"I am. Are you?"

"Definitely. Are you glad you are alone with me?" he teased. "I have been waiting to hold you in my arms all day."

"I am." He smiled at me.

"Can I get a kiss?"

Here was my chance to tell him that maybe we should back off and that we needed to end this.

After some hesitation, I surrendered to him. I wrapped my arms around his neck. I didn't say anything, I just nodded.

"Thank you, baby." He wrapped me in his arms and took me captive. His kiss was more gentle than usual. It took me by surprise.

We stayed in his tub for an hour. Things didn't progress any further than kissing. It was a sweet intimate moment. And I was starting to think that maybe I had a thing for him.

16

Jealous

"Wrath is cruel, anger is overwhelming, but who can stand before jealousy?" *Proverbs twenty-seven:4*

Quinton

I really couldn't explain what happened that fateful weekend between Rayven and I. We had just made up a month ago, but I was already starting to see her in a different light. I was starting to enjoy her company a little too much.

One night, I was hanging out with her and Desiree at the house. We were throwing back Coronas and reminiscing. We got on the topic of food, realizing that none of us had ever tried Greek food. Taking my cue, I decided to invite the girls out to a popular Greek restaurant near my job. They both quickly accepted. I figured that I could call Tyler later to make it a foursome.

However, when Friday rolled around, Des had to go on an unexpected business trip and 'I' had prior plans that could not be broken. That just left me and Rayven. I figured that there was no reason to cancel on her. The two of us could have fun without our friends. By 6:30, Friday evening, I was knocking on her door.

"What's up, Q?" she asked, opening the door.

"Not much. What's the deal with you?"

"I am here, chilling, waiting on you all. Come on in, Q."

"Thanks." I walked past her.

"So where are Des and Tyler? Are they meeting us here or the restaurant?"

"Desiree didn't call you?"

"No, she didn't. Why? What happened?"

"She had to leave out of town at the last minute."

"On business?"

"Yep."

"Wow. We never get to spend any time together." She was beginning to look sad. I got nervous because I wasn't in the mood for drama between the two girls. I had already heard this from Des.

"She feels the same way." I offered her some consolation.

"Well, then I guess that Des and I are going to have to talk about this later," she said, thankfully dropping the subject. "So whats up with your boy, Tyler?"

"He can't make it.'

"Oh okay. Well, it's just us I see." Something flashed in her eyes. "Are you ready?"

"I am. Are you?"

"Yes."

She looked lovely in some ripped jeans and a tight tank. It fit her in all the right places. She wasn't thick and curvy like my girl, Des, but she held her own. She had nice eyes and a great smile. She always knew how to attract a lot of attention.

Dinner was nice. I wasn't sure if things were going to be awkward between us, but they weren't. It didn't feel like we hadn't hung out alone in years. Things felt natural.

The only time the conversation turned uncomfortable for me was when we started talking about Desiree. The last person I wanted to talk about her with was her best friend. I couldn't afford to have Rayven detect any feelings on my end.

"So how is it living with Desiree? Does living with her make you feel uncomfortable?"

"Nope. Why do we have to talk about this?" I asked, reaching for my drink and leaning back in my chair.

"Why not? Is it painful for you?"

"No," I lied. "I am straight."

"Then whats the big deal?"

"I never said it was a big deal." I took down the rest of my drink. "What is it that you want to know, Rayven?"

"I honestly just wanted to know if it was weird living with her considering how you use to feel about her."

"It's not weird," I said, laughing a little nervously.

"Really? So why do you laugh?" Oh my goodness. Why was she calling me out?

"Because this is funny." It wasn't funny.

"No it's not. How is it funny? You know what I think?"

"I am honestly afraid to hear what you think."

"I think you still have feelings for Desiree." I swallowed hard.

"Why do you think that?"

"I see the way you look at her."

"How do I look at her?"

"The same way you did five years ago." I just stared at her. What could I say? Desiree still consumed my heart, but I couldn't admit it. "You want to hit that?"

"Well, I do," I said, slowly. "That means nothing."

"Of course it does, Q."

"Not really. It just means that I find her attractive. The woman is freaking beautiful, but so are you. I am a man. I would love to go there with either of you."

She stared at back at me, obviously taken back. I was satisfied that I finally shut her up. She was digging too far.

"We already went there,' she said, throwing a spoon at me.

"Under happier circumstances."

After dinner, we headed back to her place. We sat close to each other on her couch while watching HBO, but we didn't touch. I felt like I was fifteen on my first date. I was terrified to make any move.

As always, my mind moved to Desiree. I missed her. I wished that she was back at the house, waiting for me. I wanted one of her hugs or her addictive kisses. I was not excited to go home, knowing she wasn't there.

When I woke up the next morning, I was not in my bedroom. I was stretched out on Rayven's couch, fully clothed. I did have a pillow and a blanket. I was confused. What happened?

As if she heard the question in my head, Rayven appeared dressed in a short blue dress. Wow. She looked gorgeous.

"Hey, sleepyhead."

"What's going on?" I asked, sitting up.

"Nothing.' She laughed, loudly. "Don't worry, we didn't do anything. We weren't drunk enough."

"Okay," I laughed.

"You fell asleep during the movie and I kind of left you there."

"It's crazy how I don't remember anything."

"I don't know what's up with your memory lapse. I didn't slip anything into your drink, I promise." She winked at me.

"That makes you seem guilty," I joked. She smiled. "So where are you headed to?" I asked, standing.

"I am going shopping with my mother."

"I hear you. Have a good time. I am going to head on home. Call me later if you would like to do something," I said, kissing her forehead. Was I trying to ask her out?

She did call me. She told me that she was invited to a co-workers dinner party and wanted someone to accompany her. I was gamed because I had nothing else planned. Des was still out of town and Tyler was still pre-occupied. It was Saturday night and I was not trying to sit at home.

I put on some dress slacks, a shirt and tie and headed to Rayven's house. She looked incredible in her fitted floral dress. She got into my car smelling divine.

"Hey, Q." She leaned over and kissed my cheek. "Thanks for coming with me. I wasn't trying to sit at home and do nothing."

"Me neither, so I am glad you called."

"Cool. You look pretty good," she said, throwing me a smile as she leaned back in her seat.

"Not as good as you."

The party was way across town. It was not in the best neighborhood so I was glad that she called me. There was no way that she needed to come out here alone. Not at night at least.

As we stepped outside, Rayven quickly latched onto my arm. When her nails dug into my arm, I knew she was uneasy. I looked over at her and smiled. It was good to see her vulnerable for once.

Once inside, Rayven relaxed, quickly turning into quite a social butterfly. For a minute, you would have thought she was the hostess. She grabbed my hand and started introducing me to all of her co-workers. I could tell that most of them assumed that Rayven and I were together. Some of them made it obvious that they were measuring me up.

Eventually, I was able to let my guard down and have a good time. Everything was nice. The company was cool, the alcohol selection was pretty good, and the music was on point. Thankfully, there was no drama.

On the ride home, Rayven was extra talkative. I just enjoyed her conversation and laughed at her jokes. I had missed out on some valuable time with her. She was someone that I could spend time with.

When we got back to her spot, she invited in me in for some drinks. I quickly accepted and followed her inside. As soon as I sat down, I undid my tie and unbuttoned my shirt. She just smiled in my direction and gave me a look. I don't know why, but I turned away.

As Rayven changed into something more comfortable, my mind drifted to Desiree. I missed her so much. Every now and then my mind would go a little crazy thinking about her. She was coming home tomorrow and I could not wait.

I hadn't seen her in two days, but it felt like a week. I hadn't kissed her in a week and that felt like a month. My body was yearning for hers, and I couldn't help but think this was ridiculous. I shouldn't want a woman who wasn't mine so badly, but I did. I needed to put an end to it all, but not right now.

"Are you hungry?" she asked, returning to the room.

"Are you serious?" We had eaten two hours ago.

"Yeah," she laughed. "Didn't Des tell you? I eat like a horse."

"Well, so do I. I will have what you are having."

She fixed bacon, egg, and cheese sandwiches. It hit the spot.

After our midnight snack, we settled on the couch with some Ciroc. I was ready to wash my troubles away with this girl. I didn't want to focus on anything, especially not how much I wanted her best friend. I needed this tonight.

I didn't intend on drinking that much. I had to drive home and I wasn't trying to sleep on this couch again. I preferred my bed, no matter how lonely I got.

The Ciroc tasted extra smooth to me, and apparently to Rayven, because before I knew it, the bottle was empty. I could feel it too because I had started moving really close to Rayven. Or maybe it was the other way around. Either way, she was starting to look like someone to take my mind off of Desiree.

I am not sure which one of us made the first move. The next thing I knew, she was in my lap and her lips were on mine. My hands were up her shirt and hers were down my pants. And I was seriously entertaining the idea of taking this woman to bed.

Something clicked in my mind, though. I don't know if it was common sense or guilt, but something made me put a stop to it all. She practically jumped out of my lap when she felt me pull away.

"What was that?" I asked.

"I don't know," she mumbled.

"I apologize. I didn't mean to make you feel uncomfortable."

"No need to apologize. I think that this was on the both of us. This is why you never drink too much. You never know what might happen," she joked. "You may not be able to control your actions."

"You are right," I laughed, nervously. I reached for my tie and stood. "I guess maybe I should leave. It's getting late."

"True. I think that I do need to go bed. I have church in the morning. I need to spend some time with God." Me too, I thought. I needed to ask God what was going on with my life.

"Well, let me go." I did kiss her cheek. "Thanks for tonight."

"No problem. Thank you."

I got out of her house as fast as I could. What just happened? Whatever it was, it scared me. It felt nice, but I was not trying to hook up with Rayven. I wanted more than anything to be with her best friend. I knew I didn't have a chance with Desiree, but I didn't want her to cut off the intimacy between us. I was greedy for her.

On the other hand, kissing Rayven was lovely. I think I wanted it all to happen. I was pretty sure that it was not the alcohol.

As soon as I got home, I went to bed. My mind was racing and I didn't want to think of anything else. I just wanted Des home.

I got up early the next morning to go to church. I thought that would be appropriate considering how confused I was feeling. I was able to pick up little Quinton and take him with me. After church, we went to my parent's house because I thought it would be beneficial for us to be around family. My son loved running around the yard as a carefree three-year-old. India never provided him with that opportunity which was a shame.

By the time, I dropped Quinton off and argued with his mother, Desiree was at home. I smiled as soon as I saw her car in the driveway. I needed to see her for my sanity.

I was so excited to see her that I was scared. I was so afraid of my reaction that I stood outside longer than I should have. I needed to get myself together. I felt like I needed a cigarette and smoking wasn't my thing.

I headed straight for her room. I prayed that I wasn't about to make a fool of myself. Usually, I would walk in, but today I knocked.

She kind of hid behind the door when she opened it. That drove me crazy because I just wanted to feel her arms around me. She did give me that smile. My heart started to beat faster.

"What's up, Quinton? What can I do for you?"

"I just wanted to say hi."

"Hi, sweetie."

"Are you okay?" She still hadn't opened the door.

"I am fine."

"I am glad that you made it safely."

"Thank you. How was church?"

"It was great. Much needed."

"Church lasted all this time?"

"No, I went to my parent's house. I spent the day with my son."

"Oh okay. How is everybody? Little Quinton?"

"They are good. He is happy." Disappointment was settling in.

"Good to hear." She was preoccupied. Maybe someone was on the other side. Maybe she didn't really go on a business trip. It took everything in me not to push the door open and see for myself.

"I will let you go now." Apparently, that's what she wanted. "I was just speaking," I mumbled.

"Where are you going?" she asked, grabbing my hand when I turned to walk away. "Come here." She pulled me into her bedroom. My breath caught in my throat when I saw her standing there in her red bra and panties. Red, the color of passion. The color of love.

"What do you really want?" she challenged. "Why don't you tell me the truth?" She pinned me against her door. She started to kiss me. I was in heaven.

"I wanted to see you," I whispered, wrapping my arms around her. It brought relief to my body.

"I know. Do you miss me?"

"Yeah," I admitted. "You were all I thought about."

"Are you going to show me how much?"

"Yes, right now."

"Take your clothes off!" She practically ripped my shirt off.

'I got it," I chuckled. It did my ego wonders to see her standing there, eying me impatiently. When I stood before her nude, she smiled at me. I actually blushed.

"You are beautiful," she whispered, pulling me to her.

"You're the beautiful one. Baby..."

"Quinton." She stopped me with a kiss.

I reached around and unhooked her bra. I turned her around and pinned her against her door. I proceeded to kiss every inch of her bare skin. She grew impatient, though, and started pushing me towards the bed.

"Okay, Desiree, I am yours."

"Give me what I need," she hissed at me. Her eyes were dark with desire. "Work me."

I started kissing her stomach while pinning her down to the bed. I couldn't stop. It was intoxicating and I was being selfish. She kept mumbling by name, so I whispered, "Desiree, patience."

"We haven't done anything yet, but I love you."

I stared back at her. I couldn't find the words to respond to her. I knew her words didn't mean anything. They were just words spoken in the moment of passion, but they affected me more than they should have. A jolt of momentary sadness moved through me.

So she couldn't see my face, I flipped her over and begin to kiss her back. I inhaled the scent of her. I reached for her ponytail, allowing her hair to escape down her back. I ran my fingers through it for a moment. I was trying desperately to find the right words.

"Quinton..."she whispered. I turned her back over and we started at each other. I was overwhelmed, so I closed my eyes.

When I had the courage to speak again, I whispered, "Well come here and show me how much."

Rayven called the next morning. She asked me if I could meet her over lunch. It was obvious that we needed to talk. We couldn't ignore what happened between us.

I was nervous the rest of the morning. I just didn't know what I was supposed to say to her. I was confused and could not offer a real explanation to what happened the other night. I did know that I liked the kiss and I probably should not have.

"So what's this about?" I asked when I slid into a booth at a local pizzeria close to her job.

"Don't act that way, Q." She didn't crack a smile. Wow. I realized that she was tenser than I had initially thought.

"Okay, I am sorry. You are right."

"What happened the other night? Were we that messed up?"

"No, we weren't," I admitted. "We knew what we were doing."

"That's what I thought."

"Before I knew it, you were kissing me."

"We kissed each other and you know it! Stop playing around!"

"Calm down, Rayven." I reached for her hand. "We both kissed each other. This is just weird."

"I know. I called you because this was all I thought about yesterday. I even asked God what the deal was." She smiled finally.

I couldn't say the same. I spent my night with her best friend.

"I wanted to kiss you, Rayven."

"Would it scare you, if I said that's what I wanted to hear?" She looked relieved. "I wanted to kiss you too."

"No, it doesn't scare me," I squeezed her hand. "I enjoyed it."

"Me too,' she said, blushing. "So what are we going to do?"

"Would you like to see if there's something between us? Something more than an attraction?"

"We can do that," she said, squeezing my hand.

"Cool. So how about I find some place nice to take you tonight or are you busy?"

"No, let's do this."

"Okay, then. Shall we order?"

I didn't know what I was doing? I needed someone special in my life. I needed something more than the intimacy between Desiree and I. I needed someone to call my woman.

"Wow."

"What?" she asked, frowning at me over her menu?"

"Nothing, sweetheart, I just thought of something."

I had to give up Des. I knew I didn't want to, but as soon as she caught wind to this, she was going to cut me off. Maybe, I should have put more thought into this.

Desiree

When Rayven called me and asked me to meet her for lunch, the next day, I was worried because I could tell that something was up. Lately, every time we talked, she was in tears. It was never good news anymore.

I tried not to focus on it too much. I tried not to worry. I couldn't help it. I took care of my best friend and sometimes she was an emotional basket case.

"What's up, Rayven?" I asked her the next day when I met her at Jake's, a deli spot down the street from her job. "Let me know now. I am not going to sit here the entire meal, waiting on you to spill it."

"Well, hello to you, Desiree. Are you saying that we can't have lunch together without there being a reason?"

"No, but I know there is reason. I could tell by your voice."

"Okay fine. We will do it your way. Can we order first? Will that be okay? This is our lunch."

"Fine."

"Quinton and I are dating," she blurted after ordering.

"Excuse me!" I said, almost knocking over my glass of sweet tea.

"We are pursuing something."

"You and who?"

"Quinton," she repeated. "Your roommate."

"I know who Quinton is!"

"Calm down. Why did you ask?" She looked bewildered.

"Because I am in shock, Rayven!"

"You insisted on us dating. You said we would make a great couple." That was before we started sharing more than conversation. That was before we kissed. That was before the sex.

"Yeah, but all this time, you two were denying that you even liked each other. I go on one business trip and it all changes? How did this happen?"

"It just happened, Des. You can't always foresee things." That was true, but I was still angry. My hand was trembling.

"We spent some time together alone over the weekend. Saturday night, we kissed." And then he comes to my bedroom Sunday and loves my body for hours. That was Quinton, though. He got it wherever he could. I felt like a fool.

I sat there quietly and listened to how they kissed and how he left because things got weird. I listened to how she thought about him all the next day. I bit my lip so that I wouldn't blurt out that he wasn't thinking about her because he was whispering my name half the night.

She told me how they met up for lunch the next day. How they decided to see what was brewing between them. How they went out last night. I thought it was messed up that Quinton didn't tell me.

Did they have sex?

"Excuse me, I have to pee." I felt nauseated. I needed to calm down. My blood pressure was rising. My face was red.

I threw water on my face and took a couple deep breaths. I still felt horrible, but I figured I could put on a good face for my best friend. She didn't deserve this.

Our food had arrived by the time I arrived back at the table. I took a bite out of my sandwich and a sip of tea before speaking.

"So you really do like him?"

"I do." She smiled shyly. "I want to see how much."

"And he likes you?"

"I guess so. Enough to casually date me."

"Well, I am happy for you." I was lying.

"Are you sure, Desiree?" She was frowning.

"Yeah." I lied again. I wanted to say something else but I couldn't bring myself to.

"You don't seem happy."

"I am." I sighed and reached for her hand. "I was in shock."

"Oh okay. Good. Thank you, Des. This means a lot to me." She had a huge smile on her face. I wanted to slap it off. I felt guilty.

I couldn't concentrate when I got back to work, so I faked a migraine. I was told to go home of course. No one questioned me.

I wasn't sure why I was so upset. I was the one who told Quinton and Rayven to date, but now that it actually happened, it bothered me. Maybe because I had gotten use to him being with me in a sense. We had been sleeping together for months now. Now he was dumping me because he found something he liked in Rayven. A month ago, they couldn't stand to be in the same room together.

I was going crazy. I was pissed. I was jealous. I hated sharing.

I had kissed the same lips that my best friend had. We had both been intimate with him. If she knew about what Q and I had been doing, would she feel the same way?

"If he liked Rayven, he should have left me alone!"

I was mad at myself. I was a fool for ever getting involved with him. I was a fool for allowing things to progress the way it had. I had stopped thinking logically the first night that we kissed.

He was in the living room when I walked through the door.

"Hey, what are you doing home?" he asked.

"Hi, Quinton." I breezed past him. I didn't even attempt to answer his question.

"Are you okay?" he asked, sounding concern.

"I am fine."

"Wait a minute," he said, getting up to follow me. He was quicker than me, so he grabbed me before I could shut my bedroom door. I blocked the entrance so he wouldn't come in. "What's wrong with you? Tell me."

"I don't feel good."

"What's wrong?"

"I have a migraine."

"Oh wow. Do you want me...?"

"No."

"Can I...?"

"I can take care of myself, Quinton."

"Sorry, I..."

"Right now, I would just prefer to be alone."

"Oh okay."

"Will you back up, please?"

"Sure." He did.

"Thank you." I slammed the door.

I walked into my bathroom, pulled off my clothes, turned on some bath water, sat on the edge of the tub and I cried. And I didn't know why.

17

Bitter

"Let all bitterness and wrath and anger and clamor and slander be put away from you, along with all malice. Be kind to one another, tenderhearted, forgiving one another, as God in Christ forgave you."
Ephesians 4:31-32

Quinton

Desiree didn't talk to me the next three days. I didn't understand why. I figured I did something, but I couldn't figure out what it was. When she came from work, claiming she had a migraine, I believed her because she looked sick. I was concerned and all I wanted to do was give her some medicine and hold her in my arms. She shut me down, but I respected that.

When she gave me the cold shoulder the next day, I realized that it was more than a bad headache. I thought maybe she was PMSing. I had a sister, so I knew what that was about. I wasn't going to nag her.

By the next day, I got the feeling that it was more than that. I could tell that she was mad at me. I got confused. What had I done this time? I couldn't stand her being angry with me.

By the third day, I got smart. I left her alone because that's what she wanted. I would avoid her whenever we were in house together. I figured that if she didn't see me, she would get over it. I wanted her to be completely calm before I even considered approaching her.

At work, I was now doing the 12:00 to 4:00 show, so my nights had freed up. What a blessing. That day I took little Quinton out for pizza and then brought him a new toy. Of course, India wanted to argue with me. I left irritated. I was stressed out over her and Desiree. I headed to Rayven's hoping that she could help me relax.

"What's up, girl?" She greeted me at the door. I was happy to see her. I loved how she threw herself in my arms. This was the type of affection I could get used to.

"Not much."

"Really, well I am here to change that."

I lifted her in my arms and took her over to her couch. She sat in my lap and I just held her close to me. I just wanted it to feel as if she was my girl and I was her man. I wanted this to be real. I needed this.

My mind was racing. I started to kiss her. It felt good, but it wasn't enough. Des consumed my thought which wasn't fair to her.

I didn't want to focus on Desiree or what we had been through over the months. I wanted to forget the woman. As messed up as it was, for the second time, I was using her best friend to do so.

I did like Rayven. I was digging the time we spent together. I could see myself with a woman like her. Sadly, at that moment, I liked Des ten times more. I prayed that could change soon.

Still, no matter how hot and heavy things were getting between us on the couch; it was failing to clear my mind. My mind was going crazy. I could feel Desiree in my arms. I could taste her lips on mines. Right now I was holding and kissing Rayven

I tried to force my mind to concentrate on the present. I pulled her closer and kissed her harder. I wanted to think of nothing else, but Rayven. I laid her on the couch and within moments I had her shirt and bra on the floor.

She was enjoying it. She had wrapped her legs around me. I could tell that she was willing me to take it there. Shamefully, I wasn't sure if I wanted to go there. It wasn't the right time, so I pulled away from her. She looked at me as if I had insulted her.

"I am sorry, Rayven."

"You sure like to reject me."

"It's not like that."

"Then what is it like?" She asked, quickly grabbing her clothes. How do you make a woman think she is going to get some and just stop in the middle of it?" I could see tears in her eyes.

"No. Come here." I pulled her to me. "Please don't feel that way. Those weren't my intentions to make you feel that way."

"Then what were your intentions? I am hot and bothered."

"Me too! I just don't want us to move too fast."

"Wow! I never heard a man say that to me before."

"I am serious, Rayven. If we are going to make this work, this has to be more than an attraction. More than sex."

"I understand," she said after a couple of moments.

"Cool." My reasoning didn't sound like me, but tonight it was me. I couldn't go through with it, even though I wanted to. We both ignored our desire for intimacy for the rest of the night. We ordered Chinese, sat on her couch, and just talked.

This was actually a good thing. We got around to leaning about each other. I knew Rayven, but admittedly, I wanted to know more. We talked about our families, our aspirations and even our sexual fantasies. I wanted to do more than hold her hand, but I didn't.

I liked Rayven. I was more than ready for a commitment. I wanted a woman that I could call my own whether that was her or not. I wanted a woman who could satisfy me mentally, emotionally and physically. No woman had been doing that for me lately. Most chicks were just as horny as men these days and just wanted sex.

"Has Desiree said anything to you about us?" Rayven asked.

"Umm, no." I froze. "Does she know?"

"Yeah. You mean you haven't said anything to her?"

"I haven't had the chance to talk to Des these days." That wasn't a lie. She wasn't talking to me. "I have been busy and so has she."

"Oh." I could tell that she didn't believe me.

"So what did she say?" Now things were starting to make sense.

"Well, it was weird actually."

"How?"

"She seemed pissed." Great. "She couldn't seem to understand how we just hooked up all of a sudden." I was in deep with her.

"Yeah, it was fast. But..."

"I thought this is what she wanted. She is always on my case to hook up with you." That was true, sweetheart, but over the last couple of months, Des and I had been doing some hooking up of our own. This was all before the first night we kissed or the first night we took it there. The game had changed.

"Yeah, she has been bugging me too," was all that I could offer. My throat was suddenly very dry. I didn't know what else to say.

"Then I don't get it," she shrugged. Rayven was so oblivious right now. "I do know that she was a little salty about you not telling her. She said that you should have told her."

"Really. I didn't realize that it was that big of a deal." Yes I did. "I mean for me to tell her immediately." I didn't want to hurt Rayven's feelings. "I haven't really seen her."

"I understand." You really shouldn't. Rayven grabbed my hands.

"Maybe you should think about saying something, though. You know, to keep the peace." Sweetheart, it's too late for that. The peace had been shattered.

"I will." I was going to have to say something. I was not looking forward to it. I dreaded it. Desiree could never fight fair.

"Don't worry. By the end of our lunch, Desiree was cool with the idea. She appeared happy." No, she wasn't.

"That's good." If Des was happy, she would be talking to me. "When did this conversation take place?" I wanted validation.

"Tuesday, at lunch." Oh yeah. That was no migraine.

I couldn't stomach what Rayven had revealed. I was nervous. It was time to get out of here because I felt as if I was suffocating.

"Hey, baby." I leaned over to kiss her. "I don't want to leave, beautiful, but I do have to get up earlier than usual."

"Okay, Q." She kissed me back eagerly. I could tell that she didn't want me to leave. I breathed a sigh of relief when I got outside.

"This is what I get." I didn't think things through. I didn't realize that me hooking up with Rayven would hurt Desiree.

I didn't know what to feel. Desiree meant too much to me. If my friendship with her suffered because of this, I was going to lose my mind. I needed her. If she wanted this thing between Rayven and I to end, I would do it without hesitation.

I walked into the house and there was a light on in the kitchen. She stood in the middle of the room in pink boy shorts and nothing else. Why did she have to do this to me?

"Hi." I could barely manage that. I wasn't sure she heard me until she turned slowly. When our eyes met, she smirked at me.

I couldn't control myself. I was drooling. I took in every inch of that body that I adored. I started to imagine how that body would feel. I imagined being with her. I wanted that.

I wanted to kiss her soft skin. I wanted to inhale her scent. I wanted to taste her lips. I wanted to hear her whisper my name. I could feel her lips on mine, her breath on my skin, and her nails digging into my back.

I didn't expect her to walk over to me. She stood right in front of me. She stood close without touching me. It was torture.

My body was shaking. My palms were sweaty. My throat was dry. I was breathing hard. I thought maybe I was going to pass out.

Why did she have to stand so close to me? I could smell her. I could almost taste her. She was breathing on me. I loved it.

I closed my eyes and leaned against the wall. I had to get away from her, but my legs wouldn't move. I was hypnotized.

"I hope Rayven makes you feel the way I do." She couldn't.

"Desiree." I opened my eyes. She smiled at me.

"Goodnight, Quinton." She walked away from me.

It took everything in me to not reach for her. I felt as if she had punched me in the stomach. It hurt, but she was the only one I wanted to comfort me.

I walked back to my room. I hopped into the shower. Afterwards, I climbed straight into bed. I closed my eyes, but I didn't fall asleep. The night was long.

Desiree

What I did to Quinton was messed up. I couldn't help it, though; I was still salty about him being with Rayven. I had been in my bedroom, shamefully aching for him. I wanted Quinton to ache for me in the same way.

It gave me satisfaction to watch him squirm. I saw the desire in his eyes. I saw how his body reacted to me.

I could tell what he was thinking. The same thoughts were running through my head. I wanted him tonight. It was going to be an incredibly lonely and long night.

Whenever Quinton walked into the same room, my whole body would react. I never met a man that could satisfy me the way he could. No one could kiss me the way he could. No one could touch me the way he did. No one could love me the way he had.

I lay in my bed and imagined him next to me. I could smell him. I could feel him. I could imagine him kissing me. I could imagine him touching me. I ran my hand over my body, wishing it was his hand

I was so hot. I was sweating and I hadn't done a thing. I stared up at the ceiling, breathing harder than I should have.

"Great." I slid a pillow between my thighs. "I am suffering."

I guess this what I got for being hateful towards Quinton. I was making a fool out of myself. I knew I was going to have to apologize. I wasn't going to feel better until I did.

I was so jealous. Q wasn't my man, so I didn't have to right to be. I couldn't help it. I had him first, right? I guess not, considering Rayven and him had been together that fateful night in college.

"I pray that was just once."

Q and I had been sleeping in the same bed for the last couple of months. It's where I wanted him to be. I wanted his affection. I wanted him to keep spoiling me. I wanted him to keep loving me.

If there was no Quinton, where did that leave me? Alone. I didn't need a man, but I wanted one. I wanted to be with someone.

I had to accept that I wasn't in a relationship with Quinton. Whether I wanted to admit it or not, what we had was purely centered around sex. I am sure that's how he saw it. I did love our closeness. Like any other woman, I loved being held and told that I was beautiful. Selfishly, I was going to miss all of that.

I had to give it all up. I had to give him to Rayven. Rayven deserved all of that too. If he wanted to be with her, I couldn't stop him. I couldn't be mad either.

"I am being so selfish." I wanted to keep Quinton around for reasons that were purely physical to fill an empty void in my life. Rayven wanted him on an emotional level. I knew she liked him. I could see it in her eyes. I loved my best friend, so I was willing to risk my happiness for hers. For Quinton's as well.

Why wasn't I more excited. Months ago, this is what I wanted for them. I wanted them to hook up because I thought they were perfect for each other. I should have been happy, but I wasn't. I had to figure it all out. I was going to have to find a way.

I felt the tears.

"What is this!" Why was I this emotional? I must have been PMSing. I think my period was due soon.

Maybe I was jealous because they had found each other and I had not found anyone. I was just resorting to being intimate with one of my best friends. All of the men I had recently dated decided that didn't want me in the end or they ran to another woman. Just like Q.

"Shoot!" I was getting a headache.

I would apologize to Quinton in the morning and attempt to move on. I would pretend that my two best friends being together didn't bother me. I knew Q couldn't stay mad at me and I knew he would forgive me in a moment. I was his weakness.

Finally, I fell asleep at 2:30. By 3:15, I was awake again. I had to go to him. I sighed and climbed out of bed. I grabbed a t-shirt and headed down the hall to his bedroom.

Quinton

I heard when she opened the door. She called my name, but I didn't answer. I pretended to be asleep. I didn't know what to say to her. I was scared to say anything.

She didn't leave. I could feel her presence. My body could feel her. It was yearning.

"Quinton, I am not stupid. I know you are not asleep." How could she tell? When I didn't answer, she let out a huge sigh of frustration. I heard her stomp over to the bed. She jumped on top of me, straddling me, grabbing my arms. "Look at me!" In defeat, I did.

"Are you going to mess with me again?"

"No," she said, climbing off of me. I wanted to pull her back, but I couldn't. I sat up and reached over to turn on the lamp. I was surprised to see a pleading look on her face. She wanted forgiveness.

"Why are you in my room at 3:30 in the morning?"

"I am sorry," she said, throwing her arms around my neck. I wrapped my arms around her and pulled her close. She laid her head on my shoulder. All I could feel was relief.

"I don't like when you are angry with me." I admitted.

"But, I shouldn't be. Will you forgive me?"

"Of course, sweetie." She gave me a lingering kiss on my cheek. I almost lost my mind. It was not what I wanted.

"Thank you."

"Why should you not be angry?" She had every right to be.

"Because I am just jealous."

"Jealous?" Did I hear her correctly? "Why would you be jealous?" I stuttered.

"Well, if you are with Rayven. I won't get to kiss you anymore." She stared straight into my eyes.

This was hard for me to accept. Was I ready to give Desiree up? She meant so much to me. She was beautiful, charming, and the sex couldn't get much better. I needed more, though. Desiree wasn't willing to give it to me. I wanted her heart, not just her body.

"Don't think this is easy for me. It's hard to stay away from you. What you did earlier was messed up."

She looked down for a minute as if she was ashamed, but when she looked back up, her eyes were sparkling. She smiled. I laughed.

"I am sorry, Quinton."

"No, you aren't."

"Look, I was mad that you didn't tell me. Wow, Q, you live with me. Were you purposely trying to hide this from me? Why?"

"No, Desiree, that's was not it. I stupidly thought it wasn't a big deal. I was going to tell you when I saw you. You were angry with me and I didn't realize why until Rayven told me."

"Oh, well, you know how irrational I get. You still love me?"

"I do." More than you would ever know. I reached up to touch her cheek. "I don't want to give up any of this, Desiree. I really don't. It was inevitable, though."

"Right. You will have something better very soon." I doubted it

"She's not you." She could never be. "It won't be the same."

She looked taken aback for a moment.

"No." She kissed the palm of my hand. "Quinton, please don't think it was just about the sex. I'm going to miss...." She didn't say anything. "You treated me well," she finally finished.

Baby, I could treat you so much better. All Des had to do was tell me that she wanted more from me and Rayven would be gone. Des would always be a dream that would never come true for me.

"I am not going anywhere, Desiree."

"In a sense, you are." She gave me a sad look. I didn't like it.

I closed my eyes because I hated this moment.

"Des..." I just wanted to kiss her, but I didn't. Surprisingly, she leaned over and kissed me. It was short and gentle. It made my heart ache. It felt right to me. Why couldn't she feel the way I felt?

"Bye, Q." She stood abruptly and backed towards the door.

"Goodnight, Des."

I didn't get any sleep.

Desiree

I came home one Thursday night hyped up because I didn't have to work the next day. I was ready to kick off my three day weekend by getting into something.

My mood dropped when I saw there was a letter.

Desiree,

So how do you feel about Quinton and Rayven? You are better than both of them, my love.

Missing You,
The One

I didn't feel afraid when I should have. I was hurt. How dare this creep toy with my emotions? As always, I shook it off, though.

I kicked off my shoes and grabbed my phone. I would call Ray to see what she was getting into. Maybe I could convince her to get dinner with me. We had not hung out in a while.

"Hello." She picked up on the second ring as if she was expecting a call. Quinton's perhaps.

"Hey, Sunray."

"Oh, hey." She sounded disappointed. I was confused to why because she obviously had caller ID.

"Am I bothering you?"

"No, Des. Why would you ask me that?" She didn't sound too convincing. "What are you up to?"

"Nothing. I wanted to get into something. Do you have plans?"

"Actually, yes. Quinton's coming over. He is going to cook for me." He use to cook for me, I thought.

"Oh." There was nothing else I could say. "Well never mind."

"We should get into something tomorrow." I knew Quinton had plans tomorrow, so she would be free. I wasn't going for that.

"I have a date," I lied.

"Oh really, with who?"

"Someone I met at a dinner party."

"Oh okay, well maybe Saturday then?"

"Maybe. I will let you go then."

"I don't have to rush off the phone, Des."

"Someone's actually at the door," I lied.

"Oh okay. Well talk to you later."

"Bye, Rayven."

Why did I just lie to my best friend? I don't know. My jealousy consumed me. I still could not understand why I was so bitter about the situation, but admittedly, I needed to get myself in check before I caused unnecessary drama.

"Oh well." Alone or not, I still wanted to do something. I took off my suit and hopped into the shower. I found myself putting on some shorts, a sheer tank and some stilettoes I had never worn. Maybe I would go dine alone.

I opened the door and slammed into Tyler. He smiled as he obviously gave me a once over. I blushed, but smiled back as I took in his T-shirt, jeans and fitted. He sure did looked good in hats.

"Desiree, where are you heading looking like that?"

"Nowhere of importance. Can't I just dress up?" I shrugged.

"Of course you can."

"Thank you, what are you doing here?"

"Is Quinton here?"

"Nope. I don't think he will be back for a while."

"Why? He doing something with Rayven?"

"Yep."

"I see. It's hard catching up with that man these days."

"Who are you telling? I live with him and I barely see him."

"So nowhere of importance, huh? Would you like to have dinner with me? You look hungry."

"How do I look hungry?" I laughed.

"I don't know. I just want you to come with me."

"Oh okay." My heart fluttered a little. Tyler and I didn't hang out alone too often. I did need something to take my mind off of Quinton and Rayven, though. "Sure, Tyler."

We went to Outback. The food was on point. The conversation was nice. Tyler had me laughing the entire time and I appreciated it. I needed this for my sanity.

I reached for my check when it came.

"No." He beat me to it. "I asked you to come with me."

"Yeah, but…"

"Be quiet, Desiree. Can you sit back and be taken care of for once. I am aware of you having the ability to take care of yourself, but I wanted to do this." I sat back and stared at him.

"Okay, thank you."

"You are welcome," he said, giving me this intense stare I was intimidated so I looked away. Tyler always had that effect on me.

"What is it that you want in return?"

"Nothing, Des. I just want your company," he smiled. "What kind of man do you think I am?"

I better not say," I joked.

Ty took me home. It was still early, so I invited him inside . I made us drinks and we settled on the couch to watch a movie. The last thing I could remember was him pulling me closer to him. He smells wonderful, I thought. If he wanted to kiss me, I was gamed.

Quinton

I got home around midnight, so I expected Desiree to be in the bed. When I walked in, I heard the TV blaring. Good, I thought, smiling to myself. I headed to the living room to say hi.

I stopped when I saw she wasn't alone. She had company. I had not seen her with anybody in a while. I thought maybe she was taking a break from dating. I guess that was naïve of me. Just because I was not seeing it, didn't mean she was not doing it.

I was about to let them be, but the dude moved his arm. I recognized the watch. What! I couldn't believe what I was seeing.

I walked closer and sure enough, it was T. They were both asleep and cuddled up on the couch. For a minute, I stopped breathing. This wasn't happening to me. My best friend could not be hooking up with my woman. The woman I couldn't have.

I was livid. It took everything in me not to grab him. I wanted to punch him in his face. How could he do this to me?

However, they were still fully dressed. That meant that they had not crossed that line. At least I hoped not.

I was confused because I did not see his car. I walked to the door and saw that a car was parked in the street near Des's mailbox. Suddenly, I remembered that Tyler said that he was driving a rental while his ride was being serviced. Still, how did I not notice?

I walked back to the couch and starting shaking him. I shook him more violently than I should have. I didn't care.

"Damn, Q. You don't have to shake me so hard."

"You wouldn't wake up."

"Stop lying. I just fell asleep."

"It's pretty late, T."

"I guess I should go." Yeah, you should. "Babe, wake up."

"Okay," she said, stirring.

"You want me to carry you." If he set so much as one foot near her bedroom, I was going to stick my foot up his ass.

"I think I am okay." She jumped up quickly. He stood and they both hugged. I didn't even want to look. If they kissed, I would lose it. That would be a nightmare.

"Thank you, Tyler."

"No problem. I will call you." For what?

"Okay." She smiled at him. She then threw her arms around me as she walked past. It felt wonderful.

"Goodnight, Quinton."

"Sweet dreams, Des." We both watched her leave the room. "Whats up, T?" I asked when she shut her bedroom door.

"Not much. How's your girl, Rayven?"

"She is cool. What are you doing here?"

"Des and I were chilling."

"I see that!" I snapped. "What kind of chilling?"

"Nothing like that," he said, frowning. "We were just chilling, Q. We are friends. Admittedly, I am not as close with Des as you are." And you will never be, I thought. "I am working on changing that."

"What are you up to?"

"Look, I came here looking for you. You weren't here. We both had nothing better to do, so we went to get something to eat. We came back here and Desiree invited me in. We watched a movie. What is wrong with that?"

"Nothing, I was curious."

"You seem agitated."

"Nope. You said nothing happened."

"What if it did?"

"It didn't, though."

"Look, so you that you know, I asked Desiree out and she said yes. I suppose that you are going to have a problem with that."

"What!" I wanted to throw up.

"I think you heard me, Quinton."

"I didn't realize that you were interested in Desiree." Well, he did tell me he was at the beach, but I guess I didn't take him seriously. This could not be happening. What had I done to deserve this? Was God angry with me?

"Now you do. Why is it a concern of yours?"

"She is my friend." And the woman who I was crazy about.

"What are we? I am your friend, Q. Why can't you be happy that I have found someone I want to pursue? She means a lot to me."

"Do you have feelings for her?" I asked. I was panicking. I felt as if I was on the verge of an anxiety attack.

"Quinton, I don't know," he said, shrugging. "It's not even that serious yet. Yeah, I like the woman, but right now, I am just trying to see where this could go."

"You are thinking long-term?"

"I don't know, Quinton! We haven't gone out on one date yet. Why are you questioning me? Do you want her for yourself? You appear jealous." I was.

"It will never be like that." That was true.

"Then? Whats the problem?"

"I am not sure if she can handle your reputation." I was reaching, but it was true. Tyler was definitely a ladies man.

"She said yes! Why would she if she couldn't handle it? You really aren't being fair to me." I didn't care. "You have your own reputation, yet Rayven still spends time with you." She wasn't Des.

"Man, you have done way more than I have," I said, getting defensive. I knew he was speaking the truth, but it's not what I wanted to hear. Not right now.

"We are one in the same!" His eyes were blazing. I had made him angry. Good.

"You are right." I admitted. I felt defeated.

"So again, what is the problem? What's the real issue here?"

"I don't want you to hurt her," I admitted. Or me.

"You think that I would hurt Desiree?"

"Yes. Did you really just ask me that?"

"Okay, okay. Considering my track record, I understand where you are coming from. I would be concerned too. Des is different."

"How??"

"Believe me, Quinton; I do care about her unlike half the women in my past." How much did he care about her? "I won't hurt her, I promise. I know she means a lot to you. I don't want to do that to you." Too late. I was already devastated.

"Okay, if you say so."

"Cool. Its late, so let me get out of here."

"Talk to you later." I followed him straight out of the door.

"Where are you going?"

"To Fridays."

I needed a drink. I couldn't handle all of this right now. I just knew that a drink was the only way that I was going to get to sleep.

I woke up the next morning with the worst headache. I guess it was to be expected after drinking at Friday's and then coming home to continue my pity party with half a bottle of vodka. So much for drowning my sorrows.

I took a quick shower and grabbed the first T-shirt and first pair of jeans I saw. Luckily it matched. I grabbed some Bayers and headed to the kitchen. I headed straight for the fridge, ignoring Desiree who was standing in the middle of the room.

"Well hello to you too," she said, giving me a bewildered looked.

"What's up," I mumbled.

She tried to converse with me, but I wasn't having it. I gave her the cold shoulder. I couldn't talk to her. I couldn't look at her. If I did, I wasn't sure what would come out of my mouth. I was more angry than I thought and I didn't want to blow up at her.

When she realized that I had a serious attitude, she stopped talking. She finally walked out of the room, mumbling, "What is your problem?" She didn't want to know.

I was in a nasty mood the rest of the day. After work, I headed straight home. I was so tense, that I immediately hopped in the shower. I was standing there in daze, trying to feel nothing but the warm water, when she stormed into my bathroom and pulled open my shower door.

"Whats up?" I closed my eyes.

"So what kind of game are we playing today?"

"Desiree, please." I needed for her to go away.

"No, look you are not going to continue to give me the cold shoulder. I am sorry; I thought you had forgiven me?"

"I did."

"Then why are you angry with me? I didn't do anything." I didn't respond. "I talked to T. He said that you didn't seem too happy about us going out. I didn't want to believe it, but now I am guessing that it does have something to do with your attitude."

"I didn't think he was your type."

"How do you know whats my type?"

"You said that you would never date me. T is just like me."

"But he is not you, Quinton. We are too good of friends to ruin our friendship over trying to pursue anything further."

"But you sleep with me, though."

"Yeah, I know." She couldn't really say anything to that.

"Desiree, I just don't want Tyler to hurt you."

"I know that you are concerned for me, but I am grown. I can take care of myself. If I get hurt, it's unfortunate, but I will survive."

"That's impossible for me. It's hard for me not to care."

"I didn't say not to care. Just don't worry."

"I can't do that either."

"Quinton, worry about Quinton."

"I will try."

"Cool, now again, am I forgiven?"

"Yes. I am sorry, Des."

"Thank goodness! Now hurry up and get out of that shower so that you can cook for me. I am starving."

"Alright," I laughed.

She turned to leave the room, but I grabbed her hand.

Desiree

He should not have grabbed my hand. When I turned around, I had to look at him again. I had to take in his nakedness. I had to take in the water and the suds dripping down that perfect body of his. I was turned on.

I sighed. Why did he have to be this beautiful? Why was I this easily mesmerized by him?

I did my best to ignore all of his glory when I first walked into the room. I had entered at my own risk. I knew he was in the shower. When I had confronted him, I was fine, but now I was drooling.

Quinton was staring into my eyes, pleading. Without thinking rationally, I moved towards him. I wanted just one kiss and I would move on. Of course things didn't go the way I intended for them to.

Obviously, he was waiting for me to make the first move. He lifted me and placed me in the shower with him. I should not have, but I let him kiss on my neck. His hands burned through my clothes.

"Quinton, this is wrong." I was moaning, though.

"Feels good to be wrong." He lifted my shirt over my head.

"What are you doing?"

"Getting you naked." I let him unhook my bra. With my mouth, I was protesting, but I was helping him throw my clothes onto the floor until I stood before him naked.

He kissed me roughly. I liked it. When I wrapped my arms around him, he pulled into him. However, I lost my balance, pulling him back with me. I was now pinned against the wall. There was no way out now.

"Quinton, sweetheart, you can't…"

"I love the way you feel," he said, ignoring me. I shivered slightly as his hand lingered between my thighs.

He kissed me again. We made out until the water turned cold. Afterwards, he lifted me and sat me on his floor. We stared at one another as we toweled off. He started to lotion my body, so I began to do the same to him.

He pushed me towards his bed. Quinton then proceeded to give me a massage I wouldn't forget. He massaged me with his hands. With his lips. The combination had me hypnotized. I would have done anything he asked.

I almost fell asleep as I was under his trance. He threw a sheet over me and leaned down to kiss me.

"You relax here. Take a nap. I am going to cook us something. When I am done, I will wake you."

When he woke me up, he handed me a plate of spaghetti. It was delicious. I didn't stop until my plate was empty. I smiled over at him, too shy to ask for more.

When we finished eating, Quinton pulled me close. I snuggled up comfortably to him. I couldn't resist if I tried.

"This is wrong," I said for the second time.

"Says who?" I couldn't answer. We both knew this was not right.

We stayed in bed all night. We watched Showtime. We talked. We made out. We didn't have sex, but it was still a perfect night.

I was supposed to call Sunray, I thought before drifting off to sleep. Oh well. This was better than going to some club.

Sadly, I didn't really think about her. I should have, considering I was in bed with her new man. I may have been horrible, and I may have been selfish, but I didn't care. I couldn't care. What Quinton and I had was so special to me.

I had him first. She took him from me. I took him back.

I couldn't resist his kisses. I couldn't resist his touch. I couldn't resist him. I couldn't say no.

18

Trustworthy

"Blessed is the man who makes the Lord his trust, who does not turn to the proud, to those who go astray after a lie!" *Psalm 40:4*

Desiree

Saturday night was my date with Tyler. He said that he was going to take me to a nice restaurant. After that, he had a big surprise for me. He said that it was going to blow my mind and it wouldn't be a date that I would forget soon.

I did admire his confidence. To me it was sexy. It turned me on. He was not overly cocky where I couldn't deal with him.

I always had a thing for Tyler. I had never wanted to admit it to anyone. I didn't tell Rayven. She didn't know Tyler too well, but if she had of known that he was Quinton's best friend, she would have asked me what I was smoking.

"I don't know, though," I chuckled to myself.

Apparently, her disdain for Quinton was a front after all these years. Secretly, she had been digging him. So if she was going to date Quinton, then she could not say anything about Tyler. As far as I was concerned, they were one in the same.

How could he not have a special place in my heart? He was my high school crush. He was the man who unknowingly took my virginity. That would always mean something.

"And here we are ten years later."

I promised myself that I would never date Tyler. He was not boyfriend material. He didn't want to settle down. He wasn't capable of treating me the way I wanted to be treated.

"So why did I say yes? Why am I going out with this man?"

I knew he was a whore. I knew he had plenty of women lined up. He had broken hearts all over the city. Some of those hearts belong to women I knew.

He was good-looking. He intrigued me. He made me laugh. He treated me well. I just couldn't resist.

What was the harm? I was grown. If I want to go out with a self-proclaimed player, I should be able to without being judged.

Who was judging me? No one, but myself. I was trying to convince myself that it was okay. I was the one with the issue. Tyler was very charming and I didn't want to end up as another statistic.

I needed to chill out. It was not like I was trying to settle down with the man. I just wanted a change of pace. My dating life had been non-existent and I needed to ramp it up. I wanted to know what it felt like to date someone like T. I wasn't trying to be his girlfriend.

Maybe I just wanted to get a piece of that. I laughed to myself. I was curious, but I am not sure if I wanted to sleep with Quinton's best friend again. However; Q was off limits to me now because of my best friend. I shouldn't have to feel guilty.

I got up from my spot on the couch and headed to the shower. It was time to get dolled up. I had to look my best tonight. I was on Tyler's arm and he usually attracted a lot of attention. That meant the spotlight was going to be on me tonight. I didn't just have to impress Tyler, but his many female admirers.

I took a long shower. I rubbed on my shea butter. I sprayed on my sexiest perfume. I put on my skimpiest pink thong and bra. I applied my make-up flawlessly. I wore my hair curly, pinning it up.

I was trying to put on my diamond necklace that complimented my studs and my Pandora bracelet, but because I was nervous, I couldn't close the clasp. I needed help.

"Quinton." I knew he was in his room. "I need your help."

"Okay." Within seconds, he appeared. His eyes grew big as he took in my appearance. I ignored the desire that I saw. "With what?"

"Will you hook this?" I asked, handing him the necklace.

"Wow," he said when I turned around. "A thong?"

"Can't have panty lines."

"I don't think you will have a problem." I held my breath as his hand brushed across my neck. Goosebumps. I really wanted him. "There you go."

"Don't leave me yet." I stepped in my strapless red number. It was mid-thigh length, so not too hoochie. It was daring enough to turn a few heads, but classy enough to make me seem like a lady. "Will you zip me?" He nodded. "Were you shaking?" I asked when he finished.

"Yes."

"Why?" I asked, staring up at him.

"You make me nervous."

"Why?"

"I want you," he said, flatly.

"Don't say that to me," I said, touching my face.

"I am just being honest."

"I know." I smiled at him, but turned away quickly. I sat down and slid my feet into some Jimmy Choos, all the while aware that he was watching me.

I grabbed my clutch and stood in front of the mirror. Was I good enough? I was no supermodel. God knew I had my insecurities, but I think I looked pretty decent tonight.

I turned to Quinton in hopes of an honest answer.

"How do I look, Quinton? Be honest with me."

"You look beautiful as always."

"Are you sure?" I didn't believe him.

"Are you really asking me this, Desiree?"

"Yes. Why?"

"You're gorgeous and you know it." Did he roll his eyes?

"Okay, thank you."

I could tell that he was in bad mood. I was going to leave him alone. I didn't have the time to deal with him.

I was thankful for the doorbell. It gave me a reason to get away from him.

"Bye, Quinton," I said, walking out of my own room and leaving him behind. "Thank you. You are always so helpful."

"Hey, Tyler," I said, opening the door.

"Wow, Desiree, you are breathtaking."

"Thank you," I looked down because my face started to burn.

"Are you ready?"

"I sure am."

He looked good. He was in a nice gray suit that fitted him perfectly. Even in his tailored suit, you could tell he had quite a body.

I smiled as he grabbed my hand and led me to his car. I was surprised to feel his hands were clammy. I could feel him shaking.

"Tyler, are you nervous?"

"Yeah, I am. Thanks for calling me out."

"Why?" I asked, stopping in my tracks.

"I am under a lot of pressure. I am trying to impress you. Make you happy. I want to have you hooked by the end of the night."

"Maybe, I am already hooked," I admitted. I leaned over and kissed his cheek before sliding into the passenger seat. "Relax."

"Okay," he said, giving me an appreciative smile.

Quinton

Did she really just walk out of here with my best friend? Was she really going to be with him all night? She was with him, not me. I felt like crap.

I had a headache all day. From the moment she woke up, Des was grinning. Her eyes were bright with excitement.

"It's going to be a great day," she blurted to me with a huge smile. She sipped her orange juice and stared out into space.

"How so?" I asked, curiously.

"I can just imagine," she said, shrugging at me.

I knew then that her happiness was over Tyler. I had a sister, so I recognized that look. It was always over some dude.

She was giddy the rest of the day. Every time I looked at her, she had this dreamy look in her eyes. The happier she got, the more irritated I felt. I couldn't understand why she was so happy about going out with my boy. He wasn't worth anything.

How could this happen to me? I wanted this woman for years. I fell in love with this woman. Loving this woman almost destroyed me and my relationship with all women. She hurt me and I had to push all of that aside so that I could salvage our friendship.

I had struggled. Some days were better than others. I tried to never act on my feelings. I always wanted to make a move, but I wouldn't. I stayed away as I should have.

I get here and the game changed. She looked at me and I was trapped inside her prison. She was the warden and she had the only key. I was trying to escape, but was failing, slowly losing my mind in the process.

She kissed me that night and it was all over for me. It felt too good. It felt right. And then there was the sex. There weren't many words to describe it. And there was a nagging feeling telling me that the fire was still burning between us. It wasn't over.

"I don't want to ruin our friendship." I could hear her voice over and over in my head. I had news for her; our friendship would never be the same. Didn't she know that friends made the best lovers?

"We would be so good together." No matter how hard I tried, I could never convince her of that.

I couldn't believe how beautiful she looked as she walked out of here. That red dress was so sexy. She wore her hair up which she never did. And I couldn't forget what was under that dress if I tried

"Oh, Lord, help me," I pleaded, dropping my head into my hands. My head was pounding harder by the minute. I fell back on the bed. Now my stomach was hurting.

Ty was a whore. And despite his reputation, Des still chose to hang on to his arm. Meanwhile, she consumed my heart. At this point, I wasn't sure how I was going to win it back from her. Prayer.

Realizing that I was still in Desiree's room, I stood and headed to mine. I grabbed my car keys, deciding that I needed to get out of this house. I was contributing to my own headache by thinking of what Tyler and Desiree was doing. I needed to focus on me.

I headed to Rayven's. Initially, I had plans, but I canceled. I called Rayven and asked if she wanted to do something. She quickly accepted. At first I was down for it, but right now I wasn't quite sure if I was in the mood. Regardless, I was going to do it. I needed to have a good time with Rayven for my sanity.

When she opened the door, she immediately threw her arms around me and kissed me. It felt wonderful. I felt as if she wanted to be with me, although, I was unsure of how much I wanted to be with her. I liked the girl, but whenever we were together, the thoughts of Desiree were overshadowing. That had to be a sign.

Why couldn't I concentrate solely on Rayven? She was just as beautiful. She had everything going for her. She was smart, funny and kept it real, which I loved in a woman. She was the perfect woman. Just not the perfect woman for me.

"I am hungry," she said, finally pulling away from me.

"Okay me too." I wasn't really. "Let's go."

Dinner was good. I didn't think about Des. The food was on point. Rayven and I were vibing. The chemistry was flowing nicely. She sat closely to me which made it impossible for me to think of anything else but her. For a rare moment I was feeling good about her. I left the restaurant with a smile on my face.

Neither of us could think of anything else to do, so we stopped for some wine and headed back to her place. We watched a romantic comedy from her collection. Everything was going nicely for a while. We were laughing, we were snuggling and I was feeling better about things. After the movie, she climbed into my lap and we made out for a while. When she moved away, things changed for the worst.

"Where's Des tonight." Thanks Rayven. I had been doing well.

"She's on a date."

"With who?" she asked, her eyes stretched wide.

"With Tyler." I shifted uncomfortably in my seat.

"Tyler? Your Tyler?"

"Yep."

"Wow. When did they start dating?"

"Recently."

"She didn't tell me."

"She doesn't seem to tell you anything," I joked.

"That's not funny, Quinton."

"I am sorry."

She had messed up my head again. All I could focus on was the two of them together. What was Tyler doing with my girl now? Was he spitting his game, trying to get her hooked as he called it?

Had Tyler seen that little lacy pink number? I didn't want to think about them being in bed together. I could even stomach the thought of Tyler touching her the way I had. Or the thought of Desiree kissing him the way that she had kissed me many times.

I was no good after that. I could barely say anything. Rayven did most of the talking. I pretended to listen. When she asked me questions, I managed to answer. I couldn't formulate much more than that because the image of my best friend and the only woman I had ever loved kept running through my head. Right now, I hated Tyler.

Finally Rayven asked, "What's your problem, Quinton?"

"I don't have a problem?"

"Oh, yes you do. All of a sudden, you are in a pissy mood. Since I brought Des's name up, you have barely opened your mouth." I loved her realness, but I hated when she called me out.

"Not true,' I lied. "What does Des have to do with anything?"

"That's what I am wondering"

"You are not making sense, baby."

"Oh, I think you understand me. Are you jealous, Quinton? I am convinced that you still have this thing for her."

"That's not true. Why are you tripping tonight?"

"Am I tripping? Or am I hitting close to home?" She stood and so did I.

"Why would I be with you Rayven if I had a thing for Desiree?

"I don't know why!"

"Come here," I said, pulling her to me. "I want to be with Rayven right now."

"Okay," She definitely looked at me as if she didn't believe me, but she kissed me anyway. The next thing I knew, she was pushing me on her couch.

"I don't know what else is on your mind then, but you need to get it out of your head. You need to focus on this, she said, pulling her dress over her head. Within moments, she stood naked in front of me, offering me something that I could not resist.

I stood, lifted her in my arms, and headed to her bedroom. I was going to let her give me something else to focus on. I needed this. If this couldn't make me forget Desiree Harris, nothing could. But then again, this didn't work the first time either.

Desiree

When Tyler brought me home, he laid a sweet lingering kiss on my lips. He told me that I was perfect and that he had a wonderful time. He was going to call me at 3:00 tomorrow.

"I am not playing around with you, Desiree. I really like you. You are too wonderful to let get away."

I walked into the house with a big smile on my face. Tyler had been very good to me tonight. He was a gentleman, opening every door, pulling out my chair and giving me his jacket when I grew chilly. He kissed me until my knees buckled.

I had to calm down. This was the first date. All men were on their best behavior in the beginning. That could have been his representative. Men treated you like a queen in the beginning, but after months and years, you prayed that they would even notice you.

Until the day Tyler got comfortable and started to act up, I was going to hang in there with him. I wanted to see if he could make me happy. I am not sure if Tyler would make a good boyfriend, but maybe I could try him out. I was ready to settle down and he appeared eager to be with me. I could get a man. The problem was hooking the right one.

I was pretty sure that Tyler was not the right man, but right now I was infatuated. He had me hooked.

I had a great time. He had gone out of his way to impress me. I appreciated all the effort that he put into planning our first date. He was right; I was not going to soon forget it.

He took me to Mikel's Café. It was a huge extravagant dining room with three levels. We sat on the top level in an intimate booth. We stared up at the stars through a glass ceiling. We held hands across candlelight. It was all very romantic.

The restaurant was very soulful. Old school R&B jams played continuously in the background. When I opened the menu, I saw names like Mama Gayle's Garlic and Buttered Potatoes, Uncle Frank's Oven Fried Chicken, and Aunt Paula's Fried Salmon Patties. I was overwhelmed.

The food was delicious. It tasted as if everything was cooked by your favorite southern grandma who had spent many years in the kitchen, perfecting southern comfort food. Over Uncle Gary's Garlic Bread, Aunt Lolo's Grilled Chicken, Cousin Fred's Collard Greens, Big Mama's Macaroni & Cheese, Cousin Annie's Peach Cobbler and Papa's Sweet Ice Tea, I asked Tyler, "How did you find this place?"

"Family friends. I was asking around about somewhere nice to bring you. I didn't want to take you the same old places. You could go to Olive Garden or Red Lobster anytime. You were too special not to bring you here," he said, grabbing my hand.

He complimented me all night. He was charming, telling me what I wanted to hear. I blushed the entire night , feeling like I did when I was sixteen-year-old. Giddy.

He told me that I was beautiful. That my eyes were pretty. That I smelled good. That my smile was sexy. I looked gorgeous in my dress. He loved my hair.

The conversation flowed. He asked me questions. He seemed genuinely interested in me. I was interested in him, finding him hilarious at times. I hung on to his every word, holding my stomach because I was laughing so hard.

After dinner, Tyler surprised me by taking me to an Alvin Ailey dance show. I didn't know they were in town. I was touched because I didn't realize that he knew that I loved Alvin Ailey or dance.

"How did you get tickets?" I asked in shock. I wanted to cry.

"Connections."

"How did you know that I like Alvin Ailey?"

"I know more about you than you think, sweetheart. You were a dancer, right?"

"Yes. How…"

"I just know, baby. I did some research."

"Thank you." I leaned over and kissed him without thinking.

"Wow." He blushed. That made me smile. "Save that for later." That made me blush. Again.

He didn't make any moves on me. I had mixed emotions about that one. I was happy that he didn't just want to have sex with me. He was trying to prove to me that he wanted more. At the same time, I was annoyed because I was hungry for a little action.

He didn't disappoint with the goodnight kiss. He kissed me for five minutes outside my door. I melted in his arms. I was smiling as he walked away.

Here I was sitting in my tub filled to the top with bubbles. I was replaying tonight's events over and over in my head. I was trying to analyze how much he liked me. Coming to the conclusion that he liked me as much as I liked him, I kept smiling.

I stood when the water turned cold. I toweled off and rubbed on my Shea Butter. I found a favorite little black gown. I knew it was wrong, but I was going to give Q an eyeful. I headed to the kitchen, stopping by his bedroom to see if he had returned. Of course not.

I sighed. I am sure he was still with Rayven. I am sure that my best friend had her legs wrapped around him. I had a feeling that they had been intimate. That killed me.

When I found myself storming to the kitchen, I stopped.

"Don't be jealous," I whispered fiercely to myself.

Shamefully, I was planning on getting Tyler in my bed very soon. And then Quinton would be forgotten. That was wishful thinking. I doubted it was going to be that easy.

I had just settled on my couch with a bowl of ice cream, in front of my TV, when he walked through the door. He walked into my living room without his shirt, smelling fresh out of the shower. I stared at him and he stared back.

"What's up?" I asked.

"Not much. With you?"

"I am chilling. Where's your shirt?"

"Where's yours?" He asked, obviously taking in my appearance.

"I am comfortable."

"Well so am I." He sat down beside me. Please don't sit here!

We sat in silence for a few moments before he asked, "How was your night?"

"Really nice actually. Yours?"

"Good."

"Did you just shower?"

"I did."

"Why?"

"Sweaty."

They had sex! Don't get jealous, I urged myself. I didn't want to show him a reaction, so I started shoving ice cream down my throat.

"Stop that." He finally took the bowl out of my hand.

"Thanks, Quinton, I wasn't eating that." We stared at each other. He could see through my distraction "Did you sleep with my best friend?" He looked away and sighed. He didn't want to answer the question. He didn't have to. I knew the answer.

"Yes, I had sex with Rayven. How does that make you feel?"

"I don't really like that," I admitted. "I am jealous." His eyes grew wide as if my admission surprised him.

"Why?"

"I don't want you having sex with my best friend."

"You said we should be together."

"That was before us." He continued to stare at me as if he didn't know how to respond. I saw something unrecognizable in his eyes.

"I had to tonight, Desiree."

"Why did you have to?"

"I couldn't stop thinking about you."

"Why were you thinking about me?"

"I am always thinking about you."

"Why?"

"I don't want to answer that question."

"Okay." We both sat there, looking anywhere but each other.

"Desiree, I don't want you sleeping with my best friend either."

"You don't? Why?"

"I am jealous too. I know I can't stop you."

"I haven't slept with Tyler, yet." His eyes grew wide.

"You sound as if you like him."

"I do." More silence.

I didn't expect him to jump on me, but he did. He pushed me back on the couch. He kissed me was so much raw passion that it almost scared me. I loved it though. I placed my hand on his cheek and he just stared down at me.

"Quinton." I closed my eyes, my forehead on his shoulder as he reached down and slid my underwear off.

"I'm always hungry for you, Des."

"You really shouldn't be."

"How do I stop?"

"I don't know."

He kissed me for a long time as his hands lingered between my thighs. We both wanted so much more but we didn't take it there. It was hard. The chemistry between us was threatening to explode.

He laid his head against my breast and I rubbed his bald head.

"What are we going to do?" I asked him.

"I don't know." Silence. "Des?"

"Yes."

"I love you so much. Please don't you ever forget that?'

"I love you too." I wanted to cry.

He finally jumped up from me as if he didn't like what I said. It startled me. I jumped up behind him. We stared at each other. I didn't expect to see the hurt in his eyes.

"Quinton..." I went to touch him, but he stepped back. "I am sorry," I mumbled. He moved towards me and I stepped back. "You are right. Maybe we both need to walk away right now. Stay away for a while." This was killing me.

"I don't like that, but I will do it, Des." He leaned over and gave me a sweet kiss. His lips lingered on mine for a moment. I wanted to pull him to me and just melt, but I didn't. "Goodnight."

I kept my eyes closed until he walked away. I then headed to my room. I cried until I fell asleep.

Quinton

I lay in my bed wide awake wondering if she was doing the same. I knew she was not nearly as crazy as I was at that moment. I thought Rayven and I had a great night and I came home feeling optimistic. I took one looked at Desiree's face and I lost it. My heart ached immediately. She was the woman my heart yearned for.

I wanted her in my arms and she told me to stay away.

"I hate this!"

I scared myself in the living room on the couch with her. I told her I loved her, but she would never realize to what extent. I just knew that no other arms in this world could be as comforting to me. No lips as intoxicating.

I jumped up from her because I couldn't breathe. My heart was broken and I didn't know how to heal it. Yes, it would be better if I stayed away, but the thought of not being near her, depressed me.

I turned on the TV and finally fell asleep.

I did stay away from Desiree like she asked. I didn't really hang around her house when I knew she was home. I was either at the station, at my parents, with my son, or with Rayven. I found myself staying over Rayven's house on most nights. I had to in order to control my emotions. It was the only way I could stay faithful.

One day after work, I walked into the house and there she was. I almost walked out. I had to be a man about this, though. I took some deep breaths and found the courage to stay. I headed to the kitchen where I knew she was at.

She was at the sink in just a Charlotte Bobcats basketball jersey. I stared at her back, longing. I wanted her affection. I wanted her to love me. I wanted her to be my woman. Right now, I felt as if I was losing her when she wasn't mine to lose.

"What are you doing here this time of day?" I finally asked.

"Oh, hey," she said, turning towards me. She smiled at me as if nothing was weird between us. Then again, maybe it was just me. Maybe I was reading too much into things. "I got off early."

"Are you sick?"

"No, I am fine,' she said, turning back towards some food that she was obviously preparing.

"Cool." I had crossed the room before I knew it I stood behind her, balling my fist to keep from wrapping my arms around his waist. 'What are you making?"

"A salad, biscuits, potatoes, chicken. Tyler is coming over," she offered as if I wanted to hear that. It killed me that she was doing all of this for him.

"Oh okay." I was actually relieved when my phone rung. Unfortunately, it was India. Drama.

Desiree

Things were going great between Tyler and I. He was no Quinton, but I enjoyed our time together. He was proving to be a great distraction. I could tell he was trying hard to be a good man for me and I appreciated that. Most days, I was still missing Q and I was insanely jealous over what he was sharing with Rayven, but I did like Tyler. I was hoping one day soon that Q and Ray would no longer be a factor for me.

Tyler came over that night. We ate dinner and then we snuggled up together on the couch. I wanted desperately for him to make a move on me. We had not done much more than kiss, but shamefully I wanted more from him. I didn't want to push him, though. I could tell he was trying to prove to me that this was more than something physical. He was really trying to make it work with me.

However, I found myself climbing into his lap. I was trying to move things along. I figured he needed a little help. He took the bait.

He pushed me down on the couch and proceeded to yank on my clothes. I closed my eyes as his hands moved feverishly over me. My breath quicken when he began leaving a hot trail of kisses down my body. I was burning up and loving every moment.

"Desiree. You are so beautiful," He whispered, stopping to stare at me for a moment.

"Thank you." I pulled him back to me and begin yanking on his clothes. I was excited that he was about to give me what I had been longing for from him. He loved me once when he was a boy, but I wanted to see how Tyler the man could please me.

I was disappointed when he stopped and pulled away.

"What are you doing?" I was frustrated.

"We should stop."

"Why? You are taking this let's wait a while thing a little too far."

"Desiree. This is not good idea." I pushed him away and begin grabbing my clothes. I wanted to cover up. I felt humiliated.

He grabbed my hand.

"Desiree, have you told Quinton about us in high school." It was the first time either of us had ever mentioned it.

"Why are you bringing Quinton up?" Now, I was annoyed.

"Answer the question."

"No, I haven't. Have you?" I didn't know how to bring it up.

"No." He let go of my hand and sat back on the couch. I closed my eyes. A headache was coming.

"What do you want to do, Tyler?"

"I want to be with you, Desiree, but before we take it there, we need to talk to him."

"Why?"

"Desiree. Quinton has a right to know. It's been bothering me lately. I want to know that he is okay with us going further." For goodness sake, why? Quinton didn't think about me when he decided to take things further with Rayven.

I didn't say that, though. I could tell that this was bothering Tyler. I could see guilt in his eyes. I didn't want him to struggle.

"I can't bring it up to him, Tyler." The thought of discussing that moment with Quinton terrified me. Tyler didn't know that Quinton and I had been intimate as well.

"I will do it, Des."

"Good."

"I need to do this okay," he said, pulling me to him. "I hope that you can understand where I am coming from."

"Okay."

"And hopefully everything will be cool and we can concentrate on us." I wasn't quite sure if that was going to work out in his favor, but I didn't say anything. We would do things his way.

Quinton

I didn't feel like talking to Tyler these days, but he insisted that we talk. About what? He had decided to date Desiree despite how nervous that made me. Then again, I don't think Tyler truly knew how I felt about her. He didn't know that I was struggling to get over her while being in a relationship with her best friend.

"Whats this about, T?" We had met up at the basketball court. I figured the exercise from throwing the ball around would be beneficial considering how stressed I had been.

"Quinton, there's something I need to tell you. I have been keeping something from you a while. I hope that we can move past this, but I need to take the risk because it's been eating me up."

"Whats this about, Tyler?" I could see something was bothering him and I didn't like where this conversation was headed.

"Desiree." I felt sick to my stomach.

"What about her?" He was the last person I wanted to discuss Desiree with. He had won her and I hadn't. Why torture me?

"In high school, something happened between us." I stared at him. I closed my eyes because I didn't want to imagine what he was about to tell me. I knew I wasn't going to like it.

"What happened?"

"We had sex." I stared at him. I felt as if he had thrown the ball into my stomach. I wanted to throw up. I couldn't find words. "Q."

"What do you mean, you had sex with Desiree." Why was this happening to me? "When?"

"Prom." I closed my eyes. I knew what that meant.

"You are the one who took her virginity?" I couldn't help myself, I blurted it out.

"What! I don't know about that…."

"She lost her virginity at prom." His eyes grew big and then he looked away.

"I didn't know that, Q."

"It doesn't matter!" Of course it did. No wonder, Tyler was so special to her. He would always be in her heart.

I wanted to cry. I turned away because I didn't want him to see how much I was hurting. This was a nightmare.

"I am sorry, Q."

"Why the hell, didn't you tell me?"

"I didn't know how. I liked Desiree, but we didn't go further in high school. I was scared. I don't think she wanted you to know."

How could Desiree keep this from me? I was started to question everything. I was questioning my significance in her life.

"Do you forgive me?"

I hated him. I hated him for being with the only woman I had ever loved, but Tyler didn't know my heart. I couldn't hold that against him. I couldn't end my friendship over this.

"It is what it is," I said, quietly.

"Quinton, if me being with Desiree is painful for you, just tell me. I don't want this to come between us."

"I'm good."

"I don't believe you."

"Let it go, T."

This was one of the worst days of my life.

For the next couple of weeks, I continued to ignore Desiree as much as I could. With the way I was feeling these days, I didn't have much to say to her. However, everything exploded one weekend when Tyler, Desiree, and Rayven wanted to double date. I was forced to sit there and watch Desiree and Tyler interact in my face. I had never dreaded anything so much in my life. I wasn't sure if I could do it, but I was going to try. They were my closest friends.

Our little date didn't end so well. Desiree ended up storming out of the restaurant and I was ready to kick someone's ass. I was not pissed for myself, but for Desiree. I didn't like anyone hurting her.

We were at the Cheesecake Factory, trying to pretend things weren't weird between the four of us. I was on edge, but everything seemed to be going well. No one else appeared to be as nervous or uneasy with this situation as I was. While everyone else conversed, I sat there in my own world. I tried desperately not to look at Desiree because I didn't want to get lost in her eyes.

The drama erupted when Desiree accidentally picked up Rayven's phone which was identical to hers. She looked down at the phone and then suddenly looked up with rage in her eyes. When Rayven realized Desiree's mistake, her face grew red. She dropped her face into her hands

"What's going on?" I spoke up.

"You and Tyler have been texting! About going out!"

"What!" I looked over at Tyler and he just threw his head back.

"I can explain, Des," said Rayven. There was fear in her eyes. Why did people say they could explain when they couldn't?

"Explain then!" When she didn't say anything, Desiree turned to Tyler. "Can you explain?"

"I…"

"I didn't think so." She stood and so did I. "Why have you been bullshitting me this last month, Tyler? Why waste my time? I thought you had change. You are who I thought you were."

"Des, please listen. I haven't, I…"

"Shut up! Rayven, you are supposed to be my girl. You are supposed to put me before a man!"

"Des, you are everything to me. I…."

"There's nothing else for you to say to me!"

No one expected Des to throw her water in Tyler's face. He looked stunned. Rayven covered her mouth with her hands. Desiree stormed away. Tyler stood to go after her, but I pushed him down.

"Stay away from her." I started towards the door, but turned back. "Rayven, you could have put a stop to our charade because we weren't working out anyway. You didn't have to do Des like that."

"As for you, T. I want to kill you right now, but I am not trying to go to jail tonight. If you want Rayven, have her. I don't really care, but I asked you not to hurt Desiree and what did you do? You messed up like you always do."

"Quinton," he said, standing again.

"Nope, don't say anything. I suggest that you both stay away from us." When I turned to walk away, Tyler grabbed my shoulder. "Man, your best bet is not to touch me right now. I guess you two can handle the bill. I mean it's the least you can do."

Desiree was outside, leaning against the wall. Her arms were crossed. There was rage in her eyes, but there were no tears. She was shaking. That scared me because it was eighty-five degrees outside.

"I figured that you would come eventually."

"Let's go home," I said, sliding my arm around her waist. Neither of us spoke on the car ride home. She clung to my hand. It felt as if she was going to break my fingers, but I didn't say anything.

"I am going to take a shower," she announced to me.

"Okay." I did the same.

I was in the kitchen waiting with a roll of cookie dough when she walked in. When she saw it, she stopped dead in her tracks.

'How did you know that I wanted that?"

"Because I know you. It's your comfort food, right." The tears finally came. She walked over to me and wrapped herself in my arms.

"I am sorry," I whispered.

"It's okay."

"I know you really liked T and..."

"I didn't like him that much. It's just the principle of the matter. Rayven is my best friend. I am supposed to be able to trust her."

"You are right."

"I just want someone to love me and only me."

"Des..." If I knew telling her that I adored her would make her feel better, I would have told her.

"Every man wants to play me, cheat on me, or run away from me. Is anybody going to stay?" I never wanted to leave her.

"You just haven't found the right man to treat you the way you should be treated."

"Quinton, when is it my turn?"

"Soon, I am sure."

"How come you are not upset?"

"Desiree, Rayven is not the girl for me. You were wrong there."

"I sure was!"

"All I care about is that they hurt you."

"You are the sweetest,' she said, finally looking up at me.

I leaned down to kiss a tear away. My lips found hers and I couldn't help myself. I held her in my arms and kissed her as if she was precious. I wanted to kiss her pain away.

I was leaving the station on Monday when I found Tyler and Rayven waiting for me beside my car.

"Q, we really need to talk to you." Tyler spoke up.

"I really don't have anything to say to either of you."

"Quinton," said Rayven, "We really need to explain this to you."

"Why is it that you couldn't explain two days ago? Instead, the both of you sat there and looked stupid. Now what are you trying to do? Are you going to stand here and tell me some sad story that you both came up with over the weekend?"

"No!" said Rayven. "We got caught. We were stunned."

"Okay."

"Can we explain?" Tyler was pleading with me.

"Talk, Tyler." I was being too nice to both of them

"One day last week, we ran into each other and we talked over an hour about you and Desiree. We both had to face reality."

"That doesn't tell me why you two were texting each other about hooking up, Tyler."

"We hit it off, Quinton."

"Whatever. I thought that you hit off with Desiree."

"I really like her, but so do you. It's time for y'all to stop playing around. Just be together if that's what you both want.."

"You don't know what you are saying."

"Q, when I told you Des and I was going out, you were jealous. I was scared that you were going to punch me then. All you had to do was tell me and I wouldn't have messed with her. Why didn't you tell me? I never felt right being with her. I feel like I hurt you."

"I wasn't jealous."

"You are lying, Quinton" said Rayven. "That night when Ty and Des when out, you were devastated. You could barely look at me. You barely talked to me."

"So." I didn't know how to respond.

"I knew you were thinking about her the entire night."

"No." I really was. I couldn't admit it, though.

"Yes. I found the nerve to start texting Tyler because I knew you didn't really want to be with me. I was getting tired of being second best. I will always be second best to Des, Quinton." She was right. "You were right, Quinton, we weren't working out."

"What's your excuse, T. How did you find the nerve?"

"Q, you are my best friend. I didn't want to hurt you. I see the way that you look at her. You lied to me. You told me that you were playing about Desiree in college. I believed that for a while."

"So," I shrugged. "It still doesn't really make what happen right. What does all of this have to do with the present?"

"Everything," said Rayven. "You never got over her."

"Rayven, how many times do I have to tell you that I am no longer in love with Desiree?"

"Quinton, how many times are you going to lie about it?"

"Why do I have to be lying?"

"I don't know why you have to lie."

I stood and stared at her for a moment. I was trying to think of the best way to respond. All of this was stressing me out. Maybe, it was time to be honest, I thought.

"What if I am not over her? What if I do have some feelings for her? What if I was jealous? Or hurt? Or thinking about her when I was with you? None of that means anything or makes a difference."

"Of course it does."

"How? Desiree doesn't have any feelings for me."

"Sure she does. How would you know?"

"She practically told me."

"Okay, so why was she upset when I told her that you and I were going out?"

"She wasn't upset."

"She was pissed. I was there."

"That doesn't mean anything."

"You two are intimate."

"Excuse me!"

"You two were intimate! I think you still are!"

"What business is that of yours?"

"Q! Will you tell me the truth! Are you and Des intimate?"

"We have kissed." I shrugged. Why was this happening?

"How long have you two been making love?"

"Huh? We aren't making love." Well, I was. I loved Des in the only way she would allow me to.

"How long!"

"We are not getting it on!" I was trying not to kiss and tell. I wanted to be loyal to Desiree. She didn't want anyone to know.

"She is jealous because you two are intimate and I got in the middle of that." I stared at her for a minute. How did she know this? How could she read me so well? This was crazy.

"Please don't tell her that we talked about that."

"I won't. She is not talking to me," she said, tears sliding down her cheeks. "I know Desiree. It's going to take her forever to forgive me. She may never do so."

"Tell her that I am sorry! That I love her and that I wasn't trying to hurt her. It may be hard to believe, but I was thinking of her happiness. I was letting you go so that she could have you."

"Rayven, that's not going to happen. Nothing more will ever come between us."

"I know Desiree cares about you. You should consider saying something about how you feel." I couldn't.

"I will tell her that you are sorry."

19

Anger Management

"For if you forgive others their trespasses, your heavenly Father will also forgive you, but if you do not forgive others their trespasses, neither will your Father forgive your trespasses." *Matthew 6:14-15*

Quinton

Rayven was right. It was going to take Desiree a long time to forgive her. Whenever Rayven tried to call, Des would not answer the phone or she would just hang it up in her face. If I tried to talk to her about it, she would cut me off. One day, I brought it up, she practically cursed me out.

It got to the point that I thought about telling her about the accusations of us wanting to be together. I was willing to embarrass myself to help save her friendship. As soon as I walked into the room, she let me know what the deal was, though.

"Do I have to keep telling you I do not want to talk about it!"

"I didn't say anything, Desiree."

"You didn't have to. You look guilty."

"Why should I be guilty?"

"I saw her name forming on your lips. I mean it, Quinton. Please don't start with me today."

"Seriously, Desiree," I said, ignoring her request. "Don't you think that you could at least talk to the girl? You two have been friends too long."

"Why should I?"

"That's your best friend."

"A friend that I can't trust."

"But couldn't you just hear her out. I talked to her and Tyler…"

"Oh, so they are a couple now?"

"Are you jealous?" I was finding it difficult to believe that she hadn't caught some feelings for T. He would always hold that special place in her heart. Apparently, she was feeling him in high school.

"No, Quinton, it's not that I am jealous. I am just pissed."

"I don't think that you are being honest with me."

"Oh well," she shrugged. "That's not my problem."

"Why can't you talk to me without getting an attitude, Desiree? Why can't you let me be your friend? Does it really make you feel better to bite my head off every day about this?"

"I am sorry." She didn't mean it.

"What is the main issue here?" I walked over to her.

"I take it that you believed what they had to tell you?" It frustrated me that she didn't answer my question. "What did they say, Quinton?"

"They just made some accusations," I mumbled. "They were pretty crazy. None with any truth to it."

"Then why are you acting as if everything is okay?"

"I can see where they are coming from." I felt nervous.

"Let's see if I can see where they are coming from. What did they say?" I didn't want to go there anymore. I had been willing when I walked into the room, but she just seemed cold and unreceptive.

"Ask Rayven. I think you should listen to her."

"I think you should stay out of my business." Wow. What had I done to her?

"Fine."

"Just tell me!"

"I am going to take your advice. I am staying out of this situation as of now." I turned to walk away, but she grabbed me.

"What did she say?"

"That we wanted to be together. You and I."

"Excuse me!" She frowned. My heart started beating fast. This was going to be humiliating for me.

"They think that you and I want to be together, Desiree." I was feeling so sick. "That we belong together. By being in relationships with either or us, they would be standing in the way of something."

"That's crazy!"

"I mean you kind of set things off when you got mad at Rayven when the two of us started going out."

"I wasn't that mad."

"Bullshit! You wouldn't talk to me for three days. You were jealous. We have already talked about this. Don't lie to me now."

"I…" She could find words. She just bit her lip and stared at me.

"I almost lost my mind when you started going out with Tyler. You already know this. I had sex with Rayven, you were upset." She stared at me blankly. I stepped closer. "Let's be honest, Desiree."

"About what else, Quinton? We were having sex. That's all it was!" I stared at her. That's not what she said previously. It was so much more to me. Her eyes were black with anger. "Say something, Quinton!"

I am not sure what made me flip out on her. It wasn't her fault, but no matter how hard I tried, I could not get over her. I wanted her to hurt like I was doing at this moment.

"I don't understand what I have ever done to you!" She looked confused, almost guilty. "I didn't have anything to do with this, Desiree. It's not my fault that Tyler and Rayven hit it off. I can't help what they think either."

"I guess you are right. We are just having sex. The bottom line is that they know that we are having sex. We were having sex while dating them, so we were wrong too. If you wanted all of this to be a secret, you failed."

"I never said…"

"Don't start the lying either. Respect me." She looked stunned.

"Are you calling me a liar?"

"I didn't call you anything, but you aren't being honest. Why don't we be real? We both were jealous. We looked stupid and they both noticed. And as crazy as their accusations may be, they are valid. To someone who doesn't know better, it seems like it was more than sex as you call it. You may think it's absurd that they think we want to be together, but I don't."

It was half true. I did want to be with her. She didn't want to be with me.

"We know it's not true. We were having sex. You made that clear to me. All that matters is that we know what we were doing."

I couldn't leave it at that. I wanted her to know it was more than sex for me. Taking her to bed was the only way she would allow me to be with her. It was the only way I could express myself.

"Wait, I am not going to tell you what you want to hear. Why does it just have to be sex? I care about you!" Her eyes grew big. "I can't help what they think, Desiree! You can't either. You should be forgiving, though? Don't be mad at them for misunderstanding what was going on between us."

"That's not what I am mad at, Quinton."

"You said they were crazy. You knocked down the accusations."

"Because...." I didn't want to hear her bullshit anymore.

"I know you are mad at them for sneaking around and you should be, but let it go. We were sneaking around too. How many times did we kiss while I was dating your friend?" She looked guilty.

"Rayven is sorry. Tyler is sorry. Don't lose your best friend over this. If they have something between them, we shouldn't stand in the way. I am happy that Rayven and I ended because we weren't working out. We were killing time together. You said you weren't feeling Tyler like that. Unless you were lying to me about that."

"Huh?" Her face was priceless.

"Do you have feelings for him?" I knew the answer.

"What! No!"

"I think that you do." Why me? She chose Anthony and T over me. Out of the three of us, I was the one that wanted to be with her.

"Q!" She looked as if she wanted to cry. I couldn't comfort her.

"I have to go." She spent a matter of weeks with T and she was feeling him like that. She knew me for years. We had been intimate for months and yet, all she saw in me was sex.

"Quinton! Will you please listen to me?"

"No. I have to go. Bye."

I am not sure how I did it, but I stayed away from Desiree in the next week. Maybe it was my pride, my ego, or just me being plain unreasonable, but I avoided her. I didn't see her and I made sure that she didn't see me.

I didn't understand why I was being this way. The day I kissed her, I expected nothing but desire in return. It's not like I expected her to profess her love for me. Why was I tripping this much? Did I expect all that to change with good sex?

God only knew how much I missed her, though. I missed her face. I missed her kisses. I missed her smile. Her voice. Her laughter.

It scared me how much, though. It had only been six days, but it felt like much longer. It was one of the hardest things I had done.

I didn't lay eyes on her until the next Saturday. Somehow we both ended up at the same party. It was at a mutual friend's house. I was in the middle of the living room dancing with this girl, Crystal, having a good time, when she walked in.

I looked up because a group of brothers around me were getting loud. Jamal, a dude I played ball with back in the day, practically knocked me over.

"Q, man, is that Desiree Harris." I turned my head so fast that a sharp pain went through my neck.

"Yeah,' I said, swallowing hard. Why was she here?

"Wow," he said, openly staring at her. "I didn't think she could look better than she did in college."

Des did look beautiful. Her hair was still long, but dyed jet back. She wore white ripped jeans and a fitted pink tank. I loved it.

My heart started beating so fast that I actually grabbed my chest. I felt dizzy. I was starting to sweat. I couldn't breathe. I didn't realize that I had stopped dancing until Crystal poked me in the ribs.

"Hello, what's up. This is my song! Who is she, your ex?"

"What!"

"Bye!" she said, rolling her eyes. She walked away quickly.

I watched three guys walk up to her. It took everything in me not to walk over to her in a jealous rage. I knew right then that I was in for a long night. Des had ruined my night. As always.

I tried dancing with another chick, but I kept turning around every two minutes to find Desiree. There was always some dude in her face. Someone always had their hands on her. I was annoyed.

When the chick finally walked away, I scanned the room for Des, but she was nowhere to be found. I don't know why it made be nervous, but it did. I started to panic. I started pushing through the crowd with only intentions of finding her. Once I did, I didn't have a clue to what I was going to say or do.

I was halfway to the door, when she grabbed my arm.

"Quinton!"

"What's up?" Just like that, I was cold again. I was still very hurt.

"What's up?" She repeated. "How much longer are you going to avoid me, Quinton?"

"What are you talking about, Desiree?"

"How can you ask me that?" Now she looked hurt? Was I taking this thing too far?

"Why don't you calm down?"

"Don't you think that we should talk about what is bothering us?" she asked. She was pleading with me. "I hate this."

"We don't have anything to talk about, Desiree." She looked at me completely dumbfounded. I knew immediately that I hurt her feelings. That didn't settle to well with me. Before I could respond or apologize, I was being pulled away by my friend, Terrence.

I tried to listen to my boy, but I could feel her eyes burning through my back. I turned to look at her and she rolled her eyes. She walked away.

I was on pins and needles. Terrance was talking a mile a minute, but I wasn't hearing anything coming out of his mouth. I thought I was doing a good job at pretending, but he called me out.

'Q, what's up? What's on your mind?"

"I am sorry. I am going to lose my mind. Where did she go?"

"Why didn't you tell me that you were trying to get with her?"

"That's not it," I mumbled.

"You don't have to explain anything to me. That beauty is right over there. Go get her, Q."

She was over there with Jamaal. I didn't like it. I didn't like him touching her. I didn't like when he leaned over to kiss her cheek. Before I could even think about it, I was moving in her direction.

"Q, calm down. Don't start anything," I heard Terrance say.

"I am not starting anything," I mumbled. "Des, I need to talk to you." I pulled her away from Jamaal.

"Q, what are you doing?" Jamaal looked confused.

"What do you think you are doing, Quinton!" Desiree said, angrily pulling away from me.

"What are you doing?"

"I am trying to have a good time. Go away."

"You said that we needed to talk."

"Leave me alone!"

"I can't do that!"

"Why not! You have been doing so for the last six days!"

"Yeah, but now we should talk!"

"No, we don't. Get away from me!"

She turned and headed back to my boy. She embarrassed me. I stared at her but she ignored me. Jamaal started back at me, baffled.

I headed straight for the door. There was no need to hang out here anymore. It would have been near impossible for me to enjoy the rest of the night. I wasn't really trying to get in any fights. I was definitely in a confrontational mood.

I was almost to my car when I heard my name. Terrance.

"Quinton, you can't drive this mad. Calm down for a minute. Wait up." I did. "Are you okay?"

"I'm fine." I had been better, but I didn't want to get into it.

"I am going to be honest. You are looking crazy mad, bruh. I am a little scared of you."

"Well, I am going to be alright.'

"Okay. good." He was quiet for a moment. "Is that your girl?"

"Nope."

"Were you working on that being your girl?"

"Des will never be my girl. It doesn't matter how hard I try."

"Why not?"

"She doesn't feel me like that," I shrugged.

"So you are crushing and she is not?"

"Something like that."

"Does she know you want her this badly?"

"Nope."

"It's pretty obvious."

"She's clueless." She had always been.

"She has to be. Tell her."

"I can't do that, Terrance."

"Why not? You need to. You are all bent out of shape."

"To Desiree, it's just sex." I know I should not have put my business out there like that, but right now I was not thinking clearly.

"What?" Terrance eyes grew big. "You are sleeping with her. I thought you two were just friends."

"It's complicated."

"No wonder you are tripping, Q. Wow, man. I don't know what to say."

"Most dudes would be happy in my situation."

"You are right about that."

"She means a whole lot more to me than some good sex."

"I can see that."

"I wish she could."

"Here she comes. Tell her." Sure enough, Desiree was walking in our direction. She had this look on her face that made me nervous. She stopped directly in front of me. She stood so close that I could smell the mint on her breath.

"Terrance, we need privacy,' she said without looking at my boy.

"Looks that way. I will give you what you need. Talk to you later, Quinton. Keep in touch.'

"Will do." I shook his hand without taking my eyes off her face. He walked away.

"What is wrong with you, Quinton?"

"I am sorry, Desiree."

"Do you even know why you are sorry?"

"I am sorry that I have been in a bad mood, for avoiding you, for causing a scene, for getting you pissed at me."

"Thank you for admitting it. Why were you avoiding me? Why were you so mad at me?" I heard the tremble in her voice. I could see tears forming in her eyes.

"You called it just sex. I didn't like that. I care about you."

"I know," she said, her voice finally softening.

"And I don't think you are being completely honest with me."

"About what?"

"About T. I know it's none of my business, but I don't like you with him. In fact, I hate the idea. He doesn't deserve you. He proved that to you."

"Quinton, you don't understand."

"You seem really upset about it. I know about you two in high school. I know he took your virginity." She nodded and looked away for a moment. After a couple moments, she grabbed my hand.

"I know what this must look like to you. T and I do have a past, but since that moment at prom, nothing has come between us. This may be hard for you to believe, but I don't care about your boy."

"Then can you please just tell me what's wrong."

"I am just tired," she whispered.

"Of what?"

"Of things going wrong for me. I am ready to be loved."

"You deserve that."

"Tyler was a good time, but he is not the one for me. This whole situation with him and Rayven just set something off inside of me."

"I hear you."

"Do you believe me now?"

"Yes."

"Good." I boldly reached for her waist and she let me pull her into my arms. Where she belonged. "Am I unlovable, Quinton?" I almost choked. If only she knew.

"No, baby. Don't believe that for one second."

"I will work on it. What's with you causing a scene?"

"I was jealous. I don't like any other man touching you."

"Why?" she asked, smiling at me.

"You mean that much to me." I pushed hair out of her face.

"Quinton, I have not been with anyone but you since you set foot in my house." I tried not to show her how I relieved I was. I was so happy that she didn't give it up to Tyler again.

"I'm all that you need. I can fulfill all of you needs."

"You think so?"

"I can be your one and only." She laughed, but I was serious. "You mean the world to me. More than you will ever realize."

"Stop it, Quinton," she said, blushing.

"I really mean that," I said, lifting her chin. "I really missed you." I couldn't help it. This woman weakened me.

"You missed me?" she smiled. "It's only been six days."

"And that's too long."

"Well, it's your fault."

"I know. I am so stupid."

"I agree." She leaned in to kiss me. Before she pulled away, I could tell where the night was headed.

"You missed me too?" I joked.

"Don't deprive me again." She ran her finger across my lips.

"I won't."

"Okay. Now take me back inside. I want to dance with you."

We went back to the party. The first person I saw was Terrance. He just gave me a knowing smile. When I walked past Jamaal, he grabbed my shoulder."

"Q, you should have told me that was your girl. I would not have done that to you."

"It's cool."

I just held her in my arms the rest of the night. As far as I was concerned, she belonged there and nowhere else. She felt perfect.

"You have been stressing, right?" I whispered in her ear.

"I have. Why?"

"Come away with me. I have to go to Vegas next week."

"That's right. You told me. For your station, right?"

"Right. Come with me." I wanted her with me. I didn't think that I could stand her being so far away from me for an entire week. I hadn't seen her in the last six days and it almost killed me.

"To Las Vegas! Quinton, I can't do that. I have a job!"

"Tell them that you need to get away. Family emergency."

"Are you serious?"

"Yes. You deserve it. Let me take your mind off of being wronged for a whole a week." She stared at me for a moment. I was glad to see that she was contemplating it.

"Q, I don't know.'

"Will you try? Do it for me."

"I will see what I can do."

"I am not taking no for an answer, sweetheart."

Desiree

A couple days after I resolved my issues with Quinton, I gave Rayven a call. Q was right, this was my best friend. It was time for us to make up.

I could hear the tears in her voice. She was relieved to hear from me. I knew that she had been waiting for me to forgive her, but I kept the conversation really short. I didn't want to get into anything with her over the phone, so I asked her to meet me for lunch the next day. We needed to do this face to face.

Rayven was already at the restaurant when I arrived the next afternoon. I could tell that she was nervous. She was sitting there, twiddling her thumbs. She looked as if she was about to throw up.

"Hey, Rayven." She went to stand, but I quickly put a stop to that. "There is no need for that. I am not that special."

"Okay,' she said, attempting to smile. "How have you been?"

"I have been a little stressed out. Admittedly I have been a little off the wall. Girl, I really have not been myself."

"That's no good, Des!" She all of sudden looked really concerned. "What have I told you about that? You keep it up and you are going to run yourself down."

"I know, I know, but you know me. I am a hard worker."

"Stubborn is more like it."

"Yeah, yeah," I laughed. "I get it from my daddy, I guess."

"I think you need to take a break soon."

"Don't worry; I have been thinking about doing so. My boss knows that I have been acting crazy lately. We are working on something for me. So what's been good with you?"

"The same ole. I am surviving somehow."

"That is all you can do. Have you ordered yet?"

"No, I was waiting on you. It's a wonder that I held off for so long. You won't believe how hungry I am right now."

"Oh, I can believe it. What I can't believe is that you remained a size four after all these years."

"Don't start. You have lost weight!"

"No, I haven't."

"Yes, you have. I am concerned." I believed her because Rayven took notice of everything. She wouldn't lie either. The chick was too real for that.

"Interesting."

"Yes it is. You don't need to lose weight, so get that in check."

"I am not doing it on purpose, but what's the big deal. I could stand to drop a few pounds."

"You have an amazing body. You are voluptuous and curvy. Men love it. I have wanted those titties and that booty for years."

"Oh please!"

"I hate you for it. I use to stuff my bra hanging with you."

"Shut up," I said, laughing loudly. "Let's get the waiter."

"Okay." I flagged the waiter down so we could order. As soon as the girl walked away, Rayven apologized, "I am so sorry, Desiree."

"Look, don't worry about it, Rayven." I woke up this morning and decided that I simply wasn't going to care anymore." I still felt that I was wronged, but I honestly believed that under normal circumstances, Rayven would never betray me. I had to admit that Quinton and I weren't innocent. Our situation made things sticky.

"No, you can't tell me not to worry about it. This is definitely something that I need to apologize to you for. I never meant to hurt you, but I did. I wasn't thinking clearly. I was wrong."

"I have forgiven you, Rayven. It's okay, I promise."

"I know you do, Desiree," she said, shaking her head. "You have the biggest heart that I know. You may forgive me, but I know you don't understand why this happened. I need to explain myself."

"I understand," I mumbled. I wasn't in the mood to hear any of this right now. I just wanted to move past this entire situation.

"No, you don't. Please, Desiree." She was pleading with me.

"Quinton kind of explained," I said, taking a sip of my sweet tea.

"I really want you to hear it from me."

"Okay," I said, slowly. What could I say to that?

"Thank you." I watched as she took a couple deep breaths. "T and I ran into each other a couple weeks ago. We talked about everything. He talked about you and I talked about Q. He told me that he had a feeling that you and Quinton had something going on."

"Why did he feel that way?"

"He told me how the night that he asked you out, Q didn't looked too thrilled. In fact he thought Quinton was going to punch him in his face." Q was so possessive over me. "And then he said when he told Quinton that you two had sex in high school, he looked heartbroken." I didn't know that. Tyler left that out.

'Quinton is very concerned for me, what I can say! He doesn't want anyone to hurt me."

"He seems more than concerned, though. Quinton cares about you like no other woman in his past."

"We have been close since we were ten-years-old."

"You definitely have an undeniable closeness."

"That's okay, isn't it?"

"It is, but you two seem to have more than a friendship."

"It's not more, I promise." She stared at me for a moment. "What! What's that look for?"

"We decided to get some lunch and we continued to talk about our suspicions." She ignored my question. "Before he walked away he asked for my number and I gave it to him. He told me that he was going to use it when the time was right."

"I felt guilty, Desiree. I sat at that table alone for thirty minutes, beating myself up for what I had done. In the end, I convinced myself it was for the best. T and I felt that our relationships with you two were doomed from the beginning. You and Q are not meant to be with us. We don't think either of you wanted to be with us."

"Wow, Rayven."

"I know you, Desiree. You think this is all bull, but it's not." I knew she was telling the truth.

"I understand where you are coming from, considering the situation between Q and I. I know it appears that it's more than it is."

"Are you sure?"

"We are just friends!" Horny friends.

"Okay," she said, slowly. "Well, I am glad that you understand."

"I do. So you and T actually have a connection."

'Yes, we do," she said smiling hard. When I saw the blush on her face and the sparkle in her eyes, I knew there was something special between them. I didn't need to stand in the way of that because I was afraid of being alone.

"Well, I am happy for you. You deserve to be in a healthy and loving relationship. I pray that you will be happy in it."

"Thank you, Des, but so do you," She reached for my hand.

"Yeah, I know I do. I will get what I deserve in due time. I guess for now, I will enjoy being single."

She stared at me for a moment before asking, "Are you and Quinton really sleeping together?"

"Yes."

"How often?"

"On a pretty regular basis," I said being completely honest. I was tired of the secrets. There was nothing else to hide.

"Wow." She shook her head. "How did it come to this point?"

"We kissed one night and there was so much sexual tension between us. Eventually, we took it there."

"This is just so not like you. My mind is completely blown."

"Why?" I laughed.

"This can't be healthy! It can't be!"

"How is it unhealthy? We are grown!"

"You two are really just having sex?"

"The sex is addictive, Rayven. I don't know what I have gotten myself into, but I don't know how to stop either. He does it for me."

"Wow. Sex in general is addictive, though."

"I get hangovers and withdrawals from this man. He keeps me on a high and I don't want to come down."

"Desiree!" She dropped her face into her hands. It took me a moment to realize that she was laughing. "Are you serious?"

"I am."

"You are honestly telling me that there is nothing between the two of you? You don't have feelings for Quinton?"

"I love him because he is my friend, but that's it. I am so attracted him. There is no denying that. Why do you keep asking me that, Rayven?"

"Desiree, I just think that you don't realize how much Quinton adores you. It's more than you will ever know."

There was a letter waiting for me when I got home.

Desiree.

It's killing me that we aren't together. First Quinton, then Tyler, now Quinton again. If only they were half the man I was.

Missing You,
The One

"Q?" He flipped me over and pinned me underneath him.

"Yes, baby."

"About Las Vegas?" I managed to ask as he kissed me.

"You are still going, right?"

"Of course."

"Thank God," he said, biting my ear.

"Well, about the sex."

"You want to stop?"

'Nooo." I moaned as his hands become a distraction.

"Then what about it?"

"I...." He kissed me. I couldn't formulate any words. When I opened my eyes, I was staring into his. I was hypnotized "Q..."

"Why don't you stop talking? Let your body talk to mines right now." My body wanted to do more than talk.

"I lost my train of thought anyway."

"Good, don't think. Just lay there so I can make you feel good."

"I already feel good."

"Not good enough. I want..." I closed my eyes as he described exactly what he was going to do to me. I blushed.

I don't know why I was feeling the way I was feeling. My mind couldn't begin to think about anything else. I was in this indescribable mood. Right now all I wanted was for him to love me. I needed him.

I was scaring myself. The intensity of our lovemaking was not something I was used to. Our bodies moved to a new rhythm. I surrendered to him in a way that I had never done before.

His kissed me more passionately. His touches were more seductive. He had me sweating harder. I was moaning louder. I couldn't stop whispering his name. Things had never been so intense.

When it was over, he rolled away to give me space, but he held onto my hand. I didn't have the energy to move. All I could do was lay there. I couldn't think clearly. I tried to think about what had just happened between Q and I, but I couldn't

I felt guilty.

Yeah, maybe it was true that we weren't hurting anybody, but as Rayven pointed out, this couldn't be healthy. Q and I were too good of friends to let sex get in the way. If I had been thinking straightly when he kissed me, none of this would have happened. It was too late, though. I already knew things were going to get complicated.

Wow. How were we going to put a stop to this when neither of us wanted to? It should not have been this difficult.

I was going to have to figure it all out eventually. I was going to have to cut myself off from this man. Just not right now.

Quinton

What was that? Right now I was confused about what just happened. I was blown away by how Desiree acted.

She clung to me. She gave all herself to me. It was as if she felt the same way I did. It felt like it was more than sex. And to me, she should have realized that.

I knew she didn't, though. That's why I was confused. There was something very different about our lovemaking. The intensity was out of this world.

Lovemaking? I don't know why I called it that. I was making love to this woman, but she didn't love me in return. With her, it could only be sex.

I moved my arm so that she could come to me. She did. She snuggled right up to me. She wrapped her arm around my waist and laid her head against my chest. It felt perfect.

"That was incredible," I said, kissing her forehead. "You deserve to be tired."

"Thank you."

"Can I get a kiss first?" I was kissing her before she could respond. She may have been tired but those lips of hers moved feverishly under mines. We kissed for a long time. I only pulled away when I felt things heating up again. I wanted her to rest.

"You are amazing, Desiree."

I felt her shiver. I quickly pulled the sheet around her and held her tightly in my arms. I watched her sleep. Just watching her tugged on my heart strings.

I sighed in frustration. I started to pray. I prayed to the good Lord that he would help me get over this woman. Hopefully sooner than later. All good things came to an end, right? I had a feeling that the ending was coming soon.

Would I be ready?

20

Sin City

"Or do you not know that your body is a temple of the Holy Spirit within you, whom you have from God? You are not your own, for you were bought with a price. So glorify God in your body."
1 Corinthians 6:19-20

Quinton

What was happening to me at the moment felt unreal. I was heading to Las Vegas for a week with the only chick that I had ever cared about. When I asked her to accompany me, I never expected for her say yes. She did, though, and I had not felt this excited in a long time.

During the plane ride, I looked over at her. Her eyes were closed. She looked peaceful. I wished that I could feel that same peace. Despite my excitement for her being here, I was anxious.

What was this trip about? Desiree tried to ask to ask me the other night, but I didn't really have an answer. I purposely distracted her so I wouldn't have to answer the question. Why was I dragging Desiree to Las Vegas? Why did she say yes?

Even though it felt wonderful to have her with me, asking her to come was a terrible idea. I was an idiot. I don't know what I thought all of this was going to lead to, but I was setting myself up for huge disappointment. She was going to pull me further into her trap and it was all going to be my fault.

We were both aware of what was going to happen. Sex and fun in this crazy city. I am pretty sure that's why she was here with me. I knew I could satisfy her. And she could definitely satisfy me like no other woman that I had ever encountered.

The hold that she had on my heart scared me. I was falling in love all over again. By the end of the week, I knew this woman was going to have complete control over my mind, body, and soul. She was going to hurt me. I was going to leave Vegas more vulnerable than when I arrived.

"What are you thinking about?" she asked, grabbing my thigh.

"What do you mean?" I asked, trying to play dumb.

"You look as if something is on your mind. It looks serious."

"Nothing really. Just work."

"It's more than that. You don't want to tell me. I will let it go."

"Okay." I was grateful. " I am glad that you are here with me."

"I am excited. Thanks for inviting me." She touched my cheek and then leaned over to kiss me. My whole body reacted.

"No problem. I wanted you here," I said, grabbing her hand

We arrived at McCarran International Airport around 3:00. We were in the taxi by 3:30. We were dropped off outside The Cosmopolitan by 3:50. By 4:10, we were checking into our suite.

The bellboy couldn't keep his eyes off Des in her shorts. His tip was me telling him to keep his eyes to himself. I made sure Des didn't hear that as she did her laps around the room.

"Are you really this exited?" I laughed at her childlike behavior.

"Yes!"

"Why?"

"I have never been to Vegas, remember?"

"That's right. Well it's a good thing I invited you. Come here," I said, pulling her to me. "Let's do something with all of this energy. What would you like to do?"

"I just want to see this place. Let's explore this beautiful hotel and then hit the strip."

"We can do that."

"As long as I am with you, I am happy," she flirted. I blushed.

"Go take a shower. We will get an early dinner, some drinks and the rest of the night is young."

"Sounds like a plan. I am hungry."

I almost followed her to the shower, but I didn't. I stood at the door when she finished and watched her. She wrapped herself in her towel and walked towards me. She kissed me as she walked by.

"I hope you enjoyed the show."

"Oh I did." I went to grab her, but she slid away from me.

"Not time for that, Quinton. Hit the shower."

I showered and dressed in some nice tan slacks and a nice button down. I felt like I looked good, but Desiree as always took my breath away. She wore a yellow sundress with no back. Mercy me.

I possessively wrapped my arm tightly around her waist.

"You look beautiful." We headed towards the elevator.

"Stop it," she said looking towards the floor. Her face was red.

"Can you walk in those," I asked, looking down at her wedges.

"Yes, I am fine."

"All night?"

"Yep and if I get tired, you can just carry me."

"How do you know I will carry you?"

"Because I asked you to." I couldn't say anything because she was right. Her dark eyes challenged mine. She had a way of staring at me that made me feel helpless.

We explored the hotel before hitting the strip. I enjoyed watching her being excited. I smiled as she took pictures of everything, including herself. I held her like she was mine when she demanded that I get in the pictures with her.

We went to Serendipity. Over burgers and sundaes, we reminisced and laughed. Her laugh was infectious and for a moment I was at peace with her.

"Whats next, baby."

"We did pass this candy store."

"Baby," I said, taking her hand into mine. "You should realize by now that you can have anything that you want."

"Okay," she said, giving me that smile that could melt my heart.

We walked around a while, sat down near some fountains, people watched a little. After that, we headed back to the hotel, had a couple of drinks, played some slot machines, and snuggled up on a loveseat in the lounge. I am not sure if it was the alcohol or just being in a new place, but Desiree was more affectionate than usual.

When she whispered, "It's time to be alone" in my ear, we headed back upstairs

Later on as we lay in the bed, my head resting comfortably on her chest, I was floating on cloud nine. Desiree rubbed my head and whispered what she wanted to do to me in my ear.

"Quinton," she said, pulling my face up to meet hers. She kissed me. "How did this happen? You and I? How did we start all of this?"

"With a kiss." She thought I meant the one in her bedroom months ago, but I was thinking about the kiss on the balcony five years ago.

"We are good friends, though. We should not be sleeping together. I never imagined that this would happen between us." I had been imagining it for the last five years.

"It's too late now, baby. No point in worrying about it."

"Can you imagine what our mothers would say?"

"I hope that you aren't telling your mother about what you do in the bedroom." I joked. She shoved me. "Come here." I pulled her around so that she was on top of me. "Whats wrong with me making you feel good."

"Nothing," I was just thinking..."

"Don't think." I grabbed the back of her head and pulled her face to mine to kiss her.

"Okay, baby. Help me free my mind."

I woke up early the next morning because I had work to do. I had to do interviews and attend a press conference for an upcoming music awards show. I hated leaving Des, but I had no choice.

I stared at her before leaving out. God she was so beautiful. I sighed and leaned down to kiss her forehead.

When I arrived back to the room around noon, she was still tangled in the sheets. It was an unbelievably sexy look on her. What I would give to wake up to this sight every morning.

"Beauty," I said, rubbing her cheek. "Wake up." It took a couple of moments, but her eyes finally flew opened.

"I haven't been in bed the whole time. I ordered breakfast and decided to lie back down. You kept me up late," she said, smiling.

"Well you deserve the rest." I leaned down to kiss her, but she turned her head. "No kisses! I have morning breath!"

"I don't care about your breath." I moved her hands away so I could kiss on those succulent lips.   .

"Whats up for today?" she asked, sitting up.

"I have tickets to this fashion show. Are you game?"

"Really?" she said, her eyes grew big.

"Yeah. Go shower. I am going to order some more room service because I am starving and we will head out."

"Cool." She stood. My mouth fell opened. She was naked.

Desiree proved how daring she was when room service delivered my burger and fries. She walked out of the bathroom in her lacy red bra and red thongs. I almost choked on my lemonade. The dude from room service almost tripped over his feet.

"Really cute," I said as she leaned over and stole a fry from my plate. She stared down at me. "I like that. You are confident." I leaned back in my seat. "Stop acting as if you are so insecure then." She smiled and shrugged. "I will dream of you in that outfit all day."

"And I will dream of you taking this outfit off of me later."

"Baby, I think I love you," I blurted, feeding her another fry.

"I know," she giggled. "And I hope you will show me how much sooner than later."

She wore a little orange dress that drove me crazy. It showed off her legs and I loved that. As we walked, I kept my hand possessively on her back. I couldn't help myself.

Desiree loved the fashion show. I smiled as she sat on the edge of her seat watching today's fashions moving down the runway. I was pleased. Her joy was everything to me.

After the show, we did a little shopping. I brought a couple things for myself. Spending money with Desiree was contagious.

My favorite part of the day was when she pulled me into a dressing room of a lingerie store. She pushed me down in the chair. She climbed in my lap and proceeded to make out with me.

"You do realize there are security cameras?" I pointed out, sliding my hand up her dress. "They know we are in here."

"Whats your point?" she breathed with her tongue in my ear.

"You don't mind, baby." She was surprising me. She couldn't possibly be as shy as she had been insisting.

"No because it feels good." She slid her hand down my boxers.

"You take my breath away." I buried my face in her neck.

"No one knows us in Vegas."

For dinner, I romanced Desiree by taking her to the Eiffel Tower Restaurant in the Paris Hotel. We sat in the corner with a spectacular view of the Bellagio and its famous fountains. She was impressed. She actually held my hand as we sipped on wine.

Des was being charming. I was hooked to her every word. I hadn't laughed so hard in a long time. I pushed the thoughts of her not being my woman to the back of my mind.

"You're amazing," I whispered as she fed me from her plate.

"Stop, Quinton," she said, blushing.

"No, I won't stop. I am serious." I reached over and lifted her chin. "Why are you single?"

"I don't know."

"Someone should be loving you. You deserve that."

"I agree." I saw frustration. It was the same frustration I felt.

"Is it because you aren't letting anyone get close to you?"

"No. It's not my time. Right now I just don't have anyone who wants to love me this point in my life." I felt a lump in my throat.

"That's not true."

"How would you know if that's true or not?" she asked, her dark eyes gazing into mine.

"I just don't believe that," I said, looking away. I felt like I was going to cave under pressure.

"What is it then? Why am I still single?"

"The wrong men."

"Obviously."

"What do you want from a man?"

"Huh?" she responded as if the question was a difficult one.

"What kind of a man do you want?"

"Someone who can satisfy me," she said, sipping on wine while giving me that seductive looked.

"I can do that," I said, pushing a piece of hair from her face.

"Yes, you can. Someone who can make me laugh."

"We laugh together."

"We do. I just want a man who is intelligent and ambitious. Someone who is loving and passionate. Someone laidback, carefree and who just loves life. Someone who is stylish, charming, beautiful, caring, generous, open. A family man. A sensitive man."

"Most importantly, I need a man who is not afraid to put God first." She had a dreamy looked in her eyes.

I sighed to myself. It was a long list, but not an unreasonable one. I could be all of those things if she would let me.

"Do you think that is too much to ask for?"

"Not at all." I raised my arm for the waiter.

"What are you doing?"

"I am going to order us that chocolate cake that you wanted and then I am going to get you back to the hotel."

When we got back to the room, she took control. I had never seen her so aggressive. It blew my mind

"Can I be yours tonight, Q?" She pushed me down on the bed.

"Anytime you want." She could be mine every night.

After our dance between the sheets, we got dress to hit up one of the clubs. We danced like teenagers, getting tipsy off of vodka. Then together we stumbled down the street. We stopped at Fatburger's and then walked hand and hand back to the hotel.

In the middle of the morning, we sat outside on our balcony in just our underwear, not caring who saw us.

"This is nice,' she whispered. "I could get use to this."

"Me too. Let's get married and move here."

"If only it was that easy. How do you feel, Quinton?" Happy.

"I feel wonderful. How do you feel?"

"I feel amazing," she smiled. "Can I ask you something?"

"Whats that?"

"Why did you allow us to kiss that night?"

"I don't know."

"You don't. I think about that a lot. We weren't even drunk."

"I just wanted to, Desiree. You were irresistible."

"You were irresistible. I am the one who initiated everything."

"Were you?"

"Yes." She looked away, her face red.

We sat there in silence for a couple of moments.

"Des…"

"Shush, she said, pushing her finger against her lips. She sat back in her chair, reaching over to squeeze my hand. "Quinton, we don't have to figure anything out. Let just enjoy this."

I left Des in bed the next morning again to do my job. I returned to the room, expecting to find her in bed. She was nowhere to be found. I was sure she was fine, but it didn't stop my heart from beating like crazy. I picked up my phone, ready to call her.

Within seconds, to my relief, she walked through the door.

"Hey, gorgeous." She smiled up at me.

"Where have you been?" I asked taking in her very tiny shorts. She sure knew how to torture me.

She grabbed my hand and gave me a quick kiss. "I was just exploring the hotel. I was killing time."

"I am sorry. I don't mean to overreact. You know how I do."

"I do know. Can we go now? I am so hungry."

After brunch, we changed into our swimming suits. We hung out by the pool before heading to the MGM for a pool party. We had fun dancing and sipping on drinks with umbrellas at Wet Republic.

I couldn't keep my hands off of her. She had on a tiny black bikini. She looked amazing as always.

After the party, we walked down the strip, eating hot dogs from Pinks and sipping on Cherry Cokes. We shared popcorn and ice cream cones. We started goofing off and taking silly pictures in front of each hotel, creating memories that I would not soon forget. It was a wonderful carefree afternoon.

When we got back to the room, we snuggled up on the couch in front of the TV. Desiree fell asleep against my shoulder. I fell asleep watching her as I often did.

She was my woman in Vegas. She had surrendered to me, and that meant the world, but it was going to end soon. I wasn't sure how I was going to deal with everything once back in Charlotte.

That night was the award show. I was grateful I didn't have to work the red carpet. I could enjoy it with Desiree. We both were able to get dressed up and be fans.

She took my breath away as usual. I was standing on the balcony, waiting patiently when she joined me. I could barely speak. It took me many moments before I could manage a "Wow."

"How do I look?" She asked, giving me that smile.

"Words can't begin to describe how you look. The word beautiful is not even good enough." Her face turned red. She put her hands on her cheeks.

"Quinton! Thank you!"

"You are welcome.' She wore a long fuschia dress. It plunged in the front and in the back with a very high split. It was definitely sexy.

"You look gorgeous in your tux, Quinton."

"Thanks, baby. Shall we go?"

I walked over to her and hugged her. I didn't want to let go. She felt wonderful in my arms. She smelled wonderful.

"Not your normal perfume. What are you wearing?"

"Heavenly Kiss."

"I love it. Being with you is like heaven on earth for me."

"I can't believe that you just said that. Why are you even single, Quinton Alexander?" Because you won't love me.

"Will you be mines?" She just smiled and grabbed my hand.

I kept throwing her looks as we headed down the elevator. She really was the most beautiful woman that I had ever seen. Or was it because I was crazy about her? Either way, she had my heart working overtime. I wanted to kiss her.

"I bet she wouldn't let me mess that lipstick up"

"Whats that?" She asked.

"Nothing, sweetheart."

"Didn't your mama teach you that it's not nice to keep secrets?" I had a bigger secret than that, sweetheart.

"I must have missed that lesson."

She almost cried when she saw the limo. I had to grab her waist because I thought she was going to fall back. I knew she was going to look too good to ride in a taxi. After the show, the limo was going to take us for a ride around the city.

"Quinton, this is too much."

"No, nothing is too much for you, Desiree."

"I don't deserve how nice you have been to me."

"I don't deserve all the time you have spent with me."

"You are so sweet. When did you get so sweet? Why didn't I know this about you?"

"I don't know," I shrugged.

"Well, I want to learn more," she said, touching my cheek.

After the three hour show ended, we rode around the city. We ate chocolate covered strawberries and sipped on champagne. And then we started to make out. That heat followed us back to our room. I only took my hands off of her long enough to watch that dress fall down that delicious body of hers. Then I pulled her into my arms and proceeded to love her as if was our last time together.

Hours later, as Desiree was sleeping, I laid beside her watching her. She looked peaceful and beautiful. She stirred a little and I leaned over and kissed her shoulder.

"I love you so freaking much." She stirred again and my entire body froze. I felt numb. I thought maybe she had heard me. I was relieved when her breathing returned to normal.

I lay completely on my back and closed my eyes. I took a couple deep breaths. Those words took the life out of me. I wanted to throw up. I was upset that I had allowed myself to fall in love all over again. I knew it, but I didn't want to admit it.

I climbed out of bed and grabbed a bottle of Ciroc that we had been sipping on. I took a seat in the corner of the room. I tried not to let the emotions overtake me. I tried not to beat myself up over my failure to get over her. I tried not to think too much at all.

I sat there and stared at the wall. I wanted to drown my sorrows with this vodka. Hopefully then I could fall asleep.

I froze when I heard her move around. She sat up.

"Quinton," she whispered. Even the sound of her voice could affect me in the way that it should not have. I swallowed hard because I couldn't formulate any words. "Quinton? Where are you?"

"I am over here, baby."

"Why? Why aren't you over here with me?" The urgency in her voice made me get up and go to her.

"Whats wrong, lovely?"

"You aren't beside me." I couldn't think. I grabbed her face and kissed her. I made love to her. I surrendered to her. It was the only way I could express myself to this woman.

I held her afterwards until she fell asleep. I then stood, grabbing some clothes. I grabbed my phone, room key, and headed downstairs. I skipped the elevator. I rained down eight flights of stairs. I had dialed Tyler's number before I hit the street.

"What are you thinking, Q?" was how he answered the phone. Do you know what time it is?"

"5:00 in the morning here and 8:00 there. You should be up?"

"Yeah, but it's my day off."

"I am sorry. I just needed to talk to someone." I heard a female's voice. I could tell it was Rayven. For a moment, I was jealous. Not because he was with Rayven, but because he was with a woman who cared about him.

"Is something wrong with you or Des, Quinton?"

"No we are both fine."

"Yeah, baby, they are okay."

"I need to talk to you because I am struggling."

"Alright, alright." I could hear him getting out of the bed and leaving the room. "Talk to me.

"I love her."

"I know."

"The only woman that I have ever loved is upstairs asleep in a bed that I have shared with her this entire week. I whispered I love you to her. I thought she heard me. And then she woke up, calling my name and we ending up making love. It was hands down the best sex that I have ever had."

"I should be on cloud nine, but I am not. You want to know why? Because I can't have her. She will never be the woman in my life. To her, it's just sex. She doesn't feel what I feel. When we are together, I feel so much more than that."

"Quinton, don't tell me this. I don't want to hear this craziness. I can't believe any of this. It's absurd."

"Call it what you want, but I am expressing to you how I feel. I can't to her. I don't want to go home because I know everything is going to change. Here in Vegas, Des surrenders to me in a way she never has. When we get back to, she is going to distance herself."

"How do you know this?"

"Because she had told me," I said, reliving the argument we had in the kitchen the other week.

"That can't be true."

"Why would someone like Desiree want to be with me?"

"Rayven is with me."

"And you are lucky," I said, honestly.

"You are right."

"This is getting hard, T. I keep falling more in love with her every day. I don't know how I am going to get through the next couple of days."

"Don't make it hard."

"How can I not? In the back of my mind is the fact that when I get home, this will be all over for me. Desiree is not someone who is going to stay single long. Someone is going to snatch her up soon. I am going to be there to see it." My heart broke at that thought. "I am not going to handle that well."

"I know."

"I am so stupid."

"You're not stupid for being in love."

"With Desiree I am. I shouldn't have kissed her. The last couple of months should not have happened."

"I doubted that you could have helped yourself."

"I have been down this road once already."

"When did you stop loving her, Q? You never got over her."

"You are right."

"Look, I know it's hard. Hang in there. Stay strong. Enjoy the next few days. Come talk to me when you get back into town."

"Alright."

"Go upstairs, hold her, kiss her, and love her. Don't stop showing her how you feel. You don't have to vocalize it. Don't go acting differently. Desiree will call you out on it and then you are going to be left trying to explain."

I walked around the hotel for a while. I needed to get my mind right. If I went upstairs now and she was awake, I would crumble. I sat down near the casino, staring at every woman who walked by. I was trying to find a distraction. None of them did a thing for me.

When I walked back into the room around 6:00, I was hoping I could slide back into bed unnoticed. I didn't want to have to answer any questions. As soon as I touched the bed, her eyes flew open.

'Where do you keep going?"

"I am sorry. I took a walk."

"Why do you keep leaving me alone?"

"I am not trying to leave you," I said, pulling her close.

"When I woke up, you weren't there." She sounded upset.

"Desiree, are you upset?"

"I am just worried about you."

"Don't worry about me. I just can't sleep."

"Is it me?" Yes. I was quiet for a moment, thinking how I should respond. She started to move away from me. "Quinton!"

"That's stupid. Why would it be you?"

"Well, you took a long time to answer."

"I did, but it's because so much is on my mind. It has nothing to do with you. I just can't sleep. I am not sure why?" I hated lying.

"I am sorry, Quinton," she said, rubbing my chest. "Is there anything that I can do for you?" Love me.

"No need for you to worry about it. I am just restless. Go back to sleep," I said, squeezing her.

I lay there wide awake for a while longer, staring up at the ceiling. I was trying not to focus on the future too much. No matter how hard I tried, I couldn't avoid the inevitable. Desiree and I had an expiration date.

21

Broken

"The rod and reproof give wisdom, but a child left to himself brings shame to his mother." *Proverbs 29:15*

Desiree

"Quinton is ignoring me."

"What are you talking about, Desiree?" Rayven asked, flopping down on the couch beside me.

"We come back from Vegas and he starts ignoring me."

"Do you mean he is not talking to you, Desiree, or he is not taking you to bed every night?" I just stared at my friend. Did she really ask me that? I had to admit, though, I was bothered by both.

"He's not doing either of those things."

"So which one is bothering you the most?" I stared at her again. Was I that transparent? I wasn't going to give her the satisfaction of knowing that I was horny.

"How are you going to ask me that question, Rayven?"

"I want to understand where you are coming from. I am a little confused." Was she smirking at me? She was being condescending.

"Of course I am upset that he is not talking to me. He is so moody. Sometimes I feel like I am living with a chick. We are living under the same roof and he acts as if I barely exist. How do I not exist in my own home?"

"I don't know. Let's be honest, though, Des. The no sex thing is killing you. Keep it real with me." She was the realest chick I knew. That's why she was my best friend.

I sighed in frustration.

"Fine! It's killing me! I am horny as hell. Don't you think that I have the right?"

"The right!" She was amused. She wasn't taking me seriously. I was legitimately upset.

"Q and I have been going at for the last five or six months. We go to Vegas and we have the best sex that I ever had. We come home and he just puts a stop to all of it. He won't come near me, he won't touch me, and he won't kiss me. He barely wants to talk to me."

"Wow."

"I feel like if I go near him, he is going to bite my head off. I just stay away. That's what he wants. How could he do this to me?"

"Des, to be honest with you, it's not really all that healthy for you and Q to be involved in this sexual relationship. You are either platonic or you are not. He has a right to stop anytime he wants, despite what you want. And you can't get mad at him for that."

I closed my eyes and took a deep breath. I didn't like what she had to say. Of course she was right, but I didn't want to admit that.

"Why, though? How could he just stop cold turkey and not tell me that's what he wanted? I feel like I got played in a way."

"Why do you feel played?"

"We spent all this time alone in Vegas. It was not just about the sex. It was more than that. Things between us were intense. They were intimate. He was sweet and romantic. He said some things that didn't fail to amaze me. He made me feel good about myself and no man has done that for me in a while."

"Oh, my Dessie," she said, rubbing my hair.

"I guess that's what you do when you are a ladies man."

"Desiree, Quinton would not play you. He puts you on pedestal and you know it."

"Why would I be any different than any other female?"

"Because despite what you are cooking up in that pretty little head of yours, you know that Quinton cares about you. So deeply."

"Then why is ignoring me?"

"I wish I could tell you. I hate seeing you in distress about this. I would love nothing more than to make you feel better about all this."

"Thank you, Sunray."

"I think Quinton started to realize that things between you were getting a little too hot and heavy. You just alluded to how intense things were getting. Maybe he was getting a little too attached to you and needed to distance himself. You have to admit that you two made things complicated." I nodded.

"You need to stop all of this anyway. Sex between you two is just messy. You don't want to risk jeopardizing your friendship."

"You are right. What can I say? I never meant for any of this to happen. It just did."

"I know, sweetie, but now it's time for you both to move on."

"You don't understand, Rayven."

"Yes! Yes, I do. Quinton pleases you like no other man has done before. Well guess what. More than one man can please you. You may find someone even better. Someone who you love, Desiree."

"I know," I laughed. "I have just gotten attached to this man."

"Well get unattached."

"If only it was that easy."

"They say in order to get over one man, you need to…"

"I don't know, Rayven. Quinton is pretty special."

"Seriously, Desiree. You are scaring me."

"I am sorry. Quinton has me going through withdrawals. This is an addiction. Eventually I will get over him." We sat in silence. I closed my eyes. I needed to stop tripping over this.

"Desiree, are you sure nothing is going to come of this?" I turned to looked at her. She was looking at me seriously. I frowned.

"No, Rayven, nothing else is going to come out of this."

"Neither of you have feelings for each other?"

"I care about Q so much, but he is not my type." Who was I fooling? I was out of his league. I wasn't going to tell her, though.

"I just think that you two would be perfect for each other."

"Well, I don't and I don't think Quinton does either."

"Speak for yourself."

Quinton

"So how are things going for you, my man?" T asked.

Tyler had been on my case about us talking ever since I got back from Vegas. I had already decided to cut Desiree off. I had no choice but to distance myself. Still, I thought maybe it would be beneficial to talk with him. I was hoping that he could reassure me that I was making the best decision.

We decided to meet at my favorite seafood spot. I figured that I could attempt to relax over beer and crab legs.

"Not all that great," I answered honestly.

"I am sorry to hear that."

"It's cool. It's just a little difficult." I hadn't spent much time with Desiree since we had come back. I truly missed her.

"So you are really going through with this? You are just going to cut Desiree off like that."

"Man, I really don't have a choice."

"Q, you can't just cut the woman off like that. That's wrong."

"You don't understand. When I am with her, I feel great. She makes me feel that way. I love her."

"But?"

"When I am with her, it hurts."

T signed and leaned back in his chair. He looked as frustrated as I felt. He shook his head and said, "Love shouldn't hurt."

"I realize that."

"And I can't persuade you to tell Desiree how you are feeling."

"No. That will never happen."

"May I ask you why?" Was he kidding me? I had been through the humiliation once. I couldn't put myself through it again.

"Because I will not be making a fool out of myself. Desiree has already made it clear where I stand."

"Where is that?"

"She has told me more than once that it just sex. She cares about me, but it is what it is. We are too good of friends to pursue anything more." I couldn't even look at Tyler when I said that. Here I was, a man who had avoided commitment, actually wanting more from a woman and she wouldn't let me have it.

Tyler just stared at me blankly before commenting.

"I don't believe that. Desiree can't really mean that."

"Believe it. She told me that I could never get with that."

"I am confused. You told me that she was opening up to you. You said things were intense."

"She was and they were. That still doesn't mean anything."

"You can't tell me that you don't mean something to Desiree."

"I am not saying anything like that. Of course Desiree cares about me. She loves me. As her friend, though. Our families go way back. Our mothers were best friends. The bottom line is that I can be her friend and I can be her lover. I will never be her man."

"Why not?"

"It's not hard to understand, T. I am not the man for her. She's my type, but I am not hers. She's not feeling me."

"I am sorry, Quinton. I just want you to be happy. You two would be good for one another. This is unfortunate."

"Yeah." I felt numb. "I guess love will come my way eventually."

"Of course. It will. Women love you."

"Never the right ones, though." I laughed. "Women are crazy."

"Who are you telling?"

"Maybe I need some professional help."

"Don't come with that nonsense. Why would you need professional help?"

"I am not falling for another woman until I get over this one."

"You will."

"Not on my own. I haven't done it all these years."

"I don't know if you will ever get completely over her."

"That's good to know," I mumbled.

"Maybe if you get away from her, you can learn to live with it. It would make things a lot easier."

"That's what I am saying. It's hard being in that house with her."

"How much longer before your house is ready, bruh?"

"About three months. Thankfully, we are ahead of schedule."

"Okay, good. How's Desiree handling all of this? How did you just put a stop to everything?"

"She just stares at me," I laughed. "She never says anything. I think I hurt her feelings, T. I hope she doesn't think that I am playing her." Knowing Des, that's exactly what she was thinking.

"I hope not."

"I want to tell her. I really do. I wish I could make her understand where I am coming from. It makes me sick thinking that I could have hurt her."

"You are going to have to tell her something."

"I will."

"I wish you would just tell her how you really feel."

"I can't. She is not trying to hear that. I lost faith a long time ago. I was dumb for allowing us to kiss."

"You needed to."

"I…" I could feel a tear. I looked away because I didn't want him to see it. "Just give it up!"

"Why!

"Because I already did."

I never thought that I would be nervous about seeing Desiree at home, but I was. Shamefully, I was hoping that she wouldn't be there, but when I pulled into her driveway to find her car parked outside, I realized I had to face reality. I sat in the car for a few moments to attempt to get my mind in a better place.

She was in her room. Everything was quiet. Normally, I would head to her bedroom to see what was up, but things had changed. Her door was closed and I hoped that it stayed that way.

I just prayed no one was on the other side. Just because she wasn't being intimate with me, didn't mean she wasn't going to seek it from elsewhere. I didn't want to think about that.

I shook my head and headed to the kitchen. I grabbed a beer. I needed something to relax me. I was definitely tense.

Before I got to my room, she opened the door. She walked out in her tank and her panties. I was instantly turned on. Why did she always have to do this to me? I knew she did it on purpose.

"What's up, Desiree?"

"I am going to fix me something to eat. Are you hungry?"

"Nope. I already ate." She narrowed her eyes at me. What did that mean? "How have you been?"

"I have been good. How have you been?"

"Pretty good," I lied.

"Wonderful. I haven't seen you in a while," she said, moving noticeably closer to me. I swallowed hard. She was suffocating me.

"Yeah. Unfortunately I have been busy."

"You are so busy that you can't deal with an old friend?" She touched my arm. I couldn't even handle her touch right now. I tensed up. I didn't realize that she noticed until she jerked her hand back. Her eyes grew dark. "Never mind, Quinton. Don't bother answering the question because you already did." She pushed past me. I was hurting her.

"Des, wait! Please let me explain," I said, trying to grab her arm.

"You don't have to explain anything to me!"

"I owe you an explanation."

'You don't owe me anything. You are a grown man! You can make any choice you want."

"It's not a choice that I want to make. I just have to. I wish I could make you understand…"

"I think that I understand perfectly well."

"No, Desiree. You really don't."

"I get it, Quinton!" She looked as if she wanted to cry and I felt terrible. I was so regretful. I should have never kissed her.

Before I could get in another word, there was a bang at the door. My day got a lot worse as that bang was followed by India's loud voice. I took a deep breath and closed my eyes. I was about to break so I needed to calm down. I was not emotionally ready for drama.

"You might want to tell your baby mother that she needs to stop banging on my door before I teach her a lesson."

"I am sorry, Desiree. I really am." I grabbed my head because I was starting to get a bad headache.

"Quinton!" India screamed. "Open this freaking door." I was going to kill her. I could hear Quinton screaming in the background.

Des pushed past me. She walked to the door and flung it open.

"Why scream, sweetheart! Next time use the doorbell instead of banging on my door like you are the freaking SWAT team."

"If I was the SWAT team, I would have kicked you door down!" India screamed at Desiree, trying to get in her face.

"You are in my house, sweetheart," Desiree said, rolling her eyes. Like a grown woman, she walked away.

"You need to tell your girlfriend to put some clothes on, Quinton!" Desiree laughed, but kept it moving down the hall.

"India." I couldn't stand this woman, but I tried not to laugh. "Why are you here? And where is your common sense? You don't come to someone else's house and start something."

"Whatever! You can insult me all that you want tonight. Here, take your son," she said, pushing my son towards me. He was screaming. He threw his arms around me and clung to me, shivering.

"What's going on? Why is my son crying?"

"He fell," she said, backing away. She was trembling.

"What do you mean he fell?"

"I made him fall!" She was hysterical. "He hurt himself!"

"What!" Suddenly I was filled with rage. I looked down at my son. His lip was bleeding. "What did you do, you freaking bitch!"

"Q." Desiree said, coming up behind me. I turned and could see that her anger had dissolved. I saw sadness. "Give him to me."

"Thank you." She took Quinton out of my arms and then touched my shoulder as if she was telling me to calm down. I knew right then that I would never love another female as much as I loved Desiree at that very moment.

"So what is she going to do? Play his mother now," India jumped in sarcastically.

"Why not," Des said heading down the hall. "You are obviously not doing a good job at it. Some women just don't deserve kids."

"I will beat…" India lunged for Desiree, but I shoved her back. Maybe it was a little too roughly, but I didn't care.

"You will not put a hand on her!" I backed her into a corner. She was scared. "What did you do to my son?"

"I pushed him down!"

"What!" I wanted to punch her. "You pushed my son! So hard that his lip is bleeding!" I said through clinched teeth. I felt like a bull about to charge. I had her pinned against the wall.

"Yes," she said, starting to sob.

"Have you pushed my son before?"

"No, I promise I haven't, Quinton!"

"Why! Why did you do it?" I backed away in disgust. I didn't want to hit her. My mother had taught me better than that.

"He pissed me off!"

"What do you mean he pissed you off? He is three-years-old!"

"I couldn't stop myself. I've been screaming at him all evening."

"Are you high? Did you shoot up tonight!"

"Yes!"

"Why are you this stupid?"

"This is why I am here. I can't deal with him anymore!"

"If you lay off of that crap, maybe you can acquire some motherly skills. You need to do what you have to do for your child!"

"I don't want to!"

"You have no choice!"

"Yes I do! I give up. You can have him!"

"What are you talking about?"

"I am giving you sole custody." I stared at her for a moment in disbelief. What kind of woman would just give up her parental rights to her child just like that?

"India, Quinton needs his mother."

"Let her be his mother."

"She is not his mother and she is not going to play his mother. This is your son and you are his mother."

"Well, I don't want to be his mother anymore."

"How could you do that to him? How could you just walk out on him?" My heart was breaking for my son.

"Look at what I did to him tonight."

"Yeah and that disgusting of you, but if you get some help…"

"I don't want to!" she screamed at me. "I am through being a mother, Quinton. Accept it!"

"That's selfish!"

"You are right," she said, nodding. "It is."

"What kind of woman are you!"

"Not much," she said being brutally honest with me. "I don't deserve that little boy."

"You are right. You don't. But God gave him to you. You…"

"Don't preach to me!"

"Maybe you should pay church a visit."

"It doesn't matter what you think. I am giving you sole custody."

"This is crazy."

"Sorry," she said, pushing past me and heading out the door.

"Wait a minute," I said following her outside.

"We are done, Quinton!"

"What is this little boy supposed to think? That his mother chose drugs and sex over him. That his mother didn't give a crap about him. You want him to grow up knowing that!"

"Shut up, Q!" she screamed. "I can't do it. He deserves you!"

"He deserves a mother!"

"A better one than me. He can't have a future with me. Why can't you understand that? It is for his well-being to be with you."

"No, India, I don't understand!"

"Well, whatever. But I loved that little boy, so you make sure that he knows that I loved him enough to give him to you." She stared at me sadly with tears streaming down her cheeks. She shook her head and walked away.

"India!" She ignored me. "India!" She got in her car. She drove away. "India, please," I whispered, knowing she couldn't hear me.

I stood in the middle of the driveway and stared after her for a while. I was in complete disbelief. The last twenty minutes had been a nightmare. This could not be happening to me.

"Q." Desiree voice interrupted my thoughts. I closed my eyes instead of answering her. I wanted to feel her arms around me. I wanted her to kiss me. I wanted her to tell me that everything was going to work out. None of that was going to happen, though.

"Quinton. Your son wants you." Little Q had his arms stretched towards me. He needed me even if no one else did.

"Daddy." I walked over to him and took him. I held him tightly. He clung to me. I clung to him. He was my heart.

"Sorry, little buddy. Daddy loves you."

"I love you, daddy." I closed my eyes. How could India do this to him? How could she hurt him?

"Thanks Desiree for taking care of his lip."

"You are welcome, Quinton."

I finally found the courage to look at her. She stared at me. I couldn't read her. She had no expression on her face.

"Desiree, back to me and you."

"Put your son to bed, Quinton." She walked back inside. I sighed. She was killing me.

"Why can't we have the women we need, little man?"

"I don't know, daddy."

The kid was asleep within five minutes of me laying him down. I intercepted Desiree before she reached her bedroom door.

"Please let me talk to you."

"Q." She was clam. "There is really nothing to explain. It was sex. I will get over it. You men are so willing to please." Wow. "I am just upset that you feel that you have to avoid me. We are still friends, aren't we? That's not how you treat a friend."

"I am sorry. I wanted to distance myself. I had to."

"From me?"

"I don't want to stop, but..."

"Come on, Q! It's sex, babe. We can both move on and find it elsewhere." I didn't want to move on. I didn't want her to. She would never realize how much that hurt me. "Why do I make you tense?"

"Because I want you so badly." I didn't mean just physically. I meant I wanted her in every sense of the word. It's what she wanted to hear. That I only wanted her for sex. She thought I was still incapable of loving a woman.

She would never know how I felt, especially right now. She would never know that I was not incapable of loving, but incapable of loving anyone but her. She would never know how broken my heart was.

"I see. I am not one of your conquests. Don't forget that."

"You mean more than that to me. Seriously, Des. Give me some credit here. After all we been through, this is how you think of me?"

"I know." No you don't. "Go to sleep, Quinton, you have had a long night." I tried to respond, but she wouldn't let me. "Just be quiet. Goodnight."

She leaned over and kissed me. She then disappeared into her room. I stared at her door. I yearned to be on the other side. I yearned for her affection. I yearned for something I had never had. The love of a woman.

"Are you really serious, India?"

I had convinced her to have breakfast with me the next morning. I thought maybe she would sleep off of her high and regain some sense. She didn't.

"Quinton, I know you hate me right now, but I told you that I can't do this anymore." Her eyes were puffy and she looked pale. Although she looked under the weather, she had never looked so normal. No bright colored weave. She wore her hair neatly pulled back. She had traded in her hoochie wear for a tank and jeans.

'You have to give me more than that. You have to make me understand why you are walking out on your son."

"Because I am not emotionally stable. I can't raise him like he deserves to be raised. I can't give him a good future."

"You can if you try."

"No, I can't," she said, starting to cry again.

"You can change, India. You just have to work hard. You shouldn't give up. You are never supposed to do that."

"I know I can change and I am going to. I can only change my ways, not who I am. I will never be a good mother to our son."

"India…"

"I flipped out on that little boy last night. I pushed him. His lip was bleeding. That's not something a mother does to her child."

"Who's to say that is going to happen again?"

"And who is to say that it's not! I don't trust myself. I don't want to keep him in a house full of drugs and sex."

"Can't you just put a stop to all of that?"

"It's not that easy. I am in this really deep. There have been people hanging around me that Quinton doesn't need to be around."

"Like who?"

"Last night, I had a threesome with two of my friends. One male and one female. Quinton Jr was in the next room." I closed my eyes. I couldn't believe some of the things that India did. "I am addicted to sex, Quinton. I am not feeding you some bullshit. This is real."

"Oh, God." I needed God right now.

"And that's not the end."

"What else happened?"

"The chick left, but the dude stayed around and we got into it. He started to get rough with me. I tried to get him to leave, but he wouldn't. He pushed me down and he raped me."

"What!" I wanted to throw up. "Are you okay? Did he hurt you? Did you call the police? Did you go to the hospital?"

"Nope, I am not worried. It's happened before."

"You've been raped before?" She nodded. "How many times?"

"Who knows, I lost count." I didn't have any words. "I got hysterical afterwards. Little Quinton started crying. I flipped out and took it out on him. I pushed my own son. All he wanted was his mommy. He was screaming mommy and I could not comfort him."

I could not look her. I was scared to.

"These men are dangerous. I am not just afraid for my safety. I am afraid for his. He could get hurt." I wanted to hug her and kill her at the same time. "He needs you more than me. You are stable, Quinton. You would be better for him. He loves you to death."

"He loves you too, India."

"I know and he is my heart. He is the only good thing that has come out of my life."

"Then why give up the good thing?"

"Because I don't want to ruin his life."

"Okay, so he will come and live with me."

"Not good enough. I am giving you all parental rights. Once I tell the courts whats going on with me, you will be granted sole custody. I won't be contesting that in any way."

"Once you do something like this, you can't change your mind."

"I have been thinking about this for a long time. Last night was the final straw. It proved that he doesn't need to be with me."

"I don't want him to grow up without his mother. What am I supposed to tell him?"

"Quinton, the way you love that boy, I know he won't be deprived in any way. There won't be a lack of love in his life."

"Of course not,' I said, emotionally. I wanted to cry.

"Tell him that his mama love him, but she didn't know how to be his mother. Tell him that I was very sick."

'I don't want to lie."

"You wouldn't be lying. I am more than emotionally sick. I am addicted to sex, weed, crack, heroin and ecstasy."

"What!"

"I have got to go," she said, standing.

"Let me help you, India," I said, grabbing her hand. "It's never too late to change your life."

"Quinton," she said, squeezing my hand and gently pulling away. "I am HIV positive. To me that as good as dead."

I felt as if I had been punched me in my chest. She had shattered what was left of my heart. She was never my favorite person, but she was my child's mother. I didn't want anything bad to happen to her.

"I am so sorry," I said, pulling her into my arms. She clung to me and cried into my shoulder. She was trembling.

After a few minutes, she pulled away. She kissed my cheek and then turned to walk away. I didn't stop her. I knew she didn't want me to. I knew she was gone once and for all.

I dropped down in my seat. I sat completely still. I couldn't move. Fate had just dealt little Quinton and I a terrible card.

Finally I was able to get up. I dragged myself out of the restaurant and to my car. I drove to my mother's house where I dropped my son off that morning. I played with him for a while and then laid him down for his nap. I sat my mother down to share with her India's shocking confessions.

"Oh my lord. "My mother started crying. I comforted her. I stayed with her until it was time for work.

Somehow, I struggled through the four hours at the station. It was the last place I felt like being, but I got through it. My listeners didn't care about my issues.

After work, I headed straight home. My mom decided to keep my son overnight. She insisted that I needed rest. All I wanted was Desiree. I was hoping that she would comfort me despite the tension between us.

Desiree

When Quinton walked in, I was chilling on the crouch with my friend, Lance, from work. He was a cutie who had been flirting with me since he started at Pink Legacy a couple months ago. I really wasn't into him at first, but we had become good friends. He was sweet, though, and he could make me laugh. He was also persistent. He didn't give up on asking me out on a daily basis.

Today, I decided to say yes. My love life was nothing exciting. Why should I turn down a good man because he wasn't my type? I needed to take more risk and date someone who I didn't normally go for. Perhaps I had been wrong about my type.

"Desiree," Quinton called out.

Lance and I weren't even cuddling. We were sitting very closely. His hand was on my knee. We were watching TV. When Quinton saw us, he looked at us as if we were getting it on.

"Yes, Quinton."

"Oh, um nothing. I see that you are busy right now. Never mind. It really wasn't all that important. I am sorry." It was obvious that he was lying to me. He looked as if he had the day from hell. It was apparent that he wanted to talk to me.

"Quinton, wait!"

"No, just carry on." He tried to smile, but failed miserably. He proceeded down the hall to his room. He didn't slam the door, but I felt as if he had.

"Lance?"

"Yeah, whats up? Who was that?"

"Quinton." That's all I offered. I wasn't giving any details.

"Are you sure that's not your man?"

"If he was, I don't think that you would still be sitting here."

"You are right. He is bigger than me too. I know that he could have easily taken me."

"Stop, Lance. Seriously, though, Q is going through something rough right now and I think that he wants to talk to me about it."

"I understand. He did look a little agitated that I was here. I don't believe that my presence is desired," he said, standing.

"Thank you, Lance," I said, hugging him.

"Go handle that, beautiful," he said, kissing my cheek. "I had a good time with you. I'll talk to you tomorrow," he said as I walked him to the door. "I will take you out to lunch."

"Great. I would like that."

I headed to Q's room as soon I as I shut the front door. I knocked, but there was no answer. I banged a little louder. It took him a minute, but he finally opened it.

He was in his boxers and I tried not to take it all in. He looked as if he was in need of some serious affection. I was willing to give him some. I wasn't sure if he would accept it.

"Talk to me, Quinton."

"It's cool," he mumbled. "Go back to your company."

"I made him leave."

"Why?"

"You obviously need me."

He stared at me in disbelief. When I moved closer to him, he reached for me. He crushed me into his body. He covered my lips with his. All I could do was cling to him.

"I do need you."

"I am here," I whispered.

Before I knew it, we were both naked, rolling around on his bed. I comforted him in a way that we both desired. Afterwards, I wrapped my arm around him and pulled him closer.

"Whats wrong, Quinton?"

He told me everything. He told me about India's addiction to sex and drugs, about her being raped, and her being HIV positive. By the time he was finished, I was in tears. I could feel his pain.

"With God's grace, everything will be alright, Q."

"How do you know?"

"Because he will never leave you. Your son's lucky to have you."

"I am lucky to have him."

I rubbed his cheek and kissed his lips.

"If you two need me, I am here for you."

"We thank you. We love you for it, Desiree."

"No problem, sweetheart."

22

Ex-Boyfriend

"Remember not the former things, nor consider the things of old. Behold, I am doing a new thing; now it springs forth, do you not perceive it? I will make a way in the wilderness and rivers in the desert." *Isaiah 43:18-19*

Quinton

The next few weeks proved to be both difficult and hectic for me. I barely had the time to eat or sleep. I was so stressed out that if I wasn't careful I was going to get sick. If I wasn't already bald, my hair would have probably fallen out. I wasn't sure how much I could bear. Only God would know that.

As promised, Desiree was there for me and my son. She did it all. She cooked for me and made sure I ate. She listened to me and comforted me. She encouraged me and she motivated me.

Desiree watched little Quinton when I needed her to. She accompanied me to the Lawyer's office. She kept my life from falling apart. She was my best friend. I loved her with all my heart for it.

I was the sole provider for little Quinton at this point. It was all surreal. Although, after many battles with India, I had wished for it, I never thought I was going to be a single father, raising my three-year-old on my own. I honestly didn't want that for my son. I wanted him to know his mother, but I had to come terms with the reality that he probably never would.

It was painful to watch my son long for his mother. In the first couple of days after India's departure, he was fine. Soon, though, he started asking for her. Every day he cried for her. Sadly, I didn't have an answer for him.

What was I supposed to say? How could I explain it to such a young child in a way that he would understand? I asked my parent's, my sister, my brother, T and Des what I should do. They all gave me the same solution. I would have to sit Quinton down and tell him that mommy was sick. She had to go away to get better.

"When is mommy going to get better?" he asked looking down at the floor.

"I don't know. It may take a long time, buddy."

"Oh." He looked as if he was thinking "Am I staying with you now, daddy?" He was such a smart little boy.

"Yeah, buddy. Home is with me now."

"Yeah!" he said, hugging me. I almost cried. "I really like that."

"Good," I said, hugging him back. He was the best thing in my life. "I really like that too." He kissed my cheek, climbed off my lap and ran down the hall in excitement.

"Very precious," Desiree said coming out of nowhere.

"You think so?" I pulled her down into my lap.

"Yes. I think that your son will be just fine."

"I think that you are right. He doesn't understand yet, though."

"True, but in time, he will."

"I hope so," I said, staring at her lips. I wanted to kiss her so badly, but I was too afraid to make that move. I wasn't supposed to do that anymore anyway.

"You feel tense." She slid her hands up my shirt and rubbed my back. "Let me help you relax," she said, unbuttoning my shirt.

"I love how you treat me."

` "You better love me," she smiled, putting my shirt to the side. I do, baby, I thought. She kissed me softly, rubbing her hands over my chest. Addictive.

"One day you will make someone very happy," I said when she pulled away. I felt a small lump in my throat. I smiled, though, not wanting to let on how depressing that thought was. She just blushed.

"My sweet Quinton." She kissed me again. This time things started to get hot and heavy, but she had the good sense to pull away. "We can't go there right now. We have a little one in the house."

"Yeah, I know."

"Well." She stood. "Isn't it time for little Quinton's nap?"

"It may just be," I said, standing as well.

"Well, if it is, come see me," she said, disappearing down the hall. I stared after her. I was supposed to have been leaving her alone. Here I was in the same position, wanting her. I was weak.

I couldn't help it. Desiree provided me with comfort that I could not find anywhere else. I needed her to stay sane.

I checked on Quinton. Amazingly, he had climbed on my bed and fell asleep. I laughed. Wow, thanks, little buddy. I could now spend time with Desiree without feeling guilty.

I took a quick shower. After showering, I grabbed the Jergens, sprayed on the Curve, and wrapped myself in my towel. I headed straight for her bedroom. I knocked and she opened it within seconds. She greeted me in a towel as well.

"Lay on the bed," she demanded.

"What are you going to do?"

"Take care of you, Quinton."

A week later, after Thanksgiving, a judge granted me sole custody of little Quinton. As soon as the judge heard half of the things India had done, she quickly agreed that my son needed to be with me. She lectured India on how disgusting her behavior was. My son's mother ran out the courtroom in tears. I did feel sorry for her.

As I walked towards the door, I knew I probably would not see her again. My family all hugged in relief when I walked out of the courtroom. I was glad that it was over. It had been difficult times.

"It's for the best," my mother whispered as she hugged me.

Quinton was waiting with Des. When she saw me coming towards them, she stood. She headed towards me.

"Here you go, daddy," she said, handing him to me.

"Thanks." I leaned over and kissed her. I thought maybe she didn't like me doing so in front of my family, but she didn't react negatively. She actually smiled.

We had dinner at my parent's house that evening. Des, Tyler and Rayven were all included. These days, they had been like family to me as well. It was hard to find friends who supported you in tough times.

Later on that night, I chilled on the couch with Des and my son. It felt wonderful to have two of the most important people in my life with me. I wished more than anything that we could be a family. I wished Des would fall in love with me. That wasn't happening.

I had gone to the bathroom when I heard my son say, "I love you" to her. I knew right then that he was starting to look up to her as a motherly figure. It was not surprising since India was no longer in his life. I felt sick knowing that one day soon, I was going to tear him away from Desiree too. I had to do so in order to stay sane.

"I love you too, sweetie," she said in return. Great! My son gets to hear those words, but I couldn't. I must have lost my mind. Why was I jealous of a three-year-old?

"Little man," I walked back into the room. "Time for bed."

"Okay, daddy." He threw his arms around Desiree and stole a kiss before following me down the hall. He hadn't even started kindergarten and was already a charmer. He was too much like me. I had always been a flirt.

"I love him," Des said once I rejoined her on the couch.

"Me too." I pulled her close to me. And I love you, I thought.

"I want a baby, Quinton."

"Well, let's get started," I said, kissing her neck.

"You don't want a baby with me," she giggled. She was ticklish.

"Yes, I do. You would make a wonderful mother and we would make a beautiful baby."

I didn't sleep too well that night. I woke up the next morning feeling pretty lousy. Even the sight of Desiree didn't cheer me up. I had one of those gnawing headaches that I felt was going to hang around the entire day. I had a nagging feeling that this was not going to be my day.

My brother was having a fifth birthday party for my niece, Joelle, that afternoon. I was of course taking my son. Desiree had made it clear that she didn't have plans, so I quickly invited her along.

We were at the toy store picking up a gift for my niece when I saw him. I was immediately disgusted by sight of Anthony, Desiree's ex. The ex that I hated the most. I couldn't help but feel that Anthony was aware of how I felt about Desiree and he took every opportunity to rub their relationship in my face.

I prayed that he didn't see us, but he stopped right in front of the glass window. He stared directly at us. I stared back at him for what felt like forever. Desiree's back was to him so she had not notice. I was hoping that he would think that Desiree was with me and would just do us both a favor and disappear. I had learned a long time ago that you didn't always get what you wanted in life. He walked in and headed straight for us. Before I could vocalize his presence to Desiree, she spotted him.

"Shit! Will you hide me?"

"Too late. I think he sees you, Des."

"What does he think he is doing?" she whispered fiercely.

"Well hello," he said, approaching us. I could tell that he was just as arrogant as ever.

"Anthony," Des and I both said at once.

"How are you two doing?"

"I am great and yourself?" Desiree asked. She was nicer than I because I could care less.

"Pretty good, Desiree. You look beautiful."

"Thank you."

"Cute kid, Alexander. He looks just like you." I didn't want to accept his compliment, but I wasn't going to be rude.

"Thank you."

"Who is he, daddy?" Quinton asked. He was giving Anthony a distrusting looked. I wanted to laugh, but I didn't. Even at three, my son obviously had a great judge of character. I wanted to tell my son that he was a sorry excuse for a man, but I kept my mouth shut.

"A friend of Desiree's."

"Alexander, you mean to tell me that you never considered me a friend?" Why was he always so smug? I chose not to respond. I just stared back at him, praying that he would disappear and leave us alone. He was a nightmare.

"Whats up, buddy? I am Anthony. Whats your name?"

"Quinton." He then turned his attention back to the toys. He didn't want any parts of Anthony. I couldn't blame him.

"Just like you, Q. Desiree, can I borrow you for a moment?"

"No," she said flatly. "We are in a rush."

"Come on, baby. It won't take long."

"I haven't been your baby for years now, so you can chill with that. Why can't you say what needs to be said right here?"

"Because I rather talk to you in private," he said, giving me a smirk. I know we learned in church to never hate a person, but I was pretty close to hating Anthony.

"Fine." She rolled her eyes, but like always, she gave into him. She followed him right out of the store. "I will be back, Q," she said to me without giving me or my son a backwards glance.

I tried not to be annoyed, but it was near impossible not to be. Seeing Anthony had made my headache worse. As well as my mood. Knowing that him and Desiree was that close sicken me. So many bad memories came flooding back. I didn't need this stress today when I was already feeling horrible.

I quickly grabbed a game and a doll that Desiree and Quinton Jr. had picked out for my niece. I also grabbed a toy that my son had picked out for himself. I paid for the toys and headed out the door. I needed to get out this mall as soon as possible. If they weren't finished with their conversation, I was going to grab Desiree and march her right out the door.

When she saw me, she quickly put an end to her conversation with Anthony. He smiled after her. He smirked at me after he saw I was glaring at him. He then saluted me and walked away.

"Are you ready?" I could tell by the simple looked on her face that she had agreed to something that she should not have. Her lack of eye contact told me that she didn't want me to ask about it.

I was seething inside, so I didn't converse much with her. She tried to talk with me as if nothing happen, but it wasn't happening for me. She quickly caught on to my mood and got into a mood of her own. At my brother's house, we both avoided one another.

Desiree stayed by my sister, Peyton's, side all afternoon. Peyton adored Desire so she loved every minute of it. I stayed to myself because I was afraid that I was going to take someone's head off if they said anything out the way.

When we arrived home and Quinton was in my room playing with his new toy, Desiree laid into me.

"What is your problem, Q!"

"How do you figure that I have a problem?"

"Don't play dumb. It's obvious that you have an issue with me."

"Whatever." I tried to put an end to the confrontation, but she grabbed me. She got into my face.

"Do you have a problem with me?" When I didn't respond, anger flashed in her eyes. "You mean to tell me that you have an attitude with me so you decide to take it out on your family?"

"Desiree, you really don't know what you are talking about."

"I know you have been acting like a moody bitch all day."

I should've kept my mouth shut, but I couldn't. What she did was none of my business, but I couldn't help myself. I had pride.

"Why are you making stupid decisions? You are going out with him, aren't you?"

"I am letting him take me out for dinner. Really that is none of your business, Quinton."

"Why?"

"Because I want to. Why is it a concern of yours?"

"I can't be concerned for someone that I care about?"

"For what! I am not concerned."

"Obviously. This man cheated on you, Desiree."

"I know, Quinton. I don't need your background check."

"Why would you let a man, willing to be so careless with your heart, take you out again? Why would you set yourself up for something like that?"

"It's just dinner, Quinton. I am not dating him again."

"He doesn't deserve that."

"Quinton, I know."

"You are quick to pounce on me for my past. Women say that men are no good and that all men are dogs. Yet, you all flock to the ones who hurt and disrespect you the most. But I'm the dog, huh? I would never cheat on a woman that I supposedly love."

"I don't understand why you are getting so defensive. This has nothing to do with you."

"No, but you need to quit giving men like me a bad reputation when you choose to mess around with men like Thompson." She looked hurt, but right now, I was hurting.

"You don't understand!"

"You are right. I don't and I am not trying to. Goodnight."

It was only 9:30, but I needed sleep. It had been a bad day.

Desiree

"He is right," said Rayven. "I can see where Quinton is coming from. Not that I have much room to talk. I did go to dinner with Mike Both you and I have been quick to dog Quinton about being a ladies man. And now you are deciding to accompany Anthony out to dinner and he did you so dirty, Desiree."

"I know. That's why I was left looking stupid in the face. You both are absolutely right."

"Then Desiree, why are you going out with him. Again, I don't have much room to talk, but you gave me a hard time, so I have to do the same. Plus, no one likes Anthony. He is a jerk. I don't get what you ever saw in him."

"I don't expect anyone to understand. I barely do."

"I am relieved to know that you don't have high expectations. Why, Desiree?"

"I need closure."

"Closure?" she repeated with a frown. "What kind of closure do you need? He is a scumbag who obviously didn't love you enough to keep his little wand inside his pants and out of other women. I think you already know that. But then again, Mike did the same to me."

"I do know…"

"What else do you need to know? Are you sure that you want closure or do you want to know how much he misses you?" She gave me this look. She was too real for her own good.

"Okay, whatever, Rayven. I am not trying to sleep with the man. I just want him to answer some of my questions. Why did he cheat on me? Did he even love me?"

"Are you sure that you can handle what he has to say?"

"I think so. Rayven, I am not still in love with the bastard. It's been three years. I just want to know where he is coming from. Plus, I was never able to give the man a piece of my mind. We didn't have it out like you and Mike."

"True. Well, I am all for that. Look," she laughed, "I love you and I want you to be happy. I just need for you to be careful. And I think Q just wants the same for you. We both had to watch him hurt you once and neither of us is going to sit back and allow him to do that again. I can't stand the fool, so if he makes one foul mood, I will not hesitate to kill him."

"Okay, assassin! Down, girl!"

"Whatever. I went on my closure dinner, so I can't stop you. Let's find something scandalous for you to wear. You do have to show the jackass what he is missing."

The night that I was to go out with Anthony approached quickly. I dressed in my pink wrap dress and stilettoes. I pulled my hair back and applied my make-up as flawlessly as I could. I pulled out my finest jewelry. When I finished, I felt I looked good enough to make Anthony squirm throughout dinner. I knew how to press his buttons.

I stopped by Quinton's room on the way to the door. I didn't like being at odds with him. I wanted to clear the air and let him know that I appreciated his concern for my well-being.

"Q." I knocked on his door and walked in at the same time.

"Whats up?" he asked, throwing me a quick glance. He was on the floor. He was reading the bible. I felt guilt. I needed to do more reading of the word myself.

"Where is little Quinton?"

"You came to see my son and not me? My feelings are hurt."

"Be quiet."

"He's staying with my Mike tonight. To play with his cousins."

"Nice."

"Yep. What is that you want?"

"Wow," I said sitting on his bed near him.

"Look, Des, I can see that something is on your mind."

"I just want to say that you are right about me going out with Anthony. And I am sorry for judging you. What you said made sense. I am being stupid and I probably should not have said yes."

"And you are right; none of this is my business."

"No, but you are my friend. I just wanted to say that I need closure, Quinton. And I was being rude to you when you were just showing concern for me. That means a lot to me."

He stared at me for a moment before saying, "I just want you to be careful, Desiree. And happy."

"I will."

"You look incredible."

"Do I?" I covered my face with my hands. Quinton could make blush with just a look. His words made me look away. The combination was impossible for me to handle.

"Yes," he said pulling my hands away.

"Thank you."

"I do want to say that the other night I was having a bad day. I am sorry for taking it out on you and everybody else."

"Forgiven. Can I get a hug or something?" A kiss would have been nice. It would have calmed my nerves.

"Okay," he said standing. "Come here." He pulled me to him and we hugged. We may have hugged a little too long. I sort of buried my face in his neck.

"You smell good," I blurted. Suddenly I didn't want to go see Anthony. I wanted to stay in Quinton's arms.

"You feel good." We stared at one another for a moment. He wanted to kiss me, but he wouldn't. I was disappointed when he pulled away. "I am not about to kiss you when you are headed out the door on a date with another man."

"This is not a date, Q."

"Well whatever it is. I still can't kiss you."

"That has not stopped you before," I said thinking back to Justin and Malik. Q didn't really respect boundaries.

"It's time we both work on controlling things between us." I didn't like the sound of that.

I opted to meet Anthony at the restaurant. I didn't want him to know where I lived. I didn't want him in my personal space. I didn't want him back in my life in anyway. No one may have understood, but all I wanted was a sense of closure from him.

He was waiting outside the restaurant when I arrived. As far as I was concerned, Anthony only had a few good traits about him and one was being on time. His other traits were questionable. Love had made me very blind. I couldn't turn a blind eye when I caught him cheating, though. It was the last straw.

"Hey, baby." He did look lovely in his suit.

"Please don't call me baby, Anthony."

"I apologize. You look beautiful tonight, Desiree." I stared at him. Anthony rarely complimented anyone.

"Thank you, Anthony. You look nice as well."

"Thank you." Wow, no arrogant response. Maybe the man had grown up in the last three years. It was too early to make that call.

Before being seated, we held harmless polite conversation. How have you been? Where do you work? What have you been up to? Once we were seated, I couldn't help myself, I laid into him.

"Why are we here, Anthony?"

"Wow, Des. Do we really have to get serious before we even order? Why don't you let me order your favorite wine first? Maybe that will help you relax." I ignored his comment. I felt it was condescending as always.

"I only agreed to meet you here because you said that you wanted to talk. I am not here to have a good time. This is not a date." I wanted closure and nothing else from this man. After I got what I needed, I intended on leaving.

I could see now that Anthony was going to make this difficult. He was a difficult man. I sighed. Maybe I did need some wine.

We did order. Anthony did order that wine. When the waiter poured it into my glass, I took a huge gulp of it.

"Wow, Des." It took everything in me not to tell him to shut up.

"Get to talking Anthony or you will find yourself dinning alone."

"I miss you, Desiree."

"Really?" I laughed. "What exactly do you miss about me?"

"Everything. I think about you all the time, especially recently. I couldn't believe my luck when I saw you in the mall the other day. It was like an answer to my prayers."

"Really, Anthony. Your prayers?"

"Yes, I have been praying about it. I wanted to see you again."

"I hope that you are not surprised when I say that I find all of this difficult to believe. In fact, I think all of this is a bunch of BS."

"I knew that you were going to feel that way. I assure you that I am being honest."

"You lied to me throughout our entire relationship. Why all of a sudden would you be honest with me?"

"I grew up, Desiree. I was a boy then. I am a man now. Cheating on you was one of the worst mistakes that I have ever made. You were the best thing that has ever happened to me."

"Funny that you would say all of this to me, considering you treated me like crap."

"I deserve that assessment. Despite what happened between us, I never wanted to lose you. I hated myself for causing us to end."

"Well what did you expect? Did you expect to play me and that I was going to stick around and just be your loyal girlfriend."

"I never expected you to find out."

"Of course not. No one ever does, but you were sloppy. If I had not caught you screwing the heifer in our bed, I would still be with you. Everyone would have talked about how stupid I was to stay with a man who obviously didn't love me enough to stay faithful."

"Cheating on you was not a regular occurrence. I did it once. I got caught and lost you all in the same night." I didn't believe him but I didn't call him out on it.

"Once is all it takes to destroy a relationship. It proved everything that I needed to know, Anthony. You didn't love me."

"Bull! I loved you very much!"

"Very odd way of showing it. If that's how you love a woman then you need to stop it."

"That was my past. I made a huge mistake."

"Huge is not the word. Detrimental is more like it."

"Obviously because I lost you, Desiree, but I am human."

"So am I. So I didn't come here to hear you excuses. I would never dishonor a relationship or commitment to someone for sex."

"What else can I say to you, but I am sorry."

"Sorry doesn't really cut it, Anthony." He hung his head. What did he expect? I was no longer the easy going girlfriend who turned a blind eye. I had grown up to in the last three years as well. "Why? Why did you sleep with her? I didn't fulfill your needs?"

"No, I was fulfilled." I was always willing to please him.

"Did I not pay enough attention to you?" I catered to the man.

"No, you did. You made it clear to me that you loved me."

"Love wasn't enough for you?"

"Desiree, love didn't have anything to do with it. Plain and simple, I was drunk."

"Usually when you were drunk, you couldn't get it up to bat."

"Believe me, it was not a good experience."

"You sure about that? She sure was having a good time."

"She was drunk too."

"Look, you can keep the details to yourself."

"I'm sorry. Alcohol was involved and I wasn't thinking rationally, Desiree."

"Okay." I needed more wine. I wanted to slap this man.

"I know that it may sound as if that's an excuse, but it's the truth. If I had not been drinking, that night would not have happened. I would not have slept with the girl." He would have. He was lying like always.

"Was that supposed to make me feel better about you cheating? Drinking is not a good enough excuse. Don't drink if you can't handle it. You were tempted already and alcohol made you fall right into the devil's trap."

"Look, I never got the chance to apologize for hurting you. That was my biggest regret. I am very sorry."

"Oh, I know you are."

"And I did love you," he said ignoring my sarcasm. "I did not appreciate what I had at the time. The day I lost you was the wort day of my life. I wanted to marry you." I almost choked on my wine. He could not have been serious. "Are you okay?"

"I am fine." I stared at him for a moment and then I picked up my wine glass and finished it off. I then proceeded to flag down the waiter. I needed another."

"Wow, Desiree. Do you think you need to drink this much wine tonight?" I know he was not lecturing me on drinking. I kept my mouth shut, though.

"I need it." After the waiter brought more wine, I excused myself. I spent ten minutes in the bathroom. I wanted to make him wait. I was trying to play all of this cool. Plus I needed to calm down.

Once I had gotten myself together, I headed back to the table. I was ready to handle things a little differently. I was here to grab my closure and move one.

"Okay, Anthony, let's talk."

He put it all out there. Why he loved me. Why he was so insecure. Why he did what he did.

"I didn't think that you would marry me," he confessed.

He told me how he missed me. That there had been a void in his life. He still had nightmares about that night. I didn't tell him about the nightmares that I had after we broken up. They lasted six months.

"You would think that by now, I would be over you, Desiree, but I am not. I still love you. When I saw you with Alexander, I thought I was going to lose my mind."

"Because I was with Quinton?" I didn't understand. I just knew the two did not like each other.

"Yeah, aren't you two together now? I almost laughed.

"Well, not exactly."

"What do you mean by not exactly? Are you having sex?"

"Yes, we are." It was none of his business, but I didn't feel like lying about it. If it made him jealous, then I loved it.

"Seriously? Wow. I didn't think that you would say yeah."

"I am not going to lie to you."

"I see. I had that feeling."

"How did you have that feeling? You saw the both of us for all of ten minutes."

"I saw the way that he was looking….oh never mind. Do you love him?" I almost said yeah, but I was going to remain honest.

"No."

"Does he love you?"

"No. Why?" He didn't respond. "Look, we are close friends. We cherish each other. We will always love each other in that sense, but we are not in love. We just have explosive sex."

Anthony got a crazy look on his face and I almost laughed.

"I want to talk about how I felt. About how hurt I was. How I did love you, very much." I let out all that I had bottled up the last three years. And finally I was started to see the closure that I so desperately needed. I had forgiven him.

By the end of the night, we had both relaxed enough to have a pleasant conversation. We were able to enjoy the dinner. When we walked out the restaurant, I actually hugged him.

"You sure that you can drive?" I had consumed a lot of wine.

"I have built a high tolerance. I am okay."

"Are you sure?" He had asked me three times now.

"Yes! Wow. Would you like to follow me home just to make sure? And then you can go on about your merry business." What was with this change of heart, I thought.

"I would feel more comfortable."

"Okay, let's go." I should have sent him on his merry way, but I didn't. I invited him inside. "Do you want coffee or something?"

"I would love some." He gave me this look. I rolled my eyes. I headed towards the house with my ex on my heels. "You did good, Desiree. Nice spot."

"Thanks." Before I realized what he was doing, he pushed me against my kitchen counter."

"Wow, Anthony."

"Baby, you look so beautiful. I wanted to kiss you all night. It's all I have been thinking about."

"Why prolong?" It felt great to have his lips against mine again. His hands burned through my dress. I squealed as he lifted me in the air and place me on the counter.

Things started to get hot and heavy. I don't know if it was the wine, but I was seriously considering letting him take me to bed. I use to love what he could do to me.

I reached up to un-do his tie. I unbuttoned his shirt. My hands slid across his chest and his stomach. I closed my eyes as he kissed my neck. I moaned a little as his lips touched my spot.

I wanted to go there, but common sense kicked in. Anthony didn't deserve this. I deserved more. I grabbed his hand.

"Stop!" He stepped back and stared at me. He started to nod.

"I get it. You can't do this. I understand."

"I am sorry, but it's a bad idea." Why was I apologizing? "Actually, I am not sorry, Anthony. I don't need this."

"No need to explain." He buttoned his shirt. He leaned over and kissed my forehead. "Thanks for tonight. I will see myself out."

"Thank you. Bye."

I sat there and stared after him. I remained there even when I heard the front door close. I wasn't sure why I let him in my home. I wasn't sure why I let him touch me, but I was glad that I regained my senses. I would have regretted that. I would not have told anyone.

I took a shower. Afterwards, I toweled off and rubbed myself down in shea butter. I didn't grab underwear, just my silk robe. I headed down the hall to Quinton's room. It was dark and empty.

"Where are you?" I asked feeling very frustrated. I could have sworn I saw his car parked outside.

In defeat, I walked back to my bedroom. I turned off the lights and turned on the TV. I slid all the way under the covers. I tried not to beat myself up too much.

"Lord help you, Desiree. You are so stupid sometimes."

Quinton

I left the house in a hurry. I didn't think. I just grabbed my keys, my phone, and my wallet. I got in my car and drove. I didn't really know where I was going until I pulled up outside T's spot on the other side of town. I didn't get out of the car immediately. I felt numb. I had literally thrown up during the drive over.

I heard when Desiree came in. I assumed that she would be alone, so I walked out to say hi. Instead I found her on her kitchen counter, making out with her ex. I was so appalled that I couldn't even put one foot in front of the other. I watched this man put his hands all over the woman that I had loved for half a year now. She was moaning the same way she did with me. I couldn't stomach it.

It felt like I was in college all over again. It was just like that fateful night five years ago where I endured the pain of watching her with Anthony. Once again, she was in his arms and not mine. I could do nothing but leave the house.

For months, Desiree was the only woman that I had been consistently intimate with. She was the only woman that I had desired to be with. I loved her with all my heart and had been holding on to false hope. Seeing her with Anthony was a slap in my face.

She had a right to be with whoever she wanted. She wasn't committed to me. I still hated knowing that she was with someone else. It did something horrible to me to know that another man was touching and loving her the way I was. Knowing that man was Anthony was almost unbearable.

"Quinton!" Tyler scared me. He had walked up to my car without me noticing.

"You scared me, bro."

"Whats up, man? Why are you sitting in your car staring off into space like you are crazy?"

"I needed somewhere to escape to for a couple of hours. Do you mind if I come in?"

"Of course you can come in," he said opening my door for me. "Whats wrong? You don't look good at all."

"I feel horrible. It's been a bad night."

"Oh wow. Desiree?"

"Yeah. What else is new?"

"I suppose that you don't want to talk about it?"

"Not particularly."

"I respect that."

"Thanks."

"No problem. Here," he said, throwing me a corona once we were inside. "Help yourself. There is more if you need it."

"Thanks I'm going to sit on your patio and drown my sorrows."

"Go for it. Look, you need to get out of that house."

"Eight weeks, T." There had been some delays.

I didn't sleep that night. I just stared at the stars in the sky, feeling sorry for myself. I had to be the dumbest man alive. I should have not allowed this to happen again.

23

Unfaithful

"Lying lips are an abomination to the Lord, but those who act faithfully are his delight." *Proverbs 12:22*

Quinton

When I saw Desiree the next day, I acted as if nothing happened. I refused to ask her how her dinner was. I knew she would lie because she was probably embarrassed by her actions. I would have called her out if she didn't tell the truth. I didn't want to put myself in that situation. I was too jealous.

I forced myself to move on. At least I made an attempt to. I was counting down the days that Quinton and I were moving out of Desiree's house and into my own. There was no way that I could get over this woman when I had to see her daily.

It had been months since I had gone out on a date with another woman. There had been no one since Rayven.

I desperately needed to go out with someone. I knew getting back in the game would be good for me. And I wasn't just looking for a good time. I wanted a woman to fall in love with.

My luck changed one day before Christmas. I had been focusing on making it a good holiday for my son, so I hadn't been focusing on myself. I was in the grocery store, picking up some things that Desiree needed. A female walked past and she was the first woman in a while that could take my breath away. I thought she was African American, but I heard her accent while she spoke on the phone and my guess was that she was Dominican. She had beautiful brown skin, a curvy body, a captivating smile and long curly hair. She had a sexy walk and carried herself with an undeniable confidence.

I was in awe, but something kept me from approaching her. I attempted to ignore her and concentrated on the ingredients for Desiree's lasagna tonight.

Ignoring her was difficult. Somehow she was on every aisle that I turned down. It didn't take her long to notice me. Pretty soon, she was making it obvious that she was checking me out. She stared me down as if she was daring me to say something. I refused to do so.

She refused to let it go. I was almost to the check out when she stepped in front of me. I had to stop abruptly.

"It's a little rude of you to stare at me and not say anything."

"Oh so you noticed," I joked. "Well I apologize."

"It's okay. What's your name?"

"Quinton."

"Veronica," she said sticking her hand out. She had a nice firm handshake. I loved that.

Before walking out of the store, I had her number saved in my phone and she had mine. By the end of the night, she had called me. She asked me out. I was not use to that. Before hanging up, we had made plans to meet for lunch since I was off the next day.

I saw Desiree the next morning. She had cooked breakfast. I tried to ignore her pencil skirt, her tight button up shirt, and those heels. I tried to ignore the urge to take her into my arms. Every time, she breezed by, I tried not to inhale her perfume which I loved.

It had been days since I had kissed those lips. Normally, I would go for it, but it was time for me stop allowing myself to fall into her trap. I had to get over her.

"Quinton!" Her voice interrupted my thoughts. "I've called your name five times and you have flat out ignored me."

"Sorry, I was deep in thought."

"I see. I asked did you want to do lunch today."

"I would love to, but I already have plans."

"Oh." She gave me that look. "You never do lunch with me anymore. You use to stop by anytime."

"We will do lunch one day this week, I promise. It may have to be an early lunch because this is my only day off.

"Deal. So who is the lucky girl?" How did she know?

"Veronica."

"Yuck," she frowned. "I knew a Veronica and she was horrible."

"Not this one."

"Hope not. You deserve a good woman. Have fun, my friend. I will treat you and Quinton to Chuckie Cheese's tonight. 7:00?"

"Sounds good to me."

"I will see you then." She kissed my cheek. I was disappointed. "Hey, sweetheart." I turned and my son had entered the room, wiping the sleep from his eyes. Desiree leaned down and kissed him, and then she breezed out of the door.

"I love that woman," I said lifting Quinton into my arms.

"I love you, daddy."

"I love you too. What do you want for breakfast?"

"Oatmeal." Of course.

"One bowl of Oatmeal coming right up for you, buddy."

"What are you smiling at, daddy," Quinton asked when I sat him down to fix his breakfast.

"Today is going to be a good day, my son. That's all."

After breakfast, I sat Quinton in front of my TV and took a long shower. I opted for slacks and a sweater instead of my usual jeans and button down. I was out to impress.

I dropped Quinton off at daycare. I then met my interior decorator at the furniture store to pick out some last minute items. All the while, I focused on Veronica. I was anxious to see her today. I hoped that she had something more to offer than beauty.

Veronica wore this cream pants suit that fitted her in all the right places. It accentuated every curve on her body. I smiled to myself when she took off her jacket, revealing a very skimpy shell. Wow. Was that something she always wore or had she done it for me?

"If not anything else, she is sexy," I mumbled.

"Excuse me."

"I said that you look very beautiful."

"Why thank you, Quinton."

I quickly realized that Veronica's beauty was more than skin deep. She was classy, smart and witty. She was very sarcastic which I loved. She made me laugh. I could tell that she had a fun spirit to her and I was digging that. To me she was perfect. She was unlike any of the women who I had recently gone out with. They had been completely wrong for me.

She invited me out for brunch the next day. I was thinking along the lines of dinner. She responded with, "Let's do both because I would really love to get to know you better, Quinton Alexander." Since I was into this girl, I agreed. I was extremely excited.

We went out twice every day the next few days. I was barely home. I was definitely grateful for my mother who had asked to keep my son for the remainder of the week. When I told her that I had a taken a strong interest in a female, she grew excited. I knew she was praying every day for me to settle down.

I barely laid eyes on Desiree. That was probably a good thing. I did, however; catch up with her on Thursday morning.

"Whats up, girl?" I was cheerful, but she wasn't. In fact, she seemed a little agitated with me. I could not figure out what I done because I had not been around lately.

"You've been busy." She peered at me over her coffee.

"Yeah, I have had a full plate these days."

"I see. How's Veronica?"

"She is wonderful." I tried not to gloat.

"You really like her, I take it?

"Well, yeah, how can you tell?"

"You have this goofy smile on your face. So do you have plans today too, Quinton?"

"Yeah, Veronica is taking me out for brunch. You know how you women are, always trying to prove to men how independent you are," I joked. She didn't crack a smile.

"I don't have to prove anything to anyone."

"Oh." What had I done?

"Well good for you.." I was about to ask her what the deal was but she didn't give me the chance. "Well, Quinton, have a good day. I must leave before I am late. Goodbye." She was out the door before I could respond. She didn't get past me before I noticed her dark eyes. Obviously I had pissed her off.

I stood there thinking until I figured it out. I had promised her that we would do lunch this week. I had been so wrapped up in Veronica that it had slipped my mind. She was hurt. I hated that I was the one to make her feel that way.

I avoided making plans with Veronica on Friday. I planned to have dinner with her at her spot on Saturday. I wanted to fix things with Desiree as quickly as possible. Things didn't go as planned.

"I was wondering if you wanted to do lunch with me today." I didn't have to be on the radio until 2:00 today, so I was free.

When I asked her, she actually stopped to look at me. "What? Veronica canceled on you?" Was she hurt? Or was she jealous?

"Nope. I purposely left Friday open for you and I."

"What? Since yesterday when you remembered that you had failed to keep your plans with me? Well, you should have cleared those plans you had with me. Now, I have plans."

"With who?" I asked. I felt that familiar jealousy.

"With a friend. He is taking me out for lunch," she said, raising her eyebrow at me. "I guess that we need a rain check. Bye now." She left me in the kitchen, feeling like a fool. Only Desiree could humiliate me the way that she did.

"Wow." I had messed up royally this time. My day was ruined before it had begun. I was going to have to spend the rest of the day trying to figure out ways to make it up to her.

Despite the heat I was in with Desiree, I was still very excited about my rendezvous with Veronica. When I wasn't thinking of ways to get back on Desiree's good side, I was thinking of my Dominican beauty. The woman was amazing.

Even my mother was excited for me.

"Are you sure that you don't want me to just keep Quinton until Sunday, sweetheart? It's not a problem?" I was picking up Quinton to spend time with him Friday night and Saturday during the day.

"Mother, I will bring him back tomorrow night. I have barely seen him all week. I would like to spend time with my son. I am cool, but thank you," I said, kissing her.

"Well, alright."

As soon as we got home, Quinton ran to Desiree's room before I could stop him.

"Dessie," he yelled.

"Hey, cutie," she said, her eyes actually brightening. I loved that she was happy to see him.

"I miss you," he said stretching his arms towards her.

"I miss you too," she said, lifting him so that she could hug him.

"You look pretty."

"Thank you," she laughed. She was just wearing a towel. That's why I didn't move closer. I was imagining what was under that towel. "You are just like your father." She finally looked up at me. The look in her eyes made me feel like an intruder. "You are such a flirt." Something told me that was an insult.

"Is that a bad thing?" my son asked.

"Of course not." She kissed his forehead before sitting him down. He left the room. "Quinton." She finally addressed me.

"Desiree. How are you?" I tried to overlook her coldness.

"I am good. Yourself?"

"I am surviving. Are you heading out tonight?"

"Yes, I am."

"A date?"

"Yes." Not the answer that I wanted to hear.

"With who?" I couldn't help myself.

"You wouldn't know him." Ouch.

"Where are you going?"

"I don't know. If you are done questioning me, I have to finish getting dress before I am late." I almost lost it when she dropped her towel. My mouth was suddenly dry. My heart was beating quickly. "Bye, Quinton." She rolled her eyes as she walked over, shoved me out of the way and slammed her bedroom door in my face.

"Apparently, I am your fool," I said heading down the hall.

I was sitting on the couch, Quinton in my lap, watching cartoons, when there was a knock at the door. I knew it was her date, but I was being spiteful. I was not going to answer it. It probably wasn't going to help my case, but I didn't care.

She appeared out of nowhere in her skinny jeans and her sweater. She looked as breathtaking as ever.

"Lord, please help me right now," I mumbled.

"Quinton, why are you being rude? You could have answered the door." I could have.

"I didn't hear it." I didn't care that I was lying. "I was daydreaming. I am sorry."

"Grow up! I don't even want to talk to you right now." She walked over to my son and kissed him once again.

"Goodbye, sweetie."

"Bye, Dessie." She looked down at me before walking away. She looked as if she was going to say something else, but she didn't. "Daddy, is Dessie your girlfriend?"

"No son." I felt a lump in my throat. "She's not my girlfriend."

"Why not?"

"She is just daddy's friend."

"Oh. I wish she was, daddy." I almost said me too.

"Really? Why?"

"She is pretty and she is nice to me."

"Okay." I felt sadness. I was really hoping that Veronica could help me out since Desiree wasn't willing to.

"Is Dessie mad at you?" Wow. My son was observant.

"Yes, very," I admitted. I was not going to lie to him.

"Why?"

"Because daddy is an idiot." In love.

Little Quinton and I decided to sleep in the next morning. Once we were dressed, I took him out for lunch. After lunch, I asked him what he wanted to do. I almost flipped when he said that he wanted to hang out with Desiree.

"Little man, I don't think that I can make that happen."

"Why not, daddy?" He started whining.

"Don't whine. You are supposed to be a big boy."

"I am a big boy, but I want to play with Dessie."

"I am sorry. You can't always have what you want. Des is busy."

I had a feeling that she didn't come home last night and that bothered me. There were endless possibilities to why she didn't going through my head. All the speculation had given me a headache.

I took Quinton to see a new Disney movie. After that, I took him to buy a basketball and a mini sized hoop because he had expressed interest in the sport. I believe that he had decent talent for a kid going on four-years-old. He was just like his daddy.

He was exhausted by the time I handed him back to my mother. He was fast asleep.

"What did you do to my grandson? Spoiling him?"

"Not much. I just gave him the world. Can you really blame me? He is my only child."

"Hopefully not for much longer."

"Bye, mother."

I headed straight to the shower when I got home. I shaved. I dressed in a button up and jeans. I didn't want to do too much. We were just hanging out at her place.

When I arrived at her condo she greeted me in lingerie and stilettoes. She gave any Victoria Secret model a run for their money.

"Wow." I was actually speechless. This had not happened before. Not quite like this.

"Do you like?" she asked, spinning around.

"Come here," I said, pulling her to me. "I love it."

"Thanks." She kissed me for a long time.

Veronica threw down in the kitchen. She made spaghetti and the best garlic bread that I had ever tasted. After the main course, she sat in my lap and fed me chocolate covered strawberries.

"Do you have room for more dessert, Quinton?" she asked, sticking her tongue in my ear.

"I do have a big appetite."

"Good to hear." She grabbed my hand and led me to her bedroom. She pushed me down and started yanking on my clothes.

"I am not going anywhere, sweetheart." I joked. She didn't respond. She gave me this hungry look as she kept pulling on my clothes. She then grabbed some whip cream. "Where did that come from?" Again, she didn't respond.

I really didn't come here for sex. I was looking for love and I wanted to see if she could offer me some. However, I couldn't turn this woman down. She was very convincing.

We lay there afterwards in silence. We both were trying to catch our breaths. I closed my eyes and willed myself to calm down.

"I think we are compatible," she said finally.

"Me too," I said, squeezing her thigh.

"Good. You will be seeing a lot more of me, Mr. Alexander."

"I like that."

"Well, alright." She leaned over and kissed me. "Goodnight." She then turned off the lights and turned her back to me.

I laid there for a moment, staring up at ceiling as I often did. I thought about how incredible Veronica was, but as always when I was alone without a distraction, my mind drifted to Des. The thought of her annoyed me. I wanted to think of anything else, yet I kept wondering whose arms she was lying in right now. It didn't matter how much I like Veronica, I wanted to be with Des at this moment.

I barged into Desiree's office on Monday morning on a mission. I had to get this woman to forgive me. I carried a vase of three dozen pink roses in one hand and a basket full of chocolate, her favorite wine, a teddy bear and a gift certificate to her favorite spa.

"What are you doing here?" she asked once her secretary let me into her office. Her eyes grew big at the sight of the gifts that I was bearing. I knew she adored pink roses.

"Desiree, I need you to forgive me."

"You can't buy me." Yet she was eyeing the gifts instead of me.

"I am not trying to, but I will do anything to get back on your good side. I hate it when we are not talking to me."

"Quinton, I am not..."

"You are mad. I'm sorry that I forgot about us last week. Believe me, I missed out because I cherish every moment I can spend with you. You are my best friend." I am not sure when that happened, but Tyler had taken a back seat in the last year. I could tell that I had touched her because the look on her face changed. I breathed a sigh of relief. "I was selfish and I want to apologize for that."

"It's okay."

"No it's not. Please say that you forgive me. I miss you. Little Quinton misses you too." I knew that would make her smile.

"Really?"

"He keeps asking about you. I miss you more, though," I teased.

"I miss him too."

"You don't miss me?"

"Not like I miss him."

"Why not?"

"He is more adorable. We are good, Quinton. I forgive you."

"Thank God. Can I get a hug?"

"You are asking for a whole lot."

"We are making up." She rolled her eyes, but she threw her arms around me anyway. It felt good to touch her again.

"Thank you for my gifts."

"You are welcome. You smell amazing."

"Thank you," she said looking away.

"Are you going to let me completely make it up to you or not? I want to finally take you out to lunch," I said, rubbing her belly. "I know you are hungry."

"You are right. Let's go," she said, grabbing her purse.

"What would you like?"

"Chicken and Waffles."

"Whatever you want. I know just the spot."

"And then I want a French Vanilla Cappuccino from Starbucks."

I took in her short navy skirt and her fitted cream sweater. She looked as beautiful as ever. It didn't matter what she had on, she always took my breath away.

"How did you get away with this?" I asked, placing my arm around her waist. I loved when she did the same to me.

"With what?"

"Your outfit is so inappropriate."

"Oh," she laughed. "I don't look good?"

"You are as beautiful as always."

"Well, that's how I get away with it."

Desiree and I had Christmas at her house. Little Quinton enjoyed his many gifts under the tree. Both of our immediate families came over for the dinner that we had cooked together. Everyone had a good time. I loved that because family was everything. Tyler and Rayven stopped by before the night ended.

For New Years, Tyler, Rayven, Des and I all went out. Veronica was out of town with her family in New York. The four of us got drunk while catching up over vodka. It was a wonderful time. I couldn't help but feel a tinge of jealousy as I noticed how in love Tyler and Rayven were. I was proud of Tyler, but annoyed that he found love before me.

Two weeks later, I was getting ready to leave the house early one morning when there was a knock on the front door. I just assumed that Desiree would get it. When the knocking continued, I realized that she wasn't. Hopefully nothing was wrong.

I was annoyed to open to door to find Des's new boy toy, Lance. I didn't refrain from looking at my watch. It was 7:45. I frowned up at him.

"Whats up, man?"

"I am on the way to work. I came by to check on Des."

"Huh? Aren't you going to see her at work?"

"That would be impossible. Desiree has the flu, Quinton. You didn't know?" he asked looking at me as if I was crazy. "Des does say that she doesn't see you much anymore." I wanted to punch him in his face. I just gave him a look.

I turned and left him standing by the front door. He could fend for himself. I headed to her room. I didn't knock. I just walked in. There she was laying in the fetal position, watching the news.

"Well, hello."

"You didn't tell me that you were sick."

"I haven't seen much of you." I had been spending a lot of time with Veronica these days.

I almost flipped when Lance pushed past me. He took a seat beside her. He pulled her into his arms. I didn't like how that made me feel. I felt devastated.

"You came!" she said smiling.

"I told you that I would."

I was hurt. She had called for him and not me. I use to be the one to comfort her.

"Do you need anything?" I asked, cutting in.

"No, Quinton. I am fine." She said, barely looking my way. "My mother is coming over."

"Well, if you need me, let me know."

"Okay, Quinton. Thank you."

"Doesn't seem like you need me anymore," I mumbled. I left quickly because obviously I wasn't who she wanted right now.

No one could ruin my day the way Desiree could. I snapped at everyone from my boss to Veronica, to my mother and even little Quinton. I was pissed and I really couldn't understand why. I just knew I was going to have to do a lot of apologizing tomorrow.

I avoided home. I left Quinton with my mother. I couldn't face Desiree. I felt humiliated by the morning. The woman I loved was sick and I wasn't aware. She didn't bother to tell me.

Why did that hurt so badly? Why did it bother me so?

When I got home later that night, I didn't get out. I just turned up the radio and comforted myself with a Corona. I was alone with my thoughts. I finally realized why I was so angry.

Desiree use to need me, but she didn't these days. Another man was in her life and that killed me. How many more people did I have to watch her with? How much longer was she going to torture me?

I felt like I was losing her when I still needed her. She was acting strange around me these days. She was distancing herself and I didn't know why. I couldn't do anything about it, but watch it happen.

Before I knew it, I was dialing the number to my radio station. Marcus was the Love Doctor. His voice filled the airwaves from 10:00 to 2:00 every night.

"You are on the air with Dr. Marcus Love. Who's calling?"

"James."

"Whats up, James."

"I have some issues."

"Let's talk about them."

"I am losing the woman in my life."

"Why, man? What happened?"

"I fell in love."

"Doesn't make sense," he said after a moment of silence.

"Well, let me explain."

Desiree

I could not believe that the woman Quinton was seeing was Veronica Ramirez. This was the same whore that Anthony had chosen to destroy our relationship over. She was the woman who tried to destroy my confidence and everything I stood for. I didn't let her win, but I could not stand the sight of her, even to this day.

I was out to lunch one day the other week alone. Initially when I spotted Quinton with Veronica, I was shocked to see them together, but then I got angry. I sat there and watched the happy couple, getting sicker by the minute. I was sick at the fact that Veronica was the one making Quinton this happy. She was the reason that he had been neglecting me.

I had been tempted to go over there and give them both a piece of my mind. I was going to tell her exactly what I thought of her. I was going to ask Q why he would do something so insensitive to me. But then I remembered that he didn't know all the details behind my break up with Anthony. He just knew about Anthony cheating. He didn't realize that the other woman was Veronica.

I struggled with the decision whether or not to tell Quinton about her. I knew Q would stop dating her without a second thought. But then I thought about how happy he seemed to be. I didn't want to be selfish. I didn't want him to sacrifice his happiness for mine. As much as I hated every moment of it, he was digging the chick.

I kept quiet about it all. I never told Q about seeing him with his new girlfriend that day. It was hard. Although he was not intentionally doing anything wrong, I still wanted to scream at him. I wanted to ask him what he was thinking. And then I would realize that I had nothing to do with who he was dating. No one said I had to like the women in his life.

Seeing Veronica brought back all the memories that I had tried to bury. I didn't want to remember what happened, but I did. I remembered every messed up detail. Vividly.

I met Veronica halfway through my second semester senior year when we needed to pair up for a marketing class project. I had always noticed in her class. She was a beautiful girl, so it was hard not to. She seemed really cool so we started to hang out when Ray wasn't available. I thought she was my girl. She had me fooled.

When I introduced her to Anthony, neither seemed overly impressed by each other. In fact they were barely cordial. They gave me no reason to suspect anything. Two years after graduating, I was still friends with Veronica and I was still dating Anthony.

I went out with Rayven one weekend while Anthony was supposedly at a party. I let myself into his apartment in the wee hours of the morning. I was expecting to find the apartment empty because I figured Anthony would be too tipsy to drive home. I headed to his bedroom, ready to fall into bed and wait for him.

I was in for a shock when I pushed open his bedroom door. I turned on the lights to find Veronica on top of my man. I actually laughed in complete disbelief. I was exasperated.

"Shit! Desiree!" Anthony pushed Veronica off and stumbled towards me. He tried to reach for me, but I would not let him.

"There's no reason to touch me."

"It's not what it looks like."

"It sure looks like you just screwed me over, literally!" Before I knew what I was doing, I had punched him in the eye. "You are a piece of shit!"

"I know, baby. I just made a huge mistake. Can we please talk about this before you just leave?"

"No, we have nothing to talk about."

"Desiree, please," he said, rubbing his eyes. "You know that I love you. This was just sex. She means absolutely nothing to me. I don't even like that girl."

"Too late. No need to insult the girl now. Apparently you were pretending as if you didn't like her. I believed your performance, Anthony Thompson. Good job."

"I don't like the whore! I was drunk and horny. She stayed in my face all night, so I brought her home." He made it sound as if it was no big deal. I was ready to punch him in the other eye.

"What! In hopes that I didn't find out!"

"I wasn't thinking," he shrugged.

"Anthony, you never do."

I turned to Veronica. She just lay naked on his bed, not bothering to cover up as if she was expecting me. She just smirked up at me. It was obvious that she had done this on purpose. She had set out to humiliate me and destroy my relationship.

"How could you do this to me?"

"I needed what I needed," she shrugged nonchalantly.

"And you couldn't find what you needed from another man?"

"Desiree, I found exactly what I needed tonight."

"Then you must be really insecure."

"Excuse me." I moved towards her. I watched the arrogant look on her face disappear.

"You have to be pretty insecure to go after another woman's man. I take it that you can't find one of your own." She didn't respond. "How do you feel? You just had sex with a man who defines you by whats between your legs. I know this idiot loves me, but he decided to think with his penis instead of his brain. Therefore," I said, turning to look at him, "His carelessness has finally caused him to lose me. Enough is enough."

He hung his head and closed his eyes.

"Baby, please don't leave me. You can't."

"What do you mean I can't? I can and I will, Anthony. I have lost all faith and trust in you and this relationship."

I proceeded to pack up some of my possessions scattered throughout his apartment. Veronica's eyes followed me. She remained silent. Anthony followed me, pleading. I ignored him. He eventually in defeat took a seat and watched me helplessly.

When I finished, I turned to them both. Veronica glared at me, but it was apparent that she was intimidated.

"Obviously you wanted my man, well this is your lucky night; you can have him. Do know it's only because I no longer want him. He's no good to me because he's tainted. Like he said, you are nothing but a whore. Only God knows where you have been!"

"And this is shame. All the problems that women have with men these days, you go and do something like this. You are a sad excuse for a woman. Plus, I figure that dogs need to lie together," I yelled over my shoulder as I moved towards the door.

"Desiree," he called, following me out of the bedroom.

"Goodbye, Anthony."

"Stay, please!"

"No."

"She is leaving. We should talk." There was panic in his eyes.

"Why should I talk to you, Anthony?"

"If you love me…."

"If I love you!" I yelled. "You have a lot of nerve coming at me about love!" I could tell I was finally breaking. I needed to get out of here. I wanted to cry alone.

"If I didn't love you, I would stay. But because I do love you, I have to go. Now, goodbye!"

As I shut the door and headed down the hall, I could hear Anthony yelling at Veronica.

"Why are you still lying there? Put some freaking clothes on and get out of here. Get out! You are a whore! Get out!" I laughed.

"And so are you, Anthony." I said to myself.

That was the end of my two and half year relationship with Anthony. He tried very hard to rekindle our romance, but I firmly told him to, "Get out of my face and never talk to me again!"

So now Quinton was dating this poor excuse of a woman. I knew I was over Anthony, but the fact was that he along with Veronica had betrayed me. I figured that the two timing, unfaithful whore would always be a whore and I was tempted to warn Quinton.

I just didn't like meddling in other people's business. If Q was happy with this woman than who was I to get in the way of that? I would just keep my mouth shut and pray that he would never bring her around me.

Quinton

"Des has been acting funny?"

"What do you mean? Tyler frowned. He was over playing some basketball with me. Rayven and Desiree was inside cooking up something in the kitchen.

"I feel like she has been giving me the cold shoulder lately."

"You know why, right?"

"Nope, I don't." I snatched the ball out of his hand. "Obviously you do." I needed him to help me out.

"Well, yeah. Rayven tells me everything."

"Please let me know. I would appreciate some enlightenment."

"Well you know why Desiree and Anthony broke up?"

"The bastard cheated. What does that have to do with me?"

"She comes home to Anthony's apartment in the middle of the night to find him in bed with this chick. Turns out this chick was a friend of hers." I never knew that.

"That's some BS right there. Really messed up of that chick. Do I know her?" Tyler nodded and gave me a crazy look.

"Yep. That's where you girl comes in."

"My girl? Veronica?" We had been dating about a month

"Veronica Ramirez. That's the chick Anthony cheated on Desiree with. And now she is your girlfriend."

"Are you serious?" The ball slipped out of my hand and rolled away. I suddenly felt like an idiot.

"That's right," he said, picking it up and dunking it. "That's why she can't quite look you in the eye."

"Why didn't she tell me?" I asked

"Because she wanted you to be happy."

"How can I be happy when I am dating a woman who intentionally hurt her?"

"I am thinking that's why she didn't tell you."

I opted to confront Desiree much later when we were alone.

"Dinner was good."

"Thank you, Q."

"That was the best strawberry shortcake I have ever had."

"I am glad that you liked it."

I walked up behind her as she wiped down the counters. I placed my hands on both sides of her. I pinned her against the counter.

"Desiree," I whispered.

"Yes," she said becoming still at my touch. It felt good to be so close to her. It had been over a month since I kissed her and right now that's all I wanted to do. In order to keep a sane mind, I resisted.

"Why didn't you tell me about Veronica?"

"How did you find out?" she asked, turning to face me.

"Don't worry about that, sweetheart." I was not trying to get Rayven or Tyler in trouble, although, I am sure it was obvious. "Just tell me why you didn't tell me."

"Because I didn't want you to worry about it."

"I don't want to date someone who has hurt you. I refuse to."

"See, Quinton that's exactly why I didn't want to tell you. I didn't want you to break things off with her because of me."

"Why would I want to date her?"

"I just want you to be happy."

"Really?" Then be with me.

"Of course, Quinton. Despite what you think, I do care about you. You know that I love you."

"And you know that I love you." More than you would ever possibly know "That's why it would be insensitive of me to date her."

"Don't worry about me."

"Do you know how important you are to me?" She blushed. "How are you going to tell me not to worry about you? I will always worry about you."

"Well, still, don't give this woman up."

"I already cut her loose." I had called Veronica after my conversation with T. She was pissed and had called me every name under the sun. When I called her out for what she did to Desiree, she became speechless. I told her goodbye and hung up the phone.

Just that easily, I had cut her off. She was a wonderful thrill for me, but I didn't have any true feelings for her. Like every other woman, she was a diversion.

"Wow." She followed me to my bedroom. "Are you sure?"

"Yes. Will you come here?" I didn't know if she would let me, but I wanted her in my arms. I didn't give a crap about Lance.

She stared at me before slowly heading in my direction.

"Tell me that you missed me first."

"I missed you, Desiree. You have been driving me up the wall."

"How?"

"It's been too long, sweetheart."

"Well," she said, kissing on my neck, "I am always here for you."

"Are you staying with me tonight?" I wasn't letting her go.

"If you want me to stay, I will."

"I am starting to think that I don't ever want you to leave."

24

Craving

"Come to me, all who labor and are heavy laden, and I will give you rest. Take my yoke upon you, and learn from me, for I am gentle and lowly in heart, and you will find rest for your souls." *Matthew 11:28-29*

Quinton

Moving out of Des's house was bittersweet for me. It was wonderful that this dream that I had for me and my son was coming true, but I was leaving Des. She was my dream too. We had been together for almost nine months. It was nine months full of some of those most amazing and worst moments of my life.

Living with Desiree had brought us closer together. It had strengthened our relationship. I knew despite how I felt that she would always continue to be there for me. I had learned so much about her and about myself.

I really didn't have much to move in the new house. All of my furniture and appliances were brand new. I just had my clothes and personal possessions, along with little Quinton's clothes and toys. Still, Desiree, Tyler and Rayven insisted on helping.

Since there wasn't much to do, we were done early, so we hopped into Des's truck and headed to Maggiano's. After dinner, we watched movies at the house. I left everyone on my couch as I went to pick up my son from my brother's house.

Quinton ran to Des, screaming her name. She was half asleep.

"Dessie, wake up."

"Hey, bookins," she said, hugging him. "Where have you been all day. I missed you."

"We went to the movies and out for ice cream."

"What kind of ice cream did you get?"

"Chocolate."

"Well, I love chocolate."

"Me too," he smiled. My boy loved this woman as much as I did. I wasn't sure how either of us were going to deal without her.

"Did you have fun?"

"Yes! I wish you were there."

"Me too. I think we need to hang out sometimes."

"Yeah, we do!"

I was mesmerized by the conversation. Since India had left, Des and Quinton had developed an admirable relationship. I was annoyed at the way that Tyler and Rayven were smiling at me. I knew what they were thinking. They were thinking that this was a sign. It wasn't.

"It's time for us to get going," Ray spoke up. Everyone stood.

"Nooo," little Quinton said, clinging to Desiree's leg.

"Son, don't bother Des like that. We can't stop her from leaving," I said, although I felt like clinging to her myself.

"But I want Desiree to see my new room," he pouted.

"I can stay ten more minutes if that's okay with you, Q."

"You can stay as long as you want, Desiree."

"Thank you. So hospitable of you," she smiled. "Well, Quinton, let's see that room," she said, grabbing his hand.

"Yeah! Let's go," he said, pulling her down the hallway.

"Wow," said T. I really wasn't in the mood for this conversation. "They get along well."

"They do. I am thankful."

"God is trying to tell you something and you are ignoring him." I knew Tyler was going to say this. I didn't want to hear it, but I didn't want to be rude. "She is the woman for you. And for you son."

I stared doing the hall. I longed for her, wishing I could believe Tyler's words. I couldn't

"Right. I really appreciate the two of you helping me out today."

"No problem. Why are you ignoring me, man? It's time to stop doing this to yourself. Why can't you at least tell her that you want something more?"

"I do hear you, but I really don't see the point in us keep talking about it. Please don't keep feeding me false hope. It's time to move on and I am trying very hard to do so."

"You think that's whats going to make you happy?"

"I just can't do this tonight, Ty. Again, I thank you."

"Well, alright. No problem," he said, giving me a disappointed look. "Goodnight, Q."

"Goodnight." Tyler hugged me and Rayven kissed me. And then they left. Finally, I was alone with Desiree. I was nervous. I didn't want to say goodbye.

I walked slowly down the hallway towards my son's room. I stood at his bedroom door, laughing to myself as he insisted on showing her everything in his room. Amazingly, she had incredible patience, probably more than me and I was the kid's father. Seeing her with my son made me want her even more. My son needed her.

"Honey, I got to go now. Give me a hug." She knelt down.

"Bye, Dessie."

"Bye, sweetheart. I will miss you." She kissed his cheek and he kissed her back.

"You are going to miss little Quinton, but what about big Quinton?" I teased as we headed down the hall. Why did I insist on always setting myself up?

"What about big Quinton?" she asked, facing me.

"Are you going to miss him too?" My heart was breaking.

"Maybe a little," she teased.

"Just a little?"

"What do you want me to say?"

"I just wanted to know," I said, looking away. Maybe she wasn't going to miss me. Maybe it was just me that was going to miss her.

"I am going to miss you terribly and I think that you already know that." I didn't expect to look over and see panic in her eyes.

"I will miss you too," I said, pulling her to me. She clung to me for a few moments before moving away. We stared at each other.

"Kiss me," she said, wrapping her arms around my neck.

"I wanted to kiss you all night." We kissed for a few moments.

"I can't believe that you are leaving me, Q."

"I am not leaving you. I am just leaving your house."

"That's leaving me."

"No, it's not, baby. I will still be around. I will always be there for you. I hope that you know that." I rubbed her cheek.

"I do."

"It won't be the same." It wouldn't be. I knew that, but I wanted to comfort her. "I won't see you every day, but we are still going to see each other, right?" I needed reassurance.

"We both know that you're going to get busy and I'm not going to see you much. You aren't going to come hang out with me. Things will go back to the way they were." Before moving in, I didn't hang out with her as much as I should have. I was protecting my feelings.

"That was before. Things have changed." At least on my end. "We have shared so much in this last year."

"And you will find someone else to share that with. Easily. After all, you are the Quinton Alexander." Why did she think I was so much of a ladies man? I had dated a lot of women, but I had changed in this last year. I only wanted one woman in my life and she was it.

"Do you think I am just going to go out and find another woman to replace you? To share the things that we have shared?"

"Yes."

"Desiree Harris, you mean too much to me. You could never be replaced. There isn't a woman alive that could compare to you."

She stepped back, her face turning red. She covered it.

"I'm just going to really miss you, Quinton. I will be lonely again without you." What about Lance? I didn't want to think about him.

Knowing she was going to miss me really struck a chord. I knew that it wasn't a big deal, but it was to me. In the midst of my emotional turmoil, it gave me great satisfaction.

"Stay here with me," I blurted. I didn't want her to leave.

"Quinton, I can't do that."

"Why not?"

"I just can't." She didn't want to stay here. She knew she could.

"Yes you can. This is my home and I just asked you to stay. I want you to." For good. I loved her too much. I would marry this woman tomorrow if she would let me.

"No, Quinton, we both know that I shouldn't do that."

"Do what? Desiree, do you want to stay?" She smiled at me and looked away. She didn't say anything, but I could see the twinkle in her eyes. I knew then she was playing coy.

"I am not going to stay, Quinton. That's my final answer."

"So, I guess there is no need in me trying to persuade you." I grabbed her behind and pulled her to me.

"Nope," She parted her lips for my incoming ones. The kiss made me shiver with pleasure. I pushed her backwards until she was pinned between me and the wall. I couldn't help myself. I started yanking on her clothes.

"What are you doing?" she whispered.

"Pleading with you. Stay with me tonight, please."

"No." She was protesting, but was enjoying my roaming hands.

"I can make you feel so good." I started kissing her neck because I knew it turned her on. "I will do all the work."

"Quinton, that sounds good," she said, pushing me away. "I am going home to my bed tonight." Why, I thought. Was Lance coming over? Was she attempting to stay faithful to him now? I was annoyed, but I tried not to show her.

"You are so frustrating," I mumbled. She didn't hear me as she pushed past me.

"I am sorry, Q. You don't understand how much I want you tonight." No, it sure didn't feel like it. "We have to stop this. This thing between us can't continue."

I stared back at her with no words. I had tried hard to stop many times before, but I couldn't. I couldn't tell her how I felt, but I could show her. Now, she wanted to prevent me from doing that.

"Don't you agree?" I didn't trust myself to respond. There was so much that I wanted to say to her, but I couldn't. She stared back at me, nervously. "Please, don't be mad. Will you forgive me?"

"Of course. No big deal, right?" I turned to pick up some trash on my coffee table. I walked to my kitchen just so I could get away from her for a moment.

"Why would you say that," she said, following me. She grabbed my arm. "It's a big deal to me, Quinton. Don't be dismissive of me." I was speechless for a moment.

"You are the one dismissing me," I finally responded after a moment of silence.

"Because I have to!"

"Why?" I stared at her, searching for the answer. She just stared back at me without saying anything.

I turned my back to her. If she wanted to be with Lance, I had no way of stopping her. I just couldn't stomach it right now. It hurt. Seeing her with anyone that wasn't me was painful.

"Don't worry about answering. I get it. We are friends." We would never be anything more and I had to face it. I guess I was going to be single for a very long time. My heart wouldn't get over this woman even though I willed it to. I prayed constantly.

"Yeah, isn't that good enough?" Why did she ask me that?

"Better than nothing," I blurted.

"Whats that supposed to mean?" She looked hurt. She thought I was trying to insult her.

"Nothing," I hugged her so I wouldn't have to look at her anymore. "Our friendship means the world to me. Go ahead and head home. It's getting late."

"Okay." She kissed me quickly and starting back away from me. "Goodnight, Quinton."

I walked outside and stood on my porch as she headed to her car. I closed my eyes because it was painful watching her walk away. I just listened as she started the car and backed out the driveway. I didn't open them until she was far down the street.

I stood outside for a moment longer, feeling out of it. I then realized that my son was inside alone, so I walked back in and shut the door. I headed to his bedroom and got him ready for bed. Once I knew he was seconds away from dreamland, I headed to my own bedroom. I stripped down to my boxers and tried not to wallow too hard in my own self-pity.

Here I was blessed to have this brand new home for me and my son, yet I was feeling alone. I didn't have anyone to share this new king size bed with. I didn't have Desiree. While Des and I hadn't shared a bed together every night, knowing she was down the hall, there were always possibilities. They no longer existed.

She had finally put a stop to everything happening between us. It was forced. It was against her will. It was against mine.

After twenty minutes of staring up at the ceiling, I picked up my phone to call her. I couldn't begin to think about sleep until I knew she was home safely. When she answered the phone, I knew she was in bed. It killed me because she should have been here with me.

"Whats wrong?" She sounded more seductive than usual.

"Nothing. I was making sure that you were home. I thought that you would call me." Was Lance there?

"I'm sorry. I wasn't thinking. I am not use to this." Me neither.

"It's cool. Are you in bed?"

"Yes. Are you, Quinton?" The way she whispered my name excited me more than it should have.

"Yes, I am laying here. Alone. What are you wearing, Des."

"You know those lacy black panties that you love so much?"

"Yes", I said closing my eyes. She knew I loved those.

"Well I am not wearing anything. I am completely naked."

"I hate you for telling me that."

"I love you, though, Q."

"Not enough." If only she knew.

"Would it make you feel better to know that I am naked because I can't stop thinking about you? I was literally hot and bothered. I do have a pillow between my legs. I have my window open."

"That does make me feel a little better." I smiled to myself.

"I wish you were here."

I didn't say anything, though. I understood that she was trying to do this in our best interest. Under normal circumstances, ending things would be ideal, but she didn't know how I felt. She didn't know I was crazy in love with her.

My only response was, "Me too."

I know there wasn't a day that went by that I didn't think of her. It appeared that that she consumed my thoughts almost every waking moments of the day. I prayed every night that the thoughts of her would subside, but they didn't. I went through each day as if I was in a daze. I felt like I was living in another world.

I wanted to be angry with myself, but I couldn't help it. It didn't matter how hard I tried not to, loving her was like an addiction. I was started to think that I was going to yearn for Desiree Harris the rest of my days. I hated knowing that I was going to have to settle for another woman that wasn't her.

Every time I closed my eyes, I could see her face. I could see her playful grin. I could see that sparkle in her eyes. I could imagine the way she kissed me. The way she touched me.

I eventually told myself enough was enough. I could not let this woman continue to take over my life. I started focusing on other extracurricular activities. I started writing poems. I started working out more. I spent more time with my son to fill the void in his life.

Unfortunately, I was now one of those rare single fathers. I had to work hard to be both parents. Every day I prayed that I would find a positive woman that he could look up to. He loved Desiree, but she could not be around the way we both desired her to be.

Still, a week and half later, I found myself in her neighborhood on the spur of the moment. I pulled in her driveway only to discover that she wasn't at home. I sat in my car filled with disappointment.

After ten minutes, staring at her door, I left. I was now in a pissy mood because I didn't get to see her face.

I drove to Tyler's house. I really didn't want to be alone right now. My son was with his cousins so I had nothing to do. If I went home then I would be left with my thoughts. I was hoping I could convince Tyler to come out and get drunk with me.

"Whats wrong?" he asked as soon as he opened his front door.

"Nothing," I lied, forcing myself to smile. "I am cool. Why do you think that something was wrong?"

"You were looking a little down and out."

"Oh, I am straight. Just a little tired."

"Come on in, Q. So what do we owe this pleasure to?" he asked sitting down on the loveseat across from me.

"Nothing really. Can't I just visit an old friend?"

"I am not saying anything is wrong with that."

"I am sorry. I did just stop by unannounced."

"Since when have I ever cared about that?"

"What are you up to? Busy?"

"Nope, Rayven and I are just chilling like always."

"Did I hear my name?" Rayven came out of nowhere.

She looked good, I thought. She had put on a little weight, but in the right places. I guess love was benefiting her. Surprisingly her and Tyler were still going strong since that fateful day in the restaurant.

"Hey, Quinton," she said, kissing my cheek.

"Whats up, girl? How are you?"

"Oh, I am lovely," she said, finding a seat in Tyler's lap. "How have you been doing??"

"I have been okay. I am surviving."

Did anyone else feel weird? I had slept with this girl twice. Now Tyler was sleeping with her. Did he know what we had shared? I wonder if Rayven had bothered to tell him. Maybe he just didn't care because he never let on.

"When is the last time you have seen Desiree."

"It's been a while." I shifted uncomfortably in my seat. I didn't come here to talk about Des. I came here to get her out of my head.

"Why aren't you making a better effort to see your girl?" This chick sure didn't mind calling you out. She was always digging.

"We both have been very busy. Can we not get into this today?"

"I'm sorry. Whats been going in your life, Quinton."

I really didn't want to be alone, but thirty minutes later, I was ready to get out of this house as soon as possible. It was nothing like watching another couple in love when you couldn't have it yourself. Watching Tyler and Rayven was making me sick to my stomach. I felt like I needed to give them privacy."

"I am going to get out of here," I said, finally standing. I was not going to bother asking T to go out. It didn't seem as if he was leaving his girl's side tonight. I couldn't blame him. I wouldn't either.

"Why are you rushing? I feel like you just got here."

"Nope, I was just stopping by."

"Why don't you stay and have dinner with us?" No thank you. I could not stay with these two another minute. "I feel as if I haven't seen you in a while."

"No thank you. I am not all that hungry. Catch you later, Rayven," I said, kissing her cheek.

"So what's really going on, Q?" Tyler followed me out. You look like you are a little preoccupied this evening."

"Really?" I was playing dumb.

"When are you going to tell Des how you feel?" Why did we always have to go into this? I was started to feel like a broken record.

"I am not going to do that."

"Why not!"

"Tyler our love is one-sided. Telling her wouldn't make a difference. She will never be my girl. I accept that."

"You shouldn't."

"Why not?" I laughed for no reason. "I can't make Desiree catch any feelings for me. This is my problem, T."

"Why do you keep saying that love is a problem?"

"Because for the last six years, it has been for me. It has sucked."

"I hate hearing that. I just want to tell Desiree myself."

"That's not cool."

"I wouldn't do anything like that to you."

"It's cool. I know that you wouldn't. Look, I don't want to put her in an uncomfortable situation."

"I get that."

"Don't worry about me. I will be okay. I admit that I am not in the best mood today." He nodded. "I am going to get going."

"Well thanks for stopping through."

"No problem." We hugged quickly and then I was on my way.

I really didn't know what I was going to do tonight, but I doubted that I was going to be able to relax at home. I had to do something. I had to get out of the house.

I did go home and lay down for an hour instead of continuously wasting gas. I didn't go to sleep, I was just passing time. I eventually got up and headed straight for the shower. Thirty minutes later, I was dressed with my car keys in my hand. I got in my ride and just headed towards the city, singing along to Anthony Hamilton.

I went to this cozy little spot uptown. It was a lounge where young and attractive singles gathered. I didn't feel like going to the regular club where the thirsty chicks were begging for your attention. I was in search of something more mature.

I found a little table in the back of the place so I could observe more inconspicuously. My waitress was this cute chick name Yvonne, but she wasn't my type. I promised her a $25.00 tip if she kept the Coronas coming. She tried to flirt with me, but I ignored it because although she was friendly, I wasn't feeling her like that. I didn't want to flirt back and lead her on.

I was leaning back in my sit, taking in all the ladies, so I wasn't paying attention when this one chick walked up to me.

"May I sit here?" she asked, demanding my attention. She sat down before I could respond. Wow. She was bold, but I didn't mind.

I wasn't sure if I was buzzed or not, but she was looking extra nice to me. She wore a tight little black dress. She was very busty and I tried not to admire that too much, although, her cups were spilling over. Instead I tried to focus on her beautiful chocolate skin, her full lips and her exotic eyes. She had long hair and a sexy grin.

"I didn't say yes."

"I don't take no for an answer, but I know you would have."

"How do you know my girl is not in the bathroom?"

"Because I have been watching you from across the room since you walked in," she said, staring at me seductively.

"Have you? I hadn't noticed."

"Well, isn't it the point not to be obvious?" She leaned closer. I loved her voice and she smelled wonderful.

"Quinton," I said, offering my hand.

"Jada."

She didn't leave my side the rest of the night. I had to admit that I didn't want her to. I had been craving a woman's company tonight and I was enjoying myself talking to Jada. I don't think Yvonne liked it, though. She stopped talking and just looked irritated. However, she continued to work for her tip. She kept the Coronas coming.

This woman was sexy, confident and funny. I was digging her. I could tell she was digging me to, so I wasn't surprised when she asked me to accompany her back to her place.

"You want me to go home with you?" I wasn't sure how I felt about that. I didn't want to go down this road anymore.

"Yes."

"For what? Just to chill?"

"Sweetheart, don't act like you don't want what I am offering."

"I want it," I admitted. I just didn't know if I should take it. "I was trying to see if you knew what you were doing."

"Don't worry" She stood. "I do. Are you coming?" She headed for the door as if she expected me to follow. I sat there hesitant, trying to decide whether or not I should resort to my old ways and go home with this woman. I hadn't gone home with someone that I wasn't dating in so long. Where had that gotten me? Nowhere.

I don't know if it was because I was lonely tonight, horny, or a little tipsy, but I stood. I threw $100.00 on the table and followed this woman right out of the door.

"Where's your car, sweetheart?" she asked. "I rode with friends."

She lived in a condo not too far from my house, but I didn't say anything. I didn't plan on seeing this woman again. We both knew what this night was bout. Sex. The chemistry was high between us and we were doing something about it.

When we got to her place, she led me straight to her bedroom. No tour. She pushed me on the bed and proceeded to climb over me.

"You have a condom?" she asked, while kissing me.

"Of course." This felt good, I thought, kissing her back, but there was a voice in my head that was trying to convince me otherwise. Something was telling me not to go through with this. My conscience. This was not what I really wanted.

Still, I would feel like a fool turning this down. I was going to go for it. I proceeded to ignore that voice and focused on her thighs. They were thick and I loved them.

When she slid her hands down my pants, I knew it was on. I decided to lay it on her. I pushed her down on the bed and begin to kiss her on her neck. I moved my hand up her dress. She was not wearing underwear. Oh wow. That turned me on.

"Wow, Jada."

"What? You know you like that. I like the way that feels," she whispered with her tongue in my ear.

"I do." I pulled her dress over her head. Her body was beautiful. Endless curves and sexy dark chocolate.

"Beautiful," I whispered. I loved how soft her skin was. I love how full her lips were. I loved how sweet she smelled.

She quickly took control. She climbed on top of me. She started to rub her naked body against mine.

"Don't tease me," I whispered.

"I want you inside."

"Patience," I said, grabbing her bare behind. So soft.

"Actually. Stop. I have to pee."

"Oh okay. Go handle that."

I guess she was freshening up because she took a little longer than expected. That wasn't good. By the time she opened the door, I had convinced myself not to go through with it.

I couldn't go to bed with this woman when another one was on my mind. It all felt good, but I couldn't forget Desiree if I tried. I missed her. I ached for her. I needed her. I was scared for myself.

"Jada, I don't think I can do this."

"Excuse me?"

"I can't get down with you tonight. I should leave."

"I think that you owe me some type of explanation."

"To be honest with you, I only came out tonight to get another woman off of my mind."

"You have a girlfriend!"

"No, she is not. She means everything to me, though. I really care about her."

"You love her?" I refused to answer the question. I didn't know this girl. I didn't want to reveal everything to her.

"I just don't think that it would be fair to you."

"Well, I am disappointed, but I respect that."

"Good. Thank you."

"I am amazed. Most men would take sex with no strings attached in a heartbeat. You turned it down because you have feelings for someone you aren't even dating." I didn't like how her statement made me feel. I felt stupid.

"I am not most men. And this is not just any woman."

"She can't be."

"I am sorry, Jada."

"It's okay, Quinton. This is what I get anyway."

"What do you mean?"

"I don't normally bring men home. This is not something that I do. I just saw you tonight and couldn't help myself."

"I want to, but…"

"Stop explaining yourself." She give me a lingering kiss. "Get out of her before I attempt to convince you otherwise."

"Alright. It was a pleasure."

"Indeed it was." I headed to the door. "Quinton? Do me a favor."

"What is that?"

"Tell this woman that has ruined my night that you love her. Stop running."

"Who says that I am running?"

"It's obvious, sweetheart. Most men do."

The next day, Tyler and Rayven asked me over for dinner. I figured that I would just go considering that I had nothing better to do. Quinton Jr wasn't coming until later, so the house was quiet and lonely. Plus, I could use a good meal. Rayven could throw down in the kitchen.

I was standing on the patio when Des arrived. I was unaware of my surroundings. I didn't know she was there until she touched me. I should have been startled, but instead my body reacted with utter relief. I closed my eyes as she rubbed my back and then wrapped her arms around my waist. She laid her head against my shoulder.

Neither of us said anything for a moment. I was trying to get myself together and find the words that I wanted to say. My heart, as always in her presence, was beater faster than it should have.

"Quinton, I missed you," she finally whispered in my ear. My response was to grab her and pull her around so that she was standing in front of me.

She looked beautiful of course. Tight jeans, black sweater, boots. Her hair was pulled back into a bun. She was low-key, but that's when she was at her sexiest.

I was so taken back by finally seeing her that I was rendered speechless. I was consumed with emotions. I just grabbed her waist and kissed her. I kissed her hard.

"Do you miss me?" she whispered.

"Yes," I said, wrapping her completely in my arms. "Why haven't you called me, Desiree?"

"You didn't call me either, Quinton."

"This is not cool. I can't go three weeks without laying eyes on you. Without talking to you."

"So what are you going to do about it?"

"A week from yesterday."

"Saturday."

"My house. 8:00. You and I. Dinner."

"Okay."

"You will be staying." I thought she was going to give me a hard time, but she didn't to my relief.

"Okay."

"Good. Give me another kiss." She did. I slid my hand up the back of her sweater. I had not touched the softness of her skin in so long. "Still so soft."

"I am the same," she whispered. "Nothing changed."

"Thank goodness for that, baby. You haven't."

I kissed her neck. She just stared into my eyes as if she was searching for something.

"What is it, Desiree?"

"Nothing." I felt her shiver. "I am cold, Quinton." She laid her head against my chest.

She wasn't really cold. It was sort of warm out today, not your typical March day. Still I knew what she was feeling because I was feeling the same way. Something unrecognizable flowed between us. I shivered too.

25

Therapy

"Do not deprive one another, except perhaps by agreement for a limited time, that you may devote yourselves to prayer; but then come together again, so that Satan may not tempt you because of your lack of self-control." *1 Corinthians 7:5*

Desiree

I had missed Quinton more than I was willing to admit to anyone, even myself. He controlled my thoughts more than he should have. When I attempted to focus on something else, I found myself struggling. That scared me.

The house was lonely without him and little Quinton. I hated not having them around. I missed Quinton's voice. His laugh. Quinton Jr's infectious spirit. Being around them made me happy.

I waited weeks for Quinton to call me, but he never did. I knew I could have called him, but as always, I was being stubborn. Apparently so was he. Over the last nine months together, we had both played a lot of games. I knew he missed me.

Still, I lay in bed at night, doubting myself, wondering if he did. I wondered if he thought about all of the nights that we shared as much as I did. I wondered if he missed holding me in his arms. I would rub my belly at night, wishing that it was him doing so. I would run my fingers across my lips, imagining him kissing me like only he could. I would hold onto my pillow, aching for him.

Did Quinton realize what he had done to me? Could he see how complicated things had gotten between us? Our intimacy had become second nature. It was now an addiction. We both depended on it.

When I finally laid eyes on him at Tyler's house, I was a little overwhelmed. I stood watching him at the door for over two minutes, trying to figure out what I was going to do. I was a little angry that I had not heard from him, but I was excited to see him because I had missed him terribly.

I walked over to him, making my presence known. I didn't know how he would react to seeing me. He surprised me. He kissed me with raw passion and that scared me. I shivered when he touched me. I melted into his arms.

I should not have accepted dinner at house next weekend. We both knew what that was about. A night full of love. And we both knew that we needed to put a stop to everything happening between us, but I am not sure if either of us knew how to.

The week dragged along more than usual. The days were long and stressful at work. The nights were lonely. I was starting to think that Saturday would never come. After my week to forget, I deserved a night in Quinton's arms.

My stomach was in knots when I woke up Saturday morning. I had no idea why I was nervous about my upcoming night when I shouldn't have been. Something felt different. I was thinking too much into it. I was trying to make tonight more special than it was.

When it was time to get ready, I sat in a tub full of bubbles to help myself relax. I rubbed myself down in Vanilla Sugar body oil. I slipped into pink lacy thongs, deciding against a bra. I chose a pink maxi dress and my favorite black motorcycle jacket and ballerina flats. I applied minimal make up and put my hair up into a bun.

I was anxious during my drive over. My heart was racing as if this was our first time alone. I could not understand why I was feeling this way. I sang along to Beyoncé, attempting to ease my nerves, but it didn't work.

I found myself knocking on his door over ten minutes early. He opened it within thirty seconds. He looked gorgeous in his white tee and jeans. It was simple, but I appreciated it just the same.

He pulled me inside and into his arms

"It's good to see you," he whispered against my lips.

"I know." He smelled wonderful. I buried my face into his neck. I clung to him. I wanted to melt into his arms

"Desiree," he whispered my name. I looked up at him and he begin to kiss me again. When things started to get hot and heavy, I attempted to put a stop to things before they heated up too much.

"It smells good in here."

"Yes, I know you do. You always do." He grabbed my behind and I squealed in delight.

"The food, Quinton," I said, finally succeeding in pushing him away. He gave me a boyish grin

"Baby, I will wait for you. I will be ready when you are." I laughed and looked away. My face was burning. "Come on in," he said chuckling at me. He pulled me into the living room. "Give me your jacket." I smiled as I pulled it off.

"Do I meet your approval? I turned slowly. He didn't say anything at first. He just stared at me. "Quinton?"

"You look incredible like you always do. I don't understand why you don't get that by now. You always take my breath away."

"Thank you." My face was burning so I sat down. I couldn't handle his compliments. "So what are you doing? Trying to seduce me?" I took in the dim lights, the candles and the slow jams playing softly in the background.

"Yes," he said, handing me a glass of wine. Where did that came from, I thought, taking it out of his hand. Wait, did he say yes?

"Really, Quinton," I laughed. He had a serious look on his face. "You're just going to be so blunt about it?"

"Why should I lie?"

"Do you think that you are going to succeed tonight?" I teased.

"I think you know that I can seduce you, Desiree. I know what excites you. I know what turns you on. I know how to please you." He did. I took a sip of wine and stared at him.

He went in to kiss me again, but once again I stopped it.

"Dessert comes after dinner."

"Why do we have to follow these rules?"

He led me to his dining room table and sat me down. He placed a napkin on my lap. He kissed my forehead and headed to the kitchen. He returned moments later with two plates.

"Wow, Quinton," I sad when he sat a plate in front of me."

The man had cooked his famous Honey Mustard chicken with rice, green beans and homemade biscuits. It was one of my favorite meals. Mrs. Alexander had taught Quinton very well.

"Tonight is a special night."

"How is tonight special?"

"Because you are here with me, Desiree." I couldn't really respond. His comment was sweet. They gave me butterflies. I am not sure it was his intentions to make me feel that way.

"The food looks delicious, Q. Thank you for cooking this." His eyes were holding me captive. Why was he doing this to me?

"I hope it taste just as delicious." The way he was looking at me, I could tell he was not talking about the food on the table.

I devoured the food. It was that good. I was thinking Quinton could out cook me. I usually did my thing with skills acquired from my own mother. He just smiled at me appreciatively.

By the time I finished, I was sure my face was flushed. Quinton didn't say anything, but he kept undressing me with his eyes. That excited me. I knew I was in trouble when my eyes kept landing on his lips. His lips could do amazing things to me.

"How's work?" he asked. I took a sip of wine and smiled at him gratefully. I needed to talk about something mundane so that I could get my mind together.

"Pretty good." I was finally able to concentrate on something besides the sexual tension between us. I was finally relaxing. I wanted to catch up with Quinton, my friend, not just Quinton, my lover.

We conversed like old friends. For a moment, it felt like things were the way they were before we had complicated our friendship with our desires. I was glad to know that we could still be friends outside of the bedroom.

The mood changed when it was time for dessert. Quinton left the room and I went to sit on his couch. He came back with Chocolate Cheesecake.

"That looks yummy," I said, rubbing my belly.

"Yes I know," he said giving me one of those looks. I could read his mind. "You aren't where I want you.' He sat down beside me and pulled me into his lap.

"Can I tell you where I want you," I teased. "Dessert first."

We took turns feeding each other chocolate cake. He smiled when I licked his finger. When the cake was finished, the heat returned. His lips were on mine before I knew what was happening.

"Don't push me away anymore. Tell me it's time."

"I don't want to make you wait any longer."

"Thank you." He looked at me seriously. "It's been too long."

"Yes," I know I said grabbing both sides of his face. I kissed him until we were both breathless while his hands moved feverishly over me. His hands burned through the fabric of my dress.

"Take you shirt off," I whispered. He did so while kissing on my ear. I helped him. I then allowed my hands to move freely over that beautiful chest of his. I leaned down to kiss it. The sight of his muscles turned me on so. "You smell so good," I whispered.

"You…" I didn't allow him to finish because I kissed him again. "Take your dress off," he finally whispered in my ear.

"Okay." Together we pulled my dress over my head. He flung it across the room. "I wasn't going to put it back on, Quinton."

"Making sure." I pushed him on his back. I ran my breast across his chest. I knew he like that and I wanted to please him as much as we wanted to please me. He pushed his hand through my hair and pulled my face to his. His kiss was amazing. I shivered as he ran his hand across my back

"I love you," I whispered. Why did I say that? The things people could say in the moment of passion.

"Baby, I love you too." He begin kissing on my neck, his hands yanking on my underwear. "I need these off of you." I stood. He protested until he realized what I was doing. Finally I stood before him completely naked.

"You are so beautiful," he whispered sitting up. He pulled me to him but remained seated. He proceeded to plant hot kisses all over my stomach and thighs. I caressed his bald head as I basked in the pleasure. When I couldn't take it any longer, I lifted his chin so he would look up.

"Quinton, I want you to make love to me, right now."

He looked up at me startled. For one terrifying moment, I thought I had said too much. Before I could retract, he literally knocked me off my feet.

"I don't want to let you down."

With the candles burning, and Jodeci playing in the background, he did make love to me. Sweet and gentle love. It was so good to me that it scared me. It had never felt like this before, not even when we were in Vegas. It had not felt like this with any other man, not even Anthony. This was with Quinton, my homie.

He lay on his back when we were done. Sweat dripped down both of our bodies as if we were going at it for hours. I lay there trying to catch my breath while listening to him attempt to catch his. Moments later, he stood. He scooped me up into his arms. Without a word, he carried me to his bedroom. He laid me down on his bed.

"Wait here for me. I will be right back, precious."

I lay there, naked and suddenly vulnerable. I did feel good. I couldn't feel much better at this moment, but I should have been sharing this with the man that I was supposed to love. I should not have been sharing such moments with Q. I loved him dearly and he meant the world to me, but he was not going to be my husband.

"Oh goodness." Wow. When had marriage crept in my head? I suddenly felt an overwhelming sense of guilt

"Beautiful, what are you thinking?" Q asked, lying beside me. He reached for me. I was startled by his interruption so I moved away. "Whats wrong?" he asked, looking bewildered.

"Nothing." I stood quickly. "I will be back." I made a beeline for the bathroom, shutting the door behind me.

What had come over me? When he touched me, I was scared. Was it the fact that I was able to surrender to him so easily? Or that I could love him so freely? Or the fact that he could love me so freely? Or was it the fact that sometimes I felt as if needed him so badly or I would lose my mind?

"I shouldn't even be here." I should not be in his bathroom, naked. He should not have been naked, waiting for me on his bed. I shouldn't be sharing the same bed with him. I should not have been able to love him the way I had.

I was here, though. I had to be here because like a drug addict, I was craving another hit. I needed to feel the high from his caresses and his kisses. I needed to be in his arms. Tonight.

I tried not to think about the end. That was inevitable. I had no choice but to keep my word and give this up. I wasn't sure how. I wasn't sure if I was ready. Things were complicated, but amazing all at the same time.

I sighed as I reached for a wash cloth and wiped the sweat off of my skin. I stared at my reflection in the mirror. I ran my hands across my body, trying to imagine how my skin felt to him when he touched me in this way. I took a deep breath and I finally opened the door.

He sat on the edge of his bed with his head hung. I could sense that he was upset. My heart ached.

"Q." He looked up at the sound of my voice. When he stared back at me, I could see the hurt in his eyes. He looked as if he wanted to cry. "Babe, whats wrong?" I asked, blinking back some tears of my own. I walked over to him and climbed in his lap. He buried his face in my chest. I clung to him, laying my head against his.

"Are you mad with me?"

"No!" I felt bad that I was the one to hurt him. "I am so sorry."

"I thought I had upset you."

"Quinton, I am not upset." I caressed his cheek.

"Do you want to be here with me tonight?" He sounded more vulnerable than usual. I couldn't say no even if I wanted to.

"Why would you second guess yourself?" I kissed him. "I wouldn't want to be with anyone else tonight."

"Not even with whats his name?" Was he asking about Lance? I had not thought about him all day.

"No. Why are you thinking about other men, Quinton? You need to concentrate on me right now. No one else. And I am focused only on you. And this is where I want to be. Will you love me tonight? Will you hold me?"

Before he could respond, I kissed him again. I continue to kiss him until I could feel him relax.

"Quinton, will you do that for me?"

"I will do anything that you want."

"Anything?" I shivered when he kissed my shoulder. It was a simple kiss. Why did it affect me in such a way? He nodded. "Well, lay back. Let me handle things for once. I leaned down over him. I ran my hands over his body, following each touch with a kiss. I took my time because I wanted to savor every moment.

"Desiree?" he whispered.

"Yes, sweetheart." He had a look in his eyes that startled me. "Baby, what did you want to say to me?"

"Desiree….I." He caressed the back of my head for a moment without saying anything. "Never mind."

"Don't…." Before I could say anything else, he was pulling my face down to his again. He kissed me with urgency. And while we kissed, I allowed our worlds to collide. I loved him slowly until the pleasure got the best of us. I collapsed on the bed beside him.

I kept my eyes closed for a moment. I sneaked a look at Quinton. He had a satisfied looked on his face. I smiled because that made me happy. I closed my eyes again, taking deep breaths and enjoying the moment.

"Desiree." After a moment he slid an arm around my waist and pulled me to him. He pressed his lips against my shoulder. I protested a little when he moved away. "Shush. I will be back" He disappeared in this bathroom.

Seconds later, I heard the water running. After the water stopped, he returned. He scooped me up in his arms for the second time that night. We soaked in his Jacuzzi size bathtub full of bubbles.

"Am I the first woman allowed in your tub," I joked.

"The only woman," he said, kissing my back."

We soaked in that tub until we were both drowsy. The water had turned cold. We got out. We toweled off. We rubbed each other down in his cocoa butter and then returned to his bed.

He pulled me to him and kissed me for a long time. He then pulled a sheet over us. We fell asleep in each other's arms.

Quinton

I woke up the next morning, almost expecting to be alone in my bed. I just knew that Desiree would be long gone. Instead, I wake up to find her arm still draped across me and her head against my shoulder. I stared down at her, one part of me thinking how lucky I was to have her here with me. I would cherish every moment that she chose to share with me.

Something didn't feel right, though. Unfortunately, the other part of me realized that spending time with Desiree was very bittersweet. I couldn't knock the constant sadness I felt when she was around me. I had accepted that I would never win her over and because of that my heart was in a continuous state of turmoil.

A pain in my chest caused me to move towards the edge of the bed. I tried getting up without waking her, but her eyes opened.

"Is it time to get up?

"No, Des. Go back to sleep."

I pulled the sheet back over her body and then kissed her forehead. I tried not to run for the door, but I did. I found some shorts in my laundry room and flopped down in front of the TV. As much as I loved having her body pressed against mine, I needed to get away from her at that moment. I was suffocating.

Waking up next to Desiree felt right to me. She felt as if she belonged to me and no one else. I had lost hope of anything developing between us, but my heart was telling me not to give up. My heart was trying to convince my brain to fight for her. I couldn't. If I did, she was going to destroy me one day.

'This is ridiculous," I said blindly flipping channels.

Why did I insist on spending my nights with Des? Being intimate with her was not going to help me. It was making things twice as hard. My desire for her was standing in the way of my healing.

"Am I supposed to get over her?"

I was beginning to think that God put me on this earth to love her. Would he do that, knowing that she was not intended to love me in return? I really hope not.

"Maybe I should tell her." What would that solve? Nothing. It wouldn't make me feel any better. No one wanted to tell someone that they loved them, knowing that they were not going to hear the same profession in return. I was going to save myself the humiliation.

My best bet would be for me to get over this woman once and for all, but it was proving to be one of the most difficult things that I had to do. I had been in love with this woman for the last six years and I was doing nothing more than falling deeper in love with her. My love for her was causing me some serious inner chaos. I was fighting a war that I knew I was going to lose from the beginning.

Why was this so hard? Why couldn't I just give up? Why couldn't I move on? Why was I hanging on?

I was hopeless, but I couldn't convince myself to do what I had to do. I didn't want to be away from her. Without her, I felt an unexplainable emptiness. I knew it was wrong to feel that way. I should not allow Desiree to have so much control over me.

She had an undeniable spell over me. I didn't have it left in me to fight her. It took less energy out of me to just give into her. She would fulfill my every need as long as she wanted to.

Frustrated and very much disappointed in myself, I headed to the kitchen. I started preparing breakfast. I knew Desiree loved bacon and pancakes, so of course I wanted to fix her favorites. Forty minutes later, I was heading to my bedroom with a plate of food and a cup of juice on a tray.

As soon as I pushed opened the bedroom door, her eyes opened. She immediately sat up in bed and that familiar feeling of butterflies came into my stomach. She was the most beautiful woman in the world to me. She was unbelievably sexy, wearing nothing but my sheet and a big smile.

"Whats that?" she asked, her eyes twinkling with excitement.

"You know what this is," I said, laughing. I sat down beside her and placed the tray over her lap. "I thought you might be hungry."

"Quinton, you really spoil me." It's because I love you.

"Don't get used to it, though, sweetheart."

"Too late," she smiled in my direction. "I hope you made more because you aren't getting any of this."

"Luckily I did," I laughed.

After breakfast, we showered together. Our shower turned into a quick session of lovemaking. It was one sexy shower.

We spend the afternoon snuggled up on my couch, watching basketball. I laughed because she was more into the game than I was. I was too busy concentrating on her. She was driving me crazy because she was wearing nothing but my one of my old T. shirts.

Later on that evening, Des rode with me to my brother's house to pick up my son. She wanted to see him before she headed home.

"What's going on?" My brother asked as soon as Desiree left the room with my sister-in-law. "She spent the night with you, right?"

"Where did that come from?" Why was he asking me this?

"It's obvious."

"No, it's not," I said in denial. "Do you really know what you are talking about?" I asked, not really wanting to get into this with my brother. Not today.

"I do. I was in your position once, little bro."

"What position?"

"You love this woman."

"That would be stupid of me."

"Love is a beautiful thing, my man. Love is not stupid." I think he misunderstood me.

"It would be stupid for me to still be in love with Desiree." Why couldn't I tell him the truth? Why was he pushing me like this at a time where I already felt vulnerable? I headed for the door, but he grabbed my shoulder.

"Stop lying. It's time for you to tell the truth."

"Look, there's no point in telling Desiree how I feel."

"Oh my goodness, you are so stubborn. Lil bro, stop running. Toughen up and tell this woman how you feel."

"I can't do that. You don't understand."

"Make me understand, then. Why won't you tell this woman how you feel about her."

"I can't make her love me!" I felt like someone had shot me in my heart. It shattered at that moment. It hurt to say those words.

My comment rattled my brother. He didn't respond. He just stared back at me. I stared back at him for another moment and then finally pushed past him.

Little Quinton was all over Desiree, however; when she pointed out the fact that I had entered the room to his attention, he climbed out of her lap and came running towards me.

"What's up, lil man?"

"Hey, daddy."

"I missed you. I have a surprise for you."

"Yes! Where is it!"

"You'll see. Are you ready, Desiree?" I needed to get out of here.

"Okay," she said, giving me a strange look. "Whats wrong?" she asked me during the ride home.

"I am cool. Mike said something to me that's got me thinking."

"Oh, do you want to talk about it?" Not with you.

"No, I am fine, Des. Don't worry about it."

When we got back to the house, she didn't bother going inside.

"I better go."

"Oh okay. It's been nice." I said, hugging her. I didn't kiss her. I couldn't when I was feeling this way. I wasn't prepared for the hurt look on her face.

"Yeah, it was. Well, talk to you later."

"Please do. Bye, Des."

"Bye, Q."

She turned and hurried to her car. She jumped in, started it up and backed out. She didn't bother to wave or blow the horn. Something told me that I hadn't handled the situation too well.

26

Yearning

"There is no fear in love, but perfect love casts out fear. For fear has to do with punishment, and whoever fears has not been perfected in love." *1 John 4:18*

Desiree

It's been nice? That's what he said to me? He summed up our time together with three words. Three insignificant words. Was he kidding me!

I was so mad that I could barely breathe correctly. My heart was beating faster than it should have. I was so hot that I had all four windows down. I was driving over 70 mph in a 45 mph speed zone. Jay Z was turned up to the highest decibel.

I couldn't think straight. I didn't want to think. I just wanted to be pissed. My reckless driving was helping me get my frustration out, but I needed to get home before I ended up killing someone.

I did have the good sense to thank the Lord when I pulled safely in my driveway without incident. I made a promise to myself that I would have never do anything so stupid again. At least not while I was angry. I could have lost my license or caused a serious accident.

I literally screamed at the top of my lungs once inside. I didn't know what else to do. I felt as if I was going to explode.

I was surprised when the tears came. I didn't understand why I was crying. I just fell on my couch and let it all out. I allowed myself to cry until I couldn't cry anymore.

I felt stupid for crying. It was after all just words. I should not have been affected by them. Unfortunately, I was. Extremely.

Quinton and I had spent a passionate night together. Last night meant more to me than I was letting on. It was not just a night of loving, but it was a night with Quinton. I cared about him more than he could even imagine.

I assumed that he viewed last night the same way I did. He cared about me as a friend; that would always be obvious. He was very vocal about that, so I didn't have any doubts. But I was already feeling guilty about being intimate with this man, so I was desperately trying to place more significance over the night than I should have. We were strictly having sex and I somehow had to face that.

I was angry with myself, not with Q. I felt humiliated by allowing myself to give into him so freely. I was humiliated because I allowed him to love me over and over again. I was humiliated because I thought we were doing more than having sex.

"What were the last nine months?"

Other than Tyler, I had never allowed myself to become intimate with a man who I was not in a committed relationship with. I was always intimate with a man who I loved. I was never into finding a man who could just fulfill my sexual needs. I never wanted to be in a friends with benefits situation.

All of that logic flew out of the window the first night Q moved in. We kissed and my entire way of thinking was gone. As desperately as I tried to fight the fire burning between us, I was hooked. Hooked to his kisses, his touches and the way he loved me. For the first time in my almost twenty-eight years on earth, I was addicted to sex.

Being with Q meant the world to me and he demeaned it with his three words. With those words, he had embarrassed me. I realized that I had placed more significance in the situation than he had.

"Wow!" This was one of women's downfalls. We always became attached to the wrong men. I was no different.

"Forget this!" I was not about to sit here and sulk over some man who I wasn't even dating. I definitely felt stupid because this wasn't even like me. I wasn't use to tripping like this.

I wasn't going to stress over Q all night. There were too many sexy brothers out there. I worked with a couple of them who were single. I needed to start acting as if I was single too.

I headed to the bathroom to run myself a long bath. I was going to force myself to relax. I had to work in the morning and I needed to get some rest. I had a feeling that this was going to be a crazy week considering how Friday ended.

I was taking my clothes off when I heard my phone ringing from my bedroom. I stood there and listened with my heart beating like crazy. I didn't move until it stopped ringing. When it stopped, I continued to take my clothes off, folding them neatly on my sink.

My toe had barely hit the water when my phone rang again. Frustrated, I headed towards the phone on my bead. I figured that it was Quinton, but I wanted to make sure. If it was my mother, I was going to feel bad.

My intuition was right on the money. Quinton's picture flashed across my phone. Seeing his face made my blood pressure rise, but I willed myself to take some deep breaths and walked away. I was not going to give into the temptation of picking up the phone and giving him a piece of my mind.

I soaked in my tub until I almost fell asleep. Realizing that the bath had done its job, I climbed out. It was time for bed. I climbed under my covers and then listened to Quinton's voice message.

"Des, I know you purposely didn't answer the phone. Please don't do this. Baby, please don't be mad at me. You know I can't stand this." There was a small pause. "I really wish I could hear your voice right now. I am sorry, okay." That was it.

It was kind of sweet, but then again, I had learned that Quinton had a way with words. I was tempted to call him and put him out of his misery, but another part of was reluctant. Quinton didn't know what he was apologizing for; he just knew I was angry with him. Of course he was going to call and try to make amends with me.

"Mr. Alexander, I am going to let you suffer a little longer."

I threw my phone on the nightstand and turned off the lamp. Enough was enough. I was determined not to spend another moment thinking about Quinton.

Too make matters worse, I was getting stressed out about my stalker. He had stopped sending me letters for a while, but I received another one today.

Desiree,

I am glad he is gone. You are mine, not his.

Missing you,
The One

I woke up the next morning deciding today that I needed to turn a few heads. I had my eyes set on a certain coworker. While I had been seeing Lance for a while, I hadn't given him my full undivided attention. He wanted it; it was time to give it to him.

I slipped into a short black skirt with a sexy white blouse that was still appropriate for work. I had some new black and white stilettoes that I had never worn. I wanted to feel good today. After last night, I wanted to feel confident.

I got verification as soon I walked through the revolving door to my building. The security guard practically knocked over his coffee.

"Good morning, James," I said, chuckling to myself.

"Good morning, Ms. Harris. You look beautiful today."

"Thank you, James. I appreciate that."

"Girl, I love those shoes and that skirt. I must borrow," my coworker, Kendra, gushed when I breezed past her.

"Thank you. We may be able to work something out."

Before I could reach my office, I passed Kyle, one of the newer brothers in the office. He had glanced my way once or twice, but I found him a little too high maintenance. I had never held much of a conversation with him other than a hello and goodbye. Because he was very into himself, he never pushed it, but today he did a double take and stopped. He sort of blocked my path.

"Hi there. We were never formally introduced. It's Kyle," he said, sticking his hand out. I took it and smiled. I know your name, but you never bothered to know mine.

"Desiree."

"How are you doing this morning?"

"I am great. How are you?"

"I am wonderful."

"How are things going for you?"

"I am still learning, but it's been great. I enjoy it here."

"Good to hear."

"I am on my way to a meeting, but I really wanted to say hi."

"That was nice of you."

"I will see you around, Desiree." Why did he whisper my name that way? I had definitely piqued his interest.

I smiled after him. He was nicely built and I enjoyed looking at him, but I couldn't go there. He wasn't my cup of tea.

I had just settled in front of my computer to check my email when the door to my office pushed opened. In walked Kendra with a delivery man on her heels. He was holding a huge vase of Tulips. They were undeniably beautiful.

"Delivery, sweetheart."

"Wow." Quinton, I thought immediately. Who else would do this? "Thank you," I said when the man sat them down on my desk.

"Well, who did something to you?" she asked when he left.

"Q," I blurted. "He's trying to get back on my good side."

"Tulips too! Different. Obviously this one adores you."

"We're just friends, Kendra."

"Whatever," she said, rolling her eye and heading for the door. "Men don't send flowers to just friends. Only to mothers and lovers. Bye now." She winked and shut the door behind her.

I stared after her, speechless. She was right in a way. We had definitely crossed that friendship line. We had been lovers; however, at this moment, I am not sure what we were. That scared me.

Snapping out of my trance, I grabbed the card and read it aloud.

Desiree,

I am sorry. From the bottom of my heart, I never meant to hurt you. When you are ready, please come and talk to me. I will be waiting patiently. I love you.

Quinton

I sighed. I knew Quinton was sorry. I figured I meant enough to him for him not to give me some fake apology. I decided to get out of my feelings and to forgive him. I had reached for my phone to put him out of his misery when Lance walked in. Apologizing to Q was quickly forgotten. I was genuinely happy to see Lance.

"Well, hello, Lance." I walked over to him to hug him. That and a quick kiss took him by surprise. "How are you?"

"Well, I am good right now." He gave me a boyish grin. "I saw you walking across the office looking so incredible and I had to come speak to you this morning."

"Thank you, Lance."

"Come here, gorgeous." He pulled me to him to kiss me. It was our first passionate one. Despite how much we both enjoyed it, we cut it short. We didn't want to get caught in the act. "I have wanted to do that since I laid eyes on you, but I didn't have the nerve."

"Just go for it, Lance. I like for a man to take charge."

"I will from now on. How about we get dinner after work?"

"I would love that."

"Cool. I will pick you up right here around five."

"Perfect. I will be waiting."

When he left, I almost jumped up and down with excitement. I needed this. I needed him to ask me out. I needed to start dating again. I was hoping that Lance would prove to be a good distraction.

"This time, things will be different," I said aloud, sliding back in my seat. I was going to allow myself to be serious about this guy. Perhaps, Lance could offer more than I was giving him credit for.

Quinton

I had sent Des flowers this morning, hoping that I would hear from her. I was thinking after a good night's sleep that she would be over last night. By afternoon, I realized that was not the case. Apparently, I was not forgiven.

By 3:00, I was so upset that I was visibly annoyed. Before it turned 4:00, I had snapped at all of my colleagues to the point where they refused to come around me. I could barely get through my show, but somehow I managed. I wrapped the show up by 5:55, By 6:05, I was pulling out of the parking lot.

I was halfway home when I realized that I was supposed to stop by the mall. I had to pick up my mother's present from the jewelry store. I had to pick it up tonight because tomorrow was her birthday and I was taking her out to her favorite restaurant after work.

I was so frustrated that I made a sudden u turn in the road. In my recklessness, I almost hit another car. They laid on their horn, but in my rage, I flicked them off and gave them some choice words.

I walked into the mall thinking that I would be in and out within fifteen minutes. I was wrong. I had my mother's gift in my hand and was heading to the door when I spotted Desiree.

The sight of her infuriated me even more. I started to head into her direction. I knew I was not going to feel better until I gave her a small piece of my mind. I needed to express myself now or I was liable to explode on some innocent bystander. That could be dangerous and I was trying to prevent that from happening.

I was about to yell her name when I saw that she wasn't alone. I stopped walking so fast that this small kid slammed into my leg. The little girl looked up at me and went running into her mother's direction. Instead of apologizing, I just stared after her, not feeling as bad as I should have. At this moment, the only thing that I was concerned about was how I felt.

The dude looked familiar to me. If he was familiar to me, then he had been around before, which meant that she was seeing him on a regular basis. They were obviously dating. That meant there was a possibility of them becoming serious. With a relationship came intimacy and sex. I couldn't handle knowing Desiree was doing more than casual dating.

Who was I fooling? I couldn't handle that either. I didn't want her to be with anyone but me. That wasn't going to happen, so I was in a depressing situation.

"Lance." How could I forget him? She told me not to worry about him. So she lied.

I watched the two of them walk hand and hand into a book store. They looked intimate which was driving me up the wall. Had they kissed? Had she given him some loving?

I was getting sick to my stomach. I felt like I was going to lose it when he leaned down to kiss her. It was like watching Anthony all over again. Maybe this time, it felt worst. I was desperately in love with her now. I felt as if the universe was punishing me, reminding me of how much I didn't deserve true happiness.

She looked happy and that's what I wanted for her. I just wanted be happy too. And I was never going to be content watching someone else please her the way I wanted to. Sadly there was no way I could stop it. The inevitable looked as if it had happened. I would have to accept it.

They kissed again. This time, Desiree grabbed him by his shirt. She kissed him the way she had kissed me so many times before.

My mouth was growing dry. I was starting to sweat. My heart was beating quicker than usual. I felt like I was about to have an anxiety attack. I had to get out of here and away from the both of them.

I headed towards the door once again, this time walking as fast I could. I wanted to sprint, but I didn't want to alarm anyone. I was literally a couple feet away from the door when she yelled my name. I would have ignored her and kept walking, but she called my name again. This time she was so close that it would have been obvious.

I took a deep breath and then turned to face her. It was torture.

"Whats up?" A sharp pain went through my chest. I grabbed it, hoping that she didn't notice it.

"Quinton!" I was surprise when she threw her arms around me. It was a long hug. For that moment, in her arms, I felt as if everything was okay. When she pulled away, that feeling disappeared. Nothing was okay. "I thought you were ignoring me, Q."

"Why would I do that?"

"I don't know. You were about to walk out of that door."

"Baby, I just didn't hear you," I said, grabbing her hand and quickly letting go. I hated lying to her, but I couldn't admit to her what was really going on in my head.

I know," she said, grabbing my hand again and holding on tightly. "Quinton, I am sorry."

"For what?" She looked incredible in her skirt and blouse. Her skirt accentuated all the curves that I loved. My eyes drifted up to her lips and I realized that someone else had just kissed them.

I looked away. It was unbearable to handle. I didn't want to imagine anyone being as passionate about this woman as I was.

"For being a bitch," she blurted. "There was no reason for me to act so petty towards you. Speeding off last night and then purposely avoiding your phone calls were uncalled for." I just nodded. It hurt to hear her admit it. I hated when she was angry with me.

"It's okay."

"No, it's not, Quinton. It was childish."

"I forgive you, but only if you forgive me."

"You were upset with me?" she asked, quietly.

"Of course not, Desiree." I was just…."

"Tell me later, okay?"

"When?" When was she going to have time for me again.

"I will call you later on tonight."

"Do you promise?" I asked, skeptically.

"Yes. Thank you for the flowers, they were very beautiful. I loved them." She hugged me again and it took everything in me not to hold onto her tightly.

"I know that you love Tulips."

"You know too much about me, Quinton Alexander." She stared directly into my eyes.

"Not enough," I said, staring back. I wanted to know everything and more.

"I meant to call you."

"Why didn't you?"

"I got busy."

"I see." She looked back in Lance direction. He was eyeing us.

"Oh, Lance. He wasn't the issue. I was busy with clients all day."

"Okay. Are you on a date?"

"I guess you can call it that."

"Are you serious about this dude?"

"Well, not yet." Not yet? That meant there was a possibility.

"You want it to be, though.

"I don't know," she giggled. "I better get going. Lance is waiting." I didn't give a crap about Lance. What about me?

"What do you two have planned?"

"Dinner. I'm not sure after that. I can share all the details later."

"Please spare me. I don't care to know." I had to be honest with her. She just stared back at me.

"Okay, I won't."

I watched her walk back to this dude, Lance. I wanted to yell for her to come back, but couldn't quite find the words. I couldn't humiliate myself like that. Instead, I hung my head and then turned to walk away. All I felt was numbness.

Desiree

Lance took me to this popular seafood restaurant overlooking the city. It was an unusually warm night, so it was the perfect weather to have dinner under the stars. I am not sure if it was the atmosphere or the wine, but I could feel the chemistry between us. I could feel the romance brewing.

We held hands. We stared at each other. We talked and started to really get to know one another. We had been spending time together off and on, but this was our first real date. By the end of the night, I felt as if I had been dating him for months.

"This is perfect."

"What did you say?" He looked puzzled.

"Oh nothing." I took a sip of wine and looked away.

He insisted on walking me to my front door when he dropped me off at home. He went in for the hug, but I went in for the kiss. Our embrace turned into a make out session against my door. I didn't realize the amount of sexual tension between us until my dress was practically hiked up around my waist and his hand was cupping my behind.

The only thing that stopped us from going further was me realizing that we were on full display. The thought of my neighbors peering out their windows made me pull away from him. I am sure the nosy old lady across the street was getting more than she bargained for. Plus my Aunt Karen lived a couple houses down. I didn't want her to tell my mother.

After Lance left and I was alone inside, I took off my clothes and headed straight for my shower. After my shower, I immediately got in my bed. I sighed as I slid under crisp cool sheets. After a couple moments of gathering my thoughts, I reached for my phone.

"I thought you weren't going to call me," Q answered.

"That's not how you answer the phone."

"It's late, Desiree, are you just getting in?" Wow. He completely ignored what I had said.

"I took a shower before I called you."

"Are you in bed? What are you wearing?"

"Nothing," I teased.

"Can I come over?" Please. Yes. I wanted that more than anything, but I couldn't allow that to happen anymore.

"No."

"Wow. I can't believe that you just flat out said no." I could hear the disappointment in his voice.

"I need sleep."

"I guess you have moved on to better things."

"Will you shut up? That's nonsense, Q."

"If you say so."

"I miss you, Quinton," I blurted. No filter. Goodness, Desiree.

"Really?" He sounded a little taken back.

"Yeah."

"What do you miss?"

"Everything," I admitted.

"Little Q misses you. He has been asking about you."

"That sweet, but I want to know do you miss me?" When he did not answer me right away, I got scared. "Never mind. You don't have to answer me."

"No, Desiree, I miss you so much that I can hardly function normally. I don't think it's healthy." I closed my eyes so I could absorb what he had just said. I placed my hand over my heart because it was now beating faster.

"That's what I wanted to hear," I finally whispered.

"You just want to know how much power you have over me."

"It's not about the power, sweetheart, it's about keeping me sane. I need to know that you are feeling the same way that I do."

"I am. About last night, Desiree."

"Don't worry about it, Quinton. I am past that."

"This weekend meant so much to me and I never really got to express that to you. It's not about having sex with you, it's about having you around me. I need that."

"I know." I suddenly felt stupid for my outburst last night

"Do you? You do know that us being together means pretty much everything to me these days. Having you waking up beside me is something that my soul desires."

"I do know, Q," I whispered. I couldn't understand why tears were falling down cheeks. If Quinton knew I was crying, he would think I was crazy. I was starting to think that maybe I was losing it.

"Des, I am sorry that I didn't say all of this last night, but do know I immediately felt bad."

"I understand, Q, you looked upset."

"My brother said something crazy crap to me and it fogged my mind up pretty badly. I wasn't thinking clearly."

"Are you okay? Do you want to talk about it?"

"No, I am cool."

"I am here for you," I said, knowing not to push Quinton.

"That's all I need to know."

"Come over," I joked. He laughed.

"Go to sleep, Des. We will talk tomorrow."

"I can't wait."

"Me neither."

Tomorrow came and I didn't get to talk to Quinton. I knew that it wasn't a big deal, but it bothered me more than I wanted to admit. I was aching to hear the sound of his voice. I felt as if I needed to hear it. Knowing that drove me crazy.

I started seeing a lot more of Lance over the course of the next three weeks. Every day after work, we would hook up. We were spending so much time together that it was becoming difficult to keep our relationship a secret from our fellow colleagues. I was not trying to be any part of the water cooler gossip.

Admittedly, I was having a wonderful time getting to know him over lunch, dinner or a drink. It didn't matter where our date began, by the end of the night, we were making out on one of our couches. And then we would cuddle up and talk into the wee hours of the morning. It didn't matter how heated things got between us, I managed to put out the flame.

Things changed one Friday evening. We had ordered pizza and was chilling on my couch. I left the living room to get something out my bedroom. Lance followed me. I turned around and there he was.

"Whats up?" I smiled up at him knowingly. I was very much willing to take it there if he tried.

"I want you," he whispered, pulling me into his arms. I probably should have pulled away, but I didn't. Not many women could turn down a man as sexy as Lance. He was tall and muscular with an irresistible smile. He gave Morris and Idris a run for their money.

We started kissing and I shivered as his hand moved underneath my shirt. Before I knew it, we were on my bed and he was on top of me. It didn't take long before half of our clothes were on my floor. I closed my eyes as I ran my hand freely over his muscles.

"Lance," I whispered.

"Shush." I moaned a little as he started kissing my neck. "You are so beautiful, Desiree." Something about those words reminded me of Quinton. I immediately felt guilty thinking of him while I was with another man. I attempted to push him out of my mind. "Will you let me have you?" he whispered in my ear.

"Have me?" I repeated.

I closed my eyes as his lips explored my bare skin. He kept whispering "you are beautiful" and "I want you". As sweet as he was being, I found myself thinking of the things Quinton would say to me and how he would touch me. I thought about how he could make me feel with just the brush of his lips.

Suddenly, I pushed against Lance. I pushed him on his back and climbed over him. I took him by surprise.

"Wow," he laughed.

"This is my part of the show." I smiled down at him and proceeded to take my bra off. He stared back at me with excitement in his eyes. He was obviously eager about the possibilities between us.

I made a huge mistake of looking in the direction of my nightstand. I quickly found myself staring into Quinton eyes. It was a picture of him and I. I became frozen. I just stared back at Quinton. I knew right then and there that I missed him more than I was letting on. I wanted to be with him in that moment.

'This is so messed up," I whispered. I was about to go there with one man, but was desperately wanting the affection of another.

"What! Whats wrong?"

"Sorry, Lance. I can't do this with you right now."

"You are kidding right."

I could understand his frustration. Here I was practically naked, sitting on top of him. I was in the wrong. A woman shouldn't play with a man's emotions like this. I couldn't help it. My heart was speaking very loudly to me and I had no choice but to listen.

"No!" I said, suddenly climbing off of him. "I am afraid that I am not kidding. I am sorry." I picked my clothes up off of the floor and sprinted to my bathroom. I slammed the door behind me as if I was expecting him to follow me.

I stood in front of my bathroom mirror, shivering. I was so startled by what happen that I looked terrified. I didn't recognized myself. I started laughing hysterically, but that laughter quickly turned into uncontrollable sobs. I felt confused, defeated and alone.

I jumped when Lance knocked on the door.

"Desiree, I hear that you are upset and you don't understand how that makes me feel. Can I please come in?"

"Give me a moment," I managed to get out.

"Okay, I will be right here."

I quickly pulled my clothes back on. I splashed my face with water. I needed to calm down. I grabbed a washcloth and washed away the smeared mascara that had fallen victim to my breakdown. I took a few deep breaths before opening the door. I was embarrassed to face him, but all of that quickly went away when I saw Lance was genuinely concerned.

"Are you okay?" he asked, pulling me to him.

"I am fine," I lied. "I am really sorry that all of this happened."

"Don't apologize to me. I just want to make sure that you are good because you scared me running out of the room like that."

"I don't quite understand whats going on with me," I admitted.

"It's okay. You do understand that I would have never forced you to do anything that you didn't want to do. You could have told me if you felt uncomfortable."

"It's not like I didn't want to. I was so in the mood, but I just couldn't go through with it tonight."

"Are you sure that you are okay?"

"I am going to be okay." Again, I lied. I was beyond uneasy.

"Good. Please don't ever scare me like that again, Desiree."

"I didn't mean to do that." I laid my head on his shoulder.

"It's okay. I am still going home a happy man."

"You really don't have to lie to me to make me feel better."

"I am not lying." He grabbed my face and kissed my forehead. I closed my eyes and took a deep breath before opening them. Why did that small act of affection remind me of Quinton as well?

"You have the softest skin and the sweetest lips," he whispered.

"Do I?" I forced a smile.

"Yes. You are the only thing that's going to be on my mind for a while." I wished I could say the same to him.

"I will be thinking of you too." Why was I lying to him?

"Look when you are ready just let me know. We will take things slow. Just know that I will be ready when you are." He was either acting or he had to be the most understanding man that I had ever been with. I stared into his eyes for a moment and detected sincerity. Knowing that he was being genuine made me feel worst.

"Lance, I know that our time will come." I managed to slide my arms around his neck.

"Good." He kissed me. I kissed him back with all that I could considering that Q was all that I could focus on. "I better get going."

"You don't have to rush." I wanted him to go.

"I don't want to leave you, but I have to get up early. Plus, I need to get away from you, sexy, and cool myself off." He smiled to let me know he was joking.

"Take a shower," I giggled.

"Those are my plans. And even that may not work."

When Lance left, I headed straight for my phone on my nightstand. Before I could even gather my thoughts, I was dialing Quinton's number. I couldn't quite understand why I was feeling this way, but I needed to see him right now if he would let me.

I felt as if my heart shattered when he didn't answer. I redialed his number, refusing to believe that I was not about to get what I wanted, only to receive the same results. I was so disappointed that I almost flung my phone into my bedroom wall.

I fell back on my bed and just stared at the ceiling not really knowing what to do with myself. I decided that it would be best for me to go to bed. I was settled in between my sheets by 11:30 on a Friday night. I couldn't go to sleep though. I was awake when Quinton called me back around midnight. I refused to answer. I wasn't sure if I had the right words for him.

I had lunch with my older sister, Jade that Saturday afternoon. I decided to tell her everything. She had known that something was going on between Quinton and me, but I had spared her the details. I blurted every complicated aspect of our relationship.

"I don't know if I believe you," she whispered fiercely in response to my confession. Her eyes were wild with disbelief.

"Why not? What part don't you believe, Jade?"

"You are telling me that you and little Quinton Alexander...."

"Little Quinton is not so little anymore."

"Spare me those specifics. I don't want to know that much."

"What!" I blushed. "That's not what I meant Jade. I was simply trying to point out that Q is grown. We are both pushing thirty."

"So you are breaking him off the cookie? And on the regular?"

"Yes."

"Just sex? You two don't have feelings for another?"

"We are just friends, Jade."

"I don't believe you. I just can't. This is all blowing my mind."

"Why is it so hard to believe?"

"This just doesn't sound like you."

"I know. It isn't like me at all."

"How did this happen, Des? Why did you allow this to happen?"

"He kissed me. I kissed him back. I was hooked after that night. It became an addiction. I needed it."

My sister stared at me for a moment.

"It can't be that good," she blurted.

"Oh it is," I said as seriously as I could.

"Really? Desiree you are really tripping over Quinton."

"No, I am not. It's not that serious," I lied. "I am just stuck on you know...."

"Oh my gosh," she laughed, throwing her head back. "Please stop. At this point, I can never look at him quite the same again."

"He really knows how to please me," I teased.

"Okay, Des. I think you are lying, though."

"Why do I have to be lying?"

"You don't have to. You are choosing to sit here and lie to me. I am your big sister, so I can tell that you are not being real with me."

"Jade, stop trying to make something out of nothing. I'm telling you the truth. I'm just not telling you what you want to hear."

"You are right; you aren't telling me what I want to hear. Again, you are choosing to be dishonest with yourself and me. I know you, Desiree. There is no way that you can be intimate with a man and not develop feelings for him."

"This time is different," I said, starting to shift uncomfortably. I was trying to convince myself and not just my sister.

"Why are trying to kid yourself? You are telling me that you haven't caught any feelings for, Q?" She was breaking me down.

"I do care about him. We have been through a lot together in the last year. Surprisingly, we have become even closer since he moved in. We are just friends, though, Jade."

"People who are friends don't just sleep together."

"Friends with benefits do."

"I think we both know by now that the beneficial thing between friends doesn't really work, Desiree."

"It has made things sticky. That's why we are stopping."

"It's only been three weeks, Desiree. You didn't stop because you wanted to. You stopped because you two are busy. If he called you tonight, you would be ready and willing."

"Nooo," I said, trying very hard not to smile.

"Stop it. All this lying is not necessary. You care about him, Desiree. I see it in your eyes. You have feelings for him, little sister."

"I really don't think so."

"Then what was the deal last night?"

"I miss him, Jade. I miss him so much."

"Why? Why were you thinking of him while you were with another man?"

"I don't know," I answered, honestly. "Because my reaction scared me," I said, closing my eyes. I was desperately trying not to face the truth.

"Desiree, do you have feelings for Quinton."

"Jade, I can't," I said, shaking my head vigorously.

"Yes, you can."

"We are just friends, though."

"You passed that line last year, sweetie. Why do you miss him?"

"I barely see him. I use to seem him every day."

"If you needed him, would he come?"

"Well, yeah."

"Think about what you are saying. You're confused, little sister."

"I will admit that."

"If you didn't have feelings for this man, then why would you be confused?"

"I…" She got me. I was at a loss for words.

"Admit it, Des. Whats wrong with having feelings for this man?"

"Because it's Quinton, Jade. I feel silly."

"Don't feel silly."

"I can't help it. I don't want to fall for this man."

"Too late." I sighed in frustration and looked up at the sky. I asked God why. "He has already stolen your heart."

"I guess." I was tired of denying it." I could never win with Jade.

"Think about it. Why did you let your boy kiss you?"

"I couldn't say no, Jade. I tried, but I couldn't. I wanted it."

"So maybe he had your heart before that night." Did he? "Des, be careful. Please don't set yourself up to be hurt. You don't deserve that. I want you to go home. Search your heart. Figure out the truth."

After lunch, Jade and I took a trip to the mall. Shopping was my thing but today I couldn't get with it. My mind was all over the place.

When the night came, I decided to stay in. I lay in bed in front of my TV. I continued to miss him. The yearning made my night long and restless. I barely got any sleep, waking up almost every hour.

I woke up the next morning, ate a big bowl of apple jacks and hopped in the shower to get ready for church. I decided that I was in need of some religion. I slipped into my favorite red dress in hopes of cheering up and headed to First Baptist.

As soon as I made myself comfortable on the end of a pew, I felt his presence. I turned slightly and there he was staring at me. After a couple moments, he smiled and waved. I waved back.

Knowing that he was under the same roof had me on pins and needles. For the first time in ages, I was nervous at the thought of being close to him. From that moment on, he was the only thing that consumed my mind when I should have been focusing on praise and worship. I stared at the preacher, but heard nothing he said. My service had been ruined.

I waited by the end of the pew after service, knowing that he was coming towards me. I took in how nice he looked in his suit. I quickly looked away because I was getting aroused. This was not the place. Why was I allowing him to do this to me?

"Hey you," he said, finally reaching me.

"Hello, Mr Alexander," I said, holding out my hand in hopes that he would take it. I wasn't sure if I could handle more of a touch then that.

"Really, Desiree?" Unfortunately, he ignored my hand and quickly pulled me to him. I was forced to embrace him.

"I am sorry. How have you been?" I managed to ask him. I needed to get away from this man.

"I have been decent, Des." Why was he staring straight into my eyes and no matter how hard I tried not to stare back, I couldn't look away. "How about you? What have you been up to?"

"The same ole." Was it my imagination or was he moving closer.

"Oh. I haven't heard from you in a while," he finally blurted. "I don't really like that."

"I haven't heard from you in a while either, Quinton."

"Are we going to go through this again?" he asked, this time obviously stepping closer to me. If he moved any closer, it would be inappropriate considering we were in church.

"Not if you would get you act together," I joked.

"I called you last."

"Oh, whatever. Will you walk me to my car?" I asked, grabbing his hand. If I didn't get him to follow me, I felt as if I would never get away from him.

"What are you up to today?" he asked.

"Dinner at my mother's."

"That's nice. Will you tell her hello?"

"I will. What about you? What are you getting into?"

"The same. About to pig out over my mom's cooking."

"Great. Tell her hello as well."

"I will."

"Thanks. How is little Quinton?"

"He is being good."

"I am glad to hear that. Well, I better get going." I managed to hug him quickly. "I hope to hear from you soon, Quinton."

"You know my number as well, Desiree," he said, seriously.

"I do. You are on my favorites list and everything."

"Well treat me as one of your favorites and use it."

"Okay," I whispered.

I was anxious on the ride home. I was not quite sure why I was feeling this. I just knew I wanted to be by myself for a while. I called my mother as I pulled into my driveway and broke the news that I wasn't going to be over for dinner.

"Why, honey?"

"I feel sick. I think I am due for my monthly soon," I admitted.

"Well, sweetie, go lay down."

"I will, mommy."

I was crying before I unlocked my front door. I sat down on my couch because my tears blinded me. I was breaking down.

After a while, I took off my clothes and found an old t-shirt. I fell down on my bed and cried some more. I grabbed the very picture of Quinton that had sent me into this whirlwind of emotions. I could feel my heart breaking as the confusion disappeared.

I could not deny it. I loved this man. He had somehow crept into my heart. Unexpectedly, I had fallen for one of my best friends.

I let him kiss me because I was crazy about him. I surrendered to him because it was the only way I could express myself to him. Being with him was addictive because I not only yearned for him physically, but with every inch of my soul. I didn't want things to end between us because I didn't want to be left feeling this way. Yet, here I was.

Why? When? How? How could I fall for Quinton Alexander, a self-proclaimed ladies' man. My Childhood friend.

He was definitely not the best man for me to love. I knew he was a wonderful person, but I should have not fallen for him. He said he wanted to be in love, but was he even capable of loving a woman? A woman like me?

What's a girl to do? Telling him was out of the question. I felt out of his league. I was pretty sure I was not the type of woman that he envisioned himself being with.

"If I tell him, I may never hear from him again." I couldn't avoid him because he meant the world to me. I didn't want to go through life without him. He would always be a part of me in some way even if it wasn't in the way that I wanted him to be. I am pretty sure Quinton wouldn't be cool with that either.

"Quinton, I love you so much."

I didn't understand how much I wanted to be with Quinton until now. I had been bitten by the love bug before and I knew that love was not always fair. Sometime the person in your heart is completely different form the person God has intended for you.

I would love Quinton Alexander from afar. He would never hear my profession. This was a secret that I would be taking to my grave.

27

Game-Changer

"For I know the plans I have for you, declares the Lord, plans for
welfare and not for evil, to give you a future and a hope."
Jeremiah 29:11

Desiree

It had been a day to forget. I was late for work. I had to
deal with a difficult artist. My mother called because she was upset
with my father and felt the need to vent to me. As a result, I had a
gnawing headache. All I wanted to do was shower and go to bed.

I came home, kicked off my heels, yanked off my suit, and threw
everything into a pile on the floor. I took a quick shower to help with
the tension in my body. I grabbed my favorite pajamas, drank a glass
of wine and then retired to my bed. I needed rest.

I got up a couple hours later, restless and frustrated. I watched
mindless TV for a while, sipping wine and eating leftover chicken
wings. When I finally became drowsy, I headed back to bed. I had
barely laid my head against my pillow when I heard a noise. I sat up
in bed. It sounded as if someone was trying to break down my door.
They sounded as if they were relentless.

My heart dropped. What was happening? Why was this
happening to me? Was this the person who had been harassing me
off and on for the last year? It had to be.

Frantically, I jumped out of bed. I opened my bedroom door
and peered down the hallway. I didn't see anything, but I could hear
them rattling my doorknob.

"Who the hell is it?" I screamed. "Go away!"

The rattling stopped for a moment, but then started back again. I
slammed my bedroom door. I stood in the middle of my floor,

pulling on my hair, breathing hard with tears falling down my face. Feeling as if I was in the middle of a Lifetime movie nightmare, I was having a panic attack.

"What are you going to do!" I started to pace the floor. I was trying to calm myself. It wasn't working. "Come on, Des!" I took a couple deep breaths as I looked towards the sky. "God, help me!"

"Fight!" I had to defend myself. I wasn't going to allow some lunatic to break in my house and terrorize me. No one was going to rape me. No one was going to take from me. I wasn't going to allow this person to do this to me.

I flung open the door to my closet. I grabbed the shoebox from the corner and pulled out the gun. My parents were paranoid when I moved out alone and wanted to make sure that I had a way of defending myself. My father brought me a gun, took me to the gun range and taught me everything I needed to know.

"Our Father, which art in heaven…" I leaned against my bedroom door and repeated the Lord's Prayer twice. I needed his strength and his protection.

I flung opened the door. I headed down the hallway. The rattling of my door stopped. For a moment, I leaned against the wall and heard nothing. I thought the person had given up and retreated.

Just as I was about to breathe a sigh of relief, I heard the door open. For a moment I froze, but then I realize that someone was in my house and that I had to move quickly. I moved down my hallway, closed my eyes and fired a shot. I missed.

"Stop! The police are coming." I lied. The person dressed in dark clothes had their face covered. I couldn't tell whether it was a man or a woman. "Who are you! Why are you doing this!"

With my gun, pointed at their head, the intruder begins to back towards my door. I let them because I wanted them to get away from me. They hit the porch and took off running.

I collapsed onto the floor and begin to sob!

"Thank you, my Lord!"

Thinking the perpetrator would come back, I stood. I quickly shut my front door. I moved down the hallway and grabbed my phone. First I called 911 and then I called the only person that I wanted to comfort me. Quinton.

Quinton

A week had passed since I had last saw Desiree. I was only able to interact with her for a moment at church, but it was better than nothing. The three weeks that we hadn't talked before had been pure torture. I could have given in and called her or I could have taken a trip to her neighborhood, but I wouldn't allow myself to do either one. Unwillingly, I was trying to distance myself from her. I got the feeling that Desiree was trying to do the same because she had not made any effort to get in contact with me either.

That bothered more than I was willing to admit. I was distancing myself because I was attempting to protect my heart. Why was Desiree distancing herself from me? Was she losing interest in our relationship? Was she too preoccupied to work on maintaining whatever it was that we still had between us? I didn't want to think it about it too much because it was going to get me worked up, but something told me that it was because she was too busy with another man. With Lance perhaps.

I obviously didn't want to think about her dating anyone else. I foolishly tried to convince myself that she was intimate with me only. I could no longer hide from what was more and likely the truth. Lance was probably Desiree's man.

In that case, I didn't want to be around her. As selfish as it may have sounded, I wanted her to be happy, but I sure didn't want to see it. I didn't want to disrespect her relationship in anyway. I knew myself. Anytime I laid eyes on Desiree, taking her into my arms would always be a temptation.

I went out with some of my boys from college on Saturday night, leaving my son with my brother. My brother had been really understanding towards me since our conversation a month ago. Knowing that I was in a constant state of grieving, he told me that I deserved the chance to go out.

For five hours, I didn't think about her. My night was full of alcohol and beautiful women. I was in temporary bliss. I was so tipsy that I made out with this young chick that followed me to the bathroom. When she tried to come home with me, I resisted. I was a changed man. I was not trying to take things that far.

T, the designated driver, dropped me off in the wee hours of the morning. As tipsy as I was, I lost my high as soon as I set foot through my door. I headed for the shower. After that, I made myself a sandwich. I devoured my ham and cheese and then headed to bed because I was exhausted. I was out for the count as soon as my head hit the pillow.

I was in pretty deep sleep when my phone ranged. I was more than annoyed because I was having a pretty pleasant dream. I tried to ignore the phone when I realized it was 4:00 in the morning; however, the person on the other end was proving to be relentless. I grabbed the phone and answered it blindly and angrily.

"Who is this!"

"What do you mean!" a female voice sobbed. "It's me. Did you erase my number already?"

"Des!" I quickly sat up in bed. "What's wrong?" A nauseated feeling took over my stomach. "Why are you crying? Are you sick?"

"No, but I really need you right now."

"Okay, Okay, I am coming," I said, immediately stumbling out of my bed to find my clothes. "Can you tell me whats the matter?"

"Someone just broke into my house!"

"What!"

"I am so scared," she whispered. "What if someone wants to hurt me! Someone has been stalking me and I don't know who it is!"

"What do you mean someone has been stalking you? Did they touch you!" I tried to remain calm, but I wanted to lose my mind.

"I shot at them, so they left." She had a gun?

"I am on my way, right now. Did you call the police?"

"They are on the way."

"Good. Hold tight. I am coming for you. Hold on to that gun Go to your Aunt Karen's house."

I drove like a maniac trying to get to my woman. If anything happened to her, I honestly believed that I would lose what mind I had left these days. To me, she would not be safe until she was in my arms. As soon as I got to her, I wasn't letting her go for a long time.

The drive from my house to hers took about 15 minutes, but I got there in less than ten. I ran many red lights, but luckily I didn't see any blue lights behind me. I wasn't stopping for them regardless.

When I got to Desiree's, the cops were already there. I rushed inside only to have one of them block my path.

"Sir, do you live here?"

"No, but…"

"Well, I am sorry, sir, but I can't let you in."

"I need to get to her."

"The police are questioning her."

"I don't care!" I felt my blood boiling, but I stopped myself. Cops didn't like brothers like me, even when they were brothers themselves. "Look, sir, I just want to get to my girl. She needs me."

"Quinton!" Desiree came running towards me.

"Are you okay?" I whispered, pulling her firmly against me.

"No, I am not," She started to sob into my shoulder. "I am really freaking out."

"I am right here."

I walked past the young dude and gave him a hateful look. I wanted him to know that if he took my girl from me, we were going to have some serious problem. He understood where I was coming from because he threw his hands up and backed up.

"Miss," an older officer approached us. "We do need to finish asking you a few questions."

"This is too much for me! Please give me a minute."

"Baby, you need to calm down."

"I'm trying." She wrapped her arms around my waist and clung to me. I could feel her trembling.

"Will you give us just a moment?" I asked the officer.

"I understand that she is upset. I will give you five minutes." It was difficult getting her to calm down, but I finally did so.

"I am right here, Desiree and I am not going to let anything happen to you."

The officer returned and finished questioning Desiree. I stood beside her with my arm around her shoulder. If I so much as moved, she would dig her nails into my side as she continued to cling to me.

I was shocked to find out that someone had been harassing her for over a year. She received texts and letters normally. She never once disclosed that to me. I felt sick knowing that someone could have potentially been trying to hurt her.

"Can you stay?" she asked. "I am going to freak out if I have to stay in this house by myself. Well, to be honest, I am going to freak out regardless, but I would feel better knowing that you are beside me." I stared into those hypnotizing eyes as she pleaded with me. I rubbed her face and refrained from kissing her.

This was a bad situation, but it did something to me to know that she still needed me. It satisfied me. I was relieved that she called me and not Lance. He could not have possibly been her man.

"Pack your bag, sweetheart and come home with me. You are not going to get any sleep here anyway."

"You are going to let me spend the night at your house?" I almost laughed. I couldn't believe that she asked me that. If she had any clue to how badly I wanted her in my house every night, she would have grabbed her bag already.

"Really, Desiree. Come on," I pulled her towards the bedroom.

I helped Desiree pack an overnight bag and lock up her house. After that, we hopped into my ride and headed back to my spot.

"Where do I sleep?" was the first question out of her mouth. I stared at her. "Baby, where do you think?"

"The guest room?" That would never happen. After all that we had been through, she wasn't allowed to sleep anywhere but in my bed. I am not sure what she had going on with Lance or any other man, but tonight, she would be mine.

"That's not going down. I will pick you up and throw you on my bed if you move towards the guest room." She smiled up at me. "I have to keep an eye on you."

"Right," she said, moving towards my room. She threw me a look over her shoulder. She was so sexy, even when she was this vulnerable. I shook my head. Get it together, Q, and refrain from making a move.

I finally followed her into the bedroom. I tried not to stare as I watched her undress, but I failed miserably. It didn't matter what she did, she fascinated me and this time wasn't any different.

"Get in, Desiree" She stared at me while climbing in.

"Are you coming?"

"Yes." I pulled off my clothes, climbed in beside her, and then reached over to turn off the lamp beside me. To my surprise, I didn't have to reach for her, she came to me immediately. I almost breathed a sigh of relief when I wrapped my arms around her. She belonged there. When she was with me, I was sane.

I lay there and listened to her breathing. I was restless. I thought about Des being in danger earlier and me not being there to protect her. If something had happened, I would have killed someone.

Knowing that the night could have ended in violence sent chills through my body. There were so many thoughts running through my head. I felt as if I was on the verge of a panic attack. I managed to remain calm for Desiree's sake, but I was in for a long night.

We laid around in bed the next day until about noon. We made brunch and then sat down and enjoyed her favorite channel, HGTV. We then got dressed and headed to her parent's house. Desiree wanted to let them know what had happened to her.

I was amazed every time I saw her mother. Mrs. Harris, who was in her mid-fifties, didn't looked a day over forty. She was a beautiful older black woman with an amazing presence. When I stared at her, I could see Desiree's future. She was the splitting image of her mother. She would always be just as strikingly beautiful.

I loved Mrs. Harris. She had always been like a second mother to me. Too bad, I couldn't see Desiree as my sister. I yearned and ached for her daughter in a way that I had for no other woman.

"You will stay for dinner." She insisted because I had not been over in months I would never turn down dinner with the Des's parents. They were like family.

Her parents almost lost their minds when she told them about her stalker and the breaking and entering. Her mother became so hysterical that she practically fainted. Desiree wrapped her arms around her mother and they clung to each other.

'Why didn't you call us, baby girl?"

"I am sorry, mommy. The first person I thought of was Quinton. He was very good to me." She squeezed my hand.

"You have always been the best big brother to Desiree."

I bit my lip. Would her mother freak out if she knew how much I had been taking care of her daughter? How I had been fulfilling her sexual needs? How loving Des had become my drug? My addiction?

Des peered over at me and stared at me knowingly. She bit her lip a little and I looked away. I could tell she was turned on. Knowing that, turned me on as well. This was not the time, nor the place.

"I would do anything for Desiree, Mrs. Harris." I had to because I loved her. Of course neither of them realized that.

"Stay here, baby," her mother pleaded.

"No, mommy, I will be okay"

She wasn't. The fear returned to her eyes as soon as we walked through her front door. She was putting on a brave front, but I could tell she was still freaking out. I knew she was not ready to be alone.

"Thank you, Q." She hugged me. "I appreciate everything."

"Des, you know I would do anything for you. Are you sure that you are okay?" She pulled away and forced a smile. "No, you aren't."

"I am okay, Quinton."

"So I can leave and you will be fine alone tonight?"

"Yes," she whispered, looking down.

"Pack your bags, Desiree."

"I can't."

"You will."

"I have work in the morning."

"You can stay with me for a week or so. As long as you need, darling. If you need to stay longer, please do."

"But…"

"Are you really arguing? It's not like you want to be here by yourself. Just come with me. I want you to. You want to. Be with me for a while." I prayed that she couldn't hear desperation in my voice.

"I don't want to do that to you."

"I want you to come." I grabbed her hand. "Please." Was I begging? "I still miss you. I don't know how to not miss you."

"Do you?" She gave me that irresistible smile.

"I do." She stared at me for a moment and then she grabbed my face and kissed me. She gave me one of those sweet gentle kisses that made my heart ache. "Does that mean that you will come?"

"Okay, I will stay with you for a while."

I was not the only one happy to have Desiree in the house with me. As soon as my son laid eyes on her that evening, he was all over her. Every time they interacted over the next couple of day, I thought about how she would make a wonderful mother.

I was taking a nap one evening and dreamed about Des getting pregnant. She had a beautiful baby girl who looked just like her. Anthony was the baby's father. I woke up in a sweat.

Later on that night as bedtime drew near, things became difficult for me. I wanted to make a move on her, but I was afraid to do so. I was not quite sure if she had closed that chapter of our relationship. Maybe she didn't want me in the same ways that I wanted her. She had been with Lance after all.

When I heard her whisper my name, I knew the deal. I could hear the desire in her voice. I could feel the passion in her touch. I am not sure who kissed who first, but once our lips collided, things between us exploded. We frantically yanked at one another clothes and proceeded to make love all night.

Things quickly went back to the way they were before I moved out. She was willing. She was vulnerable. She was surrendering.

Things felt very real to me. She felt like she was mine in every sense of the word. I had to keep reminding myself that she wasn't. She would never be that.

I wasn't ready for her to leave at the end of the week, so I convinced her to stay another week. She agreed. My heart was happy to hear the word yes, but my mind knew that I had done the wrong thing. Having her here with me was not healthy, but I didn't care.

I watched Desiree attentively every day. I memorized everything about her. When we weren't together, I would daydream about her. I imagined the way she smiled at me when I talked to her, at how she would bite her lip when she watched TV, or how she rubbed her belly when she got hungry.

I had noticed that she had been rubbing her belly a lot lately. Every time I turned around, she was eating. It was as if she couldn't get enough. She was devouring everything in sight.

I walked in one evening to find Desiree on my couch eating straight out of a container of a gallon of Rocky Road Ice Cream. I chuckled to myself as I took a seat beside her

"Hey, beautiful," I said, pulling her to me. "How are you?"

"Great," she mumbled with a spoon in her mouth. "You?"

"I am good." I laughed. I reached over and rubbed her stomach. "Are you hungry, sweetheart?"

"All I could think about was this ice cream all day, Q. I could barely get through the day. I was excited when I got here."

"You could have taken you clothes off and put on something a bit more comfortable. She was still in her dress and her stilettoes.

"There was no time for that."

"You look good in that dress," I said, sliding my hand up her thigh and kissing on her ear.

"Do I?" I could hear the smile in her voice.

"Yes." I took the ice cream away and sat it on the table. "Do you know what else?"

"What else. Tell me," She whispered, sliding her hand up my shirt and beginning to kiss me. I shivered slightly at her touch as always. She lay back on the couch, pulling me with her. "Actually, why don't you tell just show me? I want you to make me moan your name, Mr Alexander."

"I intend to do that."

She had my shirt off and was working on my jeans when my phone rung. We both tried to ignore it. We couldn't. Whoever was trying to reach me, called me again.

"Really!" I moved away from Des, ready to cuss someone out.

"Calm down. I am not going anywhere."

"You better not." I was ready to catch a terrible attitude, but it was my mother. I almost felt guilty.

By the time I got off the phone, Desiree had changed out of her suit and into a tank and some very small shorts. She was back in front of the TV, digging into that ice cream once again.

"Can I have some?" I asked, pulling her to me.

"No."

"You are greedy," I laughed. "You have been eating a lot these days." I was treading dangerous waters, but I had to say something.

"I know." To my relief, she didn't get angry.

"Are you pregnant?"

"Umm…" She looked away and a funny expression came over her face. I immediately got nervous. "I don't know."

"What do you mean that you don't know?"

"I don't know if I am or if I am not."

"Are you telling me that you could be having a baby?"

"I could be," she said, shrugging.

"What makes you think that you are?"

"I haven't seen my period in two months."

"Okay. How are you are this calm?"

"I am not calm," she said, finally turning to look at me. I could see the terrified looked in her eyes. "I am scared out of my mind. I haven't found out yet because I am scared of the results. I am pretty sure that I am pregnant, Quinton."

"You need to get to a Dr."

"I know."

"I will go with you."

"Will you?" she asked, eagerly grabbing my hand.

"Only if you want me to."

"I want you to."

"Okay, we will go together."

"Why would you be that nice, Quinton."

"Because I care about you." Because I love you.

"Okay," she whispered. She buried her face in my shoulder.

"Please don't cry," I whispered moments later. I wanted to cry too. Was she having my baby? Or was it someone else's. The thought of her having another man's baby was unbearable. "It's going to be okay." I said, lifting her chin.

"How do you know that?"

"Would you be having my baby or someone else's?" I was afraid of her answer, but I had to ask her.

"Quinton, I haven't been with anyone else, but you, since you set foot in my house." She didn't know how relived that made me feel. She didn't hook up with Malik. She didn't hook with Lance, Tyler or Anthony.

"I will take care of my baby, Des. And you too."

"No...."

"Don't argue with me right now."

"Okay." She sighed. "I am really sorry, Quinton."

"Don't say that. A child is a blessing. A gift from God."

"I know..."

"I want to have more kids."

"Not with me, though, Q." Especially with you.

"You are already the most important woman in my life. You are more special to me than you could ever imagine," I said, rubbing her cheek. She gave me this adorable look. I wanted to tell her how much I loved her. I didn't want to keep it myself anymore, but I didn't want her to be uncomfortable. "You will mean the world to me."

"India didn't."

"You are not India."

"I am not your woman either." I closed my eyes. She wasn't, but that wasn't my choice.

"Sometimes, I feel that you should be." I couldn't believe that I said that to her. She just smiled at me.

"With all that we go through, it amazes me that I am not." So why aren't you? "So it's okay if we are pregnant?"

"Of course, baby."

"I am not sure if I am ready, Quinton."

"Me neither."

"Then what would we do?"

"Get ready together," I responded.

I should not have been as calm as I was. I should have been losing my mind at the fact that I may be having another baby. I didn't just get any woman pregnant, but the only woman I had ever loved. The one woman who I couldn't make my mine. The woman who would never love me the way I so desperately wanted her to.

I knew Desiree was pregnant. I really didn't have much doubt in my mind. As soon as she told me that it was possible, I accepted the inevitable. She was going to give birth to my second child. I think deep down I wanted it.

I didn't believe in viewing pregnancy as a mistake. A child was a gift straight from God. Sometimes we weren't ready to receive God's gift. This baby was meant to be somehow. It was a product of my love for this woman. Desiree was unwilling to give me her love, but she was giving me someone else I could love. Someone who would love me back.

The next day I went with Desiree to her Doctor. She confirmed our suspicions. Desiree was pregnant. She was two and half months pregnant. Our lives were about to change.

"I think that you should move in for good?" We were on the living room floor eating Chinese when I blurted that out. I had been thinking about her moving in since we found out that Des was pregnant. I was trying to go for everything that I wanted.

Plus, I had almost lost my mind when someone broke into her home. My mind was at ease when she was with me. I couldn't bear having her staying alone when her stalker was still at large. Her stalker had not contacted her since she had been with me.

"Why?" She didn't even look up at me.

"Desiree? I am serious."

"You can't be. I can't move in with you!"

"Why not? Give me a reason, Desiree." She stared back at me.

"I can't."

"You can't? Are you telling me no just because you don't want to stay with me and little Quinton."

"That's not it."

"You have to give me a reason for me to accept no."

"How would it look with me and you living together?"

"Really, Des? What are you talking about? I lived with you for almost nine months."

"That was for a reason."

"This is for a reason."

"People are going to wonder why I am living in your house when I obviously have a place to stay."

"I think that people will realize why when they see that you are going to have my baby."

"Have your baby?" she repeated as if she was still in shock. "I can't believe that I am having your baby."

"Why not?" I was afraid to hear her response. I knew I wasn't the man of her dreams. I knew she didn't have feelings for me. I knew she thought I was still some sort of player. I was pretty sure that she didn't respect me.

"Because you are Quinton. Look at our friendship. What happened? What happened this last year that allowed our relationship to develop into one that would create another human being together." A one-sided love.

"It could be worst, right?" I looked away. "You could hate me."

"Did I say it was bad at all?" she said, turning my face back around. "I want a baby boy who looks just like you."

"We are having a baby girl."

"How do you know?" she asked, climbing to my lap. "How do you know that I am not having another mini you?"

"I have this feeling." I thought back to the dream I had recently. I remembered Des had a girl. In my dream, that little girl belonged to Anthony, but in reality, she would belong to me. A daddy's girl.

"Well, I wouldn't mind a beautiful baby girl either."

"Me neither. Now back to us."

"You really want me to move in with you?"

"Yeah. I don't want you to worry about what other people may think about us. All that matters is that I want you here with me."

"Really, Q. Have you thought this through?"

"Desiree, I don't want you away from me!" She looked taken aback. I knew she didn't understand. If she had any idea of how much I needed her, she would know why I was pleading with her. "I need both of you," I said, rubbing her belly.

She placed her hand over mines and closed he eyes. We sat there for a while, neither of us saying anything. I just stared at her.

"Why do you need me here? Why do you want me here? I would never keep your child away from you. Don't you worry about that."

"I know, but I want you here. I…" I wanted to tell her. I wanted to tell her that I loved her. "I just want you here."

"Why?" She started to kiss me. I don't know how she expected me to answer with her lips on mine and her hand down my pants.

"This isn't the reason," I whispered against her lips. She begins to unbuckle my pants all the while kissing me. I moved her hands, so I could touch her. I wanted her naked.

"No, but this is how the baby got made."

"It's a wonder that you are just getting pregnant."

"I hear sex makes the labor easier." She pulled me on top of her.

"Let me help out with that. I will have sex with you every day."

"A reason to move me in huh? Sex when I want it?"

"Whenever you want it." She laughed at that. "Please move in." I said, kissing her shoulder. She didn't answer me. She just started yanking on my jeans. I rolled off of her long enough to get them off. She slid out of her shorts and her panties at the same time. She then yanked on my boxers.

I begin to love her on the floor. She showed me her appreciation by digging her fingers into my back. She moaned softly in my ears.

"Move in," I pleaded.

"Answer me," she said, biting my ear.

"You are the only woman that I want to be with. I want to be there for you. I don't want to miss anything. I could go on and on…" She made a noise that I had never heard before. "Are you listening?"

"No, just love me."

"Whatever you want."

We lay there afterwards, side by side, attempting to catch our breaths. We lay there so long that I almost dosed off. In my groggy state, I barely heard her say, "Okay, I will move in."

"Good girl," I said, pulling her close to me.

"Are you sure that you want me here?"

"Yes, I am lonely here without you," I admitted.

"Well," she said, touching my cheek. "We are here to stay."

Desiree

I was scared to live in the same house with Quinton again. Things had definitely changed since he moved out a couple months ago. When I left, I had not admitted to myself that I had feelings for the man. These days, he was all that I could seem to think about.

For two weeks, I felt as if I was wearing my heart on my sleeve while in his presence. It was a wonder that he had not noticed. I was convinced that I was not good at hiding my feelings very well. That was something that I was never good at.

I had no intentions of ever agreeing to his proposition, but Quinton was extremely persuasive. Somehow, he always seemed to get what he wanted from me. Easily.

It was hard enough to resist some men. It was even harder to resist a man like Quinton. It was nearly impossible to resist a man who you were in love with.

"I want you here." That was all it took. It was all I needed to hear him say. I wanted to be here too. Plus after what had happened to me and my stalker still being at large, I felt safer with him around.

I had not accepted the fact that I was pregnant yet. I definitely couldn't get over the shock of being pregnant with Quinton's baby. The only thing that I understood was the fact that I was terrified. And for that reason, I needed Quinton and I think he knew that.

If he was willing to take care of me for a while, I was going to let him. I was going to let him take care of me for as long as he desired. It was definitely wishful thinking, but maybe one day he would realize that I was the woman for him.

I wasn't naïve, though. Just because a woman has a man's baby, doesn't mean that man wants that woman. I didn't believe in trying to trap a man. That usually brought resentment.

I didn't want to be in this position, but I was. I wanted kids, but I wanted to be with a man who loved me. Married. Things weren't going as planned, but as always, life was full of the unexpected.

Every day after work, I brought more of my belongings to Quinton's house. As the week progressed, I started to feel guilty. I felt as if I was invading his space. I constantly brought this up to him, but he would cut me off.

I had just stepped out of the shower one evening to find Quinton on the other side of the door, greeting me with a towel.

"How are my girls? Come and give daddy a kiss." I rolled my eyes, but I gave in.

"We are fine. How are you?"

"I am great actually. Did you move in more of your things?"

"Yes, I did, but…"

"Don't start, Desiree."

"I feel like I am in your way. I can't help it."

"Why do you feel that way?"

"Because this is your brand new home and I am just moving in."

"I want this to be your home too, Desiree."

"I know you do. Are you sure that you don't want me to stay in the guest room at least?"

"No, why would you stay in the guestroom?"

"I don't know."

"Look, I am not going to tell you this, but one more time. I want you in my life, in my home and in my bed every night. Is that more clear to you, babe."

"Yes. I was just asking."

"Do you want to stay in the guest room?" he teased, rubbing on my behind. His hands somehow burned through my towel.

"No," I smiled. "What if I said yes, though?"

"I would have to convince you otherwise."

"I bet. I want to be right beside you every night," I blurted. My face felt hot as soon as I said it. I don't think he noticed because a huge grin came across his face.

"That's what I want to hear from you. Now since we have finally settled this issue, please put some clothes on. Little Q and I would like to take you out for dinner."

I didn't ask Q whether he had doubts anymore. The guilt was still there, but it diminished a little each day. Q appeared sincere and I believed that he wanted me here with him. I just wished it was because he loved me and not because I was caring his unborn child.

"I sleep in his bed every day, but I am not his woman." Wow. How did that look?

Over the next weekend, I moved the rest of my belongings into Quinton's home. Things felt final. I had turned the electricity and the cable off at my house. There was no turning back. Quinton and little Quinton were my family.

A couple nights later, Quinton and I met T and Ray for dinner. I was nervous because I was going to tell Rayven about my pregnancy. She would be the first. I was too terrified to tell anyone else. My stomach became nauseated every time I thought about telling my mother. I was not sure how I was going to get through that.

We met at the Cheesecake Factory. The four of us shared a meaningful and intimate conversation over good food and delicious cheesecake. I enjoyed myself more than I had in a long time. I needed that time with my best friends.

After dinner, we took a walk around downtown. It took a while, but I finally took a couple deep breaths and pulled Rayven aside to relinquish my secret. I was not quite sure what she was going to think about me for allowing this to happen. What was she going to think of Quinton being my baby's father?

"Sunray, can I talk to you for a second?" I asked, pulling her away from the boys. Quinton gave me a knowing look.

"Um, sure. Whats up, Dessie?"

"I have something to share with you?"

"Really?" She frowned. She was giving me a weird look. "Well, I guess I have some sharing to do of my own." I took notice that she appeared a little uneasy herself. "You go first, Des."

"Promise not to judge me, Rayven." I squeezed her hand.

"Desiree, I love you. I would not judge you. What is it?"

"Well," I said, grabbing her hand and placing it on my stomach. "I am pregnant."

"Are you serious? You're being honest?"

"I am very serious, Rayven. I wouldn't lie to you."

"Desiree, this better not be some joke. Are you really pregnant?"

"Yes," I frowned. "What? Why don't you believe me?"

"Oh my goodness!" I could see tears in her eyes. She threw her arms around me and clung to me."

"Why are you crying? Please don't cry."

"No, you don't get it!"

"Get what?"

"I am pregnant too!"

"Really, Ray!" I threw my arms around my best friend, this time clinging to her. We both held each for a while. Neither of us said anything. We just cried together. "We have been best friends for so many years and we have been through so much together, but I would have never imagined that this would have happened."

"I know." She finally pulled away from me. "This is wonderful though. I was so scared, but having you go through this with me is indescribable. I can't even express how much this means to me. How many weeks?"

"I will be three months in a week, Rayven. What about you?"

"Almost four months."

"Wow, and you didn't tell me."

"I was afraid, Des."

"I understand. You are going to be a beautiful mother."

"Whatever, you are the supermodel?" She wiped my tears away. "Are you really having Quinton's baby." I hadn't mentioned Quinton, but obviously she assumed. She assumed correctly.

"I am. I have moved in to his house."

"So you are going to be a family."

"For a while," I said, shrugging. I felt a moment of sadness. Q and I weren't in love like Tyler and Rayven. They were going to be the real family. It almost felt as if we were pretending.

"You deserve each other, Desiree." That was not the response that I expected from her. I was taken aback. "It's obvious how much you two care about one another."

"True, but...."

"You are just right for each other." I frowned at her. Where was this coming from? This was definitely a 360 from over a year ago.

"Rayven, I..."

"Please don't bother arguing with me tonight. Just go with it. I love the possibility of you two."

"I see."

"And you are having a baby together. What does that even mean?" It means that we were careless. It didn't mean anything more.

"I don't know."

"Do you have feelings for him, Des?" Wow. She was going in tonight. I couldn't take it. I couldn't tell her how I really felt. I didn't want to cry. I didn't want her to know that loving Quinton was breaking my heart.

"I don't know." I wasn't ready to tell her the truth. I would one day when I was sure I could handle it.

"What do you know?" she joked.

"I know that I am carrying his child and he seems to be happy about that. He promises me that he will take care of us. I also know that I need him right now."

Her eyes danced with excitement. She grabbed my hand and just stared at me before responding. I felt as if she was searching for something more.

"Give me a hug. That's sweet."

"What about you? What does this mean for you and Tyler? Enough about me."

"I love him with all my heart, Des. I know that he is my soulmate. I now see why things didn't work out with anyone else."

I stared at her with a lump in my throat. She seemed so happy and that meant the world to me. Envy was a deadly sin, but I couldn't help but feel it flowing through me. I wanted love. I wanted my soulmate. I wanted to feel her emotions and experience her joy. I didn't want to be in love with a man who didn't love me, but I was.

"I am so happy for you, Rayven. And for Tyler."

"Thank you."

"Everything okay?" Quinton and Tyler walked up behind us. I turned and his dark eyes held me captive for a moment.

"We are done," I whispered. My throat felt dry. I closed my eyes for a moment and then took a deep breath. He noticed.

"Are you okay?" He pulled me to him and I just pressed my forehead against his shoulder.

"I am." I said, stepping back after a moment. "Guess what? Rayven is pregnant too."

"Are you forreal? T, Rayven's pregnant too." I laughed. I guess it was not official until it came from Tyler's mouth.

"Yeah. Wait a minute. What do you mean is she pregnant too?" He looked really confused. He looked from Quinton to me. "Desiree, are you pregnant?"

"I am pregnant, Tyler."

"Seriously? With Quinton's baby."

"Yes with Quinton's baby."

"Q, you are about to have another kid?" I laughed again. What was with these two? Even Rayven looked at me and shook her head.

"Yeah it seems that way," he said, placing his hand on my back. He kissed my forehead. "Congratulations, Tyler."

"Oh wow, man. This is crazy. Thank you! Congrats to you too, man." He walked over and hugged me. "Congrats to you, Desiree."

"Thank you, Tyler."

"Let me buy you a drink. Your first kid too. We should celebrate." Quinton kissed my lips quickly and then kissed Rayven on the cheek. "Congrats, Rayven."

"Thanks, Quinton.

We stood and watched the two best friends head to the bar. You could tell they were both overcome with joy. It was good to see.

I linked arms with my best friends.

"Let's get some ice cream."

"That sounds like my kind of celebrating."

Do you really think we are going to have a little girl?" I asked Quinton as we snuggled up the couch later on that night.

"Yes, I do."

"Why?"

"I just have this feeling. Would you be happy with a baby girl?"

"I am happy as long as our baby is healthy."

"Good." He kissed me for a couple moments. My heart started beating faster. I kept my eyes closed even as he pulled away. I didn't want him to see how much his affection affected me.

"I have something to ask you, baby."

"Whats that?" I asked, finally opening my eyes."

"When are we going to tell our families? Especially our mothers?"

"Soon. I have to be honest, though. I am scared."

"Don't be."

"How can you say that?"

"They will accept their grandchild, Des."

"How do you know?" I was talking crazy. Of course they would accept their grandchild. That didn't mean that we weren't going to receive judgment.

"If we are okay with it, then they should be as well."

"Q, you really don't know my mother."

28

Affirmation

"And you will know the truth, and the truth will set you free."
John 8:32

Desiree

"What exactly are you and Quinton now? Are you two officially dating?" Rayven asked. We were in the middle of Quinton's kitchen one Sunday afternoon, attempting to create a delicious dinner. Rayven and Tyler stopped by after church. We of course invited them to stay a while.

"No mam!"

"Calm down. Your face is red." I touched my cheeks and turned away, embarrassed.

"It's hot in here," I lied.

"Girl, bye! Stop it! I was just asking?"

"Why are you asking me that?" I sniffed. The onion I was cutting had me tearing up.

"Are you crying?"

"Rayven, you know I hate cutting onions. Now whats up with you asking me that question?"

"I don't know," she shrugged. "You are acting like a couple. You are all up under Q. He can't stop touching you. And the pet names are out of control." I laughed. Was it really like that?

"None of that means anything. We have always had an affectionate relationship. Quinton has always flirted with me and I have always flirted back. None of that means that we are a couple."

"I didn't say that you two were a couple. I was simply asking if you two were dating. Why did you move in again?" she asked, leaning against the counter, becoming preoccupied with the brownies that Quinton Jr and I had made the night before.

"He wants to be a part of the pregnancy, especially because he missed out on the pregnancy of his first child." I was laying it on thick, attempting to validate why I was here.

"You don't have to live with him for that to happen."

"No, I don't, but he wants me to be here."

"I bet." I didn't like the tone in my best friend's voice. I looked over my shoulder and she gave me a knowing smile. What was going on in that head of hers?

"What does I bet mean, Rayven?"

"Q is crazy about you, Des and you are too blind to realize it."

"Will you stop!" I wanted to believe that, but I couldn't

"Why should I?"

"I am asking you to, Rayven! I don't want to go there today!"

We both just stood there and stared at one another. Suddenly, I was consumed with emotion and felt the urge to cry. I hated feeling this way and she wasn't helping.

"Don't cry. I am sorry. I wasn't trying to upset you."

"I know, I…" I had gotten pregnant by a man who I wasn't in a relationship with and I felt some type a way about that. I was disappointed in myself.

"Whats up, ladies" We both stared at Q with guilt. "Are you sure that you two don't need any help?" We both shook our heads. "What's the matter?" He frowned. He moved in my direction.

"Nothing," I said, holding up my hand to stop him from grabbing me. I couldn't deal at the moment. "I will be right back." I dropped my knife and headed to the bedroom, leaving both Rayven and Quinton looking confused.

I went into the bedroom that I shared with Quinton. The man who I adored and loved. The man who didn't feel the same way about me. The man who had given me a precious gift. Unwillingly.

I placed my face in my hands and just cried. I was throwing myself a pity party and I desired no interruption, but I got one. Quinton knocked before entering.

"Can I come in?" I wasn't sure if I wanted him to come in, but this was his house and I didn't want to tell him that he couldn't.

"Sure."

"Whats wrong?"

"I don't know," I said, standing trying to get myself together. "I am just in my feelings today. It's okay."

"No, it's not. Are you and Rayven fighting? I will ask them to leave." I stared at him for a moment. Why was he this concerned? Would he really ask our friends to leave just because I was upset?

"No, please, no. We weren't fighting. I don't know why I am crying, Q Its just my hormones, I am sure."

"Oh." He stared through me. I could tell he didn't believe me, but I was relieved when he didn't push it. "Come here."

I floated into his open arms. After a couple moments, I found myself accepting one of his kisses. I begin to focus less on the empty feeling in my heart and more on the heat rising between us.

I allowed him to push me on the bed. He pushed up my skirt and pulled down my panties, flinging them across the room. I smiled up at him as he unbuttoned his belt and quickly dropped his jeans. I open my arms and held him against me as he loved me quickly. I buried my face in his shoulder to quiet my moans.

We lay there, side by side, holding hands afterwards. I smiled in satisfaction up at the ceiling. I turned to look at him and he was staring at me. My face grew hot.

"What?" I asked.

"Did I satisfy you?"

"Of course. Don't ask absurd questions. Don't you always?" I leaned over and kissed him before jumping up to smooth my clothes.

He sat up and stared at me for a moment, before standing to adjust his own clothes. I bit my lip as I watched him.. I would have loved to cuddle in bed right now instead of facing the questioning looks of our friends. Quinton's arms could be so comforting.

Knowing that my best friend's child was a product of a loving relationship while my child was the end result of just raw sexual passion between Q and I, made me feel incredibly small. Whatever Quinton and I shared, felt diminished in comparison. I felt guilty.

"What are you thinking about," Q asked. He was watching me. "It looks like you have a lot on your mind."

"I am fine." I quickly hugged and kiss him. "We should get back out there before Rayven comes knocking on the door."

"I wouldn't put it past her."

"Sorry about that. I am back." I avoided eye contact with Rayven when I returned to the kitchen. I just washed my hands, and then picked up my knife and continued where I left off.

"Desiree," she placed her hand on my arm to stop me. "I didn't mean to upset you. Forgive me."

"Of course. I am not mad; I am just a little emotional."

"I understand," she said, heading back to her side of the counter. "Was it good," she mumbled.

"Was what good?" I couldn't help myself. I started smiling.

"Your hair is a hot mess."

"Oh!" I started giggling and couldn't stop. Apparently it was contagious because Rayven started laughing as well. It was a much needed tension killer.

"I needed it," I finally managed to get out.

"I bet." She hugged me and we both resumed cooking

It had been a couple weeks since we found out that we were expecting and neither Q nor I had told our parents. I wasn't going to lie, I was downright scared. And despite Q trying to keep it together for the both of us, I had a feeling that he was a little apprehensive. I kept telling myself that it was going to be okay, but was I prepared to have the conversation with my parents? Especially my mother?

"Oh gosh," I sat down because I started to feel dizzy.

I just knew that I was over three months pregnant and I was showing slightly. We couldn't wait until I was five or six months to tell our folks. They needed to know yesterday. Whether we were ready or not, the conversation was inevitable.

I was distracted for the rest of the evening. Quinton and I were washing dishes after dinner when I dropped a glass.

"Wow! That's just great, Desiree. Quinton, I am sorry. I didn't mean to break your glass."

"Baby, it's just a glass. Don't look so shaken up about it."

"It scared me."

"Don't worry about it. Just tell me whats wrong," he said, pulling me away from the broken glass.

"Nothing, really."

"Stop lying. Go sit down in the living room and let me handle this," he said, grabbing a broom.

"But what about the dishes?"

"Des, we do have a dishwasher. I will load it later. Right now, go have seat. I will be there in a few minutes."

"Okay." I walked to the living room and took a seat in front of the TV. I started flipping through the channels. I wasn't really noticing what was on the screen.

It was all so sad. I didn't even notice that Q was beside me until he took the remote out of my hand. He turned the TV off and then pulled me to him. I closed my eyes and laid my head against his shoulder. I thought about how much I loved him in that moment. I thought about how I wished I could tell him what was in my heart.

"Whats really bothering you, Des?" he finally asked. "And please don't deny it. I am not blind. It's written all over your face."

I sighed in defeat. I closed my eyes and took a deep breath. I said a quick, "Help me now, God" prayer and then found the nerve to look at him.

"Are you scared?"

"No."

"Why not?"

"I have faith that we will be just fine. If you are fine, then the baby will be fine. Why? Are you scared?" He rubbed my hand.

"Yes, very much so."

"It's okay to be scared. I have a child. This is new for you. Plus, you are the one carrying the baby. Our experiences will be different."

"True. I am scared to tell my mother."

"You need to tell her."

"I know. You need to tell yours."

"You are right, I do. Admittedly, I have been procrastinating. And I have been doing it on purpose."

"Why? Do you think that your mom's going to disapprove?"

"She will accept it, don't worry about that. I just know that she is going to give me a lecture. I love my mom, but I don't really want to hear her mouth. We are both adults and this is going to happen. I don't need to hear a speech about being careless." I wasn't sure that I wanted to hear her mouth either, but I didn't say anything.

"So are we are going to tell our parents soon?"

"Yes and we are going to do it together. I won't leave you hanging. I know that you are very nervous about this."

"Okay, thank you. What are we going to say, Q?"

"What do you mean?"

"I can't exactly tell my mother that you and I have been hooking up this last year. She is going to assume that we are more than friends and I am going to break her heart by telling her…"

"Desiree, calm down." I had started to become hysterical. I closed my eyes and took a deep breath. He rubbed my cheek with the back of his hand. I grabbed his hand and kissed it. I just wanted to jump his arms and tell him I loved him, but I couldn't. "I am sorry. I don't know if I can do this."

"Des, you have been my best friend and my lover. Now you are going to be the mother of my child. Tell her that. You are more than my friend. Far more."

"Are you sure about that, Quinton?

"I wouldn't have wanted to share this last year with anyone, but you." I stared at him. He couldn't have meant that. "Desiree, are you my girl? No, let me rephrase that. Are you my woman?"

"I…"

"Let's stop playing games. We need to be together right now. I want you in my life. Just say yeah." He started kissing me on my neck. I closed my eyes and basked in the pleasure for a moment.

Had he lost his mind, though? What he was suggesting was ludicrous. He didn't want to be with me. He was doing this for his unborn child. He was trying to step up, but didn't have to go this far.

"You don't have to do this," I blurted. You don't have be with me for the baby sake. We can…"

"Desiree, will you be my woman?"

"A relationship, Q?"

"Yes or no, sweetheart? Just be honest with me. I can't make you do anything that you don't want to do."

I stared at him. I searched his face. I was searching for emotion. I wanted to know why he was offering this proposition. I knew he didn't feel the same way about me as I felt for him. What was the reason behind this if it wasn't for the baby sake?

I wanted to scream yes and kiss him. I didn't want to be with anyone, but him. Could I be with him knowing that it wouldn't lead to love? Could I do this?

"Yes," I found myself saying.

"Say what?" He looked as surprised as I felt. "I can't believe you said yes," he said, pulling me to him.

"I think it's for the best right now. I really need you."

"And I need you. This is right, Des. We need to do things this way." I closed my eyes and nodded. I laid my head against his chest. Of course he didn't really believe that. He was just trying to step up and do the right thing. I, on the other hand was being selfish. I didn't want another woman near him.

"You're mine now," he said, his hand caressing my thigh.

"Quinton, no need to get possessive," I joked.

Quinton and I decided the next day would be the day. It wasn't fair to our families to keep our pregnancy a secret. We wanted to be able to share this moment in our lives with them. As scared as I was to become a mother, I was determine to enjoy this entire experience.

When Q got home, we headed straight to his parents' house.

"Hey, ma." He kissed his mother. "Where is dad?"

"Not here, sweetheart. He is helping a friend."

"Will he be back anytime soon?"

"Unfortunately he won't be back until later on tonight. Why?"

"Um, can I talk to you for a moment?"

"Sure," she said, turning away from the stuffed peppers that she was making. She eyed Quinton suspiciously. "What is this about?"

"I am not going to beat around the bush or try to sugarcoat things. You are going to have another grandchild, ma."

"Oh, son." She took her glasses off and sat them on the counter. She covered her face. For a moment, I thought she was crying. I started to panic. I had the feeling this wasn't going to go well.

"Relax, mother."

"Not again, son. We have already been down this road."

"This time things will be different. I know that things were crazy the first time around."

"How are things going to be different? You have to stop doing this. You have to learn some self-control." She walked over to the kitchen table and sat down. "Why do you insist on sleeping with these women that mean nothing to you? Are you in need of that much of a thrill? What happen to you using protection?"

"Mother, please listen to me." He knelt down in front of her and grabbed her hand.

"Why are you being so careless? I know your father and I have taught you better than this." I shifted uncomfortably. Was telling my mother going to be this hard?

"You did." Quinton looked up with guilt on his face. I started to feel the same guilt. "Life just happens."

"Life didn't just happen. You need to hang up your player card, son. You are almost thirty. It's about time that you find a decent girl to settle down with."

"I agree with you, mother. I really do."

"I'm not sure that you do. Who did you get pregnant this time? Quinton, I can't deal with another India. She put us through too much. Now look at you. You are already raising a child by yourself."

"I can't deal with another India either."

"Who is she?"

"Desiree, mother." He stood and reached for my hand. I grabbed it and he pulled me towards him.

Her eyes grew huge as she looked up at me. I was terrified for a brief moment that she wouldn't accept me, but the expression on her face started to change. I decided to speak up.

"Mrs. Alexander, I am carrying your son's baby." I was surprised to see tears forming in her eyes.

"Desiree, oh wow!" She stood and threw her arms around me. I felt instant relief. "Sweetheart, I can definitely deal with you. You are a whole different breed of woman." I was taken back. I wasn't sure if I deserved such a compliment.

"That's good to hear." I felt tears of my own forming.

"I am so relieved."

"I told you things were different this time around, ma."

"Can you really blame me? Your track record has sucked. So are you two together. Please tell me that you are dating."

"Yes," I volunteered quickly before my apprehension for lying to her got the best of me. Yes, Q and I were dating now, but I felt as if our relationship was a huge façade. We weren't together for the emotion, but for the convenience.

"Praise God!" she said, clasping her hands together and looking towards the sky. "I have always wanted you for Quinton."

"Mother, please don't embarrass me." His face was red.

"I couldn't ask for a better mother for my next grandchild."

"Thank you so much, Mrs. Alexander."

"How many months, Desiree?"

"Over three months actually."

"Wow, you are that far!" She placed her hands on her cheeks. "I am so pleasantly surprised, though. Treat her well, my son. Take very good care of her. She is going to need you."

"Can you have some faith in me, mother. I am older this time around. I have grown."

"I know, but it's your fault I am like this. You scare me sometimes. I just want whats best for you."

His mother tried to get us to stay for dinner, but we had to get to my parent's house. I prayed the entire ride over that this inevitable conversation would go half as well as it did with Quinton's mother. I didn't need the stress that would stem from her disapproval.

"Hey, mommy."

"Hey, sweetheart," she said, greeting me with a hug. "And how are you, Quinton?"

"I am fine. How are you, Mrs. Harris?"

"Wonderful. So what do I owe this surprise to? Why didn't you call? I could have had dinner ready for you both."

"We were just dropping by, mother. We aren't staying."

"Well, okay." She looks disappointed I thought. My mother loved hosting people.

"I wanted to talk to you about something pretty important."

"Okay, Desiree. What is it?"

"Well..." I looked back at Quinton for support. He just nodded and squeezed my shoulder.

"What is it, child? Just spit it out." I took a deep breath.

"Mommy, I am pregnant." She stared at me and I felt as if time was standing still.

"Don't play with me, little girl."

"I am not playing with you, mother. Why would I do that?"

"This is not funny."

"This is not a joke. I am very much pregnant." She stared at me once again. I felt as if she was looking through me. At first I could tell she didn't believe me. She searched my face for the truth. When she realized that I was being honest with her, the disbelieving look on her face turned into one of defeat.

"Oh, my daughter."

"Mama, it's going to be okay, though."

"How do you know? Are you sure?"

"Yes. Please don't cry." I could feel a lump forming in my throat. I looked away for a moment because I wanted to collapse on the floor with emotion. I hated disappointing my mother.

"I don't know if I should be happy or sad."

"I rather you be happy."

"I don't know if you are going to be okay."

"Mrs. Harris," Quinton said, speaking up, "I promise that I will take very good care of your daughter. Things are going to be okay."

"You will?" she asked. She frowned up at me at me and then at Quinton as if she was trying to put two and two together.

"Yes, mam. I will take care of Desiree and my child."

My mother didn't say anything at first. She just took it all in. Finally, tears spilled down her cheeks.

"You are having a baby with my little girl?" she whispered.

"Yes, I am."

"Oh, my children." She grabbed both of our hands.

"Mommy, please just find a way to accept this because this is going to happen," I said, rubbing my belly. "We didn't plan for this. It just happened. Please just don't lecture me today."

"I am floored, but I will save you a long speech today."

"Thank you."

"How many months, Desiree?"

"Three months, mother."

"Seven months before we have our baby girl," Quinton blurted, sliding his arm around my waist."

"You are having a girl!"

"Come on, mother. I have two months before knowing the sex of our child. Quinton just thinks that we are having a girl."

"Aww that's sweet," she laughed. "That would be nice, though."

"Mommy," I said, taking her hand inside of mine. "I really hope that you are not disappointed in me. The guilt of knowing that I have made you unhappy with me is not something that I want to bear."

"No, sweetheart. I can't be unhappy knowing I am about to have a grand baby. When you and your sister became women, I allowed myself to dream of this moment. I just didn't want you have to go through all of this alone, but knowing that Quinton is beside you all of the way, eases my heart."

"Good," I smiled.

My heart was beating fast. I could tell my mother liked knowing that Quinton and I were together. Mrs. Alexander was overjoyed. In a way, we were lying to them all. I prayed the guilt of deceiving them wouldn't consume me.

I dreaded going to work the next morning. On top of the morning sickness, I felt uneasy. I didn't want to run into Lance who had been away on a leave of absence He had returned about two weeks ago thinking that we would rekindle our affair. Instead of being met with open arms, I offered him reluctance and no explanation. I had successfully avoided him until the day before.

Lance cornered me and asked me what was up? I was on my to a meeting so I was able to easily escape confrontation. Today would more and likely be different. That difficult conversation was inevitable. I figure that I would invite him to lunch and put it all out there. Until I did so, I wasn't going to be able to move on and fully enjoy my pregnancy.

I didn't get a chance to extend that invitation. Lance came marching into my office the next morning. He looked annoyed.

"Well, good morning," I said, standing.

"Do you have a minute? I think that it's time that the two of us have a conversation."

"I agree. We do need to talk."

"Whats up, Desiree? You are obviously avoiding me. Can I get some type of explanation to your disappearing act?"

"I have been avoiding you," I responded honestly. Although, he was the one who blurted it out, he seemed shocked by my admission.

"Wow. May I ask why? I thought the two of us were trying to see where this could go."

"Lance, things have really changed over the last month."

"Such as? If you aren't interested in me, be a woman and keep it real with me. Just say so. I am not into games."

"I am not into games either," I said, defending myself. "Please don't throw accusations."

"I am not throwing anything. I just made a simple statement. I just feel as if maybe you wasted my time."

"I don't want you to feel that way, but if you do, what can I do?"

"I feel as if you owe me more than you are giving me."

"I am pregnant, Lance. Practically three months."

"What!" He backed up a little. He looked at me as if I was carrying an STD, not a child.

"Yes." I moved towards him. "My child's father and I share a long history. We decided to be together."

"I see."

"Look, Lance, I am really sorry. I wasn't trying to hurt you or play any games. This is my life, though. I didn't plan on getting pregnant, but I did."

"I can understand," he said, shrugging. "I would want to be with the mother of my child. I wouldn't want her being with other dudes."

"Right."

"I don't like that we didn't have our chance."

"I don't like it either."

"Sure." He looked at me as if he didn't believe me. I wanted to say something more, but I couldn't find the words. "Take care, sweetheart." He walked over and kissed my cheek.

"Take care." I closed my eyes as he walked away. I was very much in love with Q, but I knew he would never return my feelings. Lance cared about me. He was a good man. I was disappointed.

My thoughts were all over the place, so I didn't get much work done. I decided that I needed an early lunch. I was gathering my things, when my phone rang.

"Desiree."

"Yes, Kendra."

"You have a visitor, girl." From the tone in her voice, I could tell it was a male. "He insists on seeing you."

"I am on my way to lunch. I will be out in a minute or so."

I got ridiculously excited at the thought of Quinton surprising me for lunch. I didn't want to imagine anyone else on the other side of my door. I almost tripped over my feet as I swung open my door. I practically skipped towards the front, ready to run into his arms.

My heart dropped when I saw Anthony.

"Anthony? What are you doing here?

"I was wondering if we could talk." Not again, I thought.

"Um, yeah sure."

He looks nice, I thought. He had a fresh cut. He wore dress pants and a button up. He had stepped up his game today. Maybe he was on a lunch break, I thought?

For the first time, when I looked at him, I felt nothing. I didn't feel nervous. I didn't feel excited. My heart didn't beat fast. I had moved on. I was completely over him.

I smiled to myself in satisfaction of knowing that. However, I was a little annoyed. Why was he here? What did he want? I wanted Anthony to disappear completely from my life.

We decided to take a walk in a nearby park. We walked for five minutes in silence before I said anything. I was more than uncomfortable in his presence.

"Anthony, I really don't have a lot of time. This is my lunch break. What is this about? You said you wanted to talk."

"I wanted to talk about us," he said, turning to face me. "To be completely upfront with you, I miss you, Desiree. I have been thinking about you a lot lately."

"Why?"

"How messing things up between us was one of the biggest mistakes of my life." Hadn't we been through this? "I think about what my infidelity cost me. I lost you and that was painful."

"Okay." Why did he insist on reliving this?

"I know that you are perfect for me. I really don't think another woman can replace you. There is a void in my life." What did he want me to do about it?

"Anthony, to be completely honest with you, I don't know how to respond to any of this. You are making me uncomfortable."

"I don't mean to make you feel that way."

"What are your intentions? Why have this conversation again?"

"Well..." I could tell he was nervous about something. I could see sweat forming on his forehead. "I still want to be with you." I started shaking my head vigorously. "Yes, I do. Desiree, I still love you very much." It had been years now. How was that possible?

"No!" I practically yelled. Why was this happening to me now?

"Yes, I love you. I know that you don't love me anymore, but I know that you loved me once. We were good together. Maybe you can fall in love with me again. I will work hard for that." This man has lost his mind, I thought. "I don't want to be with anyone else. Just you. Forever."

"Anthony, you need to stop this foolishness. Don't say any of this to me." There were tears in my eyes. I didn't love him anymore, but I didn't need this right now. I was too vulnerable.

"I have to tell you, Des. I want you to marry me."

"What!" I covered my mouth with both hands. This was absurd.

"I have a ring."

"No!" I closed my eyes, hoping that when I opened them, this nightmare would be over. This had to be a dream. When I opened them he was holding a ring with a huge diamond. I stepped back from it as if it was poison.

"I want you to carry my name, Desiree. Please be mine."

"Anthony, I think that you know that I can't marry you."

"You can learn to love me again."

"No, Anthony, I can't."

"Why not? You loved me once, right?"

"Yes, I did, but if we were meant to me, that last night would not have happened. We ended for a reason." He stared at me with wide eyes. He didn't say anything for a few moments.

"Can't you think about it?" he finally asked.

"I don't want to marry you, Anthony." I didn't count on him looking as hurt as he did. His eyes darkened and I could see tears.

"I see," he said, looking away.

"Anthony," I said, reaching for his hand. He pulled away quickly. "I would like to explain."

"No point." He slipped the ring in his pocket and started backing away from me. "I rather you not explain anything. I didn't really expect you to say yes." I didn't owe him an explanation, but I wanted him to know.

"I am pregnant, Anthony."

"Say with?" He stared at my stomach for a moment before backing away even further.

"I am with the father of my child now."

"I see." I watched as in took it all in.

"My future is laid out for me. You can't be a part of that."

"Quinton?" he asked. I blinked. How could he have known that?

"Yes," I admitted. "I am with Q now. I am having his child."

"Oh gosh!" I could see both pain and anger in his eyes.

"I am sorry." I wasn't. Why was I apologizing? I felt as if I was about to have a panic attack. My entire body was tense. I wanted to run away and not look back.

"I am going to be sick." He covered his face with his hands.

"I don't know how to respond to that."

"Don't say anything else. I knew this would happen. He was going to get you eventually, considering…." He didn't finish his.

"Considering what?"

"Do you know that he could never stand me?"

"Oh, yes I know." I wasn't going to lie to him. Quinton despised Anthony and he didn't hide it from anyone.

"Of course he was going to make a move on you."

"What are you talking about? This has nothing to do with you if that's what you are implying."

"Don't be so naïve, Desiree." He was beginning to annoy me. "It was inevitable that you two would get together."

"I guess so." I was not going to tell Anthony that Q and I were only together for the baby.

"Well, I should go." Please go. Get away from me. Far away.

"Okay. Look, I never meant to hurt you."

"It's okay. It is what it is. I guess this is karma. Bye, Desiree."

"Goodbye, Anthony." I turned and walked in the opposite direction, back towards my job. He called out to me.

"Wait!" What now! I turned, hopefully for the last time. "Look, I am really upset right now, but I am happy for you. Congratulations."

"Thanks."

He turned and walked away. He looked devastated. He moved dejectedly with his head hung low and his hands in his pockets. I didn't like hurting him, but I had no choice. There was no room in my heart for Anthony. My heart was pretty full these days.

I sighed and turned to head back to work. I had thirty more minutes of lunch, but I decided to skip it. I had lost my appetite. I felt sick to my stomach. My head was hurting.

Why me? Why did the last thirty minutes have to happen? If only I could turn back the hands of time. I would have told Anthony that I was busy.

My day was ruined. This day would be infamously known as the day that my ex proposed and I turned him down. I was done for the day. I was pretty sure that I wasn't going to get anymore work done. The nightmare was the only thing that consumed my mind.

29

Intervention

"And to aspire to live quietly, and to mind your own affairs, and to work with your hands, as we instructed you" 1 Thessalonians 4:11"

Quinton

Today had been a crazy day. It was a day to forget. It had left me with a pounding headache and a bad taste in my mouth. I was feeling out of it by the time I walked through my front door that evening. I was grateful to be home.

All I wanted was to see was my girl.

"Des!" I called her name but received no answer. I knew she was home because her car was in the driveway.

I found her in the bedroom sleeping peacefully. When I saw her, my heart did a somersault. This was the mother of my child. Every time I was in the same room with her, I was consumed with emotion.

I sat in the chair across from the bed and just stared at her. I took in how her chest moved as she breathed. I watched her roll over until she was comfortable. I stared at her belly.

Wow. I couldn't get over how there was a baby growing inside of her. Desiree was almost four months pregnant and I was excited to be able to share this experience with her. I would be able to go through all the motions and see the progression of my second child.

I missed all of that with India. I didn't go through the morning sickness or the cravings. I didn't get to feel my child kick or see his heartbeat. I wasn't there for the contractions or when her water broke. I didn't get to hold her hand as she gave birth to my son.

I was determined not to miss any of that with Des.

I stood and walked over to the bed. I stared down at her, debating whether or not I was going to reach out to her. I wanted to touch her, but something was holding me back. It was as if she was something fragile. I didn't want to disturb her in any way.

I finally sat down beside her. I reached over and rubbed her back. She shifted a little as a small sound of appreciation escaped her. She didn't open her eyes but she smiled in my direction.

She was having a baby girl. I couldn't knock the feeling. Or maybe having a daughter was something that I so desperately wanted. I wanted her to have her mother's curious eyes or her mischievous grin. Either would melt my heart.

Desiree was my woman right now. We had the relationship, but we didn't have the emotions. We had the admiration, the respect and the friendship, but where was the love? I had it for her, but I couldn't have her love. At least for a while, I could prevent another man from having it. I was being selfish, but this woman was too precious to me to trust another man around her. She was carrying my child.

I dropped my head into my hands. I had a bad headache and if I didn't take care of it right now, it was going to turn into a migraine. Right now all I wanted to was take a shower and then come hold Desiree in my arms. She was comfort. She was peace for me.

I walked to the kitchen and grabbed a bottle of water. I came back to my bathroom, opened my medicine cabinet and found my prescription for migraines. I popped two pills and drowned the entire bottle. I then took off my clothes and jumped into my shower.

It was instant relief when the water drops hit my body. I could feel the tension letting up. I closed my eyes and imagined todays stress going down the drain.

The madness began when I dropped little Quinton off at my mother's house. I intended to be in and out, but my mother didn't allow things to work out that way. She sent my son into another room and proceeded to quiz me on my relationship with Desiree.

"How is Desiree?"

"She is fine, mother. She will be four months soon."

"I am still trying to get used to it all."

"I am too, mother. Desiree was about two and a half months before she found out that she was pregnant."

"Oh really?" she asked, raising an eyebrow at me.

"Yeah. Are you truly cool about this? Are you happy for us?"

"Of course, sweetheart. A child is a blessing."

"Thank you," I said, leaning over to kiss her cheek.

"Uh huh. Do you love her?" Wow. Where did this come from?

"Huh?" was my response. I really wasn't trying to go there with her. Especially not this early in the day.

"Do you truly love Desiree, Quinton?"

"What do you think?"

"How would I know? I wouldn't have the slightest idea. I didn't even know that you two were dating."

"It hasn't been that long."

"Okay. So do you love her?" She wasn't going to let this go until I told her what she wanted to hear.

"Of course I do. I love Desiree very much." I could never lie to my mother. "She is my heart. She means everything to me."

"That's really nice to hear. I am ecstatic to know that you are actually serious about a woman. Desiree loves you?"

"I assume." I said it in jokingly manner, hoping that she would take my reply and let all of this go. Of course the statement wasn't really true. I didn't have the heart to tell my mother that I knew Desiree didn't love me. I didn't want to disappoint her in anyway.

"Quinton, this all eases my mind? I never dreamed that you would hook up with Deborah's daughter. Desiree has always been a beautiful and intelligent young lady. I think she is perfect for you. I am just beside myself with joy knowing that you have settled down with a woman who is worthy of your time and affection."

"Yeah." I looked away to avoid eye contact. "It's amazing."

"What are your intentions with this woman?" Why was she asking me these questions? I didn't have an answer. I didn't even know how long Desiree and I were going to last.

"What do you mean, mother. We are just going with the flow right now. We are more concerned with being good parents."

"But are you two aiming for marriage?"

"I don't know," I said, shrugging. My throat was suddenly dry. "That would be ideal." Making Desiree my wife would be a dream come true. A dream is all it would be, though. I prayed that she would stay with me long enough to give birth to our child. "Okay, well mother, I better get going."

"Sure, sweetheart. I will see you later."

"Bye."

I really didn't need to have this conversation with my mother this morning. Talking about my future with Desiree always depressed me. While I loved, I would never experience love.

I was going to think about her and my unreciprocated feelings for the rest of the day. I was going to also focus on me not being completely honest with my mother. I would be humiliated if she ever found out the truth about our relationship.

After I got through the difficult conversation with my mother, I had to endure another one with my little sister. She was in town for a couple days and wanted to catch up. We decided to meet up for an early lunch before work.

"Hey, big brother," she said, hugging me.

"Hey, little girl."

"I am a woman now, Q. Get it right!"

"Whatever, I don't want to hear any of that. How are you?"

"I have been okay."

"Breaking hearts these days?"

"Not really. I have been too busy."

"Good because those poor fellas don't deserve what you put them through," I joked.

"Whatever, I learned from the best." Oh, here we go. "I hear your time playing the field has come to an end."

"For the moment."

"Congratulations."

"Thank you, Peyton."

"I can't believe that you are going to make me an auntie again. I am really hoping for a niece."

"I am hoping for a daughter," I admitted. "I have this feeling that Desiree is having a girl."

"So it's Desiree, huh?" She took a sip of water and eyed me the same way my mother had. She looked just like her.

"Yeah, it's Desiree. What are you getting at, Peyton?"

"I cannot believe that Desiree is the woman that is about to give birth to your child. I thought you two were just friends." She looked exasperated. I almost laughed.

"We are still friends."

"Q, you know what I mean. This is all little ironic isn't it? The woman who you once wanted so badly is now going to be the mother of your child." She made it sound unfortunate.

"Yeah, what's your point?" I was trying to be nonchalant.

"Come on, big brother. This means that she is yours now. You finally got what you wanted."

"Not exactly. We are exclusively dating, but she is not really my woman." Even I had to admit to myself how confusing that sounded.

"What! That makes no sense!" She leaned forward and just shook her head as she stared at me.

"We are only together for the baby, Peyton. And to save face around our parents."

"These days, that's not even necessary."

"It's a mutual decision we made."

"Okay." She sat back in her seat, looking disappointed. "This woman is just so beautiful; inside and out. She is perfect for you."

"Don't you realize that I know all of this?"

"I just want the two of you to be together already." Me too.

"Don't you think that I want that?" My frustration was at an all-time high right now.

"Just do it, Quinton. Make this woman yours."

"I can't believe you came out your mouth with that. How do you suggest that I go about doing something like that? If it was that easy, don t you think I would have done that by now?"

"Will you just stop being stubborn and tell her how you feel?"

"I don't plan on ever telling her."

"Do you love her?" With everything inside of me, I loved her.

"She is my heart, Peyton."

"Quinton!" I could see tears in her eyes.

"Are you about to cry?"

"Yes, I am. This breaks my heart."

"Don't worry about it." I grabbed her hand and squeezed it.

"I just want you to be happy, big brother."

"I am still happy. I am grateful that she plays such an imperative role in my life. She will always be in my life. We are forever bonded. Knowing that brings me joy."

"I hear you, but come on, Q, you deserve this woman."

"I...I don't know about that."

"Why won't tell her? What is stopping you?"

"I know she doesn't feel the same. What would be the point?"

"The point is that she deserves to know."

"I don't believe that she would want me to say anything."

"Take it from me, Q. I am a female. She would want to know that you are in love with her."

"Even if she doesn't love me back? Wouldn't that make someone feel uncomfortable? I know if it was the other way around and I couldn't return those feelings, I wouldn't want to know."

"She may feel slightly awkward, but she would still appreciate knowing." I didn't believe that for a moment.

"I don't think I can tell a woman that I love her if I knew I would never hear it back."

"How do you know that she doesn't feel the same, Q? How do you truly know? Have you ever asked her?"

"Look, Desiree would never date me. She has admitted that to me on numerous occasions."

"Yet you two are dating now."

"Only for the sake of our child."

"You say that, but I don't believe it. Do you believe that, Quinton? You truly believe that's the reason that she agreed to be in a relationship with you?"

"She wouldn't be with me under normal circumstances."

"She is willing to sleep with you, though?"

"That's different."

"Desiree just doesn't seem like the type of woman that would sleep with just anyone."

"She isn't that type and I am not just anyone."

"Why would she sleep with you, Q?"

"The chemistry between us is crazy."

"Good sex? So your whole relationship is based on sex?"

"Amazing sex," I joked. I attempted to lighten up the mood.

"I refuse to believe such nonsense, Quinton."

"You don't have to," I shrugged.

"I guess that you are just going to let her walk away from you."

"She has to do what she wants to do. I want whats best for her."

"So you are okay with another man loving her." My chest was starting to hurt. I didn't need any of this right now. Why was my little sister stressing me out like this?

"Of course I am not okay with that, Peyton. I am scared out of my mind every day that she is going to fall in love with some other dude. And as much as that thought hurts me, I know I can't stop her. I don't have the right."

"Why put yourself through that?" She looked horrified.

"What would I do about it? She is going to be with who she wants to be with."

"That could be you."

"Look, I just want her to be happy. I am happy if she is happy."

"Bullshit! I don't understand why people say that when they don't mean it."

"I do mean it."

"You are telling me that you are going to be happy for this woman if she falls in love with another man. A man that's not you." I couldn't respond for a moment. We both knew I wouldn't be.

"It would hurt like hell, but when you love someone, you want them to be happy," I said finally. "Her happiness is everything to me." I was being honest.

"What about your happiness? Stop running. Stop breaking your own heart, Quinton."

"I will be fine." She stared at me and shook her head.

"Okay, Quinton, continue being the stubborn man you are." She sighed. "Do you know what you want? I am ready to order."

The conversation with my mother already had me tense, but this one had sent me over the edge. The situation with Desiree was a nerve-racking one as it was, but everyone around me insisted on adding salt to the wound. I was being tortured. At this point, I wasn't sure how I was going to get through the rest of the day because my mother and sister had ruined it. I just wanted to go home to Desiree.

"This day can't get much worse."

Little did I know that I had spoken too soon?

After work, I headed to the mall. My only destination was Godiva's to pick up the chocolate covered strawberries that Des had been craving. I was done and halfway to the parking lot when I heard my name and then that despicable voice in my ear.

"I take it that she's craving." I turned around and there was Anthony. For once he didn't have that stupid grin on his face. He looked stressed.

"What are you talking about?"

"Desiree. Quinton, I know that you two are expecting."

"How did you find that out, Thompson?" I hated knowing that Desiree was still in contact with this clown.

"You mean Desiree didn't tell you?"

"Tell me what?"

"Wow. I guess this is the validation that I needed. She is obviously over me."

"What are you talking about?" I asked, balling up my fist to keep from blowing up at him.

"I surprised Desiree about a month ago at her office." What! Why didn't Desiree tell me? I could feel my temperature rising. "Calm down. Don't get so worked up. I am sure she didn't tell you because she knows that you hate me." At least he wasn't confused about how I felt about him.

"Go on, Thompson."

"We went for a walk. I told her that I still loved her. And then I proposed." I stopped breathing for a good ten seconds. I was rendered speechless. Did I hear this fool correctly? "I know that you are heated." That was an understatement.

"You proposed to my woman!"

"Look, Alexander, there's nothing to get worked up about. You don't have to worry about anything because she quickly rejected me. She didn't get excited, she wasn't pleasantly surprised, nor was she touched by my proposal. She looked at me as if I was pathetic and then she proceeded to tell me that you two were having a baby. She told me that you two were together."

"So what's the purpose of this conversation?" I could have done without all of this. I didn't need to know.

"You really can't stand to talk to me." I didn't care to, but I didn't want to come out and say it.

"I just want to know why are you telling me all this. Are you trying to rub it all in my face?"

"Rub what? She rejected me. That's not something I want to broadcast or brag about." True, I thought. "You have always made it obvious that you couldn't stand me."

"I'm sorry." I shrugged as if it was not a big deal.

"It's not like I was looking for you. I ran into you and I think it's about time that we make amends."

"Amends?"

"I understand. I get why you didn't like me. We wanted the same girl. I just want to be able to speak my peace with you right now."

"Go ahead." I was hesitant because I just wanted to get home, but I was curious to see what he had to say.

"We were never friends and that was because of Des. I always knew you had a thing for her, so I purposely acted an ass towards you. I needed for you to back off because I knew the she was out of my league. I wasn't about to let you take her away from me."

"I never made a move on her while you two were together."

"I'm not saying that you did. Deep down, I knew that you weren't the type of dude that would. I just saw the way you looked at her. It was the same way, I looked at her. I also know that you think that I never loved her, but you are wrong."

"Am I?"

"Yeah. Des was the best thing that ever happened to me."

"Then why did you cheat? If she was so amazing, why did you risk losing her?" His face seemed sincere, but I didn't believe a word coming out of his mouth. Maybe I didn't want to believe him.

"I was young, dumb and naïve. I loved her to the point that I was scared of my own feelings. Like a little punk, I was running. Running from commitment." I guess I couldn't speak against that. I had done some running of my own.

"That night I cried like a baby. I hated myself for losing her. It is the biggest mistake that I have ever made. Just know that I loved her and I still do after all these years. However, I respect the love that you have for her."

"Thank you." I didn't know how to receive what he was saying.

"I always knew that you two had the potential. That's why I always resented you. I couldn't stand how close you two were. I knew that you two hooking up was inevitable."

He closed his eyes for a moment. I couldn't really say anything. I wasn't about to comfort him. I did feel sorry for him, though. I shouldn't have because he blew his chance.

"Quinton, I just wanted to congratulate you on your relationship and your new kid. I pray that Desiree's pregnancy goes well and that your child will be healthy."

"Thank you." I stuck out my hand and he shook it.

"No problem," he shrugged. He looked at me very seriously. "Consider yourself very lucky, Alexander. You are very blessed to have her. I would trade places with you in a minute."

"I am sorry that it didn't work out, Thompson." No, I wasn't. What was with this change of heart?

I was in a state of shock the whole way home. I didn't know what to think. I just could not believe that Anthony had proposed to my woman. Desiree had not mentioned a thing to me and I wondered why. Was it really because of my dislike for him? Did she not want to upset me? Or was it something else?

By the time I got home, I had made the decision not to say anything to Desiree. I didn't want to get her all worked up. She obviously didn't tell me for a reason. Maybe she just didn't see it as a big deal. I was just going to respect her decision not to tell me.

All that mattered was that she said no. I prayed that she didn't still love Anthony, but if she did, something told me that she didn't have it in her to marry him. She couldn't marry a man when she was carrying another man's baby, could she? I wasn't convinced she was over Anthony, but I hoped so.

Realizing that I had been in the shower over twenty minutes with my mind drifting, I turned off the water. I was freezing. I quickly dried off and slipped into some pajama bottoms.

I walked over to my bed to join Desiree. Without hesitation, I reached over and pulled her to me. She turned over and wrapped her arm around my waist. She laid her head against my chest. My body felt instant relief. I could feel the stress of today slowly disappearing. She was my peace.

"Hey, baby. How were you today?"

"I was okay. I did deal with some morning sickness."

"Poor thing" I said, rubbing her belly.

"I feel a lot better. How was your day? How are you feeling?"

"Wonderful," I lied. "I am just really glad to see you."

"Really?" She smiled as if she was surprised.

"Yes, really. Are you hungry? What do you want to eat?"

"I don't know. How about you? What do you have taste for? I will cook whatever you want."

"No, I will cook you some macaroni and cheese. I know you have been talking about it."

"You don't have to…"

"Shush. Don't you want some?"

"Sounds yummy, but I haven't done much today. I can cook dinner. You don't have to keep spoiling me. Keep it up. I am going to get so spoiled that you may never get rid of me." That was the plan. "You are going to get sick of me."

"That's not going to happen," I said rubbing her cheek.

"Okay, we shall see. Where is little Quinton?"

"With his grandmother."

"He didn't want to come home."

"Nope. My mother called and asked could she keep him. My parents are going to take all the grand-kids out for dinner. She is going to bring him home tomorrow."

"Good. I miss him." That touched me. I adored her for loving my child. "It's me and you tonight, huh?"

"Is that okay?"

"I am not complaining." I was ready for her kiss. The softness of her lips and sweetness of her tongue was all I needed after this long day. I protested when she pulled away. "Oh do you like that?"

"I love that," I said pulling her on top of me.

"I can show you that and a lot more that you will love."

Later on Desiree and I sat in front of the couch watching TV. My mind kept drifting back to the conversation I had with Anthony. I had made the decision not to say anything, but curiosity was getting the best of me. I wanted to hear what Des had to say.

"I ran into Anthony today."

"Did you?" Amazingly the look on her face did not change.

"Yeah. We had a little talk."

"So I guess he told you about his proposal?"

"Yeah, he did. I was wondering why you didn't tell me."

"I know he's not your favorite person, Quinton. I really just didn't want to upset you."

"You think that I would have been upset?"

"You would have been pissed."

"Oh, of course. Pissed is not the word, sweetheart." We both laughed. "I still wished that you would have told me."

"I am sorry. She grabbed my hand and looked up at me with puppy dog eyes. "Please forgive me. I was naïve in thinking that you wouldn't care to know."

"It's cool. This is not something that I choose to be mad at."

"What did you think when he told you?"

"I thought Thompson had lost his mind. You didn't say yes?"

"Really, Quinton? I am a firm believer that you should love the one you marry." I guess I could never convince her to marry me.

"You aren't in love with Anthony anymore, Des?"

"He does nothing for me. I am so over him. I actually felt pity for him when he got down on one knee."

"You broke his heart."

"Oh well. He broke mine. My heart healed. So will his."

"I am glad you said no." I rubbed her cheek.

"Did you really think I could marry him while having your baby, Q? What would that look like?" That was all I needed to hear.

"I wouldn't have let you marry him. I would have fought you all the way." I placed my hand over her stomach. She placed her hand over mine and looked up at me with a serious expression.

"We belong to you." If only that was true."

Desiree

One Saturday afternoon, I was standing in front of the mirror, studying the changes in my body. Time was flying. I was over four months pregnant. I was showing nicely.

My pregnancy was no longer a secret. Our families knew. Our friends knew. Even our coworkers knew. I loved and appreciated everyone for being supportive and not judgmental. Although, many were concerned, most people were excited.

None were more excited than little Quinton. Surprisingly, he wanted a sibling. He wanted a sister. He told me every day. We would sit on the couch together in the evenings and he would rub my belly and talk to his brother or sister.

I was just standing there, naked, when the doorbell startled me. I quickly grabbed my robe. I practically tripped over my feet as I headed down the hall. I was the only one home. Quinton and Quinton Jr were spending quality time with Tyler. I was waiting on Rayven, who I expected to be on the other side of the door. Instead I was face to face with Q's little sister, Peyton.

"Peyton! Hey, girl! Get in here."

"Des!" She hugged me tightly. "You look so beautiful. You are actually glowing. It's really true what they say."

"Thank you."

"I am so excited for you!"

"Are you?" I giggled. She did looked overjoyed. Her eyes were dancing with excitement.

"I can't believe that you are having a baby with my brother."

"Well, you know how things happen."

"Yeah, life does happen. Did you guys find out the sex of the baby? I need to know ASAP if I am having a niece or nephew. I can't wait to go shopping."

"You and me both! We don't know yet. We should find out some time next month."

"Oh okay. Do you guys have a preference or inkling?"

"Your brother seems to think that we are having a baby girl. I keep thinking that we are going to have a baby boy."

"A girl would be nice."

"I agree. It's what Quinton wants. It doesn't matter to me. I just want a healthy baby."

"That's definitely whats important. Any names?"

"No idea. We haven't gotten that far."

"Okay. I have to ask. How did you end up with my brother?"

"We have spent a lot of time together this last year." I wasn't about to tell Peyton that our relationship was based on sex.

"What do you see in him?" I laughed at her expression.

"That's not a fair question. It would be impossible for you to see your big brother in the same way I do. He is very good to me."

"He better be. Do you care about him?"

"Of course I do."

"Do you have feelings for him?" Don't ask me if I love him.

"I do" I was cautious with my words. "He should know that."

"Does he?" She had a strange look on her face. "Do you know he has feelings for you? I am probably stepping all on Quinton's toes, but I feel like I have to say something." Why?

"What are you talking about?"

"My brother is crazy about you. I am not sure that he knows how to tell you. You are perfect for him. I hope that he doesn't mess things up."

"Peyton…"

"Desiree, I am serious. He loves you."

"Should you be saying this to me?"

"No," she said covering her mouth with her hands. "I shouldn't be saying any of this. He would kill me. I am sorry, Desiree. My biggest downfall is my mouth. I tend to just blurt things out."

"It's okay." I laughed nervously.

"Well, I can't stay. I was just dropping by. I came to see Quinton, but I take it that he is not here."

"No. He is hanging out with the boys today."

"Oh, well, can you give him this." She reached into her purse and pulled out an envelope. She handed it to me.

"Yeah, definitely. I will make sure he gets this."

"Well, I must go. I am on the way out of town."

"Be careful," I said, hugging her.

"You are the one! Take good care of yourself. And the baby," she said, rubbing my stomach.

"I will be fine. Your brother takes very good care of me."

"I bet." She gave me a funny look. "You take care of him too. And please don't break his heart. He needs you more than he is willing to admit."

"Thanks for the pressure. Don't worry, I got his back."

"Wonderful. See you."

As she was leaving, Rayven was pulling up.

"Hey!" My best friend greeted me at the door kissing my cheek.

"Hey, beautiful." Rayven looked good with a little extra weight. Her stomach was protruding more than mine in her sundress."

"Was that Quinton's little sister?"

"Yes mam."

"Look at her! She's all grown now."

"Tell me about it."

I couldn't get over how she was prying all in her brother's business. If Quinton caught whiff of it, he was going to be angry and I couldn't fault him. He didn't have to worry, though, because I didn't believe a word that she said.

A couple hours later, the boys returned home. I was in the kitchen popping Rayven and I some popcorn when little Quinton came running into the room.

"Dessie." He lifted his arms up for me to pick him up.

"Hey, baby boy. I missed you!"

"I missed you too. Look what daddy got me!" He had a DVD.

"Cool. Can I watch that with you later?"

"Yeah, I would like that," he said, hugging me.

"Good. What did you get me?"

"Nothing, but daddy got you something."

"Oh, did he?"

"Yeah, food." Q entered the room, carrying bags of Chinese.

"Thank goodness, I am hungry."

"I bet you are," he laughed. He smiled at my, obviously taking in my outfit.

"What are you smiling at?"

"Nothing." He took his son out of my arms and sat him on the floor. "Go put that up and wait in the living room until I call you."

"Okay." He took off down the hall to his bedroom.

"What did you bring me?"

"Don't worry about that right now, sweetheart. You look sexy," he said, pinning me against the counter.

"You find me sexy looking like this?"

"Very much so."

Before we could kiss, Rayven and Tyler burst into the room.

"We are starving and you two are making out."

"Go home, Rayven."

"You wish. I need to be fed first."

Later on that night I was watching TV when Quinton surprised with my gifts. A Pandora charm for my bracelet and chocolate. It was all I craved these days.

"Thank you, baby," I said throwing my arms around him. I loved how sweet he was. "This really means a lot." I was tearing up.

"Do you approve?"

"I absolutely love this." And you. "You are too good to me."

"I try."

We had been siting there for a while together, holding hands when I thought about asking Quinton what had been on my conscience lately. For the last couple of weeks, I had been thinking about what happened between Q and Rayven in college. Who was this mystery girl? Why hadn't he told me about her?

I had been conflicting over whether or not to bring it up. I didn't want to pry, but I couldn't let it go. I wasn't going to feel better until I asked. I wasn't sure if asking was going to get my anywhere, but it was worth a shot.

"I know about you and Rayven."

"What are you talking about?" he asked, slowly.

"About you two sleeping together in college."

"Okay, so she told you." I was surprised to see anger in his eyes. I moved away because I didn't like the way he was looking at me.

"Well, not everything."

"What do you know?"

"I know about the girl."

"You know what about her!"

"Don't worry, Q, it's not like I know who she is!" I felt nervous. Why was he getting this angry? We had graduated well over seven years ago.

"I didn't tell anyone. Rayven is the only one who found out."

"I didn't know that there was someone that you cared about."

"Well, surprise, there was. You always misjudged me."

"I am sorry. I have already apologized for making that mistake."

"You said that I was incapable of falling in love."

"And obviously I was very wrong. Again, I am sorry. How come you never told me?"

"What would have been the point?"

"We were friends, Quinton."

"So." Wow. That hurt more than it should have.

"Quinton, please don't be this way. I didn't mean any harm."

"You brought the past up and now I am angry about it."

"We can drop it. Forget I said anything."

"Good." He stood up. "I need a drink."

I stared after him with my mouth open. Did he really just storm out on me? Did he really blow up at me?

I wasn't sure how he was going to react, but this is not how I imagined this going down. Obviously, Quinton considered this to be a very dark moment in his life. There were unresolved issues. I was even more curious to find out about this mystery girl.

After realizing he wasn't coming back, I stood and went to bed. I laid there wide awake, praying that he would calm down and join me. He didn't which upset me. What had I done?

Little did I know that bringing up the past was going to be a threat to my future. Everything changed after that. The honeymoon period was over.

30

Desire

"For I know the plans I have for you, declares the Lord, plans for welfare and not for evil, to give you a future and a hope."
Jeremiah 29:11

Desiree

I woke up from the nightmare with tears sliding down my cheeks. I sat up in my bed with my heart pounding against my chest. I grabbed my stomach and breathed a sigh of relief as I realize that losing my baby had been part of a horrific dream. I closed my eyes and raised my face towards the sky.

"Thank you, Lord."

In my dream, I had awakened knowing something was wrong. I was alone. There was no Quinton to comfort or help me. I called Rayven. My best friend and Tyler rushed me to the hospital. I gave birth and my baby wouldn't breathe. I had been devastated, but was now relieved that I truly didn't have to experience that heart break.

There was some reality to my dream, though. I looked over and saw that the spot beside me was still empty. Quinton not being here brought tears to my eyes. I just wanted to be held by him right now. I desired his comfort and he wasn't here to give it to me.

Q's cousin was in town for the weekend and he wanted to go out on his last night. In his defense, Q asked if I wanted him to stay with me. I did, but I found myself telling him to go. It wasn't as if he was much company to me these days. Our conversation about the mystery girl in college had really changed things between us.

I stood up still very much affected from my dream. I walked over to the mirror and stared at my appearance. I looked terrified and tired. I needed rest, but I was too scared to go back to sleep. I didn't want to have another dream like that again.

I sighed and headed to the bathroom. I pulled off my t-shirt and stepped into the shower. Instead of melting in the arms of the man that I desperately loved, I had to settle for the warm water falling fast against my skin. And while it did its job in comforting me, it's not what I desired. It was not the physical contact that I needed.

I started to cry. Tears of relief, mixed with loneliness fell down my cheeks. I felt joy and despair at the same time. I imagined that despair escaping down the drain with the water that pounded my skin. In that moment, I was an emotional wreck.

After my shower, I toweled off, rubbed on some baby lotion and slipped into one of Q's old t-shirts. I then grabbed a blanket and settled in front of the TV in the living room. It was almost 3:00 in the morning, but I wasn't' going back to sleep anytime soon.

Quinton arrived about fifteen minutes later. Knowing he was home brought relief. If anything happened then he would be there.

I wasn't necessarily happy to see him, though. I didn't like the way he looked at me these days. His face use to light up when he saw me, but now all I got was blank stares. He didn't smile at me anymore. That broke my heart. Was I the cause of his sadness?

"Hey." He frowned as he walked into the room.

"Hi." I glanced his way quickly without really seeing him. "How was your night?"

"Good." That was all he offered. He leaned over and kissed my forehead. I bit my lip in frustration because he used to kiss my lips. I was aching for more. "You want to tell me why you are up?"

"I couldn't sleep."

"Whats wrong? Do you feel okay?"

"I am doing okay," I lied. "I had a bad dream."

"Really?" I could actually see concern on his face when I glanced up at him. "Do you want to talk about it?"

"No, I am fine now." I didn't want to get into it. It would have been too emotional. I didn't want to go there, especially if he was not willing to give me what I needed.

"Alright. Well, I am going to bed. I am exhausted."

"Sleep well."

"Thanks. If you need me, wake me up."

"I will."

That was it. Our conversation lasted a minute. It wasn't meaningful. It wasn't personal. That's how everything felt between us these days. It felt as if we were acquaintances and no longer friends.

I should have never brought this mystery girl up. I should have left the past alone because soon I was going to be a part of Quinton's past. How much longer could we go on like this? The infamous conversation took place almost a month ago and he still continued to distance himself from me. Would he ever forgive me?

What could I do about any of these? Just continue to hurt? To feel sorry for myself? I had learned months ago that I couldn't make this man love me. I had to learn how to coexist in his world without the affection, the passion, and sadly, the friendship. This was Q's game and he had changed the rules. I had somehow chosen to abide by them because at this point, I had no idea how to change them.

It's not like he didn't talk to me. He didn't ignore me. I think Quinton knew better than that. He knew how stubborn I was and if he mistreated me, I would leave. Right now he wanted me to stay, so he could be a part of my pregnancy. He wanted me around for the sake of our child.

Quinton keeping me around just because I was pregnant is what hurt the most. We went from a state of bliss to this. He couldn't quite look at me when he talked to me. He stopped touching me with the exception of an occasional kiss on the forehead or on the cheek. And right now, in my vulnerable state, I needed his affection. I needed him to want me.

I just wanted to know that he cared. That he didn't just care about our child. I wanted him to care about me. I wasn't sure what he cared about these days. We use to talk about our days over dinner, but now he kept those details to himself. It was frustrating that he came home every night after 10:00. It was as if he didn't want to spend more time than needed with me.

He smelled suspiciously of cigars and cheap perfume. Unfortunately, I had to face the fact that Quinton potentially wanted to be with another woman. I know that we had decided to be with one another throughout my pregnancy, but I was being foolish to believe that would actually happen.

It was unrealistic of me to think that we could last together for the sake of this baby. We had no foundation to build a relationship on. If there was love lacking between us, we could never truly be a couple. Therefore, I could not truly be mad with Quinton for opting to find love with another woman. All I could do was sit in the background and yearn for something I couldn't have.

I just prayed that Quinton truly had feelings for whoever he was spending his evenings with. I would be devastated to know that he would choose good booty over maintaining a relationship with me. I didn't want to continue to judge and label him. All these years, I characterized him as someone who could not love, but obviously I was very wrong.

Ever since I brought up this unknown chick from our college days, he had been sad. It broke my heart to see how unhappy he looked these days. I hated seeing the distant look in his eyes. I often walked into a room to find him staring off into space. I missed seeing him smile. He hadn't done so in weeks.

In the beginning he was excited about the baby, but I wasn't confident in that anymore. Maybe reality had hit him. I am sure Q wasn't ready to settle down and start a family with me. Was that it?

Guilt started to consume me. What if he held animosity towards me for getting pregnant? What if he blamed me for ruining his life? What if he was not only regretting this baby, but all that had happened between us?

I was devastated at first. I cried for the first two weeks because the change in Quinton's behavior gave me anxiety. Then I got pissed. I was angry that he could treat me this way just because I had dug up some hurtful memories of his past. I was angry that he wasn't honoring me as the mother of his unborn child.

Now I just felt empty. I was confused. I was at a lost at what my next move should be.

I just knew that I wanted us to live in this house and be happy together. Right now, neither of us was happy. All of this would have to change soon or I wasn't sure if I could survive here much longer. I was not quite sure if Quinton was ready for me to walk out.

Would he let me leave?

Quinton

I really didn't have that much fun tonight. I should have. We went to this popular lounge downtown. We sat in the VIP section with some local artist. We sipped on Ciroc and a variety of appetizers. We were served by beautiful scantily clad women.

I tried desperately to have a good time, but I couldn't. I didn't want to be there. The only reason I tagged along was because my cousin begged me. Plus, Desiree didn't seem to care whether I stayed at home with her or not.

Instead of focusing on the people around me, I thought about Des all night. Was she okay? Why didn't she seem to want me anymore? Was she cool with what was going on between us?

It seemed that way. How? All of this was killing me.

I had to be completely honest with myself. We were in this situation because I put us there. I knew for a fact that I was being unreasonable, but I didn't know what else to do. After we had that infamous conversation, I got nervous. I forced myself to distance myself from her yet again.

Desiree had unknowingly humiliated me that night in college and I desperately wanted to spare her of the details. I was a little annoyed that Rayven had mentioned anything to her. When Des brought that night up, I was rendered speechless. Admittedly, my reaction was horrible, but I was frustrated and angry. Falling in love with this woman, who thought I was incapable of love, had hurt me more than anyone would ever realize.

Sadly, the details of that night have continued to haunt me over the last few weeks. I started having anxiety attacks. I started having nightmares.

I wasn't sure I could forgive Desiree for speaking those painful words of rejection. How could she tell me that I couldn't love a woman when my heart ached for hers and no one else's? She insisted the other week that I was running from my feelings. I was. I had no other choice. She wasn't willing to love me in return.

The fact that she seemed unbothered didn't set to well with me. She didn't notice how depress I felt. Or then again, maybe she did. Maybe she didn't care.

I personally couldn't stand that the affection was missing between us. Or that the emotions had stopped flowing. The passion had ceased. Either she was pretending or she didn't need those three things as much as I did.

I wasn't sure how much longer I could go on like this. I lay in bed, staring at my ceiling. I had so many needs that were being neglected. I needed fulfillment and I was not getting it. I hated this empty way of living when Desiree was right there. I wanted desperately to reach out, but I didn't know how.

She was supposed to be my girl. For one month, everything was great, but reality quickly came rushing in. I could not force what I wanted between us. A baby could not really keep us together. Without the love that I yearned for, we didn't really have a chance. Things were falling apart and she was only five months pregnant.

I wanted her beside me right now. I wanted to go into the living room and ask her to come to bed with me, but I didn't know how to ask. I didn't know how to get what I wanted from her anymore.

I hadn't slept well in weeks. I lay awake every night, listening to the sound of her breathing. I would ball my fist to resist the urge to touch her. I wanted to kiss her and pull her to me, but I didn't feel if I deserved any of that anymore.

I waited for her to come, but she never came. The space beside me remained empty. I had been in my bed, wide awake for over an hour and a half. Feeling defeated, I continue to lay there alone with just these dark thoughts in my head. I already knew I was not going to get any sleep.

Desiree

It was about 7:00 in the morning before I fell asleep. When I woke up hours later, I found myself snuggled up in Quinton's bed. At least he was still thoughtful, I thought as I sat up. I took a couple deep breaths and climbed out of bed.

I walked through the house and was greeted with silence. I assumed that Q was gone and I was home alone. I looked outside to find him washing his car.

"My goodness!"

What a beautiful man, I thought to myself. I stood there and watched him for a moment. He was shirtless, wearing nothing but gray basketball shorts. I bit my lip as I stared at that beautiful chest and those big arms of his. I thought about how many times I had ran my hands over those muscles while in moments of passion. At how many times he had wrapped those arms around me, making me melt. How many times I laid my head against that chest.

"It's a shame." One man should not look that good. I chuckled as I rubbed my belly. "Me enjoying the way your daddy looks is how you got here, precious." I was so horny. "Your daddy is depriving me of his loving too."

I sighed and headed to the bathroom. This standoff with Quinton was stressing me out. I needed a bubble bath.

I was soaking in Q's Jacuzzi-styled tub when he walked in. My eyes were closed, but I felt his presence. I took a deep breath and opened my eyes. He stood by the door.

"Would you like me to fix you something?"

"No thank you. I am okay at the moment."

"Are you sure?"

"I am fine."

"Okay." I stared after him as he walked away. I longed for him. I was wishing he would join me or at least come over and touch me like he used to.

I was hungry. I would have loved one of Quinton's omelets or a stack of his pancakes, but I was meeting Rayven for lunch. Afterwards, we were going baby shopping. I was excited because she was going to surprise me with the sex of her baby. I was not due to find out the sex of mine for another week.

I felt like standing out today. I picked a short fuschia sundress and cute sandals I had never wore before. I combed my hair down, applied some bronzer and some lip gloss. I wasn't trying to overdo it today. I grabbed my sunglasses and was out of the door.

"Whats up? Where are you going?" Q asked. He was washing my car now.

"I am meeting Rayven for lunch. I may do a little damage to the bank account afterwards."

"Okay. Well you can take my car," he said, handing me the keys.

"Thank you, Quinton."

"Not a problem." My heart did a summersault, when he tilted my chin and kissed me on my lips. It was the first bit of affection that he had shown me in weeks. "You look beautiful today."

"Thanks for noticing."

I met Rayven at our favorite restaurant downtown for lunch. It was a cute little Italian bistro. The weather was delightful, so we met outside to eat on the patio. I intended to make the best of the day, considering things weren't too great at home.

"Hey, beautiful," she said, throwing her arm around me. "I feel as if I haven't seen you in forever."

"It's just been two weeks. You look so good." She wore a cute pink sleeveless dress.

"Thank you, babe. How is everything going?" she asked as we took our seats.

"Good," I lied. "How about with you, Sunray?"

"Things are wonderful right now."

"Well! Tell me!" I grabbed her hand from across the table. "You don't understand how bad I want to know. What are you having?"

"Oh goodness!" She gave me a huge smile with tears welling up in her eyes. "Tyler and I are so happy. We are having a baby boy."

"Oh, Rayven!" I stood to hug her. "Congratulations."

"Thank you, babe. When do you and Q find out?"

"In another week."

"Well I hope that you will have what you truly desire."

It was after lunch while we walked down the street to check out some boutiques, that I decided to bring up the situation with Q. I couldn't really keep it from my best friend. I had to talk to someone.

"I asked Q about this mystery girl from college. The one he was in love with. I asked him about the night you two slept together."

"You did what!" She stopped walking and stared at me with wide eyes. "No, Desiree."

"I was curious, Rayven. I couldn't help myself. I wanted to know about this girl. I was wondering why he never told me about her."

"Oh gosh, Desiree." She started shaking her head. I couldn't understand why. What was the big deal? "What did Q say?"

Before I knew it, I was explaining everything to her. I told her how Quinton got upset and stormed out on me. How he had been unhappy. How he had distance himself from me. I even told her about my nightmare where I had lost our child. I was in tears by the time I had finished blurting out every detail.

"Oh, baby girl, please don't cry," she said, hugging me tightly.

"I don't understand why he is choosing to be angry with me."

"Des." She pulled away so she could look at me. She reached up and touched my cheek. "You will never fully understand until you know who this girl is."

"What does she have to do with me? This chick is causing him to be angry with me. I don't get it."

"Look, one day, Quinton is going to have to give in and tell you. I know he will. Just give him some more time. You know how men are. They can't deal with emotions the same way we can."

"How much more time does he need? It's been a month."

"He's going to come around."

"When? I can't live like this much longer."

"What are you saying?"

"I may have to leave, Rayven."

"You can't!" I was surprised to see a panicked look on her face.

"Why can't I? He is unhappy. I think I am the cause of that."

"No. Tell me the truth, Des. Do you love him?"

"What do you think?" Couldn't she tell?

"I don't know, Des. You have never admitted it to me. I am asking you here today to tell me the truth."

"Yes, Rayven, I love him."

"Then please don't leave."

Q left me alone again that night. This time he left me to babysit. Quinton Jr and I hung at home while he was supposedly helping out a friend he worked with. Because of everything that had been going on between us, I couldn't help but think that it was all bullshit.

Tonight, he didn't bother to ask whether or not I wanted him to stay. Instead, he kissed me and he left. He left me with his child without considering whether or not I wanted to go out and do something. He didn't even ask me did I mind babysitting.

I honestly didn't mind being with little Quinton. I adored him and loved him as if he was my own son. I cherished every moment with him because he was teaching me how to be a mother.

The two of us baked cookies and then settled in front of the TV to watch the Lego movie. Halfway through the movie, he fell asleep. I held him in my arms until the movie was over and then I took him to his bedroom. I tucked him in, kissed his forehead and stared at him for a moment. He's so precious, I thought.

I decided to head to bed myself. I was actually exhausted and didn't have much to do. If I sat up any longer, I was only going to focus on Quinton. The more I thought about him and his absence tonight, the madder I got. I didn't want to feel resentful. I was already on the brink of blowing up at him when he walked through the door. At this point, only one small thing was going to send me over the edge. Hopefully a good night's rest would calm all of that down.

I couldn't go to sleep, though. I had been laying there for about an hour when I head little feet coming down the hall. I sat up as little Quinton came bursting into the room. He had tears in his eyes as he reached for me. I climbed out of bed and lifted him in my arms.

"Whats wrong, sweetheart?"

"I don't feel good."

"You don't? What hurts?"

"My tummy hurts?" I looked at him and could tell that the inevitable was going to happen. I ran to the bathroom. Thankfully we made it there in time before he threw up. Unfortunately most of it hit the floor and my foot instead of the toilet.

"Oh my goodness." I could feel myself starting to panic. However, I knew the little boy needed me right now. I let him get it all out and then I held in my arms as he cried against my shoulder. I rubbed his back and kept telling him that it was going to be okay.

"I want my daddy." Of course Quinton wasn't here.

"Oh, baby, daddy is not here. I am here for you, though. I promise to take good care of you. Let's go get something to make that tummy feel better."

"Okay," he sniffed. I gave him Pepto Bismol and then I laid him back down in his bed. I asked if he wanted me to stay with him and he said yes.

I sung to him and rubbed his belly until he was able to fall asleep. I sat in a chair near his bed for about forty minutes to make sure he didn't wake up. I didn't want to have to call Quinton for help, but if it was necessary, I wanted to be ready.

He didn't need me. I could see that he was sleeping peacefully, so I stood and headed back to my bedroom I had been sharing with Q. Instead of climbing back into bed, I sat down in the corner of the room. I didn't turn on any lights or the TV. I just sat there, breathing slowly, attempting to calm myself down. I was livid.

From the moment that he walked out of the door, I was pissed with Quinton. I had already been angry with him for not being here for me, but tonight he wasn't there for his son. I knew that it wasn't his fault that little Quinton was sick, but I was starting to feel as if he was losing sight of his priorities. His family.

Enough was enough. I couldn't allow all of this to go on any longer. If I wasn't happy and Q wasn't happy, then I had no business continuing to stay here. A baby wasn't going to force anything to work out between us. Tonight, I was choosing to end all of this.

I was still sitting in that chair when Quinton walked in around midnight. He couldn't see me in the dark. He turned the lights on and stared over at the bed. He frowned at the empty spot.

"I'm right here." He looked up, startled.

"What are you doing?" he asked, walking towards me.

"I was sitting here while I was doing some thinking."

"About what? What's wrong?" I saw a rare glimpse of concern.

"How I can't take all of this anymore."

"Take all of what, Des?"

"I can't take you not being here anymore when I need you." The look he gave me was a priceless one. "And your son needed you. He was sick tonight and he cried for you." A look of guilt came over his face. For a moment, I felt bad.

"Oh, no!" He turned to leave the room, but I stopped him.

"No, Quinton. He is okay now. I took care of everything. He has been sleep for a while now. I rather you not wake him."

"Thank goodness. I am sorry, Desiree. I am thankful that you could be there for him."

"It's okay. I am leaving, Quinton," I blurted.

"Leaving?" He looked confused. "You are leaving to go where?"

"I don't really know."

"When? Tonight?" I nodded. "When are you coming back?"

"I am not." I headed to the closet, but he blocked my path.

"What do you mean?"

"I am moving out. For good."

"You are talking crazy." His eyes grew wide. Panic came over his face. "You can't leave."

"Why not!"

"You are not leaving, Desiree!" He sounded angry.

"Just let me leave, Quinton!"

"Why would I let you leave? What kind of man would I be?"

"Because you want me to leave! You would be a happier man!"

"I never want you to leave. I asked you to stay for a reason."

"Well, you have obviously changed your mind."

"No, now you are just making stuff up!" He grabbed his head in frustration. I could see fear in his eyes. "It sounds to me that you want to leave. Is that it?"

"Yes," I whispered. "I want to leave, Quinton. Will you let me? Will that be okay with you?" I couldn't understand his opposition. He had been so unhappy lately. Why would he want me around?

"No." I looked away. I didn't expect to see the hurt in his eyes. "I want you to stay with me, Des. Why do you want to leave?"

"Because I can't stay here anymore. I can't deal with what's happening between us."

"Whats that?" His voice was hoarse.

"You aren't happy, Q. You have chosen not to communicate with me anymore, so I am not sure where the issue lies. I just feel like I am obviously the problem. You are purposely distancing yourself from me is breaking my heart. I've been sad."

"I'm sorry, Desiree. I wish I could make you understand."

"Understand what? Look, I am sorry that I brought that night up. I am sorry that I misjudged you. I hope that you can forgive me one day. Still, do you think that I deserve your cold shoulder?"

"I am sorry. You don't."

"Are you sorry? Is that all I get from you. Can you explain to me why I am getting this cold shoulder over something that has nothing to do with me?" He stared right through me. "Of course you aren't going to say anything, though. Why be honest with me now?"

He started shaking his head.

"Des, please stay. I don't want you to go." I could hear the emotion in his voice. He was pleading with me. I was confused. I didn't expect this.

"Why! It's been over a month! How could you do this to me? I needed you, Quinton!"

"You don't need me anymore?"

"I still need you!"

"Then why would you leave me?"

"Because you don't need me," I whispered.

"I do. I need you more than you will ever know. You can't walk away. I would not be able to make it."

"I don't believe you." I felt as if he was lying.

"Des…why not?" He looked as if he wanted to reach for me, but he didn't.

"I don't know. Do you not want to have this baby anymore? Is that it? It's a little too late, Quinton."

"Why would you say that to me? You are carrying my child, woman. I want that more than anything."

"Then why don't you act like it. You haven't been treating me like the mother of your unborn child. You have barely been treating me like a friend. What has happened?"

He didn't say anything. He continued to stare through me. I stared at him, waiting for something, but was greeted by silence. I pushed past him to the closet. Suddenly, he grabbed me from behind. He held me tightly.

"Please don't this," he whispered.

"I have to do this and you have to let me."

"No!"

"Just let me go!"

"Damn, Desiree!" He quickly let go of me. "I need some air."

He walked out the room and I found myself following him. He walked out to his deck. He sat down in a chair and dropped his face into his hands.

"Can you let me go, Quinton and be at peace with that?"

"I can't stop you. I can't make you do anything that you don't want to do." It's not what I wanted to hear from him. I had been holding back tears since he came home. Those words caused them to spill down my cheeks. My heart was slowly breaking.

I am not sure how I could continue to live this way, but I wanted desperately to stay. I loved this man with all of my heart regardless of how he felt about me. I needed him. I couldn't be away from him. Not right now.

It took me a moment to realize that he was crying. I grabbed my chest. To see him this emotional touched me so deeply that it made me cry even harder. I never imagined that leaving could hurt him. I honestly thought that's what he wanted

I walked over to him and lifted his face into my hands. His teary eyes met mine. I started wiping his tears away. He grabbed my hand and kissed the palm.

"Please don't cry, Quinton. Why are you crying?"

"I...please don't go." I was speechless.

I am not sure if I sat in his lap or if he pulled me down. I am not sure which one of us started the kiss. I just know feeling his lips on mine and his arms around me, made me feel relieved. I missed the kisses, the touches, the intimacy, and the passion. And as I moaned in appreciation as his hands slid to the sweet spot between my thighs, I came to the conclusion that I would never love another man as I loved Quinton in that moment.

"I will always need you," he whispered. I just started at him.

"I…" I was rendered speechless again. I stood. He looked away. He was expecting me to go inside, pack my bags and leave. "Q….."

"Wait until morning at least. Maybe after a good night's sleep, we can work…"

"Shush." I was not sure if I could just walk away from love. Even if it was one sided. "Come inside. Love me. I need to feel you." I reached for his hand and he took it. He followed me inside.

I tried to take matters into my own hands, but he wouldn't let me. It didn't take long before he had me leaning over the dining room table. He begin to love me in the only way he knew how. I let out a loud noise and he covered my mouth. I closed my eyes and held on for the ride.

Afterwards we both pulled away nervously. Quinton backed up against the wall. I looked away and begin to frantically fix my clothes. I didn't take me long to realize he was staring at me. All I could see was sadness.

"I…." I tried to think of something to say.

"It was you, Des."

"Excuse me."

"That girl in college. The one that I loved." I felt as if my heart had stopped beating. I stopped breathing momentarily. I could feel my face getting hot. My mouth fell open, but nothing came out of it. "It was the first night that you went out with Anthony. I wanted to tell you. I came to your room that night, but…."

"Is that what you were going to tell me?" The memory came rushing back. I recalled some of the things I said to him. I closed my eyes. I had hurt him.

"Yes."

"No, no, no." I covered my mouth. I was shaking.

"I obviously changed my mind. I went back to my apartment. I cried over you. It was one of the worst nights of my life. I don't know what made me want to leave that night, but when I did there you were with him. He was kissing you…."

My stomach was in knots. I could see he was reliving that night. There was so much pain in his eyes. I wanted to throw up.

"Rayven saw all of that. She knew what I was feeling. You know what happened next. I will spare you the details."

Wow. I started to shake my head in disbelief.

"She was trying to comfort me. I didn't realize she was doing it because she liked me. Of course she didn't comfort me in the end. I felt bad afterwards, but I was so caught up in my own feelings that I wasn't able to set things straight between us. Obviously that's why she didn't like me over the years."

"Why didn't you tell me?"

"Because you were his girl. We both know how you felt about him. I knew how you felt about me and there really was no point. I didn't have a chance with you."

"Still…."

"I didn't want you to find out. It's humiliating."

"No." I made a move towards him, but he threw us his hands.

"Stop. Let me finish unbarring my soul." I nodded. "The reason I got so upset about you bringing that night up is because I am still running. The truth is that when I kissed you last year, I knew I still loved you. It doesn't matter what I do, I can't get over you. I keep trying, but I keep failing."

"Q…."

"I never wanted to tell you. I wanted to suffer in silence. I didn't want you to feel uncomfortable. I didn't want to lose you."

"Why are you telling me now then?"

"Because, you wanted the truth from me. I had to tell you so that you would understand. I want you to realize how much I need you. I am not quite sure how to live without you. If you leave me….." He didn't finish. He just looked down.

"You still love me?"

"I do. I love you. I am sorry, Des."

"No, don't apologize. You never thought I could fall in love with you?"

"You said I wasn't your type." He shrugged. "I accepted a long time ago, that I could not have you."

"But you do have me. I am standing right here. I give myself to you. Are you going to take me?" He looked up at me.

"I never wanted just the sex from you Des. I always want your love. I always wanted something you…."

"You can have it."

"You are going to give me your love?"

"It's yours. Your already have it if you want it."

"I…" He still didn't understand.

"See you are dead wrong, Quinton. I was crazy about you in college. Remember the night we kissed…." I watched him relieve that moment. "I couldn't stop thinking about that night for months. I didn't make any more moves on you because I was pretty sure I was out of your league."

"My league? That's crazy…."

"And then you kissed me when you moved in and I knew I was in trouble. You see if you didn't have a chance with me, none of that would have happened. This last year and a half would not have happen. I would not be pregnant right not."

"What are you saying to me, Desiree?"

"I am telling you that I love you, Quinton. I am crazy, madly and deeply in love with you. I need you in a way that I have never needed anyone else. I don't want anyone else."

I don't know how he moved so quickly,   but he did. He pulled me to him and broke down. We shared this incredible moment that I would have never imagined. We had finally knocked down those walls that were preventing something beautiful form happening.

"This is not a dream is it, baby?" he whispered.

"A dream come true." I couldn't stop kissing him. "We have been friends most of our lives. When did all of this change? What made you want more?" I could have never imagined any of this. My mind was blown.

"I always knew you were beautiful. I woke up one day and I couldn't stop staring at you. I kept thinking about how your lips would taste against mine. How you would feel in my arms. I wanted to do things to you. I wanted to make love to you. That's not what friends do."

His words turned me on. My breath quicken.

"Initially, I thought I was just attracted to you, but then I started thinking about the way you smiled, how your eyes sparkled, how you laughed. When you weren't around, I could remember how you smelled; I could hear you singing; I could see you dancing to no music when no one's watching; I could see you biting your lip when your concentrate. "

"All of that made me smile. The thought of you made me happy. When you were around me, I was happy. You brought peace to me."

"You made me lose concentration. You made me lose my appetite. I practically lost my mind."

"Quinton, I….what can I say? That's…." There was a lump in my throat.

"And then I moved in and I couldn't stop thinking about how sweet your lips tasted. How intoxicating you smelled. How soft your skin was. How your body felt against mine."

"I love when you stare at me and bite that lip of yours. I love how you dig your nails into my back. I love the way you moan my name. I don't want another woman to ever moan my name the way you do." I looked down because my face was so hot.

"I love when your wrap your thighs around me. I love the way you give yourself to me. I love the way your way body reacts to me. I love making love to you." He slid his hand into my hair and pulled my head back so I could look at him. "I vow to never make love to another woman again."

"Q…."

He leaned down and kissed me. Then he kissed my neck. Then he kissed the top of breast.

"I don't want another man near you."

"Never."

"You are the first face I want to see in the mornings and the last face I want to see at night. You don't realize how having you near me brings calm to my life. It brings peace to my heart."

"Your smile and your laugh mean everything to me. Giving you're the world is my life's purpose. Keeping you happy is what I intend to do for as long as you let me. A lifetime I hope."

My heart couldn't take this. He was putting it all out there for me. He was speaking words that I needed to hear. Words that I only dreamed of hearing.

"I will love you through every struggle, every heartbreak, every fear, and every tear. I will love you no matter how angry you can get with me. Even when you don't talk to me, when you speak those hurtful words or when you push me away. I will not go away. "

"I will love you when you scream, when your pout, when you nag. I don't care. I love everything good about you, but more importantly, I will love all of your flaws. I will love you in spite of."

I knew I was difficult and to hear that he would love me through all of that touched me in a way that I couldn't explain. I started to cry and I couldn't stop. He just stared down at me and wiped tears away.

"Quinton…." I struggled to find my voice. I wanted to tell him how I felt about him, but he would not let me speak.

"I'm honored that you are the woman carrying my child. I never want another woman to do that for me. Do you hear me? I will never let you go. I will fight for your love. If you fall out of love today or tomorrow, I will continue to fight. I will do anything it takes."

"I am not going anywhere." I said, grabbing the back of his head. I pulled his face to mine. He kissed me for a long time. It was full of passion. Full of hope. Full of love. It was everything.

When we pulled away, we just embraced. I closed my eyes and laid against his chest.

"You are my heart, Des. My world. You are my everything." I didn't have any words for that. I just held him tighter. I didn't ever want to let go of him.

I was so happy that I couldn't think straight. I had so many emotions that I wanted to express to him, but right now I didn't know how. Finally I whispered, "You are my heaven on earth, Quinton Alexander."

A week later, Q and I went in for my next appointment. We were excited to find out the sex of our baby.

"Last chance to ask God for any favors," I joked as he held my hand. "What do you think?"

"We are having a baby girl. God and I already talked."

Ten minutes later, Quinton's intuition proved to be true. I was pregnant with a little girl. Needless to say, we were both very pleased.

31

Joy

"Behold, children are a heritage from the Lord, the fruit of the womb a reward. Like arrows in the hand of a warrior are the children of one's youth. Blessed is the man who fills his quiver with them! He shall not be put to shame when he speaks with his enemies in the gate." *Psalm 1twenty-seven:3*

Desiree

Over the next three months, my life began to fall into place. I couldn't be much happier with the way things were going. I had everything that I wanted and more.

Quinton was good to me. Our relationship grew in ways that I would have never imagined. I had known this man since we were kids and while I always had a crush on him; I would have never guessed that I would be this in love with him. There were some days that I would just stare at him in awe. I was completely grateful.

I never knew that one man was capable of loving me as much as he loved me. I had been insecure over the last couple of years. There had been so many doubts in my mind about how he felt about me, but they were all gone. It was evident that he needed me in his life.

I knew after that night where we both professed our love in the middle of his living room, that our lives had changed. Quinton belonged to me. I belonged to him. We were in this thing for the long haul. Hopefully for a lifetime.

"I love this man more than myself."

I would do anything for him. I would sacrifice it all for him. I would work hard to keep him happy and in my life. I made sure he knew how much I loved him on a daily basis. I didn't want there to be one single doubt in his mind. I didn't want him to ever think about another woman.

I wasn't worried. I trusted him. I trusted him more than any other man in my past. As attentive as he was to my wants and needs, I couldn't see how he had any time to pay attention to anyone else.

"Your daddy is amazing. He is so good to us," I said, rubbing my stomach as my little girl starting kicking. I laughed at the thought of her trying to get my attention. "I can't wait for you to see him."

I was well over eight months pregnant. I enjoyed being pregnant; but thankfully, I only had two months to go. Our little angel was due at the beginning of the year.

My daughter was definitely a blessing from God. Maybe having her was God's way of bringing Quinton and I together. If I had not gotten pregnant, the two of us would still be playing games instead of breaking down the walls that were keeping us apart.

"Ouch!" She kicked me again. "Okay, baby, mommy is paying attention. Don't hurt me."

"Hey, you." Q entered the room. "She's kicking?" He asked, wrapping his arms around me.

"Yes," I said, grabbing his hands. "Do you feel her?"

"I do." His eyes were dancing. "Is she hurting you, baby."

"She is a little feisty, but I can handle her."

"You are incredible," he said, kissing my forehead. "You look beautiful today."

"Thank you." I smiled up at him with hot cheeks. His compliments always got to me.

"I love you." He kissed me.

"I love you, too."

"Good. Are you ready?" I nodded. "Let's get this show on the road. Quinton! Come to daddy, buddy."

Quinton Jr, who had grown us so much over the last year, came running into the room. He was all bundled up in his little pea coat and kangol hat. He had my coat dragging behind him.

"Aww, look at you." I laughed.

"Dessie, I got your coat."

"Thank you, sweetie."

"You are welcome"

"Good job, buddy. Daddy taught you well. You are being a gentleman," Q said, taking the coat from him. He helped me into it.

"Thank you to my big sweetie."

"You are welcome, baby." He grabbed my hand and we headed out of the house.

I took in his appearance. He wore tan pants and a cream color sweater that complimented his skin beautifully. Over it, he wore a leather coat. I smiled in appreciation. My man looked incredible. How did I get so lucky?

"You are so sexy," I mumbled to myself. I wanted him. I was extremely horny right now. As soon as I could after delivering this baby, I was going to jump his bones I wanted to make passionate love for hours. Quinton had a way of making my body respond in ways that I didn't think was possible.

I snapped out of it when Q Jr grabbed my hand. I looked down at him. He smiled up at me.

We were on our way to an event that was going change our lives significantly. All those nights that Q had left me alone and I thought he was being unfaithful, he was out trying to achieve his dreams. He had some help with his partners, Justin Jenkins and Monica Williams. Since we were young, he always wanted to open his own record label and tonight that lifelong dream had become his reality.

The trio wrote a business plan, rented a large space downtown, borrowed some money from family and friends, and put their vision to work. Tonight, all of those friends and family were coming together to celebrate their success. We were meeting at Fantasy records. We would be introduced to Integrity, a male trio, who would become the label's first artist.

"I am so proud of you, baby," I said in the car.

"Thanks, but you are the one we should all be proud of," he said, kissing the palm of my hand.

"Why is that?"

"Because you are carrying a little human inside of you."

We arrived at Fantasy the same time as Ty and Ray. I giggled to myself as I watched my best friend waddle across the parking lot. I found it amusing because I knew I looked just like her. We both had gotten ridiculously big. I was not scheduled to give birth for another seven weeks or so, but Rayven only had about four weeks left.

"Hey, gorgeous," she said, holding her hand out to me.

"Hey, beautiful." I kissed her cheek. "How are you feeling?"

"Like I am ready to deliver this child of mines already."

"Not too much longer."

"No, but this little boy is getting restless."

"I feel you. She has been kicking me all day. I know she just wants to keep my attention."

"Tell me about it," she smiled. "It means everything, though. Those precious moments with our babies."

"You are right, it does, but she doesn't understand how much she is hurting mommy."

"Don't I know it!"

"Come on you two," Tyler said, turning around because he and the boys were several paces ahead.

"You try to walk fast with a ten pound baby inside of you," Rayven snapped

"Wow," I laughed. "Do you really think that your baby is going to be that big?"

"Considering how big that I look right now, he better be."

"Baby, I am sorry," Tyler said, wrapping his arm around her.

"I forgive your insensitivity," she said, touching his face and then kissing him. Something about the sweetness of their interaction made me reach for Quinton's hands. I wanted to feel his love flow through me.

"Are you feeling okay?" he whispered in my ear as we rode in the elevator to the top floor.

"I am fine! Are you excited? This is a huge moment for you."

"I am. You should be excited too."

"I am. I am very happy for you."

"And I am happy for you."

"Why?"

What happened next was a blur. Rayven and I stepped off the elevator to find well over a hundred people yelling surprise. Water quickly filled my eyes. I covered my mouth as I scanned the room to see so many familiar faces applauding Rayven and I. Family members and friends. I took in the beautiful pink and blue decorations. We were being thrown a baby shower.

I looked over at Rayven and she was crying. I reached for her hand and she held it tightly. I placed my hand over my heart and closed my eyes for a moment. This was my best friend and today we were sharing something magical. We were given the opportunity to celebrate our blessings together.

"Did you do this, Quinton?"

"Yes baby, I did this for you. I had a lot of help of course."

"Why?"

"Don't you think you deserve it?"

"I guess…."

"Be quiet, my love. I promise you that you do. I love you."

"I love you."

"Good. Let's do this. We shouldn't leave your guest waiting."

It was all so overwhelming. I was touched to see my parents, my sister, my grandparents, aunts, uncles, cousins, and my good friends from high school and college. Q's close family was there as well. I don't know how Q managed to get all these people who meant so much to me here. I had a feeling my mother had a lot to do with it.

After some mingling, we sat down. Surprise after surprise started rolling in. The evening started with a beautiful ceremony where guest gave speeches, told stories, jokes or just gave words of encouragement. There was poetry and even singing. At the end, we toasted to the good health of our children with apple cider.

Afterwards, we played typical baby shower games like guessing the flavor of baby foods or how big our bellies were. There was a pool started for those family members who were trying to guess the weight of our babies. The family member who was closest to correct weight would receive over two hundred dollars. It was all so much fun. I was in tears from laughing so hard.

The dinner was delicious. The pleasant aroma of chicken wings, potatoes, meatballs, fresh rolls and so much more filled the room. I had my share of the food. Admittedly, I felt greedy. After taking down plate after plate, I still had room for dessert. We were served our favorite cake and ice cream.

Once dinner was over, we sat down to receive the many gifts from our family and friends. Rayven and I allowed the men in our lives to open the gifts while we watched in fascination. I was quite emotional thinking about the kindness of all of these special people in our lives. We received everything that we could possibly imagine. Car seats, swings, walkers, diaper bags, clothes, diapers, baby wipes and so much more.

We didn't need anyone to buy all these things for us. Quincy and I both were blessed with decent paying jobs and extensive savings. I was involved in an accident that almost took my life when I was little.

Because of that ordeal, I still received a monthly check. Quinton had inherited a lot of money from his wealthy grandfather. I was also receiving extra income from renting my house. All of this allowed us to live an extremely comfortable life. God was good.

I didn't want to forget this night. It was magical. Fortunately, I didn't have to. Q had hired a photographer and a videographer. He was so attentive. He thought of every detail.

I sat on the couch with my love much later that night. He rubbed my swollen feet. I smiled at him. My heart was so full right now. I didn't deserve him.

"That feels so good." He looked up at me.

"I like when you moan like that."

"Oh, I know you do," I giggled. "Thank you, Quinton."

"You are welcome, babe. I know how tired you get sometimes."

"I so appreciate your foot rub, but I am talking about the whole night. I can't believe that you and Tyler did that for the both of us."

"What did I tell you earlier, baby?"

"That I deserved it."

"Well, okay then. I would like for you to work on believing that. Come here." I swung my legs around and snuggled up close to him. He leaned down to kiss me. He kissed me for a while. It was gentle and sweet. I loved it and I loved him.

"I love you," I whispered.

"I love you more."

"Doubt it! I loved every moment of tonight, but what about the celebration for your label?"

"Don't worry about that. We will celebrate as a family once our little girl is born. Everyone else got to see the place."

"It was very beautiful. God knows that I am so proud of you. I caught a glimpse of a lot, but I would love to be able to see it again. I want to concentrate on it without all of the excitement. Are you going to handle that for me?"

"Yep, of course. What Desiree wants, Desiree gets."

"Do you have to make me sound so spoiled?"

"You are what you are."

"Shut up," I said, playfully hitting him. "You are the one who spoils me all the time."

"That's my purpose. I will give you and little Quinton a personal tour tomorrow."

"Thank you. Where are you going?" I asked, as he stood.

"To run your bubble bath."

"See, there you go."

"Quit complaining."

Rayven's baby boy was supposed to be born a few days before Christmas, but her due date came and went and there was still no sign of his arrival. She remained in good spirits, but deep down, I knew she was becoming understandably frustrated. To keep her distracted, Q, Q Jr and I spent Christmas Eve with her and Tyler.

"It's okay, Sunray, he will come any day now."

"He needs to come now. At this rate, you and I will be having our babies on the same day."

"Wouldn't that be something?"

"Yeah, it would, but no, that's not what I want!"

By the time we left that night, I felt as if she would be okay. I don't know if it was a night of joking while sipping on eggnog and making cookies or the thought of Christmas, but her mood was elevated. Baby boy was not a week late yet. He was coming on God's time or the doctors would just have to evict him.

On Christmas morning, little Quinton had his father and I up as soon as the sun rose. I smiled to myself as we watched him run around opening all those presents that Santa had left for him.

"Next year we will have two kids running around. Well one of them may still be crawling." He gave me a surprised look. "What?"

"You said next year. And we?"

"Did I say something wrong?"

"No, not at all. Music to my ears. I am just making sure that you are in this for the long haul." He squeezed my hand.

"Of course. What did you think? That I was going to have your daughter and leave?"

"No," He laughed. "That's not it. It's just been a rough couple of years and I am still getting use to things being this way between us. I am realizing more and more each day how lucky I am to have you."

"Have some faith in me, Q." I said, touching his face. "Will you have some faith in us? The past means nothing right now."

Quinton and I decided to trade gifts when we realized how much little Quinton was absorbed in his toys. I gave my love this watch that he had been wanting, but would not splurge on and some framed art from his favorite artist to put into his new office. The gift that made him act as if he was his son's age was the two tickets to the upcoming Super Bowl in Dallas.

"You are the most incredible woman that has walked this earth," he said, throwing his arms around me. "I love it," he said, laying this crazy kiss on me. "How did you manage to get these?"

"I know people."

"Wow." The man looked as if he was about to cry.

"You aren't about to cry, are you?" I asked calling him out.

"Be quiet, Des. There is something in my eye."

"Sure. Just remember that I love football just as much as you. The next Super Bowl that you go to, you better take me.'

"Deal, baby. Are you ready? It's your turn."

"Yes."

"Come." He grabbed my hand and pulled me down the hall to the room that I had not been allowed to enter for the last couple of weeks. There was actually a bow on the door. "Close your eyes."

"Okay!" I took a couple of deep breaths in anticipation as I heard the door open.

"Go ahead and open your eyes." When I did, all words got caught in my throat. I grabbed my chest because it felt as if my heart skipped a beat. I covered my mouth and then tears fell.

"Quinton!" I whispered, walking into the nursery. "This so unbelievably beautiful."

It was honestly breathtaking. The room was filled with pink and dark mahogany wood furniture. There was a mural of cartoon characters on one wall and a huge picture of a mother and her daughter on another. The wood floors were cover with two plush pink rugs and the windows were covered with floor length pink curtains. There was a beautiful dark mahogany circle crib with pink and cream linens, a rocking chair, a changing table, a dresser and a night stand with a pink lamp and a bible. There was a huge dollhouse, stuff animals and a large toy chest. It was a little girl dream room.

"I love it! Every inch of this place," I said, throwing my arms around him. I stared at the wall that had her name in big letters on it. Under it were black and white pictures of Quinton, Quinton Jr and I. Under them were the words, "Mommy, Daddy and Brother". We hugged for a long time. "This room is beyond incredible."

"I am glad that you love this place, but there is more."

"I don't need anything more."

"You are getting it. Come on, Des. We will come back to this."

"Okay," I said, not really wanting to leave. "Where are we going?" I asked. I frowned as we headed to the garage door.

"Baby, just close your eyes."

"They are closed." I closed my eyes in anticipation once again.

"Give me your hand."

"What's this?" He had placed something cold in my hand.

"Look." I opened my eyes to find a set of keys in my hand.

"What..." Before I could say anything, Q opened the garage door. I was face to face with a shiny black Range Rover."

"Nooo!"

"Yep!"

"You did not buy this!"

"It's no minivan, but you and the kids will look good in it. I know this is what you have been wanting."

"You can't give me this!"

"I can give you whatever I want. Do you not like it?"

"Quinton, you and I both know that I love it. You know this is what I wanted for a long time."

"I know. And I say what Desiree wants, Desiree gets. Just come and give me a kiss."

"Q!" I pressed my lips against his. "Thank you, baby. I don't know how to even show you how grateful I am."

"That's all I get," he asked, pulling me back to him. He kissed me hard, grabbing my butt.

"You wait until I deliver this little girl. I am going to show you something, Mr. Alexander."

"I can't wait, believe me."

"I know you can't. You so showed me up," I joked. "I just brought you tickets and a watch. Oh and some art."

"You are dead wrong?"

"Am I? How?"

"There is no way that I could find a gift that compares to the one you are giving me. You are giving me my first daughter. You are carrying a life inside of you. That's the greatest gift that a woman can give a man."

"I..." I really didn't have the words. I just felt incredibly blessed at that moment.

"When will you realize how so incredible you are to me?"

"I guess right now."

"Well good. Merry Christmas, Desiree."

December left and still no baby for Rayven. She was becoming more and more frustrated as the days rushed by. It was apparent that those good spirits were diminishing quickly. I was getting worried because this was supposed to be a happy time in her life. I didn't want her to be stressed in anyway. I wanted her to deliver a healthy baby boy.

Everything changed on the first day of the New Year. Our phone rang at 10:00 that night. I had been snuggled up on the loveseat, but when Q answered the phone, I sat up a little straighter. I was on pins and needles every time the phone rang these days

I tried to decipher what was going on by reading his facial expression. He gave me this look to let me know that it was the news that I wanted to hear. I clapped my hands together and thanked God. I was suddenly overcome with emotion. It was relief mixed with joy.

"I can tell by the look on your face that you already know the deal. Tyler said that Rayven's water broke and they are on the way to the hospital. Rayven wants you at the hospital like right now."

"Let's go. It won't take me long. Five minutes."

We quickly got ready. I felt bad for waking up little Quinton, but we didn't have a choice. Neither of us wanted to miss this moment. We dropped him off with his grandmother and headed to the hospital. Thankfully, it was late night because there was no traffic.

By the time, I reached Rayven's bedside, she had received her epidural and was resting peacefully. She opened her eyes when I touched her. She grabbed my hand and squeezed it.

"Desiree, I am so happy you made it. I was not having this baby without you, so thank God that you are here."

"Of course. I wasn't missing this. How are you feeling?"

"I am okay."

"How many centimeters?"

"Five."

I was by my best friend's side for hours. It was six in the morning when her doctor announced that it was time to push. I left Rayven to Tyler, her mother, and Tyler's mother. I joined Quinton and the two future grandpas in the waiting room. I laid my head against Q's shoulder and waited as patiently as I could.

Tyler Jr was born the second day of the New Year at 7:05 in the morning. Tyler's mom came out of the delivery room to make the announcement we had been anxiously waiting for. He was a healthy 8 lbs. 6 ounces baby boy. I closed my eyes and said a prayer of gratitude. Look at God!

We were able to lay eyes on Ray's little blessing around 8:15. We all agreed that he looked just like his father. Ty's mother was in tears as she gushed about how the baby looked like Ty when he was born.

"You did so good," I said hugging Rayven.

"I know," she laughed. "Thank you."

"I am proud of you and he is beautiful."

"Thank you. I agree. He is everything to me. He looks just like his father. Once again, thank you for being here. I wish you could have been by my side the entire time."

"I know me too. I wouldn't have missed of this for the world."

"I know you wouldn't have. You are one of the most loyal people I know." I smiled down at her. "It's almost your turn, Des and I can't wait to be there for you and my God-Daughter." She rubbed my belly.

"I can't wait either, believe me."

"I bet. Quinton, come here."

"What's up beautiful," he said, leaning over to kiss her cheek.

"Take your woman home so that she and your daughter can get some much needed rest. We have kept them up long enough."

"But…."

"Shut up, Desiree," They both said at once

"Fine! I am clearly outnumbered."

"Yes. Des, I am fine. Go home and get some sleep."

"Alright then." I was exhausted. I leaned over and kissed her. "Will you call me if you need anything?"

"Stop worrying and go home!"

"I am going!"

"It's almost your turn," Q said, wrapping his arm around my shoulder as we headed to the car. "It won't be long before we get to meet our little princess."

"I know."

"Are you ready?"

"Ready as I am ever going to be."

Quinton

I was in the studio two weeks later, meeting with a prospective artist when my partner, Monica, burst into the room.

"What's going on, Monica?" I eyed her suspiciously. She had a huge smile on her face.

"Sorry to interrupt. Desiree's mom just called. She says that Des's water has broken and they are on the way to the hospital. They are asking that you meet them there and not to worry about a thing. Mr. Harris is getting Desiree's things from the house."

"Oh, wow." I jumped up, almost tripping over my own feet. "You don't mind if we reschedule?" I asked the young female sitting across from me.

"No, not at all. Go and have your baby. Congratulations."

"Thanks, I owe you."

"Go, Quinton," Monica shoved me a little. "I can handle this."

"Okay, thanks a lot, Monica." I grabbed my coat, my keys and was out the door. I took the stairs instead of the elevator. I didn't have a moment to waste.

Once inside my car, I made my calls. I called my brother and asked him to pick up my first-born. I called my mother to tell her and my father to hurry to the hospital so they could meet their granddaughter. Finally, I called Rayven and Tyler because I knew how desperately Desiree wanted Rayven by her side.

I laughed to myself when she screamed in my ear. "We are on the way!" She slammed the phone down before I could respond.

I was anxious as I maneuvered as safely as possible through the traffic. I needed to get to my woman. I would not forgive myself if I missed a moment of this birth. I was getting nervous and had to ask God to calm me.

I almost took out a family trying to park.

"Sorry, everyone. I'm about to have a baby."

"It's okay. Congratulations, sir."

I ran through the hospital and up several flights of stairs. I was not going to stop until I laid eyes on Desiree's beautiful face. I was on a mission.

She started to cry when she saw me. She reached out for me and I wrapped my arms around her.

"I thought you would never get here."

"I am here for you now, baby."

"Good because I need you right here beside me."

"How are you feeling?"

"Miserable."

"No drugs yet."

"No. I was waiting on you. I wanted you here."

"Well, Desiree let's do this before it's too late." I had heard horror stories.

I didn't like seeing them stick that needle in her back, but I knew it would bring her relief. I did my best to remain calm for her. I was there for her comfort.

Fortunately, once the meds kicked in, Desiree was able to relax. She was able to close her eyes and rest a little. I stood beside her and her mother was not far by. As I stared down at her, I felt overwhelmed with emotion. I couldn't believe that this day had come. The woman that I loved was giving birth to our child.

It wasn't long before Rayven arrived. Des of course opened her eyes as soon as her best friend entered the room. They both cried out and Rayven embraced her.

"I got here as soon as I could. We had to wait until my mother could get there to watch TJ."

"No, I understand. I am glad that you are here now."

"There is nothing in this world that could keep me away from you on this special day."

"Thank you, dear friend. How is little munchkin doing?"

"He is fine. He just sleeps, poop and eat," she laughed. "But I love every moment of it. How are you, my friend?"

"I am fine right now. I got my drugs."

Tyler and I took a walk while the girls had their time together. We smoked cigars out in the parking lot in celebration. We shook our heads in disbelief at both of us falling in love and having babies two weeks apart. Amazing.

Desiree was in labor for about six more hours. Thankfully, she didn't seem to be in too much discomfort. She was visibly restless, but for the most part, remained in good spirits.

At 10:00 that night, the doctor looked at me and said, "Its time, daddy. Are you ready?"

This may have been my second child, but like Des, this was my first pregnancy. The actual delivery of a human being was an experience that was unknown to me. I thought it would be terrifying, but the birth of my daughter was both beautiful and emotional.

I wasn't sure if I was going to cry, but I did. Until this day, the only thing I had cried over was Des. I couldn't stop, though. This woman who I loved more than life itself was giving birth to a child that we had created together. An amazing baby girl.

Mia Elise Alexander was born at 11:15 P.M., weighing 6 lbs. 8 ounces. She had a head full of jet black hair. She had perfect eyes, perfect hands, perfect toes, and a perfect little face. She also had a great set of lungs on her. She screamed Bloody Mary for the first ten mins of her life.

As I smiled in her direction, I realized that this was one of the greatest moments of my life. I couldn't help but get choked up.

"You did so good, Desiree." I leaned down to kiss her. "I am so proud of you. I love you."

"I love you too," she said, squeezing my hands. "Thank you for helping me create this beautiful little girl. Thank you for being by my side the entire night.

"I was where I was supposed to be. Where God intended for me to be. Goodness, she is gorgeous, Desiree."

"I know she is. She is breathtaking."

When Mia stared at her mother, her eyes grew wide. It appeared to be love at first sight. It was a picture perfect moment.

Desiree looked over at me. As we stared at one another, so many emotions flowed between us. It was as if she was assuring me that they were my future.

"Come here, Q. she said, reaching for my hand. I took it her hand as she pulled me close to her. I sat on the bed beside her. "Look, Mia. Let me formally introduce you. This is your daddy."

When I held my daughter in my arms, I realized how much of a blessing she was. Mia represented love. She helped bring Desiree and I together. For that, I would be eternally grateful.

When she looked up at me, I felt like my life was complete. I couldn't ask for anything more. In that moment, I felt as if I had it all. She was what I prayed for. She was a mini-version of her mother.

This was my family. I promised to myself and God at that moment, that I would never let go of any of them. I would always cherish my love and my two children. I vowed to take care of them until my final days on this earth. From now on, I would live for them.

32

Devoted

"Strength and dignity are her clothing, and she laughs at the time to come. She opens her mouth with wisdom, and the teaching of kindness is on her tongue. She looks well to the ways of her household and does not eat the bread of idleness. Her children rise up and call her blessed; her husband also, and he praises her: "Many women have done excellently, but you surpass them all."
Proverbs 31:25-30

Desiree

Our little baby girl was a dream come true. If you had of asked me a year ago, I would have told you that I was not sure if I was ready to bring another life into this world, let alone raise one. As soon as Mia smiled up at me, I knew I was wrong. She was exactly what I needed and all that I ever wanted.

I was full of bias, but I truly thought she was the most beautiful baby that I had ever seen. Yes, it was true, she did look a great deal like me, but the more I stared at her, the more I saw Quinton in her. Mia had her father's nose, his ears and complexion.

I could tell that she was already a daddy's girl. A sense of calmness came over her every time he held her in his arms. She would stare back at him with awe in her eyes. He would stare back at her with the same amazement. I knew Quinton didn't think I paid attention to those moments, but I would often stand back and take it all in. I cherished it.

They would have a relationship that I would be envious of. An important one. Every little girl needed her father. I wanted her and my future kids to be raised in an environment where both parents were present. Both parents needed to show guidance and love to their children so they could survive in this cold and crazy world.

Q didn't just treat Mia very well; he was good to me in the months after my her birth. Eventually the plan was for me to return to work, but every day he would tell me that I didn't have to work if I didn't want to. He supported me. He understood me.

He would work long hours in the studio every day, but would still come home and take the baby from me. He allowed me to have some time for myself. I would take long baths, sit out on the porch, or write in my journal. During those moments of solitude, I would attempt to count my blessings and thank God for them.

I was blessed to have a man who loved me this hard. He still spoiled me. He couldn't help himself. He would come home with gifts almost twice a week. Flowers, chocolates, jewelry, or books. I loved when he would give me a card professing his love for me.

I wasn't as expressive towards him, but I loved Quinton so much. I knew that I didn't want be with another man. If he asked me to marry him today, I would say yes without hesitation. I would give anything to be his wife and prayed often that he felt the same way.

We were a family. Quinton, Quinton Jr and Mia were my life. As far as I was concerned, I had two children. I felt more and more like Quinton's mother each day. I knew he looked up to me in that sense because he had inquired about me being his new mother on countless occasions. He wanted to call me mommy, but I didn't know how to bring it up to his father.

I had a feeling that Quinton hoped that India would get her life together and return to her son's life. I couldn't really blame him. Neither of us knew what the future held.

If Quinton wanted me to be his son's mother, all he had to do was ask because I was willing. I loved that little boy. I wanted him to always be a part of my life. I didn't have to vocalize it. In my heart, he was my son.

That little boy loved his sister. Thankfully, he wasn't jealous about the attention we gave Mia. He looked at her with excitement in his eyes. And as most big brothers were, he was very protective of her. He was my little helper. He was special.

"Dessie." His voice interrupted my thoughts. I was preparing my tub for a nice long bubble bath. "Mia is asleep."

"Thanks for telling me, baby." I followed him into the nursery. She was sleeping peacefully. My precious angel. My gift from God.

"Can I stay in here while she sleeps?"

"Do you promise not to wake her?" I knew that he would not.

"Yes, I promise. I am sleepy. I am going to take a nap too," he said, lying on the floor.

"Okay, baby." I grabbed a pillow and them covered him in his favorite blanket. "I am going to take a bath. If you need me, I want you to come and get me, okay? Can you do that for me?"

"Yes. I promise. I love you."

"I love you too."

The rose scented bubbles felt like heaven against my skin. These baths were my therapy. It was one of the only times when I was able to focus on myself. I sank down as far as I could go. I leaned back and closed my eyes. I open them occasionally to check on the kids on the baby monitor. They were both fast asleep.

It didn't take long for my mind to drift to Q. I wished that he was here with me. I could use one of his sensual kisses or one of his seductive massages. The thought of feeling that hard body of his against mine started to get me hot and bothered. My breath quickened.

"Where are you, my love?' I said aloud.

The day Q and I were finally able to make love again did not disappoint. It was passion that I had never experienced before. It was addictive. We reached for each other every night. We found creative ways to be together when the kids were sleeping. The shower, the Jacuzzi, in the garage, under the stars. We did what we had to do.

Quinton's arrival interrupted my daydreams.

"Hey, beautiful."

"Hey, babe. You are home early?"

"I know. I wanted to see you." He leaned down and gave me a kiss. It was a sweet lingering kiss so I had my eyes closed. I jumped when his hands slid between my thighs to caress my sweet spot. My whole body reacted. "I have wanted to touch you here all day." He whispered while kissing my ear.

"Ohh," I was breathless.

After he teased me a while longer, he stood and told me that he was going to shower. I was tempted to sit in that bathtub and watch him, but instead I got out and toweled myself off. I grabbed my robe and headed to the nursery. I could see Mia twisting and turning a little in the baby monitor.

I scooped her up in my arms and sat down in the rocking chair. She opened her eyes and smiled up at me for a moment, but quickly closed them. I smiled down at her as I rocked her back to sleep. Once she was sleeping soundly, I laid her back in her crib. I then picked up her brother and carried him to his bedroom.

I walked out little Quinton's room and slammed right into Q. He stood before with just a towel around his waist. He smelled divine.

"What are you doing?" I asked.

"I came to get you. I have something to show you." He lifted me up in his arms. He carried me to into the bedroom, kicking the door shut behind him. He laid me gently on the bed.

"What is it that you are showing me?"

"How much I love you. Now don't say another word and let me handle things a little while." He undid my robe and began to slide his hand feverishly over my body. My body was aching to be loved by him and reacted to every caress.

He kissed my thigh. I knew what was up. I grabbed a pillow and buried my face in it as he started to send me over the edge. What he was doing to me was an acquired skill. It was fine art.

Afterwards, I reached for him. I wanted to return the favor, but he would not let me. My body remained pinned underneath his.

"Quinton…"

"Why are you talking?" My words were muffled with his mouth on mines. His lips didn't leave mine as he began to love me slowly. It left me delirious.

"Wow," was all I could say. I clung to his waist, laying my head against his chest.

"I really do love you, Desiree Harris. You are everything to me." A girl couldn't hear those words too often.

Quinton

I was convinced that Desiree was the most beautiful woman I had ever seen. I was sitting on the deck, pretending to do some paperwork while she ran around with little Quinton. Mia sat in her swing beside me, laughing while taking turns eyeing her mother, brother and I.

I really did have work to do, but I could not take my eyes off of the woman. I took in every move that she made. She looked incredible in little white shorts and a pink tank top. Six months ago, she was still pregnant, but today she looked as if she had never given birth in her life. Her body had snapped back quickly. I would have loved her just as much if it hadn't.

I loved this woman for who she was. She was brilliant with a sharp tongue, a full personality and a huge heart. Still, I had to admit she was drop dead gorgeous. Exotic looking. I watched men on daily basis break their necks to get a glimpse of her. I was so lucky.

I was lucky that she had chosen me. That she loved me. That she was the mother of my little girl. That she loved my son.

I loved watching her with Mia. They had an incredible bond. Mia started at her mother with unprecedented admiration. Even she recognized the beauty of Desiree. And one day soon, she was going to grow up looking just like her. I was going to need a gun because I was going to have to keep the little boys away from my princess.

Of course Des would stare at our daughter with so much love. Des just exuded love these days. I knew it wasn't just about me, but since the day Mia was born, our relationship was even better. She loved hard and that made me love her even more. With her, I felt as if I didn't have anything to worry about. She completed my life.

She was my future. My family. She was my backbone. She supported me. She nurtured me.

Desiree turned, waved and blew me a kiss while my son ran across the yard to get a ball. I blew her a kiss back wishing I could get a real one. I wanted to kiss her so bad that I could taste her lips.

I sat back in my char, closed my eyes and let my mind wander. I imagined that Des and I were alone in front of a fire place. I imagined exploring the softness of her skin, the fullness of her breast and the endless curves on her body. I could feel her breath against my skin. I could inhale her intoxicating scent and taste the sweetness of her lips.

I imagined her hands on my back. Her body reacting to mine. Her whispering my name. Her surrendering to me. I imagined loving her for hours.

The dream was so real that I had to open my eyes. I had to get myself together. I stood and walked into the house. I grabbed a bottle of water and downed it to calm myself.

She always did this me. All it took was one look or the sound of her voice. She had unbelievable power over me. As long as she had that power over me, I would never stop loving her. I never wanted to love another woman. She offered a kind of love that I would be a fool to give up.

I walked back outside to find Des sitting down holding the baby. "Everything okay?"

"Uh huh. She is just fussing trying to get someone's attention. I think she is hungry. Here," she said, handing me my daughter. "Why don't you two bond while I get her a bottle?"

"Okay. Hey, baby girl." I tickled her and she giggled. When Des returned, she had a bottle in one hand and the phone in another. I frowned because the house phone rarely rung.

"Telephone for you, Q. You take this call and give me Mia."

"Okay." She gave me a funny look when I reached for the phone. "What? Who is this, Desiree?"

"Just answer the phone, Quinton."

"Alright. Hello."

"Hello, Quinton."

"India?"

"Yes, its me."

"Wow. What do I owe this call to?" I didn't waste any time. I didn't expect to hear from her again. I quickly realized that I was being rude. "No, I am sorry. How are you, India?"

"I'm as good as I am going to be. You weren't being rude, let's get straight to it. Quinton, I want to see my son. One more time." I was surprised by her request, but relived. Despite all the negativity that we had been through, I would never deprive my son of anytime he could spend with his mother. I wanted that more than anything for him, especially with her being sick.

She came over that Saturday. She looked fine, but the look in her eyes told me otherwise. Ironically, she was more beautiful than she ever been. No more bright hair, long nails or revealing clothes. She looked carefree and vibrant in a yellow summer dress. Her hair was curled and her face was bare, with the exception of lip gloss.

Quinton ran to his mother when he saw her walk across the yard. They both cried in each other arms. I looked away. Seeing them together brought me sadness. Des sensing how I was feeling reached for my hand. I looked at her and a sense of calmness came over me.

"Why?" I whispered.

"I don't know, sweetheart. Its life. Life isn't always fair."

"Well, life sucks right now."

"No, it doesn't. Quinton Jr is blessed to have you. With your love, he will make it."

"I know. You are right, of course." I sighed.

"We'll be fine." When she said we, she was assuring me that she would be there for me as I struggled through this. The woman had incredible inner strength and I often found myself depending on it.

It was hard to watch a mother walk away from her son. My son sat on his bike, sadly staring at India's back. India looked as if she wanted to break down, but she attempted to hold it together as she walked towards me and Desiree. There was a lump in my throat. I had a feeling that this was the last time that we would see her. She had come to say her final goodbyes.

She stood before me and attempted to smile. It was weak.

"I wanted to thank you both for allowing me to see my son."

"No need to thank us, India. That's your son and it's your right."

"I know, but we all know I haven't been the best mother to him. I don't deserve any privileges."

"All that matters is that Quinton loves you, India. He has a forgiving spirit. No grudges."

"And I love him. He was all that I had. It breaks my heart when I look at him," she whispered. Tears spilled down her cheek.

"Don't, India, please don't." I wrapped my arms around her and let her cry into my shoulder. "Everything is going to be okay." I could feel Desiree's presence behind me. Knowing she was there gave me the strength I didn't need to break down as well.

"It's okay. I have to go," she whispered, pulling away. "Thank you, Quinton. You have always been a wonderful father to our son. As long as he has you, I know that he will be fine."

"I will make you proud, India."

"I am already proud. I love you, Quinton." She kissed my cheek.

"I love you too," I said, kissing her forehead. What could I say? She would always be the mother of my first child.

"Thanks. Goodbye. Take care."

"You take care, India."

She smiled and turned to walk away. She stopped and walked behind me to Desiree. She whispered something in her ear.

I got nervous. I thought her old ways would resurface, but I learned quickly that was not the case. Instead, Desiree grabbed India's hand and they walked away. Des turned and smiled at me. That eased my heart. I wasn't going to worry.

Desiree

I didn't know how to feel when India whispered that she wanted to talk to me. My heart started to beat a little faster and my legs grew heavy as I led her to her car. I couldn't imagine what she had to say to me. I knew Quinton was uneasy as well, so I forced a smile and tried my best to remain cool. Inside, I was a jittery mess.

"Don't worry, I won't keep you."

"Take as long as you need."

"Look, I am going to honest with you. I don't know how much longer I am going to be here. My days are very numbered. My health is failing." I was not quite sure that I was strong enough to listen to this. How was I supposed to react to someone who was telling me that they were going to die soon? I could feel the tears.

"No, I am the one who needs to cry. I am the weak one. I need you to be strong, Desiree."

"India, I am trying, but I don't know if I can."

"Do more than try. You have to be the strong one. Do you love that man? My son's father."

"He is my heart."

"And do you love my son?"

"So much, India. I love him so much."

"Then can you promise me something?"

"What's that?"

She grabbed my shoulder and stared me straight in the eyes. "Since I can't be there for him, will you?"

"Yes!" I whispered.

"I know he loves you and I want you to always love him back. I know that he will be okay if he has you. If you could be his mother now, he will make it."

"I could not replace you."

"No, but you can be his mother. I need for you to be his mother. Please satisfy my heart. Let me die in peace."

"Yes." How could I say no? How could I dishonor someone's dying wish? I loved her son as if he was my own child. I didn't love him any less than I loved Mia.

"And take care of his father. I know if Quinton is okay, his son will be. I don't think Quinton knows how to be happy without you."

"I don't plan on going anywhere."

"Good because Desiree, if you remain in their lives, then I have nothing to worry about." She looked down and didn't say anything for a moment. "You are their future."

"They are mine's."

"Then, I am happy. I am satisfied. I am at peace."

"You have nothing to worry about. I will honor you. Your life."

"Thank you, Desiree." She grabbed me and hugged me tightly.

"Thank you for today, India."

"I owe you so much."

"No. You owe me nothing."

"You are going to be the most important woman in my son's life. I owe you everything."

Little did I know that those would be the last words shared between us. India died three weeks later. She had chosen not to tell us that her HIV had turned into full blown AIDS. She didn't fight her battle long. India chose not to fight and surrendered to her fate.

We laid her to rest one humid day in July. It was sunny and very breezy. I wasn't quite sure what everything symbolized, but secretly, I took it to mean that everything would be okay.

I raised my face to the sky as we stood at India's graveside. I shielded my eyes from the sun. A breeze slapped me across my cheek. I felt in that moment that India was smiling down on all of us. I closed my eyes and listened to the wind. I imagined her whispering that we would all be fine and that God was with us.

I never forgot my promise to India in the weeks after her death. I knew if I didn't remain strong, Quinton wouldn't. If he was not okay, then his son wasn't going to be. Little Quinton needed his father more than anything these days.

Quinton remained very sad for weeks. I think he somehow felt as if he failed his son. It was as if he couldn't grasp that none of this was his fault. He hadn't come to terms with fate.

I remained patient. Even when Q started to distance himself, I understood what he was feeling. I found the strength to back off when I just wanted to scream at him. I tried to put myself in his shoes. All I could do was support and love him. I took care of him as I promised I would.

It was amazing to see how strong little Quinton was. He often seemed stronger than his father. At first I thought he would not fully understand what was going on. He proved me wrong.

"Mommy was sick and now she is with God," he whispered to me one day. I knew at that moment how special he was. I just picked him up and held him.

Still, there were days that I wanted to cry. I was saddened that India would not be there to watch her beautiful little boy grow up. I was afraid that he was so young that he would not remember her. Then I would remember that I had promised to be a mother to him no matter what and that I would do everything to honor her memory. I would remind little Quinton of his mother.

Sometimes when I was feeling vulnerable, I would sneak into the bathroom. I would sit on the edge of the tub and cry quietly. I cried alone because I didn't want to appear broken or weak. I had to be superwoman to everyone around me.

Afterwards, I would wash my face and head back out without any trace of my tears. I had to be strong for my man. I had to show him that when he was down, I would be there to pull him back up. I was going to help him get through this.

Quinton

I snapped out of my pity party one day when my mother called me. She was coming to pick up the kids because she felt that Desiree deserved a break.

"You need to go home and take care of your woman because you have been neglecting her." Without hesitation, I agreed. I hoped in my car and headed home to my woman.

I felt like an idiot when I laid eyes on Des. She was curled in a ball on the bed. She had done so much over the last couple of weeks, that she was physically worn out. She had been there for me, but admittedly, I had not been there for her. I had to change that today.

It was time to move on with my life. I had grieved long enough. I had everything that I needed and more right in front of me. With the people I loved the most surrounding me, I would be fine. God was not going to forsake me.

"Baby," I whispered. I leaned down to kiss my sleeping beauty.

"Yes?" Her eyes flew open and she sat up quickly. "I am up."

"No, don't sit up. I am so sorry, my love."

"What for? Is everything okay, Q? Did something else happen."

"Des, everything is fine." I was suddenly consumed with guilt. "I haven't been there for you, baby. And I regret that. Will you forgive me for how I have been treating you?"

"It's okay, Q. I understand that you were sad."

"No," I said, kissing her again. 'Stop making it all about me. You have done enough. I appreciate everything, but enough is enough. It's time that I start being there for you now."

"You have..."

"No, I haven't. That's going to change right now. Look at you. You looked exhausted. I am going to let you sleep a little longer and then I am going to take you out to dinner."

"I can cook us something."

"Baby, will you please stop. Listen, I don't want you to cook anything." I stared at her for a second. She appeared to be in a daze. "Stop pretending that everything is okay and that I haven't been treating you badly. You haven't grieved, have you? You can be sad too, Desiree."

"I..."

"Stop." I sat down and pulled her to me. "Cry. Let it out."

"No, "she said, shaking her head vigorously.

"I promise that you will feel better in the end."

She released everything. The sadness, the disappointment, the frustration and the exhaustion. She cried like a baby in my arms. And it felt good to be there for her. I had to stop letting her be the stronger one. It was time for me to step up and be the man that she needed me to be. The man God intended for me to be.

Afterwards, she was able to pull away and smile up at me

"I am ready to get out of here.'

I took Desiree to Century 21, her favorite restaurant. I told her to order whatever her heart desired. I ordered the best wine. I was attentive to my woman. My heart didn't feel as heavy as it had been. I could feel the stress disappearing as I stared into her eyes. I loved seeing her happy. I loved her playfulness.

She smiled and it felt as if my heart skipped a beat. She laughed and it was like music to my ears. She grabbed my hand and every hair on my skin stood at attention. Overcome with emotion, I grabbed her in the parking lot once we reached the car. I kissed her for as long as she let me.

"I have been so stupid, baby. I really do miss you."

"I miss you too, babe." She wrapped her arms completely around me and buried her face in my neck.

I took her home and I made love to her. I vowed that I would never deprive her in the way I had for the last few weeks. I would never let her go. I would not stop giving her everything that I had.

As we lay in bed, she wrapped her arms around my waist and whispered. "I need to know whether or not you are going to be okay, Quinton."

"Baby, I assure you that I am fine." I kissed her shoulder.

"No. I want for you to be completely honest with me. Please don't pretend that you aren't sad because you are worried about me. Tell me how you feel."

I could not avoid talking about my feeling with her. If I couldn't talk to Desiree, then I couldn't talk to anyone. I knew it was not healthy to keep everything bottled up. I took a deep breath.

"I have come to terms with India's death. Like you said, it's a sad unfortunate part of life. I rather her soul be at rest and not conflicted. It's just that my son will never know his mother."

"You can teach your son all about his mother, Quinton. He will never have to let go of her memory."

"And he won't. I won't let him. I just want to know that my son is going to be okay."

"He adores you. All you have to do is continue loving him and he will be just fine."

"I want him to experience a mother's love, though."

"I know." I could tell she had something on her mind. She got this look on her face. "Quinton, I made a promise to India."

"And what was that?"

"As long as we exist together, I would take care of both of you."

"What are you saying?"

"I promised her that I would watch out for you, Q. That means that I will support you, provide what you need me to and I will love you. I promised her I would look out for little Quinton as well."

"Really?" I was surprised that they had that conversation.

"As long as you keep me in your life."

"I don't plan on letting you go."

"Then everything will be okay. With God in our lives…"

"Amen, baby. You do realize that the longer you are in our lives, that Quinton is going to start looking up to you."

"That's fine. Let him."

"As a mother, Desiree?"

"I want him too."

"Are you sure?"

"Yes."

"I mean he is only five. He is just starting kindergarten next month. You realize that you would be essentially raising my son."

Did Desiree know what she was saying? Did she understand the commitment that she was making to me? To my son? If she meant it then God had answered all my prayers. A woman that I could love for an eternity. A mother for my son.

"I love him." She touched my face. "I feel like he's my son too."

My heart somersaulted. I felt if I could cry. I shook my head, thanking God for what he just provided me. Relief.

"He loves you," I said, kissing the palm of her hand.

"Good, then you are allowing me to honor my promise to India. You two can't go wrong with me in your corner."

"You don't know much this means to me. It means everything." She kissed my forehead. I clung to her.

"Are you in my corner?"

"Baby, I will be in all of your corners. I vow to protect you for the rest of my life."

"Okay." She looked down as she blushed. She then smiled at me. "I love you, Quinton Alexander."

"I love you."

I was so in love with this woman that I was scared. As I watched Desiree sleep, I thought about taking this relationship even further. It was my goal to make her my wife soon. I wanted to give her the same name as me and our kids. I wanted to make sure she would always be in our lives. God only knew how much we needed her.

33

Unity

"Though one may be overpowered, two can defend themselves. A cord of three strands is not quickly broken." *Ecclesiastes 4:12*

Desiree

"So what's up with you and Quinton?"

One weekend before Thanksgiving, I was at dinner with my sister, Jade, and Rayven. We were having a ladies night out. Rayven and I left the kids at home with their fathers. Jade didn't have kids yet, but her husband, Devin was still hanging with our loves. They were babysitting, but still huddled around Tyler's big screen watching the big game.

This dinner was much needed. Normally, I was out with the kids or Quinton. I loved being a mom, but every now and then, it was good to get away and have some adult time. Every mother needed some balance in her life and I was no different.

"What do you mean?" I asked, taking a sip of my Cranberry and Vodka. The alcoholic beverages came few and far in between. It tasted extra smooth tonight. It had been a while so I had to be careful. I was not trying to have a hangover in the morning. Plus I was the designated driver.

"When are the two of you going to take that next step in your relationship?' I looked at my sister with narrowed eyes. I knew what she was hinting at. I was not quite sure if I was in the mood for the conversation to go in that direction.

"What do you mean by what's the next step?" I played dumb.

"When's the wedding, little sister?" Oh here we go. These conversations always made me anxious.

"Wow." I laughed, nervously. I often found myself fantasizing about becoming Quinton's wife. I wanted to be Mrs. Alexander more than anything. "There's no wedding in the works, big sister."

"Oh, I am sure there will be. I am convinced that you two are destined to be together. This was a relationship handpicked by God."

"I agree." I was starting to feel uncomfortable. I loved Q more than anything. I knew he loved me just as much. I wasn't sure he wanted to jump the broom this early in our relationship, though.

"You two already have a beautiful family together."

"This is true, but it's still no reason to rush things along, though. We are both very committed to each other, but our relationship is relatively new. We have only been together about a year and a half."

"Technically, you two have been together even longer," Rayven spoke up. I looked over at her and shook my head.

"No we haven't."

"You have been together since the day that man kissed you."

"Intimately."

"He had your heart, Des and you have had his since college."

"I didn't know about that?" I responded, feeling guilt.

"Stop feeling guilty. You are right, you didn't know. Quinton is a very happy man now and that's all that matters."

"I hope so."

"You sister is just saying that marriage is inevitable for you two. We can't imagine seeing either of you with anyone else. I don't think Quinton would allow another man to come near you," she laughed.

'What about you and Tyler?" I was trying to move on from the topic of Quinton and I. I was feeling anxious. "You two have been together even longer."

"This isn't about Tyler and I." She took a sip of water. Her face had turned red. I knew then that my best friend had at least thought about marriage with Tyler. "Quit trying to change the subject."

"I didn't completely change it," I said, shrugging. "Look, I doubt that Quinton is even ready for marriage."

"Quinton is probably more ready for marriage than you are." I laughed. I doubted that. Every little girl had dreamed of her husband and her wedding day. In my mind, my wedding was planned. "Do you want it, Des?"

"I don't know." I quickly downed my drink. Rayven and Jade were killing me with these questions. I was beyond uncomfortable.

"Stop that." Jade moved the glass away from me. "You don't want to be stumbling in the house tonight."

"Oh please, Jade. I do think that I can handle one drink."

"I don't know. When was the last time you drank?"

"It's been too long." I tried to flag the waiter down to order another drink, but again, Jade was trying to assert her authority. This time, she grabbed my hand. "I am grown, Jade," I said, snatching my hand away from her.

"I am looking out for you. I don't care how grown you are."

"Fine," I said rolling my eyes.

"Answer the question, Des. Do you want marriage?" Rayven insisted on getting an answer from me.

"Why are we talking about this?" I could no longer hide my agitation. I was trying to have a good time tonight.

"You are my best friend. I just want you to be honest with me."

'Look, I am with this incredible man who I know loves and adores me. I have a five year old son and a eleven month baby girl. Right now, I am happy with my life. I am good with the life God has given me. Quinton and I are great right now. We don't have to get married anytime soon."

"Desiree, I love you, but I am calling bullshit."

"Wow," I laughed. "Look, yes, I would love to marry Quinton. There isn't a day that doesn't go by where I don't fantasize about him asking me to be his wife."

"Thank you for being honest. You should feel better now."

"There's no wedding anytime soon, so don't hold your breath."

"It's coming."

"How can you say that? Do you know something?"

"No, I don't know what Quinton's plans are. I do know that God put you two together. God intends for a man to seek a wife. And knowing the way Quinton loves you and has always loved you, I am pretty confident in saying he has found his wife."

I didn't pull into the driveway until after 2:00 that night. The girls and I had moved from the restaurant to a quiet lounge downtown. We spent the rest of the night sipping on Martinis and fending off brothers with tired lines. We laughed about everything. It was a good night, but I was glad to get home to my little family.

As expected, everyone was asleep. I laughed because they were all in the living room with the TV blaring loudly. The kids were asleep on a blanket on the floor. Quinton was asleep on the couch, clinging to a pillow.

"It's obvious who the mother around here is."

I walked to my bedroom, threw my purse into a chair and kicked off my heels. I then headed back to the living room and picked up my baby girl. I took off her clothes because she was warm and then I changed her diaper. I was able to do it all without waking her.

"I love you, baby girl." I leaned down to kiss her.

I had to wake up Quinton Jr. I made him change into his pajamas and brush his teeth before climbing into bed. He reached up to me for a hug and kiss.

"I love you, mommy."

"I love you too, sweetheart." To hear those words from him always brought an incomparable joy to my heart. Nothing in this world compared to being a mother. I was so grateful that God bestowed that honor upon me.

I took a shower before waking Quinton. It was quick, warm and much needed. I toweled off and rubbed on the Brazilian nut oil which I knew he adored. I slid into a pink tank and pink undies. I figured that I would give him an eyeful when he opened his eyes.

"Is this pillow supposed to be me?"

I smiled as I stood over him. He looked so peaceful and childlike, clinging tightly to that pillow. For a moment, I considered not waking him, but selfishly decided against it. Snuggling up to him was all that I desired to do right now. I wanted him to come to bed.

"My love." I rubbed his cheek. He started to stir. "Come to bed with me." His eyes opened and he smiled.

"Where have you been, girl?"

"Well, hello to you too," I whispered.

"It's about time. This pillow is not doing it for me," he said, throwing it aside. "Come here." He pulled me down on top of him.

"Is that better," I teased.

"Yes," he said, kissing my shoulder. "You smell good."

"Thank you. Why were all you asleep in the living room?"

"We were trying to wait on you, but you took too long."

"I didn't take that long. Yall just couldn't hang."

"You are right. These kids exhausted me." Imagine how I feel on a daily basis, I thought. I didn't say anything, though. Quinton was a wonderful father. "Did you have fun?"

"I did. We had a great time. I am glad to be home." I pulled away from him and stood. I reached my hand out to him, but he didn't take it. He stood and scooped me in his arms.

"Always trying to be my prince charming," I laughed, laying my head against his shoulder.

"You better believe it."

He took me to the bedroom and laid me on the bed. I started yanking on his clothes until he stood before me in his boxers. We kissed for a while, but didn't take things further. We were both exhausted. Instead, we climbed into bed together and held one another.

Quinton

I wasn't going to admit it to her, but I had missed her tonight. It was cool to spend time with the homies, but tonight, I rather had been with my woman. She deserved to go out, though. She was a good mother and I had to honor her by allowing her to spend time with her girls.

Desiree and I had been dating about a year and a half and I was still passionate about her. She still made my heart skip a beat. She was still the first thing on my mind every morning and the last thing on my mind every night.

I laid there and watched her until she fell asleep as I often did. I thought about how much I loved her. I thought about how lucky I was to have her in my life. I thanked the Lord above for her.

I wanted to take the next step. I wanted to marry this woman. I was ready, but was she?

I had been conflicting over whether or not to get down on one knee and ask her to be my wife for months now. I wasn't sure if she wanted that or was even ready for that. I knew how much she loved me, but did she want to share my name? I didn't have the courage to ask her how she felt about marriage, although I agonized over it daily. I had no idea how to approach it.

I needed help. I needed to talk to some key people. My brother Mike, my mother and probably Rayven. I needed reassurance. I needed Mike to tell me that I wasn't crazy or rushing things. I wanted my mother to assure me that I was making the right decision. I hoped that Rayven could tell me that Des would say yes.

I decided to get my answers a couple days later on Thanksgiving day.. We invited our families over for dinner, including Tyler, Rayven and little TJ. I saw no point in wasting time. My mind wasn't going to be at ease until Desiree said yes.

I was quickly able to pull Mike aside.

"What's up, little brother."

'I have something serious that I want to discuss with you."

"Yeah, I figured that. You look like you have a lot on your mind. What's wrong?"

"I have been thinking about asking Desiree to marry me." I looked around nervously because I didn't want anyone to hear me.

"Great. You think that you're ready as a man to take a wife?"

"I know that I am ready, Mike. I want nothing more."

"What is there to think about? Ask that beautiful woman, who has been nothing been but good to you and your son, to be your wife." I nodded in agreement.

"You don't think that I am rushing into things."

"Are you kidding me? I know people who have been together for three months and have gotten married. If you love someone and you know that's who you want to spend your eternity with, you put faith in God and you go for it. You don't worry about time."

"You are right."

"You have loved this woman since college. How much more time do you really need? I doubt there is a more perfect woman for you. No other woman is going to make you this happy."

"I don't want another woman." I looked over at Desiree. She was kneeling before my son. They seem to be having a serious conversation. "Quinton adores her."

"Like his father. You have a beautiful family. Go for it."

I did feel better after talking to my brother. I no longer felt as if I was rushing into things. Still, I wanted that reassurance from mother. Besides Desiree, there was no one's opinion that I respected more. She was a brilliant woman.

"Ma, can we talk," I said, dropping down into the seat beside her. "I want to ask Desiree to marry me." I didn't want to beat around the bush.

"Oh!" She was loud.

"Come on mother, can you be a little discrete. Well, I guess I should say that I am thinking about asking her."

"Think about what? God says that a man should find a wife."

"It sounds as if you are a fan of the idea."

"That woman is the best thing that has ever happened to you."

"She is."

"She's good to you. She's a brilliant mother. She loves Quinton as if she gave birth to him. It's difficult to find a woman with that kind of compassion these days."

"It's one of the many reasons that I love her."

"She makes you happy, baby." I could see tears in my mother eyes. 'No longer do I see the sadness in your eyes. I see joy. Why would you search for that anywhere else when you have found it?"

"I am not going to search elsewhere. She is my soulmate."

"And this family adores her." My mother squeezed my hand. "I want her as a part of this family. Make her my daughter-in-law."

"Okay, mother." I hugged her. "Don't cry."

"I can't help it. If you lose this woman, I will kill you." I laughed.

"Don't worry, mother. Living without her is not an option."

Rayven was the difficult one to get alone. It felt as if of all days, she and Des were glued to one another's hips. If I pulled her to the side for too long, Desiree would suspect something. I didn't know how to go about things and it was making me frustrated.

Finally Rayven walked out of the room and I attempted to follow her inconspicuously.

"Rayven, can I get a word with you?"

"Sure, what's up?"

"Not for too long, though. I don't want Desi to get suspicious."

"Okay." She frowned at me. "What's going on, Q? Is there something wrong?"

"No. I want to ask Desiree to marry me."

"Oh my goodness, Q! Really!" I was relieved to see the excitement on her face.

"Not too loud, Ray. You know Des is nosey," I joked.

"I am sorry. I am just so overjoyed. This is wonderful."

"Is it?"

"Yes!"

"I love her and I want to marry her tomorrow, but…"

"No buts. Why are you saying but!"

"I need to know that this is what she wants. I need to know that she is ready."

"Desiree loves you with all her heart, Quinton." I could see tears forming in her eyes as well. What was going on, I thought. "She is ready. Ask her and I guarantee you will get the answer that you want to hear. She will make you happy, don't worry."

I cornered Des in the kitchen hours later. I wanted to feel her out myself. I pulled her to me.

"What are you doing?" She smiled up at me.

"When are we going to make another baby?"

"Can Mia walk first," she laughed. "She's almost there."

"I just thought I would ask. You know I want a big family."

"We'll have another one." That's what I wanted to hear.

A couple days later, I found the nerve to approach Desiree's parents. Call me old-fashioned, but I wanted their blessing. I was on the verge of having a panic attack, but when Des's mother cried into my shoulder and her father shook my hand vigorously with tears in his own eyes, I knew they accepted me taking their daughter's hand in marriage.

I was finally ready. I got all the reassurance that I needed. I knew that I was making the best decision for me and my kids. This woman was meant to be my wife.

"Now on to the hard part." I just hoped Des felt the same way.

My father was good friends with a Parisian jewelry designer named Sophia Broussard. Rayven and I met with Sophia at her Jewelry store a couple days later. I wanted something breathtakingly rare. That's how I saw my love.

"Four carets and I want a pink diamond." Both Sophia and Rayven looked at me with wide eyes. "I love her and want her ring to be different. She is worth every penny."

"Give me 1000 dollars and I will design the most beautiful ring that you have ever seen."

"Are you sure?" I could not believe what I was hearing. I expected to pay much more.

"The difference will be my wedding gift to you."

"You are an angel from above, Sophia."

Everything was falling into place. The ring was scheduled to arrive in exactly a month. It would arrive after Christmas, but before the New Year. I had one month to plan an unforgettable night for the love of my life.

Desiree

Quinton was good with surprises. I was not quite sure what he was up to, but one Saturday in December, he informed me that he had many surprises coming my way. I'm not sure what that could have possibly been, considering he had been very good to me during Christmas. He said that he would be gone all day, but he would be picking me up at 6:30 sharp. He told me to get dolled up and to look as beautiful as I possibly could.

I really did not know what to think. I quickly came to the conclusion that we were going somewhere pretty special. I assumed maybe we were celebrating something.

I begged him to tell me where we were going. He wouldn't. He kissed me and told me not to worry about it. He took the kids so that I was left alone. He demanded that I enjoy the rare day to myself.

I had just showered and was enjoying a cup of coffee and a bagel when the doorbell rang. I wasn't expecting anyone, I thought. I quickly found my robe and headed to the door. I was surprised to open the door to find an older gentlemen wearing a tux and holding a vase of pink lilies.

"Oh wow! Hello."

"Ms. Harris?"

"Yes. I am her."

"These are for you, my lady."

"Why, thank you sir." I smelled the flowers as I took them in my hands. They were lovely.

"I have been instructed to stand here as you read the note that accompanied the flowers."

"Really?" What was Quinton up to? At least I hoped these were from Quinton. I had not heard from my stalker since I had move in here, but they were still out there. I am sure they knew where I was. I held my breath as I opened the envelope.

Hey Baby,

I hope you knew that these flowers were from me. I thought they were beautiful. Anything beautiful reminds me of you. Say hi to Garrison. Don't worry; he is a family friend so you can trust him. I hope that you know that I love you with every ounce of my soul. You and the kids are my entire world.

I have a special day planned for you. You deserve this day. You have been good to me. You have been an extraordinary mother.

I know you want to know whats going on, but I want you to go with the flow. Garrison is going to chauffeur you around for today. Each stop will be in preparation for tonight. I can't wait to see you. You will be on my mind all day.

I love you.

Quinton

I stared down at the note for a moment, trying to let it all sink in. I laughed to myself. Something told me that this would not be a day that I would forget anytime soon. I walked over to Garrison with tears forming n my eyes. I found myself embracing him.

"Thank you, Garrison."

"You are welcome, Ms. Harris. Mr. Alexander has quite a day planned for you."

"I bet he does. I am going to get dress and I will be ready in just a minute."

"I will be waiting outside."

I quickly dressed in jeans and a sweater. I grabbed my leather jacket and my purse and quickly headed for the door. I almost tripped over my own feet when I saw Garrison standing by a Bentley.

"This can't be happening."

"Mr. Alexander says that you deserve the best."

Garrison took me to a spa. I received a massage and then a facial. By the time I sat down to get my nails done at my favorite salon, my body was floating on cloud nine. I felt at peace.

After the nail salon, I had lunch at a cute little bistro downtown. After lunch, Garrison dropped me off at one of the most exclusive hair salons in town. I was immediately greeted when I walked through the door. The owner himself colored and styled my hair in a curly up do. His wife applied my makeup. The results were so astonishing that I became teary eyed at my own appearance.

"You look ravishing," Garrison said, smiling at me as he helped me back into the car.

"Thank you." I leaned over to kiss him because I was touched by his sweetness. I think I made the old man blushed.

Garrison dropped me back off at the house and informed that he would be back at 6:30 sharp with Quinton in tow. I sighed to myself. I couldn't wait to see him. When I opened the door to the house, I was surprised to find Rayven waiting on the other side.

"What are you doing here, Ray. Q has you up to something?"

"Well, of course, darling. You look so beautiful." She threw her arms around me.

"Thank you. Whats going on."

"I am here to help you get dress."

"Really?"

"Yes, come on. Close your eyes." She pulled me towards the bedroom. I tapped my feet in anticipation. "Okay, open." I took a deep breath and opened my eyes to find Rayven holding a beautiful pink strapless dress.

"Oh wow." I covered my mouth.

"I know, Des. Isn't it lovely? Your man has wonderful taste. It's Loren Gavelston." One of my favorite dress designers. How did Quinton know that?

"What is happening, Ray?" I was on the verge of breaking down.

"Please don't cry. You are going to mess up your gorgeous make up. Let me do the crying tonight. Now come here so we can see you in this beauty."

The dress fitted me perfectly. It was as if the dress was made for me. How? I remembered my mother taking my measurements recently. She said she was making me something. Well-played mother.

It hugged me in all the right places. It was strapless and glittery with a sexy split that came to my thigh. I loved the train.

I stared at myself in the mirror for ten minutes. I was taken back by my own appearance. I had never felt so beautiful. I felt amazing.

"How do I look?"

"Breathtaking. Quinton is a lucky man." She kissed my forehead. "You are ready for someone's red carpet."

"I don't know what to say."

"Say nothing. Q told me to save this for last."

"Whats that?" I shook my head at the pink pearls and matching tear drop earrings. "I must be dreaming."

"No. You are deserving." She said, hugging me. I clung to her.

"You are the best friend a girl could ask for. I love you."

"I love you. Now let me take your picture so I can put you on Instagram."

At 6:30, I was waiting for Prince Charming outside on the deck. I was staring up at the stars forming when I felt his presence. I turned and there he was looking gorgeous in a black tux. I took a deep breath. I was a lucky woman.

We stared at one another without speaking. He was taking in my appearance as well. I was confident that the look in his eyes was one of approval. I could tell he was feeling the same way about me.

"Are you ready to tell me whats going on?" I whispered.

"Don't worry about that." He moved towards me. "Go with it." I went to say something, but he placed his finger against my lips. "You look even better than I imagined. You take my breath away."

"And you take mines." I parted my lips for his incoming kiss. It was sweet and gentle.

"I couldn't wait to see you all day. You made the wait worth it."

"Quinton, you are so good to me. Today was too much."

"Never. Put this around you." It was a pink mink cape. It was gorgeous.

"Where did you get that?"

"Will you put this on before you get sick?"

"I don't know what to say."

"Good, let's go."

Sure enough Garrison was back with that Bentley. He smiled and nodded at me. He told me that I was a vision of beauty. This time I blushed.

Quinton and I rode in silence. I tried to ask where we were going once more, but he just told me to stop asking questions. I had no choice but to surrender. I just clung to his hand and prepared myself for what was ahead.

We pulled up to the Carlson Tower, an exclusive building downtown. We walked through the lobby and headed straight for the elevator. I didn't say anything on the ride to the top floor. I just wondered who Quinton knew to pull off something like this.

We walked off the elevator and stood in front of two large double doors. Quinton just smiled down at me and opened them. He had to push me through them because I could feel my knees buckle.

"What did you do?" He didn't respond. He just pulled me further into the room. We stood in a room with beautiful hardwood floors and floor to ceiling windows with panoramic views of the city. The room was bare of furniture with the exception of a single table in the middle of the floor set for two and a baby grand piano. There were candles and pink roses everywhere.

The tears fell and I started to shake my head. This was too much. I turned to say something, but again Quinton cut me off.

"Give me your coat, baby." A man appeared out of nowhere. Quinton addressed him as Dominique. When Dominique walked away, Q pulled me to him. He kissed my forehead. "Don't cry, Desiree." He kissed me for a while.

"Is my makeup smeared?"

"Nope, you are still beautiful."

Q knew I adored seafood. We feasted on fried calamari, fried oysters, salmon and steamed vegetables. We washed it down with Moscato. The meal ended with German Chocolate cheesecake. It was one of the most delicious meals that I had ever had in my life.

"Delicious." I moaned just as he begins to kiss on my neck.

"Don't I know it?" He pulled my face around so he could kiss me. "What do you have on under this dress?"

"You are just going to have to wait and see." He just gave me a knowing look. He poured us both some more wine.

I was in awe when local celebrity, Kellan Mitchell appeared. He was the newest artist at Fantasy Records. He sat down at that piano and serenaded us. It was romantic.

"Come here," Q said afterwards. He pulled me to the window. "I want to talk to you about something."

"What is it?" I felt a little nervous all of a sudden.

"Don't look that way. It's nothing like that."

"Okay." I tried to take a couple deep breaths to calm down, but I couldn't help myself. Quinton himself had a look of anxiety on his face. Still, I attempted to hide my emotions as best as I could. I took a gulp of my wine.

"Hold on." He yanked off his jacket and threw it on the floor. He undid his tie. He was sweating. What the heck was going on? "That's better."

"What is it, Quinton?" I rubbed his back.

"I love you so much, Desiree."

"And I love you just as much."

"I knew that I wanted to be more than your friend that day you came to my room mad at Briana back in college."

"Really?" I was surprised.

"I knew something was up when I couldn't stop staring at you. You were so hurt that day and all I wanted to do was protect you."

"You were so good to me."

"And then you let me hold you that night and that really messed my mind up. You were all that I could think about for weeks. I started missing you when you weren't around. And then the day we kissed on the balcony, I couldn't focus on anything else."

He fell silent for a moment. I could tell he was reliving that night. I allowed my mind to go there as well. No kiss had ever affected me the way that his had. I never admitted it, but I knew I had feelings for him that night. I would have never imagined that he felt the same way. I ignored what I was feeling and found myself stupidly accepting a date with Anthony.

"I knew I had feelings for you, but after that night, I realized how strong those feelings were. I called Tyler and before I knew it, I was confessing that I loved you."

"Oh, Q." I buried my face into his neck.

"I want you to know that I tried to fight you. I didn't want to tell you, but love was kicking my ass. I got the courage to tell you. I wanted to beg you for a chance, but then I saw you in that dress, so excited to go out with Anthony. I gave up. I gave up on love. I gave up on you." I shook my head.

"I wish you would have told me."

"Why? What good would that had done?"

"After we kissed that night, Q, you were all I could think about as well. I felt stupid, though, so I pushed those feelings I had for you aside. I truly felt that I had no chance with you. If you had of told me that you loved me, you would have found out that I was crazy about you. I would not have gone out with Anthony that night."

He didn't respond, so I lifted my face to look up at him. I grabbed my chest because I felt pain in my heart when I saw tears in his eyes.

"I am so sorry. I didn't mean to upset you." I reached up to wipe his tears away.

"You mean to tell me…" He stopped and hugged me tightly. "It wasn't our time. We weren't supposed to be together then. We are together now and that's all that matters."

"It means everything."

"I could never get over you," he continued. "The day I moved in I knew I was in trouble. I just want you to know that all those bad moods and those jealous moments were because I loved you."

I thought about all the men I paraded in front of him. Lance, Anthony, Justin, Malik, Tyler. I had caused him a great deal of pain. That didn't set well with me. I felt like a jackass.

"Don't feel guilty," he said, reading my thoughts. "It's not like you knew, sweetheart."

"Still, I am so sorry."

"You can't be sorry when you did nothing wrong." I went to say something, but he cut me off with a kiss. "And then you got pregnant with my baby. You committed to me. I was happy with that, Desiree. I didn't expect more from you."

"I just thought that if I couldn't make you love me, I could make you mine for a little while. I jeopardized all of that because I didn't want to discuss that night in college. If I told you, you would have seen how weak you made me. I was being a man full of pride. I didn't want to reveal the vulnerabilities of my heart."

"Love is powerful, though. Sometimes, it's like a drug. It was the emotion that made me weak. The emotion sent me running, but it also made me afraid to lose you."

"I never imagined you giving me your heart, Des. I never want to let it go. I want it forever."

"It's yours." I responded.

"You make life so very good. I don't even want to know what it feels like to be without you. I don't want to have a family without you in it." He didn't have to worry about anything.

"Quinton, I hope you know that I am committed to you. I am committed to this family."

"Good." He turned me around. I am not sure where the projector came from, but Quinton Jr appeared on the wall.

"Hi, mommy." I wanted to collapse with emotion. Just seeing his face and hearing his voice touched me. "I think that you are the best and I don't ever want you to go away. I want you to be with me, Mia and Daddy forever. I love you. Mia loves you. Daddy loves you."

He opened a box and revealed the most beautiful pink Diamond ring. I gasped. "Mommy, will you marry us?"

I stopped breathing at that point. I placed one hand across my chest and the other across my forehead because I felt as if I was going to pass out. I turned and Quinton was already on one knee

"Are you listening, Desiree?"

"Yes! Where did that ring come from?" He was holding that big pink diamond ring.

"Shush. You know that I love you. I won't be fully satisfied until you become my wife. Please say yes to a lifetime of happiness. I promise I will work to love, cherish, protect and honor you until I take my last breath."

"Q!" I was sobbing now.

"Will you marry me, Desiree Harris? Well, will you marry us?"

"Of course. Yes!" He breathed a sigh of relief and slipped that ring on my finger. I continued to stare down at that ring as he stood and watched me.

"Do you like it?" He pulled me to him and pressed his lips against my forehead.

"I think it's the most beautiful thing that I have ever seen."

"You are the most beautiful thing I have ever seen." I couldn't say anything. I just wrapped my arms around him and kissed him "Thank you for saying yes."

"Thank you for asking me."

Later on that night, after we were completely alone, Quinton took me into the master bedroom. There was nothing but a four poster bed in the middle of the room. Pink sheets. Pink rose petals.

"You correlated everything to the ring."

"Yes, baby," he said, reaching for my zipper. "Mercy me," he whispered once the dress hit the floor. I stood before him in my G-string and nothing else.

He scooped me up and placed me on the bed. Once he was naked, I pulled him on top of me. We kissed frantically and then we made quick passionate love. After that, we made a slow burning type of love with just the moonlight shining in on us for hours.

Hours later, while lying in his arms, he whispered. "Do you want to take a ride? Garrison left that Bentley in the garage.

"Where did you get that Bentley?"

"Don't worry about the details," he said as he slipped back into his pants and shirt. I slipped back into that Pink Mink and nothing else. "I like that, baby." His eyes had a glimmer in them.

We took a ride to a secluded part of the city. We climbed into the backseat and cuddled. It was a sweet end to a magical night. This was a story that I would be telling for years to come.

34

Rage

"Refrain from anger, and forsake wrath! Fret not yourself; it tends only to evil."
Psalm 37:8

Quinton

It had been nine months since I had proposed to Desiree. I loved referring to her as my fiancé. I loved listening to her plan the details to our April wedding next spring. I loved catching her smile down at her ring. I loved that she seemed genuinely happy.

It was obvious to me that she wanted to be my wife. I was finally confident after all these years that she felt the same way about me that I felt about her. My heart was finally at peace with that. I was finally without any doubts about our future together.

I was thankful that my son adored this woman as much as I did. He truly loved her. I knew the fact that India had died was the reason that he clung to Des. He didn't want to lose another mother. I was going to do everything in my power to make sure that didn't happen. I prayed to God every night that he would always watch over her.

I sat at my desk one afternoon consumed with my thoughts about her. I was imagining her in her wedding dress. I didn't doubt for one second that she was going to take my breath away. I knew for a fact that I was going to cry.

"Wow.' I got up from behind my desk and walked down the hall to my partner's office. "Chad, I think that I am going to head on out. I have some errands to run. You need me to take care of anything before I leave."

"We are good here, Q. Go ahead and get out of here. I am going to leave myself within the next hour. Say hi to that beautiful woman of yours."

"Cool, I will. Tell your wife hello as well."

"Will do."

I walked back to my office and quickly shut everything down. On the way to my car, I called Desiree.

"Hello, babe." She had the sweetest voice. It immediately comforted me.

"Hey, my love."

"What are you up to?"

"Missing you. I am on my way home."

"I miss you too. How did you manage to leave so early? Are you feeling okay?"

"I feel fine. I just wanted to come home early today." I didn't let on how badly I just wanted to be with her and the kids.

"Sounds good to me. You can eat dinner with us tonight. The kids and I would really like that."

"I would like that too." I had been so busy these days that I missed out on quality time with my family. "Have you cooked yet?"

"No, not yet. Why? What would you like?"

"I will take care of that. I just want you to relax."

"Thank you. I will show you my appreciation later. I will take care of dessert," she teased.

"Already looking forward to that. I am going to stop by Wegmans. I will be home shortly."

Des loved Italian food, so I was picking up some Italian bread to go along with my five cheese lasagna when I heard my name.

'Well, hello there, Quinton Alexander. We meet here again." I knew who it was before I turned around. I would have rather ignored her, but mother had raised me better.

"Hello, Veronica." She was still undeniably beautiful in her suit, pinned up hair and flawless makeup, but I still looked at her in disgust. I had lost respect for her when I found out what she did to Desiree. I had always been protective of Des and I wasn't too keen on anyone who intentionally set out to hurt her.

"Well, you don't look very happy to see me."

"I don't know what to say to that," I said, shrugging.

"How's life being treating you?"

"I am blessed. Look, I hate to be rude, but I am in a rush."

"Oh," she said, giving me a wounded look. "Well, it was nice seeing you again." Unfortunately, I could not repeat those words back to her. It would have been a lie.

"Sure." I started walking away.

"Maybe, I will run into you again." I really hope not, I thought.

"Who knows? It's a small world. See you."

"Bye, Quinton."

Her tone of voice rubbed me the wrong way. I didn't give her any more attention, though. I kept walking away. I wanted to get away from her as quickly as I could.

Thankfully, I was able to get out of the store without running into her again. I was finally able to head home to Desiree and my kids. When I walked through the door, I kissed my woman, sat her down on the couch, and poured her a glass of wine. I told her not to worry about the kids and to focus on relaxing. I took the kids into the kitchen with me while I cooked.

After dinner, I played with the kids while she took a long bath. Once I put the kids to bed, Desiree and I snuggled up on the couch to watch TV. We ended up making out like teenagers, so I lifted her, took her to the bedroom and then proceeded to make love to her.

I walked out of my office around the noon the next day to meet one of my artist, Kellan Mitchell, who was about to drop an album. I was in a rush because I had to be at the restaurant in thirty minutes. I was calling my partner to tell them I was on my way, when I saw her. My heart fell. What now?

"Veronica, what are you doing here? How did you even know I worked here?" I was irritated.

"I am here to see you, Quinton."

"How did you find me?"

"Oh come on, Quinton. Do you really think that it was all that difficult? You are well known."

"That doesn't explain why you are looking for me? What do you want?" Was this chick trying to cause trouble in my life?

"I am here to see if you wanted to get some lunch. I thought we could talk." I didn't have time for any of this.

"I am not interested. I have plans for lunch today, Veronica." I headed towards the elevator with her on my heels.

"Really, Quinton." She was quickly becoming annoying.

"Yes. I am leaving right now."

"How about another day?"

"No, I don't think so." I pressed the down button, but I turned in time to see anger flash in her eyes.

"Why be so difficult? Why are you being rude?"

"I don't desire to spend any time with you, Veronica. What's so difficult to understand about that?"

"Why is that? You use to enjoy spending time with me. In and out of the bedroom."

"Oh here we go." I rolled my eyes. "All of that is a part of the past." I stepped on the elevator. She stood and stared at me instead of walking on. "Are you coming?" I asked, becoming increasingly frustrated by this whole interaction. I let go of the button to allow the door to shut, but she grabbed the door to prevent it from shutting. She quickly stepped on.

"The past, huh? Whats holding you back?" She walked over to me and tried to push up against me. I pushed her away.

"Cut that shit out!"

"Why don't you stop acting like that? Why don't you come over tonight? You remember where I live?"

"That's not happening."

"And why not!" She snapped.

"I am really not obligated to explain myself. I don't want to."

"What kind of man turns down sex with a beautiful sexy woman," she said, frowning. She was full of herself.

"I am the kind of man that is engaged to a woman who I love more than anything! I would never jeopardize my happiness with her to be with a woman that I could care less about. Stay away from me, Veronica, if you know whats good for you."

She didn't say anything else. She just stared at me with a deranged look on her face. I shook my head and walked off the elevator without giving her a second glance.

I could feel her staring at my back. I didn't like the nagging feeling in my stomach. I never wanted to see her face again, but something told me that I hadn't seen the last of her.

My instincts were on point. I was at the park that weekend with Desiree and the kids. Des had taken lil Quinton to buy an ice cream cone and I was walking behind Mia. Mia was fascinated by a flower. I looked up and saw her. I immediately felt myself becoming furious, but I quickly composed myself in front of my daughter.

"Hello, Veronica. What did I tell you?"

"I know, but I saw you over here with this adorable little girl and I just had to come and say hi."

"What are you doing here? Are you following me?"

"No." She laughed at me. "Really, Quinton, do you think I am crazy enough to do all of that?" She turned and pointed to a woman who resembled her. The woman was glaring at me. "I am here with my sister and her kids."

"Oh."

"Whats is this precious little girl's name?"

"Mia." Mia looked up at the sound of her name. She looked up at Veronica, but quickly lost interest.

"She's adorable."

"Thanks. She looks like her mother."

"So where is this woman that you are so in love with?"

Before I could respond, Desiree and Quinton came towards us. I was afraid that Des would be angry, but she wore a smirk on her face. She shook her head and winked at me.

"Well hello, Veronica." Veronica almost tripped over her feet when she stepped back a little.

"Desiree! Well, honey, how are you?" She didn't seem sincere.

"I am wonderful. How are you?"

"Fabulous. It's good to see you. I see that you and Quinton are still good friends."

"Something like that," she said, laughing loudly.

"Mommy," said Quinton Jr. "Who is she?"

"Mommy," Veronica repeated. "I don't remember you being pregnant back in the day. You kept this little cutie a secret." This chick was not as bright as I thought she was.

"Sweetheart, this lady went to school with mommy and daddy many years ago. Say hello."

"Hi," he said, frowning up at her.

"Whats your name, cutie?" She knelt in front of my son while Des and I shared a look.

"Quinton." By the expression on her face, Veronica finally put the pieces of the puzzle together. She stood up and looked at me.

"You have a son!"

"Obviously."

Suddenly Mia commanded all of our attention by screaming, "Mommy" and running towards Desiree with her arms stretched. Des scooped her up in her arms.

"Whats wrong, baby." Mia just buried her face in in her mother's shoulder. Desiree smiled at me and rubbed her back.

"Someone's sleepy," I volunteered. I walked over and stood beside my love.

"She sure is."

"What a beautiful family," Veronica spoke up with obvious sarcasm. I smiled in satisfaction. I could see that Desiree had gotten under her skin.

"Thank you!" Desiree shifted Mia in her arms. That's when Veronica spotted that ring.

"That ring is incredible!"

"Oh, I know. Thank you, Veronica! Quinton has always had incredible taste. Baby, I am going to take Mia to the bathroom. I will meet you gentlemen by the swings."

"Okay, we are right behind you." Quinton Jr grabbed my hand. I look down to see even he was eying Veronica suspiciously. I laughed to myself. My son obviously had a great judge of character.

"Desiree Harris, huh. The finest thing to hit the campus of NC State. That's the woman that you love?"

"This is the woman that I have always loved. This will be all the proof that you need. My family is my life, Veronica. I am going to ask you one last time not to bother me anymore.

"Fine, I got it."

She turned and walked away. I took a deep breath because finally the uneasiness that I had been feeling the last week had disappeared. I was sure that she would finally leave me alone.

"Give me some ice cream, kid."

"Daddy, you can only have a little bit."

I thought my nightmare was over, but again Veronica proved me wrong. She was set out to intentionally ruin my relationship with Desiree. She was a sick woman.

I was in my office late one Friday, finishing up some paperwork, a couple weeks later. I was waiting on Desiree because we had plans to go out of town while my future in-laws watched the kids. She had taken the car to have it serviced and I was stranded. This is when the trouble started.

"Well hello, Mr. Alexander."

I closed my eyes at the sound of her voice. If I looked up at her, I was going to go off. I was trying to remain calm before I threw her out of the window. She was about to make me lose it.

"Go away," I said as calmly as I could.

"Not just yet. I just got here."

"Get out of here, now!" This time I yelled at her. I opened my eyes and she stood before me in a trench coat and heels. Crap! Considering it was 100 degrees outside that could not have been a good thing. The conniving little winch had something up her sleeve.

"Why are you so angry with me?'

"Because now you are blatantly harassing me."

"That was not very nice of you." Her eyes were very glazed. She was scaring me.

"No one is trying to be nice. I want you to go away and to never come back."

"You don't really mean that!"

"Yes, I do! What is it that you want from me? You said in the park the other week that you would leave me alone. Why are you going back on your word! Why are you here!"

"It's quite simple. I really want you!" She undid her coat and let it drop to the floor. She stood before me in a see through bra and a G-string. And while she looked beautiful in it, I looked at her in disgust. Desiree was far more desirable to me and I realized in that moment how lucky I was to have her.

"I don't want you! Put your clothes back on and leave!"

"Are you sure?" She closed the door and walked towards me.

"You are wasting my time and yours. I am really about to completely lose my temper."

'I don't think so. I don't believe that." She pushed me down and attempted to sit in my lap, I pushed her away. She then took a seat on my desk in front of me. It took everything in my power not to grab the chick by the neck and physically throw her down the stairs.

"What are you trying to do? Do you get pleasure out of harassing me? Get off of my damn desk, Veronica."

"Come on, Quinton. You may be getting married, but that doesn't mean you can't have a little fun with me on the side."

"You really are stupid! I don't want a side chick!"

"Why? I am just being passionate! I am fighting for you! We had fun together. Inside and outside of the bedroom, Quinton. How can you forget all of that so easily?" I laughed.

"We went out for like a month! Are you kidding me? There was nothing between us. I have found so much more."

"Stop resisting me!" She grabbed my hand and attempted to run it across her breast, but I yanked it away.

"Too late. I want no parts of you." Without warning, she jumped into my lap and pressed her lips against mine. "Get off me!" I pushed her off of me with so much force that she fell to the floor.

"Stop!" She screamed. I was thankful I was alone in the office and today. I would have been humiliated. "What is wrong with you!"

"What's wrong with me!" I grabbed her arm and yanked her off the floor. "You are driving me up the wall. I have asked you to stay away from me more than once and you refuse to listen. I opened my office door and flung her out into the hall.

"You don't have to be so freaking rough with me, Quinton." She said, angrily pulling her arm away from me.

"If you had of left when I told you to the first time, this entire confrontation could have been avoided. You chose to stay around and piss me off!"

"I will call the police." I shook my head. This was the type of woman who would intentionally ruin an innocent man's life.

"And when you do, make sure you tell them that you have been stalking me."

"Why are you doing this!"

"Why don't you leave on your own before I call the security guards to escort you out of the building."

"Why would you do that to me? I love you!"

"You are crazy. We dated a month," I said, laughing. I could not believe that any of this was happening to me.

"That doesn't matter. It was love at first sight for me."

"Well not for me. Let's see, I have been in love with Des since college. I was still in love with her while we dated and I still love her to this day. We have been in relationship for well over two years. This means that the two of us haven't dated in almost three years."

"You still consume my heart," she said with tears in her eyes.

"Look Veronica, I thought you were a beautiful girl and we did have fun together, but to be honest with you, you were just a distraction while I was trying to get over my girl. And dating you didn't seem to work. I didn't have feelings for you."

"I am not a quitter, Quinton. Are you telling me that I should just give up?"

"My life is full and there is no room for you. I don't want you in my life in any way."

"You son of a bitch!" She picked up a stapler and flung it at me. I grabbed my phone to call security, but froze at the sound of Desiree's voice.

"Such a temper we have, Veronica."

'Des, baby. She…" My heart was beating three times as fast as normal. I was afraid that this chick had ruined my life. I was afraid that after all this, I was going to lose my best friend and my lover. I was afraid she would take my daughter and run. How would my son and I make it?

"Quiet, Quinton." She walked over to me and placed her hand on my shoulder. "Let me handle this." I nodded and backed away.

"Veronica, are you out to get me?" Her voice was calm which meant she was pissed. Veronica backed away and I could see she was trembling. I then realized that she was very intimidated by Desiree.

"You must be out to get me. You have to be. Did I do something to you? Is there a reason that you dislike me so much that you keep trying to ruin my life?"

"Umm…" Desiree was moving closer and closer to Veronica

"Come on answer me, sweetheart." Veronica kept backing up until Des finally had her pinned against the wall.

"I…."

"You are one stupid whore. Something is seriously wrong upstairs. I don't know what you have against rational thinking."

"I am so pissed to be standing here again talking to you about trying to take my man! You better be glad that I know the Lord and I have self-restraint. The thought of my two beautiful kids is the only thing keeping me from knocking your ass out. I can't do jail time. You aren't worth it."

"Seriously, why are we in this position again? All the men in the world and you keep going after mine. Anthony was garbage, so I was thankful you ended that relationship. I let you win because I forfeited. Quinton is different. I love this man more than I could have ever loved Anthony. I am not about to allow some little cheap whore such as yourself to take him away from me."

I moved towards Desiree because I could hear her getting upset.

"No, I am fighting for Q. This is the father of my kids. His family needs him. What kind of woman tries to take a man away from his family! Why are you trying to break up my family!"

"I am sorry!" Veronica was sobbing.

"No, you aren't. I don't accept your apology because you aren't sorry. You may be sorry that you got caught again. You may be sorry that you are here standing half naked in front of a man who has rejected you."

I slid my arm around Desiree's waist.

"Calm down, baby. She isn't worth it."

"I know Quinton is not going to risk losing me for someone like you. My future looks bright, girl. I am not about to let you ruin it for me or my kids. Stay away, Veronica. Don't you ever come near Q again or it will be your biggest regret in life. Do you hear me!"

Veronica didn't respond. She just stood there and cried guilty tears. That pissed Des off because she reached out and slapped her.

"Stay the hell away! Puta!"

"Time to go, Veronica." I wrapped my arms around Des to restrain her. Veronica quickly moved towards the stairs. Desiree broke from me and ran behind her.

I laughed as Des snatched the coat out of her hands. She then shoved her which caused Veronica to bounce down the first flight of stairs. She looked up at Des horrified and then ran down the steps.

"That was petty," she said, turning to me with tears in her eyes.

"She deserved it."

"Why is she so hell bent on taking you away from me?"

"No one can take me away for you. Don't worry."

"I can't lose you," she said, giving me a wounded look. A rare glimpse of uncertainty.

"Baby, you will never lose me."

"Okay." She laid her head against my shoulder. "If any woman is going to show up in your office with a trench coat and some trashy lingerie, it will be me."

'You are the only woman I want to see in lingerie."

"Good, sweetheart. Are you ready?"

"Let me shut everything off."

Once we got downstairs, two security guards were standing beside Veronica, who was screaming. A female officer was putting her in handcuffs.

"Are you, Mr. Alexander?" The officer addressed me.

'Yes, mam."

"We caught this female trying to vandalize your vehicle."

"Oh, really." The devil was sure busy today. He didn't prevail. God had my back, though.

"Yea, Quinton,'" one of the security guards addressed me. "This chick was flipping out. We kicked her out the building because she was acting like a lunatic, plus she is a little indecent. JJ," he said pointing to the other security guard, "spotted her running for your truck that Desiree had just got out of. We went running behind her which caught the attention of this lovely officer."

"Wow,' I said, shaking my head. "Thank you," I said, shaking both security guards hands.

"No problem."

"Well, Mr. Alexander," the cop spoke up. "Would you like to press charges?"

"No charges, however; I would like to request a restraining order for me and my family. Ms. Ramirez doesn't seem to understand the word no." Veronica tried to spit at me.

"Whatever," she screamed. "I should have hurt your ass when I had the chance," she yelled at Desiree.

"Be quiet!" The cop hauled Veronica away.

Des turned and stared at me. There was a strange look in her eyes. "I think she's been in my house."

Des's suspicion turned out to be true. Veronica was her stalker. She was the one writing the crazy notes and leaving them in the mailbox. She was the one that had broken into Desiree's house that night. She had been out to hurt my woman in any way she could.

She had been watching Desiree for years. She had hired private investigators to find out everything they knew. She had intentionally tracked me down. She had set out to take me away, but she didn't realize that the only thing that was going to take me away from Desiree was death.

Desiree

It was a month before my wedding and everything appeared to be running smoothly. I had taken care of every major detail. I just had to worry about all the minor ones. I was not stressing about anything, though. I refused to be a bridezilla.

Everyone seemed to be on cloud nine, especially Quinton. I loved his childlike excitement. I expected him to be nervous by now, but he showed no signs of cold feet. I decided to ask him about his excitement one day.

"Are you really this excited about the wedding?" I asked one unusually warm March day as we sat at the table on the patio after breakfast. The kids were running around.

"Yes, baby. I love you and can't wait to make you my wife. You aren't excited about making me your husband," he teased.

"Shush. Most men wouldn't care about the wedding, though."

"I am not most men." I stood and walked over to him. I sat in his lap. I wrapped my arms around his shoulder.

"Are you sure you aren't getting cold feet?"

"You have nothing to worry about. I have never been so sure about anything in my life."

I believed him after that. I stopped worrying. I had planned our wedding and in a matter of weeks, I was going to enjoy it. I wanted our special day to be as stress free as possible. I was determined to be a relaxed carefree bride.

I came home one Saturday after running errands and meeting with the caterer to finalize everything for the reception. I felt hot and sticky so I wanted to take a shower in peace before Quinton and the kids got home. Moments like this were rare for me.

I had just put my key in the door when a car pulled up in the driveway. I frowned because I didn't recognize the black Lexus. I waited for the driver to get out, but they never did, so I cautiously moved towards it. I felt uneasy.

I stopped a few feet from the vehicle and yelled hello. The windows were tinted so I couldn't make out who it was. I didn't want to get too close just in case I had to run. Finally, the driver door opened. My heart beat quicken as I waited for the driver's identity to be revealed. They were moving agonizingly slow and it was creeping me out.

"Hello, Desiree."

"Anthony!" I frowned. "Why are you here!" I couldn't help myself. I hadn't seen in him in over two years. There was no reason for him to be here. I kept trying to close this chapter in my life, but he kept insisting on reopening it.

I didn't want to see him. I didn't want to talk to him. I definitely didn't want Quinton to come home and see Anthony in his house.

"Can I not visit an old friend?"

"How did you figure out where I lived?"

"I did some investigating."

"Why are you investigating me, Anthony?" I looked at him as if he had lost his mind.

"So many questions. I just wanted to see you, Desiree. I hear that you are getting married in a few weeks. To him." He moved towards me, but I took a step back. There was a dark look in his eyes. The tone of his voice made my skin crawl. There was something off about his appearance. I had a bad feeling.

"You heard right. Again, why are you here?" I asked, stepping back once again as he moved closer. I didn't want to be near him.

"I can't come say hi, baby?" I wanted to tell him not to call me baby, but I kept my mouth shut. He looked as if he might snap. "Why do you keep moving away from me?"

"What are you talking about? My mouth was dry.

"Come and give me a hug." He grabbed me before I could move back again.

"You are hurting me!" I yelled as he hugged me roughly.

I froze when he whispered, "Shut up!"

"Excuse me! I think that you need to let go of me!" I begin to struggle. I tried to pull away, but his grip on me was much too strong.

"Desiree, you haven't begun to experience pain yet."

"What! Anthony why are you talking crazy? You really need to let go of me!" Why was this happening, I thought.

"No. Walk inside."

"I am not letting you in my house. You need to leave!" I yelled. Where were the neighbors when you needed them?

"I am not going anywhere. Walk!" he barked. My heart broke when I felt the coldness and hardness against my side.

"What are you doing?" I looked down and saw the gun. Tears spilled down my cheek. "Why are you doing this to me?"

"Walk, bitch!"

I had no choice but to head inside. I prayed that the Lord was walking with me. It took me a few moments to get the door open because I was blinded by the tears. Once inside, he shoved me. He forced me in the living room, eventually slamming me against the glass patio door.

"I want your neighbors to see what I do to you." I started shaking like a leaf. I was very afraid. It was the most sickening thing he had ever said to me and I wasn't sure what he was capable of.

"Why are you doing this to me, Anthony?" I tried to speak, calmly. I didn't want to yell and get him angrier.

"Because you hurt me!"

"I am sorry that you were hurt!"

"No you are not," he said, sliding his hand around my neck.

"What do you plan to do to me?" God, please help me.

"I am going to make love to you and when Quinton gets here, we are going to do it again." He was going to rape me! I felt my knees buckle. I thought maybe I would pass out.

"No!" I started shaking my head uncontrollably.

"You have no choice," he said, sliding the gun between my thighs." It was the most horrific feeling.

"Stop it. You are not a bad person, Anthony. Don't try to be. What will this solve?"

"Shut up, Desiree!" He slid his hand around my neck again. "Don't try to tell me what I am. I feel like being a bad person. I want to hurt you, Desiree." I knew then that he was no longer the man that I once fell in love with or maybe he had suppressed this person. He had literally lost his mind. He looked possessed.

"You don't really want to hurt me." I was trying to play mind games with him.

"Yes, I do." This time he attempted to kiss me, but I turned my face. "Don't do that." He grabbed my face and turned it back around. He pressed his lip against mine, but I refused to kiss him.

"Why do you want be like that?" I gasped when he ripped my shirt open, sending buttons flying. He began to kiss my neck and caress my breast. I was repulsed. I was afraid to scream. I thought if I did, he would do something else to me. I almost lost it when he grabbed me between my thighs and begin to caress me there.

"Don't touch me there!" I screamed. "I don't want that from you, Anthony."

"Why not? You use to like when I touched you."

"So long ago."

"Stop crying." He didn't care that there were tears spilling down my cheeks. He didn't care that I was someone's mother. He just wanted to hurt me. He knew this would destroy me.

"Why?" Anthony and I hadn't been together in years. Why was he doing this now? Because I was marrying Quinton and not him. He couldn't stand it.

"You're so beautiful, Desiree. The most beautiful woman in my life." He begin to stroke my hair. "I loved everything about you. I am still in love with you."

"Then why would you want to hurt me?"

"Because you are marrying him. Big mistake. I have to teach you a lesson."

"I love him, Anthony. There's nothing you can do that's going to change that." My life was in danger, but I wasn't going to lie.

"Shut up. Don't ever say that to me again." Suddenly, I heard car doors and the kids laughing. I closed my eyes because I knew it was a matter of time before Q came home. I didn't want to think about the possibilities of what might happen. I wanted to throw up.

"Baby, we are home. We have a surprise for you."

"Mommy!"

"Don't hurt my kids," I said, frantically.

"Never. I love kids!" He looked crazy. Sick bastard.

"Baby, where are you. I see a car outside. Do we have a..." When Q entered the living room, he almost tripped. I could see the terror in his eyes.

"What are you doing, Anthony? Get away from her!"

"No, I don't think so."

"Tyler," Q yelled.

"What's up?" Q's best friend entered the room. His eyes grew big. Hey, my man, don't do no crazy shit!" Tyler said to Anthony.

"Who are you?" Anthony said, pointing the gun in his direction.

"Don't do that!" Tyler yelled holding his hands up.

"T!" Q pushed him out of the room. "Get the kids out of here."

"Sure, man," he said, backing quickly out the door.

Q looked about as scared as I felt, but his voice was calm.

"Why are you holding a gun to my…"

"Because she shouldn't be with you."

"She's my soulmate and I think you know that."

"I don't think so, Alexander."

"Yes," he said, moving closer to us. "You know she is. That's why you are here. That's why you are here trying to hurt her."

"Stop walking. Don't come any closer. I will shoot you and her."

"What do you suppose I do? You have ripped my girl's clothes. You have her pinned against the door and you are holding a gun to her. I will protect her and I will die doing so."

"You need to chill. Be calm."

"How can I be calm? You are trying to hurt the woman I love."

"I love her too."

"If you love her, why would you try to hurt her?"

"She's with you. That's her downfall."

"If you have a problem with me, don't punish her. You and I can handle this like men."

"No!" I groaned."

"Shut up, Desiree." Anthony covered my mouth with his hand. "No one is talking to you sweetheart." I looked over his shoulder at Q. He was begging me to stay quiet.

"Come on, man," Q continued. "We both know that you really don't want to hurt, Desiree."

"You don't know that."

"Yes, I do." Anthony kept the gun pointed towards Quinton, but he looked at me. I could see that Quinton's words were getting to him. He was having second thoughts.

"Please, let me go," I said, pleading with him.

"I don't think so." He squeezed my face and then kissed me. I didn't close my eyes. I stared at Q and saw rage in his eyes. I had never seen such a look come over him and I had seen him angry many times. I knew if he got a hold of Anthony's gun, then he was likely to shoot him.

"Let her go, Anthony! You might want to stop touching her." His voice was almost unrecognizable.

"Oh, you don't like that, Alexander."

"She doesn't either. You are forcing yourself on a woman. What does that make you?"

"Look…"

"No, you look! Your issue is with me. You are mad because she chose to be with me! Sorry about that, but you can't tear apart what God put together. Let's handle this, Thompson!"

"Oh, we are going to handle it alright."

"She will always be with me. God made her for me, not you. You lost your mind if think for one second that I am just going to let you have her. I am not going to let you harm her in anyway."

"I have already had her. I had her long before you."

"What a disrespectful thing to say. If you loved Des, you wouldn't talk about her in that way. "You are nothing but a coward." This time Anthony moved away from me and towards Quinton. I stopped breathing because he was handling his gun dangerously. "I think you are sick bitch. You always have been one. I despise you."

"Alexander, you have a lot of nerve. You are judging and insulting me while I am holding a gun. Maybe I am the one who holds your final judgment today."

"Oh you think you are so big because you are threatening me and the woman who you supposedly love with a gun. If you were an honorable man, you would be handling this with words, not violence."

"I don't have time for conversation."

"Make some."

"No, I am not."

"I see. You don't leave me much choice. Desiree, baby, go to your kids." I attempted to move slowly always from the glass door. Anthony stopped me.

"Don't you move. I am in control."

"Let her go to her children while we handle this."

"Things aren't going to go your way today, Alexander. We are playing by my rules."

"I don't think so," Q said, staring Anthony down.

"Well, I do."

Without warning, Quinton lunged for Anthony. I stood hypnotized with terror as the two men struggled. Fear ran through me as I eyed that gun. I knew something was going to go wrong.

If anything happened to Q, I was going to lose it. He meant everything to me. I didn't know if I was capable of existing in this cold world without him. I didn't want to find out.

I froze in horror when the gun went off. I knew one of them had gotten shot. When Quinton backed up and grabbed his shoulder, I gripped the wall. I screamed when I saw the blood. They both looked at me because I was about to lose it.

"Calm down, baby," Quinton said. "It's okay."

"Don't tell me to calm down," I yelled, taking them both by surprise. I jumped for Anthony. Amazingly, I had enough strength to knock him off his feet. The gun fell and I was able to grab it. I pointed it right at him. It took everything in my power not to pull the trigger. I closed my eyes and begin to pray.

"Shoot me, Desiree. What are you waiting for?"

"How dare you, Anthony. Why would you do this to me? Why would you try to hurt me and take me away from my family? Why would you try to take Q away from me?"

"I love you."

"No, you don't. Don't speak those words to me! You can't love me! And I sure as hell don't love you."

"I know," he said, beginning to cry. I was watching this grown man hit rock bottom.

"I don't feel sorry for you!" I was getting hysterical.

"Desiree, come here." Quinton grabbed my waist. He grabbed the gun He took the bullets out and then pulled me to him. I buried my face into his chest. "I love you."

"I love you Quinton. I am sorry that this happened to you."

'This is not your fault. Don't you apologize to me!"

"But he hurt you."

"He did, but God saved me. I will be fine, so stop crying. The devil didn't win today, baby, and we are going to be thankful."

"I can't help it."

"Yes you can.'" He kissed me. "I got you. I got us. God got us."

"He does." I nodded. The thought of the good Lord sparing our lives brought calmness to me. I was going to be thankful."

"Did he hurt you, my love. I can't imagine what you must of went through before we got here."

"I am okay. He didn't rape me. He just threatened me."

"Good," he said, breathing a sigh of relief. "I need to hurry up and marry you."

"You still want to marry me after this nightmare?"

"Oh the need for me to marry you is even stronger. If it's the last thing I do on this earth, I am getting you down that aisle."

"Babe. Nothing is going to break us, huh? It seems like the world is trying to do everything to pull us apart."

"We will always be together."

The police busted in after that. Tyler had called them. Anthony was arrested, not only for assault, but for a stolen gun and drug possession. I didn't know what to think. This man who I once loved had attempted to destroy me. Oh how people could change.

35

Matrimony

"Husbands, love your wives, as Christ loved the church and gave
himself up for her, that he might sanctify her, having cleansed her
by the washing of water with the word, so that he might present the
church to himself in splendor, without spot or wrinkle or any such
thing, that she might be holy and without blemish. In the same
way husbands should love their wives as their own bodies. He who
loves his wife loves himself. For no one ever hated his own flesh, but
nourishes and cherishes it, just as Christ does the church, because we
are members of his body. Therefore a man shall leave his father and
mother and hold fast to his wife, and the two shall become one flesh.
This mystery is profound, and I am saying that it refers to Christ and
the church. However, let each one of you love his wife as himself,
and let the wife see that she respects her husband."
Ephesians 5:25-33

Quinton

The wedding was approaching quickly with just a
little over a week away. Things were returning to normal. Everyone
was focusing on the wedding and trying not to think about the
traumatic events that happened close to three weeks ago. I admittedly
was very excited. I had been in love with Desiree for years and was
thankful that the Lord was finally giving me the chance to not only
love her, but be her partner for a lifetime.

However, despite the undeniable joy, I was still feeling a little
anxious. Anthony had tried to destroy me by taking my love away
from me. I had been having nightmares. I woke up in sweats some
nights and couldn't go back to sleep. Some nights, there would be

tears in my eyes. I would never wake her. I would just reach for her and allow the sound of her breathing to comfort me.

What if Des had gotten shot that day? Anthony and I were both struggling for the gun when it went off. I didn't care about being shot myself. My shoulder would heal. I would have never forgiven myself if a bullet had so much as grazed her.

I would have killed Anthony. I would not have wanted to live. I didn't want to think about existing without her. She had become my heart and soul.

I didn't want Des to know that I was struggling with this. She had seemed to move on and I didn't want to make her relive what she had been through. I didn't want her to know that losing her was my biggest fear in life. I kept quiet.

Desiree

A couple days before the wedding, Quinton Jr asked if he could see his mother. He wanted to go by her gravesite and leave her flowers. I could not deny him of that.

So one morning, I left Mia with my mother and we made the trip to the cemetery. Little Quinton picked out some tulips from the store. When we stood before India's tombstone, he laid the flowers on top of her grave.

"These are for you mommy. I just came to say hi. I hope you are doing much better now that you are with God. I have been thinking about you. I miss you."

"I am doing okay mommy. My new mommy is taking care of me. Don't worry about me okay. I love you. See you soon."

I tried not to cry. He was only six, almost seven. How could he be this wise? He was beyond special. I was blessed that God was allowing me to be a part of his life.

"Mommy!" He ran to me. I knelt down so he could throw his arms around me.

"Yes baby" I hugged him tightly.

"I love you!"

"I love you too, baby."

"Mommy, please don't leave me like my first mommy did." I felt a lump forming in my throat. How could you make such a promise to a little child?

"I won't, baby. I won't leave you." I prayed if anything ever happened to me that he would forgive me.

I did not know whether or not having our bachelor and bachelorette party the night before the wedding was going to be a mistake. All I knew was I ready to have fun and celebrate my upcoming nuptials with my closet friends. The planning was finally over and the day I was to marry Quinton Alexander was now less than 24 hours away. I didn't feel nervous; I was grateful.

With the events that had unfolded, we may have been tempted to postpone things. Finding out that Veronica was my stalker and was hell-bent on stealing my man was draining. Having Anthony attempt to rape, hurt or even worse, kill me, was the scariest experience out of my life. The last seven months had been right out of a lifetime movie. Despite it all, Q and I decided not to give into the temptation of postponing things.

This was all a part of the Devil's plan, but God's plan would always prevail. We both felt that God wanted us to move on. Anthony and Veronica had done nothing, but brought us closer together. We wanted tomorrow to happen more than anything. It was time for me to take his last name.

I was grateful that Quinton still wanted to marry me. I knew my lack of confidence was stupid because it didn't matter what Anthony did, nothing was going to stop Q from loving me. I just couldn't knock the guilt associated with him getting shot. I knew that it wasn't my fault, so I didn't share my feelings with anyone

Quinton went through each day acting as if nothing ever happen. He acted as if he was never shot; therefore, I never brought any part of the nightmare up. I assumed that he just wanted to move on, so each day I would wake up and pretend that those days that Veronica and Anthony tried to break were a part of imagination.

So now that the night before the wedding had arrived, I was not going to think about the past and was going to focus on my future. Tonight I wanted to spend a carefree night with the girls. Then I was going to lie down and dream of the beautiful day and life ahead. I was ready for this.

We didn't have a wild bachelorette party planned. My bridesmaids, my mother, my future mother-in-law, and some of my close family members booked a hotel suite. We didn't hire a stripper;

we just drank champagne and ate pizza. It was so refreshing to just laugh and relax with women I loved.

I didn't think about what Quinton was doing. I knew Tyler had arranged a poker night at the house. I hoped Q was not face to face with some stripper trying to make her booty bounce, but I wasn't going to worry. I trusted Q and I truly believed that he respected me enough to do anything stupid that would jeopardize our relationship.

Early that morning, around 2:00 while everyone was sleeping, I went outside and sat on the balcony. I was staring up at the stars, thinking about the day ahead and the two week honeymoon to Jamaica and the Virgin Islands. I was startled when my phone vibrated in my hand. When I saw that it was Quinton, I quickly assumed that something was wrong.

"Babe, whats up?"

"Hey, baby. I didn't know if you were up?"

"You were lucky. What's wrong, Q?"

"I can't sleep."

"Are you getting cold feet?" I joked.

"You know I have wanted to marry you before you even knew I love you, so that's a negative." I didn't respond. He wasn't there to see it, but I blushed. "I need you."

"I need you too."

"No, right now."

"Now?" I repeated. What was he suggesting?

"Yes. Can I see you right now?" he pleaded.

"Yes." I would not deny him.

"Thank you. Meet me at Hyde park."

"I will be there."

"Leave in five minutes. I want to get there first."

"Okay, Q."

When I got there, he was parked by a tree. He was sitting on the trunk of his car with his head in his hands. It alarmed me to see him that way. I couldn't help but feel something was wrong even though he tried to deny it. I prayed he didn't want to call off the wedding.

"Hey, babe." I hurried to him. "Whats wrong?" He lifted his head and I could see sadness. My heart started to beat fast. That scared me.

"Hey, baby." He pulled me to him. "I am so happy to see you."

"Good." I wrapped my arms around his neck and leaned in for his incoming kiss. The kiss was everything. No man could ever make me feel the way he could with his lips.

"I have been thinking about kissing you all night."

"You were supposed to be having fun with the boys.:

"I did. I had a good time. We played poker and I won. I pigged out on chicken wings and threw back some coronas."

"Not too many, I hope."

"No, sweetheart. Nothing is going to ruin our day tomorrow." I breathed a huge sigh of relief. "I couldn't stop thinking about you all night, though."

"Why were you focusing on me?"

"Because you are my favorite subject." He was the sweetest man.

"I like that." I kissed his neck. "Is this why you call me?"

"I couldn't sleep."

"Why not? Are you nervous?"

"Not about tomorrow."

"Then what is it?" I pulled back. I wanted to see his face.

"I didn't want to say anything about a couple weeks ago because I figured that you had moved on." I breathed another sigh of relief because I hadn't moved on.

"I thought you had moved on too." His eyes grew wide.

"Do you think about that day too?"

"How can I forget it?" I could feel the tears forming.

"I didn't want to make you cry," he said, wiping my tears away.

"It's okay for me to cry sometimes. I want us to talk about it."

"Are you sure?" he asked, caressing my hair.

"I am."

"Okay." He was silent for a moment. "If Anthony had of raped you...."

"He didn't, babe. Don't even think about it."

"I know, but I keep having nightmares, baby. I could have lost you. I don't know how I would have survived if something had of happened to you at the hands of that maniac."

I closed my eyes because I felt overwhelmed with emotion. Tears burned my cheeks.

"Quinton." When I whispered his name, he pulled me into his arms. "I could have lost you too. Every time I see this scar on your shoulder, I will be reminded of that day."

'It's not your fault. I really wish that you would let that guilt go because I know that you are carrying it." I just nodded.

"I will work on it. Lots of prayer."

"Yes. We will both get through this. I just know that I can't ever lose you." I could hear the emotion in his voice. I could tell that he was trying not to cry.

"God willing, you won't, baby. Please don't focus on what could have happen in the past or what could happen in the future. Focus on us and our kids in the present. We must push forward with our lives." I hoped that I was able to take my own advice.

"You are right, baby." Q slid his hands through my hair and pulled my face to his. We kissed for a while. Eventually things heated up. His hand started to slide up my skirt. He whispered "Oh, girl" in my ear when he discovered my lack of underwear..

"Surprise" He pushed me against his car. I reached for his pants zipper. We made love.

"Thanks for that," he said, afterwards. "I needed that."

We kissed once more and then went our separate way. I headed back to the hotel. When I slid back in bed beside my best friend, her eyes opened.

"Did you go see Quinton?"

"I did."

"You two could not go one night without seeing one another."

"Be quiet. Don't go there tonight."

"Fine!" She threw an arm around me. "Des, I have something to tell you. I wanted to wait until after your wedding, but I can't keep this secret any longer."

"What is it?"

"I am pregnant again."

"Seriously?"

"Yeah, I am about six weeks pregnant."

"Wow! Are you happy about this, Rayven."

"Yes, Desiree. Very."

"Then I am over the moon with joy for you." I hugged her.

"Thanks. Ty and I are getting married. He asked me last night."

"And you didn't tell me!"

"This weekend is supposed to be about you."

"Girl, I don't care about that! Congratulations. You both deserve this!" I wanted to cry.

"Thank you. We want a private ceremony. We want to get married on the beach."

"That's really romantic."

"Of course we want you and Q to be there."

"Anything for you, Rayven."

"Thanks, Des. Enough about me. I am so happy for you."

I slept like a baby. I didn't wake up on my own the next morning. Rayven had to shake me.

"Get up, sleep beauty! It's your wedding day."

I started my morning off by soaking in bubbles and sipping on champagne. I laughed to myself because if I wasn't careful, I would be stumbling down the aisle to my future husband. I had to slow down. That was a look that I was not trying to wear.

While enjoying my bath, I thought about Quinton. I thought about how much I loved him. I thought about how happy he made me. I was wondering what he was doing at the moment. How he was feeling. What was he was thinking?

I had a day of luxury planned for me and my eight bridesmaids. I wanted to thank all my girls for taking part in one of the most special days of my life. Everyone had been supportive of me and thankfully not one of them had been difficult.

We feasted on eggs, bacon, sausage, grits, pancakes, French toast, biscuits and croissants. We washed it down with mimosas. It was good times. My photographer and videographer was there to capture every moment.

We all had massages, manicures and pedicures. Afterwards my hair dresser came in and hooked my hair up. I wore my hair down in sexy ringlets. I opted against a veil and had decided to wear a bridal crown made of pink peonies, petite ivory roses and baby breath. It was gorgeous and romantic, made by one of my bridesmaids who was a florist.

After hair and make-up, we sat around and laughed over hot fudge sundaes. We mainly talked about the men in our lives. My married friends gave me advice. Despite all of their words of caution, I knew Q and I would be fine. We would keep God in our marriage.

There was a knock at the door. One of the groomsmen walked in with bags in his hand. Quinton had brought all of the bridesmaids beautiful necklaces. It brought tears to my eyes because it matched the bracelets I had given them. He knew I had conflicted over which one to give them and I had no idea that he would surprise me.

He sent me a huge vase of flowers, a box he wanted me to save for the honeymoon and a bracelet with the birthstones of my children. It was beautiful. I was crying by the time I opened his card.

To My Future Wife,

You have always been the woman of my dreams. I have loved you for such a long time without expecting your love in return. The day you told me you loved me was a gift from God. I am so thankful to have you in my life. I am so thankful to have you as the mother of my children.

I can't wait to spend the rest of my life with you. I vow to make you happy. I will always be there to love you, to cherish you, to spoil you and to protect you. You, Desiree Harris (almost Desiree Alexander), are my everything. I can't wait to see you come down the aisle towards me and a lifetime of joy.

Your Future Husband,
Quinton.

I stood in the corner and tried to calm myself. I closed my eyes and took deep breaths. I was so emotional. I was so thankful towards God for blessing me. I was beyond lucky. Not many women found a love like this.

"Desiree." Jade, my sister's voice brought me out of my moment. "Oh baby girl, I know." She wrapped her arms around me. "I am so happy for you."

"Thank you, Jade. Thank you for being my Matron of Honor."

"Of course, little sister. I love you."

"I love you too."

It was about four that evening when my bridesmaids, dressed in pink strapless dresses, helped me into my gown. It was a beautiful strapless gown with a full bottom made by Christian Jamison, a sought after designer that was popular on the east coast. Once my sister and Rayven, dressed in ivory, zipped me up and helped in my pink Louboutins, I took a deep breath and took it all in.

I stared at myself, speechless. For once, I felt confident because I knew I was beautiful. I almost didn't look like myself. I looked like a princess which is exactly how I wanted to feel

I didn't want to cry, but when I turned towards everyone else, they were crying. There didn't appear to be a dry eye in the room.

"You are the most beautiful bride I have ever seen," sobbed my best friend.

"Stop it, you are going to make me an emotional basket case."

I grabbed my chest when my mother brought Mia into the room. She looked adorable in her big fluffy white dress with a pink sash. She wore pink flowers in her curly hair.

"Mommy!" She ran towards me when she saw me.

"Hey, sweetheart."

"You look pretty mommy."

"Not as pretty as you, my precious girl." I lifted her in my arms to kiss her.

"Thank you." She kissed me back. "Mommy, I love you."

"I love you too." I just held her in my arms as she laid her head against my shoulder. She brought peace to me.

"Desiree, sweetie, the phone." My bridesmaid Gabriella handed me my phone with a smile.

"Thank you. Hello."

"Hey, baby."

"Hey Quinton!"

"Hi, daddy!" Mia said, growing excited. I laughed. She was such a daddy's girl. I put the phone on speaker phone,

"Hey there, princess."

"I love you, daddy."

"I love you too, princess. Is mommy in her dress."

"Yes! She looks pretty, daddy. You will like it!"

"I bet she is. I can't imagine how incredible she looks." I blushed. "I can't wait to see her."

"You both are making me blush."

"Stop that.'

"I can't help that and you know it."

"I will tell you that you are beautiful for the rest of your life. Now hurry up and get to me. You have another gift coming to you. I loved the watch, how did you know I wanted it." I gave him an engraved pocket watch that I knew he had been dying for, but refused to purchase.

"I pay attention, sweetheart. I also know you never buy yourself anything." He really was a selfless man.

"That's because I don't need it. You and the kids are all I need."

Before I knew it, we were leaving the hotel suite and were climbing into the limo that awaited us. We were on our way to the church. The fairy tale that I had been planning since I was a little girl was finally happening. God was good.

Everything was happening in a whirlwind. I sat outside at First Baptist in the limo alone for about five minutes until my wedding director came to get me. Once inside, she reached for my necklace.

"Jewelry change."

"Why?" I loved my pearl necklace and matching earrings. "Whats wrong with my jewelry."

"Nothing, my dear, but you have been upgraded." She reached for two jewelry boxes. She opened the biggest one and revealed the most beautiful diamond necklace I had ever seen. There were teardrop earrings to match. I covered my mouth because they were both breathtaking.

"Kira, where did you get that?"

"From your husband to be," she said, placing the necklace around my neck. "He says you deserve the best."

"He really needs to stop doing this to me" I was crying again. I reached for the handkerchief that my sister had hidden in my bouquet. At this rate, I was not going to have any mascara on by the time I reached the front of the church.

"Something tells me, honey, that you have a lifetime of surprises to look forward to."

"I think that you are right."

My father looked very handsome. He didn't look remotely close to 55. He looked more like my older brother than my father.

"Hey, princess," he said, embracing me. "You look very beautiful. You look so much like your mother."

"Thank you, daddy."

Everything hit me when the doors opened and we headed down the aisle. Quinton and I had decided to have a candlelight wedding, so candles aligned the aisles. There were pink and white roses everywhere. It was all stunning.

I was touched to see the church overflowing with all the people I loved the most. I loved seeing my girls in front of the church in their pink and ivory dresses and Quinotn friends in their white tuxedoes. Quinton Jr standing next to his father and Mia standing next to my sister is what sent the tears spilling down my cheek.

I loved my children more than anything. I lived for them. I was happy that Quinton and I could give them this. Mommy would now have their same last name.

It was when Tyler leaned over to whisper something in Quinton ear that my eyes landed on my future husband's face. An overwhelming feeling washed over me. I thought maybe that I would faint if wasn't for the support of my father.

He looked so breathtakingly beautiful. There was an intense expression on his face. I felt his soul when his eyes met mine. I could feel the love flowing between us. I couldn't look away.

When I got there, I smiled at him. His face relaxed into a smile.

"You look better than I imagine."

"Thank you, so do you."

My father cried when he gave me away. I never expected my father to show such emotion. I hugged and kissed him.

"I love you daddy, thank you."

I cried through the entire ceremony. Through the solos and the poems. I could barely get through my vows. I actually paused when I saw a tear in Q's eye. He squeezed my hand and I continued.

Quinton's vows were so moving that I looked down so I wouldn't break down in front of everyone. It felt amazing to have a man love you so much and vow to do so for the rest of his life. When I looked away, though, he lifted my chin, so I had no choice but to stare into those eyes. When he finished, I wanted to jump into his arms and just kiss him, but I couldn't.

This was my fairytale. This was my prince charming. I was the princess. And God had given me my happy ending.

"I now pronounce you husband and wife. You may kiss your bride." He kissed me and I felt as if our souls collided.

Quinton

I stood in front of the church and took it all in. The ladies had done a fantastic job decorating the church with candles and flowers. The beautiful setting prepared for what was yet to come. My beautiful bride. A beautiful life.

I waited anxiously for Des. Her girls looked lovely, but I wanted to see her. I had to keep from tapping my foot impatiently.

I was overcome with emotion when each of my children walked down the aisle. My handsome son who was growing by the day, looked very distinguish. My beautiful Mia, the splitting image of her mother, stole the show with her charm.

The musicians started playing "You are so beautiful' on the piano and on the sax. The doors of the church opened. My heart felt as if it did a full summersault. I took several deep breaths to contain myself. I knew I was going to cry.

When I saw her, I didn't want to blink because I didn't want to miss a thing. My breath kind of got caught in my throat. The song was perfect for her because she was the most beautiful woman that I had ever seen. I had imagine her to be gorgeous, but I didn't know she was going to look as exquisite as she did.

She was a Godsend. She was my angel. She made my life better. She was my soul mate. She was my future.

I was one lucky man and I was not taking this for granted. Sometimes I wasn't sure if I deserved Desiree. I didn't know if I deserved her love, but she gave me her heart. God had seen me fit to have her love, so I was going to do everything in my power to nurture her heart and to make him proud.

Desiree's love was intense, comforting, satisfying and fulfilling. Better yet, it was all mines. She was walking down the aisle to pledge that love to me. She was going to vow to love me for a lifetime.

The joy in my heart was indescribable when she spoke her vows to me. She promised to love me and make me happy for the rest of our lives on this great earth. When I gave her my vows, I made sure she realize that I was going to work to keep her happy. If she didn't realize, I wanted to make sure she knew how much she meant to me.

Our first kiss was perfect. I loved it, so I kissed her again. I didn't want her to forget that moment. The church erupted into applause at my display of affection for my wife.

The reception was at the Country Club where our fathers played Golf. We were in a ballroom with floor to ceiling and wall to wall windows. The room opened up to a huge terrace. The backdrop was a lake. The sky was star-filled and the moon was full. It was a perfect setting for romance.

Our celebration was definitely for the grown and the sexy. Our intimate setting was created for adults only. The kids were all sent home. We even sent our kids home with the babysitter. A college aged female that was a friend of the family. She was paid well.

Our 250 guest feasted on Italian and seafood at candlelit tables. You would have thought everyone was stuffed after a full course dinner. The guest became anxious for our white chocolate five tier wedding cake. Des and I had had to cut it quickly. Everyone went crazy over it.

After dessert, we all sipped on champagne as jazz played in the background. Eventually, though, the party moved outside to the terrace. Old school R&B filled the room. That's when things got real sexy. People got down and dirty on the dance floor.

I thought I would lose my mind when Desiree disappeared for a while. I had searched the entire room twice when she reappeared. She had replaced her princess gown with a very little and tight white dress. It fitted her perfectly.

I just stopped in the middle of the room as she moved towards me. I was mesmerized by the way she swayed her hips. I was already imagining what she was wearing under that dress. I was visualizing what was to come later. I couldn't wait to for our passion filled night.

"Just in time." She floated back in my arms just as Roberta Flack and Donny Hathaway's "Closer I get to you" came on. As we danced, I whispered exactly what I wanted to do to her later in the honeymoon suite. She blushed as always.

She held me captive as she begin to sing in my ear. I loved her voice. It was the sweetest sound I had ever heard.

Everyone was having such a good time that they didn't want to leave. I was pleased. The celebration didn't break up until well after midnight. Everyone cheered and applauded us with sparklers as we got in the limo around 1:00 in the morning. They banged on the limo as we pulled away.

Des cuddled up to me during the journey to our hotel. She laid her head against my shoulder. I smiled to myself. She looked adorable, half tipsy in my jacket.

We were staying in Des's bridal suite overnight. In the morning, we were going to meet our kids at the airport to say goodbye. Then we were headed to the Virgin Islands and Jamaica for two much deserved weeks.

I lifted my bride in my arms as soon as we got on the elevator. I was a man all about tradition. I didn't set her down until we were back in her room. I dropped her on the bed. She reached for me. She grabbed by my collar and kissed me hard.

"Wow, baby."

"I am sorry," she whispered, undoing my tie. "Did you need to settle in, my love?"

"I am good."

She ripped off my clothes and pushed me back on the bed. I was hypnotized as she slid out of that tight white dress. She wore a sheer pink bra and G-string. Incredible.

She then proceeded to take me to a place that my body had never been. She was in complete control and all I could do was hold onto her hips and enjoy the ride. She was unusually aggressive and I loved every moment of it.

"Wow, Des," I whispered as she collapsed beside me. We laid there side by side for a while without saying anything, holding hands.

Eventually, I reached for her. She allowed me to take control. It was music to my ears when she started moaning my name. I made love to my wife and I didn't stop until I knew she was satisfied.

The next morning, we showered together, ordered room service and then headed to the airport. My mother was meeting us there so we could say goodbye to our kids. My parents were going to keep them for the first week. Des's parents were going to keep them the second week. Our kids had not been away from us longer than a weekend, so I prayed that they could handle it.

"Daddy! Mommy!" My son came running out of nowhere.

"Hey, kid." He was getting tall, but I still scooped him up in my arms. "Were you good for grandma?"

"Yes sir."

Mia clung to her mother with tears in her eyes.

"I want to be with you, mommy."

"I know you do. I want to be with you too.'

"We should be together."

"I know, baby," she said, clinging to her daughter with tears in her own eyes. "Mommy and daddy loves you very much."

"I love you."

"Mommy will miss you a whole lot."

"I will miss you."

"If you are good for grandma and papa, mommy and daddy will bring you something back."

"I will be good, I promise."

"Good. Now I want you to go to that window with your brother and watch the plane fly away. I want you to wave so that mommy and daddy can see you."

"Okay, mommy."

We kissed the kids goodbye and then boarded the plane fifteen minutes later. I looked over at Desiree when we had buckled up. She had tears in her eyes. She looked uneasy.

"They will be fine, Des," I said, squeezing her hand.

"I know," she said, smiling at me. "I am being unreasonable. We just haven't left them this long."

"True, but they are in good hands."

"You are right, sweetheart."

Honeymooning with my new wife was two weeks of heaven. We spent our days sightseeing, shopping, laying on the beach and sampling local food. We spent our evenings getting tipsy and dancing to island music. We spent our nights making love. Sometimes we made love until the sun came up.

I looked over at her one day while she was napping on the beach and I couldn't stop staring at her. I was mesmerized by how beautiful she was. I would wake up to this loveliness for the rest of my life.

I thought about all that we had been through. I thought about falling in love with her in college and then moving in with her almost five years later to discover that I had never stopped loving her. I felt hopeless despite the explosive chemistry between us. I remember feeling heartbroken when I moved out, but then discovering that I couldn't live without her.

I remember the bitter sweetness of her pregnancy. I begged her to be with me, not believing that I could ever win her heart. I did, though. My whole life changed that day she confessed her love to me.

I would have never thought three years ago, that I would be this desperately in love. Each day, I found myself falling more and more in love. I didn't think that it was possible, but I loved her with every ounce of my soul. She was my best friend, my lover and the mother of my children. She was my biggest blessing. I didn't need anything else because I had all that I ever wanted and all that I ever needed.

Desiree

While on our honeymoon, Quinton told me that he adored my voice and wanted me to come to the studio. When we got home, Q had me recording a song that his partner had written. I was overwhelmed by how amazing the song sounded. I had never dreamed of singing professionally, although it was something that I loved to do.

I had just gotten excited about my new career when I found out I was four weeks pregnant. I sat in my car outside the doctor's office for over twenty minutes, gripping the steering wheel because I didn't know how to take it. I went straight to Q and he left work early. We both hung on the couch in shock.

The next day, we decided that this was God's doing. He wouldn't put more on us than we could bear. We weren't dating anymore, we were married. The kids were good ages at 7 and 2 and a half. We would be fine.

Both of our families were over the moon with joy. Our parents wanted more grandchildren. Rayven flipped out because we were both pregnant together again, although she was practically four months pregnant now.

A month later, we flew to Hawaii with Tyler and Rayven so they could get married. It was a sweet, romantic and intimate affair. It was so private that Q and I were the only guest.

Rayven looked like a breathtaking goddess in a flowing white sundress. Tyler looked handsome in his white pants and white button-up. They made a striking couple.

I cried. Their vows were so touching. Their love seemed so intense. It was magical. I was glad to be a part of this moment in our friends' lives. I wanted to always be there for my best friend.

Next June, I was in the hospital with Rayven as she gave birth to a beautiful baby girl. Baby Alana became my second God-child. I was in love with her as soon as I held her in my arms.

Now, it was my turn. I couldn't wait until I delivered my two baby boys. They hadn't given me many problems and didn't seem to be in any rush, but I was ready to meet my blessings.

Quinton

The day Desiree gave birth to our two baby boys was supposed to be one of the happiest days of my life. Julian and Jamison didn't give Des any issues her entire pregnancy, so we were hoping for a good day and a healthy delivery. Instead the day turned out to be one of the worst days of my life. For one dark moment, I thought my life was over. I wanted to die.

We left for the hospital one Thursday morning. Desiree was to be induced bright and early and then we would wait patiently for the arrival of our boys. Everything progressed slowly, but fine.

My wife was in labor for over 24 hours. We just assumed they were being stubborn. When it was time to deliver, she pushed for an unusually long time, still both boys came out small, but displaying their healthy set of lungs, by screaming.

That's when my nightmare started.

I was smiling at my sons, holding Desiree's' hand when she started to convulse. She was foaming at the mouth. Her eyes were rolling in the back of her head.

I yelled out for help. I was shoved out of the way, but I tried to push my way back to Desiree's side. I was hysterical.

"Let me do my job, sir."

"Please do something! Don't let her die!" Someone pushed me out of the room. Desiree's mother followed me into the hall.

"Calm down, son. Everything will be alight. It's in God's hands." I allowed her to hug me for the moment.

My family came around the corner at the worst time. They were excited with their flowers, teddy bears and balloons. They just wanted a glimpse of our boys. But with fear in my heart and tears streaming down my cheek, I didn't want to see any of them.

My mom stopped in her track.

"Why are you crying? What's going on?"

I stared back at her but couldn't speak. Des's mom spoke up. "The boys are fine."

"But..."

"Desiree is not. She is having seizures."

"Oh, no, no, no. My word."

Quinton ran from my mother's side and threw his arm around me looking heartbroken. He understood.

"No, daddy, no!" He started crying and my world felt as if it was falling apart.

"Stop crying, son."

"No, what's wrong with mommy. She said she wouldn't leave me. I don't want her to leave. I need my mommy." What was I supposed to say? Quinton crying set Mia off. She ran to me too.

"I want mommy. Let me see her! Where is she going! She didn't say bye to me."

"Mommy is in the room sweetie. She's not going anywhere." I realized I had to calm down for my children's sake. I knelt down "Mommy is sick, but the doctors are in there making it better. She will be fine. God will take care of her. We believe in God don't we?"

"Yes, daddy," they both nodded.

"Stop crying, both of you. Quinton, you are the oldest. You have to watch over Mia and your brothers. You are my solider."

"I am, daddy."

"Mia, you are the only girl. You are our little princess. Little lady of the house. Are you mommy's helper?"

"Yes, daddy. Mommy says I'm her princess."

"Yes. Mommy would want you both to stop crying." I kissed both of them on the forehead. "Go with your grandma to see your brothers. Go check on them for me." The nurses had taken them away. I looked up at my mother and pleaded with her. She just nodded and grabbed both of them.

"Come kids. Let's go see your brothers."

I leaned against the wall and prayed. I prayed that God would not take the only woman I had ever loved from me. I prayed that he wouldn't take a mother away from her kids who needed her. I prayed he wouldn't make me a single father. I wasn't strong enough.

I wasn't quite sure I could live another day without her. I couldn't function without her. I knew I would want to die rather than breathe a day on this Earth without her by my side.

Then I felt guilty. What about our four kids. I couldn't leave them fatherless too.

"God. Have mercy!"

The whole ordeal only lasted thirty minutes, but it felt like an eternity. I walked back into the room and Desire was laying there with her eyes opened. She looked exhausted, but she smiled at me. She held out her hand.

"Hey, baby. Come here."

I couldn't speak. I was too overcome with emotion. My heart was beating fast and I felt as if I was suffocating.

"What's wrong, my love? Why are you crying? Where are my babies? Are they okay?" She looked confused.

"They are fine," I said, rubbing her hair. "Baby, you scared me so badly. Don't do that again." I pressed my lips against hers.

"What are you talking about? What did I do?"

"You had a seizure. You were unconscious."

"I did. I was" she looked at me horrified.

"Yes. Scariest moment of my life."

"I don't...I don't remember." She looked at me horrified. "Why am I having seizures?"

"High blood."

"I have high blood!"

"They are getting it under control. Calm down, baby, please. Don't worry. Everything is going to be okay. Don't stress right now. I am pleading with you."

"Okay, my love."

"Thank you." I pressed my lips against hers again. She grabbed my face and kissed me back.

"I love you, Quinton."

"I love you, Desiree. So very much. More than myself."

The kids reuniting with their mother brought peace to my heart. They both climbed in beside her. They hugged and kissed her.

"How are my babies?"

"Mommy, we are glad you feel better. We prayed for you. God listened to us because you didn't leave us." My son was wise beyond his years.

"No baby, I am not going anywhere, okay."

"Okay."

"You are mommy's little prince and you are mommy's little princess. No more tears." She took them both in her arms.

Our new gifts from God, Julian and Jamison were both thankfully healthy. They were a little irritated, but both seemed to be at peace when their mother held them. They stared up her in admiration as if nothing else in the world mattered to them.

She was everything to all of us. Our lives were better because of her. God blessed us today. He allowed her to exist in our lives yet another day.

After that day, I did have nightmares, but thankfully, she didn't have any more seizures. Her blood pressure remained under control. God took care of her.

Still, on the boys first birthday, I woke up in tears. I grabbed her and pulled her to me. She threw her arms around me and laid her head against my chest.

"I love you," she whispered. "I will never leave you."

Finally, I found the peace I needed. I could not live in the past any longer. I needed to exist in the present. I needed to look towards the future.

"I promise I will always cherish you," I whispered.

The boys had a great first birthday. A Disney themed party with appearances from Mickey and Minnie. There were corn dogs, cotton candy and cupcakes. Lots of family and friends came to celebrate. Along with their gifts, they brought joy, laughter and love.

When the night was over and all the kids were tucked away, Desiree turned to look at me and smile.

"I still want another one. One more baby girl would be perfect."

My chest tightened. Could I bear her giving birth again?

"A baby girl would not be guaranteed."

"Not if I give birth." I frowned at her. "I know the thought of me getting pregnant again scares you. I don't want to put you, the kids or even myself through that. I want to adopt. I want to give a child at home. A baby girl."

I smiled as relief flowed through my body.

"If that's what you want, let's make that happen."

"In a couple years when the boys are older." She wrapped her arms around me.

"Okay. Nothing matters as long as we are together." She just smiled up at me.

"God is incredible. He gave me you, Quinton Alexander. And for that, I am the luckiest woman in the world."

I didn't speak, I just smiled at her. My heart was too full

I held her in my arms and we slow danced under the stars for a while. I savored the moment alone with the woman who had single handily turned my life around. I knew nothing but darkness until the day she told me she loved me. Today I knew nothing but joy.

She was right, God was incredible.

ABOUT THE AUTHOR

Writing has always been one of Cherrell Bates biggest passions. She began her journey as a writer while in high school. She was highly blessed to publish her first published novel, "Yield Not to Temptation". This novel is the second in her journey.

www.ingramcontent.com/pod-product-compliance
Lightning Source LLC
Chambersburg PA
CBHW030237030726
47493CB00022B/80